PLAYER MANAGER 6

PLAYER MANAGER

6

TED STEEL

Podium

Cover design by Damonza

ISBN: 978-1-0394-7473-4

Published in 2025 by Podium Publishing
www.podiumentertainment.com

Podium

THE STORY SO FAR

Max Best has recovered from a near-fatal attack and has led Chester FC's men's team to fourth in the league, while the women's team is competitive in tier six. Exhausted by performing three jobs and pushing his body to its limit, he is delighted that help has finally arrived. With a new manager and a new scout easing his burden, he can focus his efforts. His first task? Learning to deal with ultra-defensive opponents.

PLAYER MANAGER 6

"If everyone likes what you're doing, you're doing it wrong."

—Hope Solo

HOME DISADVANTAGE

Tuesday, October 24, 2023. Match 13 of 46: Southport versus Chester.

"Boo!"

We were only five minutes into the match, but the home fans were livid. They watched as their goalkeeper passed to their centre back, who passed to the other centre back, who looked around for an option and didn't see anything he liked.

"Booo!"

The ball was played forward, and their two strikers combined, venturing into the Chester half. We engulfed them, stole the ball, and Ryan Jack kicked the ball long. It spun out for a throw-in.

The crowd hushed, waiting to see what would happen. Southport cycled the ball across the pitch in a flat line, then passed it back to the goalie.

"BOOOO!"

Magnus Evergreen was next to me. He was a strange guy and a strange player. He had CA 41, which was a measure of his overall ability as a footballer, with CA (I believed) standing for current ability. There was another supremely important number that I could see floating above the heads of every footballer I watched play live. This was PA, potential ability. Almost every player had a PA higher than their CA. Magnus was an exception—his was —2. What did it mean? No clue. I felt I wouldn't understand it until Magnus reached his CA limit.

"Er, Max," he said now, with a little undercurrent of something in his voice. "Didn't you give Jackie Reaper a stern telling-off for playing defensive football last time he was here? He's been back at the club for a day and this is the most defensive performance by a Chester team . . . probably ever."

"As director of football, I'm furious," I said, but I snapped my head around to look at the home fans. I got the sense, the very distinct and clear sense, that latecomers were arriving to the stadium, asking what the hell was going on, and were being told. All around were pockets of quiet disbelief that soon turned into anger.

"BOOOOOOO!"

Magnus sensed I was preoccupied, but curiosity got the better of him. "How long do you think he can keep this up?"

"I'm astonished he's lasted this long. He's writing his resignation letter, don't you think?"

Magnus looked at the pitch, the fans, and the beleaguered manager. "I'm afraid you're right."

I gave him a friendly pat on the arm. "Forget that guy. He tried being a football manager but he's out of his depth. He's history. Magnus, mate. How's my aura?"

He looked me up and down. "Resplendent."

"Oh," I said, savouring the way the word bounced along my ear canals. "I like that. Yes, I like that a lot."

Twenty-five minutes earlier.

Southport is in Merseyside, north of Liverpool, and it was my first time there. I didn't know if Merseysiders talked about the Beatles a few percent less the farther they lived from Penny Lane, but I did know that when Red Rum won the Grand National in 1973, he was paraded on Southport's Haig Avenue pitch at halftime. Red Rum was a horse, by the way.

I also knew I'd played for Darlington against Southport and we'd swatted them aside in the first half before taking it easy in the second. That was 2—0. And in my third match as Chester caretaker manager, we'd smashed them 4—0. So if I understood maths, and I felt like I did, we would beat them 6—0 tonight. Or would it be 8—0?

Anyway, as with any trip to Merseyside, where grinning strangers called me "la" and offered to sell me "charcoal chicken an' chips," I was happy to have Jackie Reaper by my side.

The away fans were crowded behind the goal in the uncovered Blowick terrace, about 500 of them, many wearing Chester's blue and white kit, but many more wearing coats and macs, since the endless summer was finally over. For the time being, they didn't care about the impending rain. Rain was coming, but one reign was about to start.

We'd announced Jackie's new role on social media, but I hadn't been tracking the response. So now I pushed Jackie slightly ahead of me, clapped, and the fans told me what they thought of the news.

"Jackie Reaper's blue and white army! Jackie Reaper's blue and white army!"

The man himself clenched his fist, punched the air, waved for more. After a full *minute* of exultation, I pulled him away, applauded the fans, and we headed back to the dugout.

"Did you grow up on a farm?" I asked.

He did a tiny smirk and pretended to sigh. "No, Max. Why?"

"Because you milked that like a pro."

He shook his head but didn't reply. We both knew I was right. He was shameless.

We were soon back at the away dugout, where we would part ways for the rest of the evening. Livia was there, looking quite emotional, and finally some inhibition melted away and she dashed to Jackie and kissed him.

"Whoa!" I said. "This is an undeclared relationship. No public displays of affection until you've spoken to HR."

"We did that," said Jackie. "Last time."

"But you quit, mate. You're a new hire. You've got to start again."

"Yes, bosh," he said, which is Scouse for "boss." I often wondered if our new sponsors hadn't intended to call themselves BossCard and asked a Scouse IT guy to buy the domain name. Now they were stuck with the name BoshCard. It was very, very plausible. "Are you ready to play?" he said, worried I hadn't warmed up with the rest of the first-team players.

"I'm feeling a bit tense, actually. I might ask your girlfriend to give me a good rub. Is that all right?"

"Sure," he said, not rising to the bait.

I flicked my head towards the dressing room. Livia frowned. "You're serious?"

"I actually am."

"Lead the way, then."

"Bye, Jackie!" I said, overly loud, winking and giving him a Maxy two-thumbs.

His tongue poked out of the side of his mouth. Welcome back, mate! Vimsy slapped him on the back, and Jackie stayed, soaking up the atmosphere. It was obvious he'd missed it. Vimsy followed Livia and me down the tunnel.

My good mood stayed out on the pitch. The closer I got to the dressing room, specifically the *home* dressing room, the more I felt my jaw clenching and my eyes narrowing. I burst through the door to the away room and was assaulted by the familiar sights and smells of a large group of men in a small room.

"All right, shut the fuck up," I demanded.

The players were absolutely buzzing. I saw it in their smiles and ready laughs, and in the squad overview screen given to me by the curse. Morale was very, very high. The return of Jackie had lifted the entire club. The lads settled down, quiet and alert.

"Southport are going to play four-four-two," I said. So far, so normal. Everyone in the National League North played 4-4-2, unless forced into a change by playing against superior tacticians like Jackie Reaper. Or me. "Low block."

There was a huge groan.

Three days before, top of the table Kidderminster had turned up at our stadium with a plan. They would get ahead, then when I brought myself on, retreat into their shell. Turtle up. I'd done my best to get us back into the match, but no dice. I had taken the defeat with sublime grace and dignity and just the merest hint of frustration. It seemed to me at the time that the tactic would be repeated, again and again, for the rest of the season. And now, here was proof.

I had *not* expected it in away matches.

I took the marker pen and got ready to draw on our tactics board. It would have been better on a flipchart, but the less equipment we took with us, the better. Dressing rooms were often tiny. The tactics board would do, even if I was drawing over the top of a football pitch.

"Mikel Arteta inspires his Arsenal players," I said, making eye contact with my troops, "through the use of imagery. He uses *drawings* to tell a story simple enough for his players to understand." I drew a car. "You are a car. You've got four wheels. That's, er . . . the midfield? No, sometimes we use five in midfield. Cars have an exhaust. That's Youngster. He's exhausting. Rearview mirror. Something about Henri always looking at himself. Who was that Greek chap?"

"Max," said Henri Lyons, my French striker. He had current ability 58, which was very good in this division, but his improvement had stalled. I had a plan to deal with that. If it worked, it would open up all kinds of crazy possibilities. "How long did you think about this, ah, imagery?"

"Not long," I confessed. "I thought we'd turn up, slap, and go home with three points. I literally cannot believe they are doing a low block at home to a team that was nearly relegated last year. Jesus Christ." I shook my head. "There will be something like two and a half thousand people here today. That's more than we got against Kidderminster. Some matches Southport get like four, five hundred spectators. Imagine you're expecting the biggest attendance of the season and you wake up and think, *I know! I'll make the match as boring as possible!*" I shook my head some more, then vented one large, "Argh!" I drew a second car, then tapped the "Chester" one. "I've been tuning this car. Making the engine good. The engine is . . . the midfield. Shit. Look, lads, don't tell Jackie how bad this team talk was. Ah, wait, I remember my point. We've been getting faster, smoother, fewer oil leaks. And our opponents," I tapped the second car, "instead of doing the same, have given up racing and become bricklayers." I rubbed out the drawings and slid eleven yellow magnets onto the tactics board, all squashed up against the goal at the top. I jiggled both middle fingers towards the home dressing room, and took a few seconds to compose myself. "What do we do?"

"Crosses," said Henri. "These players are not as physically dominant as Kidderminster. We will score from crosses."

"Slaps," said Sam Topps, my marauding midfield terrier. He hadn't liked me at first, but the more I pushed him, challenged him, the more he tried to impress me. When it came to football, he had absolutely no problem doing things my way. "They're not as disciplined as Kidderminster. Not as well coached. If we get to the sides and cut into the penalty area, we'll get great chances."

"A mix," said Pascal Bochum, my short German forward. "We had thirty-one shots against Kidderminster. They were incredibly lucky. We don't need to change anything. If we have that many shots in ten matches, we'll win nine. I say we change nothing."

"Thanks," I said. "I agree with two of you." That made Pascal frown because it was logically impossible. I smiled. "Here's what we're going to do."

I got the blue magnets and laid them out in our 4-1-4-1 formation. It was probably my favourite way to set up the team, but I hated our left back and he was by far the worst player in the core squad. I had been using 3-5-2 recently, which allowed me to cut out the left back and utterly dominate midfield.

Today I made one slight tweak to our usual version of 4-1-4-1. I pulled all the magnets earthwards until, like Southport, they crowded around our goalkeeper.

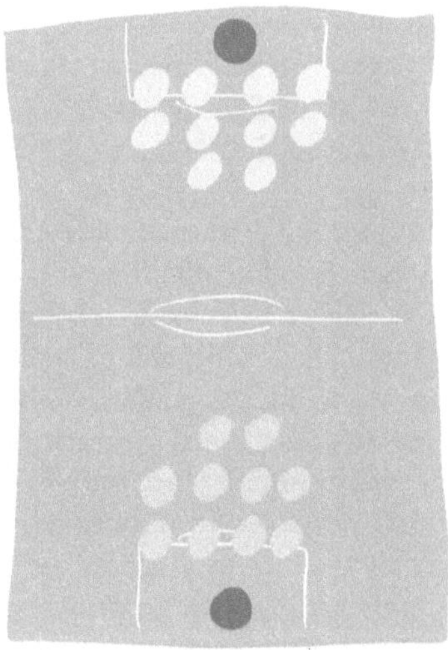

"Low block?" said Vimsy. He was my defensive coach. Not very talented and quite combustible, but he had been at the club much longer than me and I didn't have the heart to replace him just yet. I wanted to make personnel changes over years, not months. "Max Best doing a low block? Do I . . . What?"

"That makes no sense," said Sam. "They're doing a low block. We can't do a low block as well."

"Why not?" I said.

"Because . . . what will anybody be blocking?"

My assistant manager, an ex-army guy who'd been hired as my bodyguard, laughed. His name—he claimed—was John Smith, but we called him the Brig. He wasn't a football expert, but he understood comedy. When he laughed, Sam grinned, realising how asinine the situation was.

"Low block," I said, in the form of an order.

Henri, my friend and former client, sighed. "I'm sorry, Max. I do not understand this one. We're the better team. What happened to 'attack until you drop'?"

"Slight detour, *mon ami*. We're a car, yes? Driving to . . . where do we want to go?"

"Fountains Abbey," said Youngster, an incredibly talented defensive midfielder who was a devout Christian.

"Is there a Nando's there? Never mind. We're driving to see some fountains, but on the way we stop off for twenty minutes. Right? And in those twenty minutes, we get the Southport manager sacked and make everyone think twice about low blocking us."

Vimsy never could follow my logic when it got more than slightly twisted. "I still don't get it."

I nodded. Clarity was usually best. "We have something like seventeen more away matches in the league this season. I, for one, don't want to be playing against ultra-defensive teams in every one of those. It's all right if they do it at our place. That's on us to bring the heat, isn't it? But if you're at home, in front of your own fans, you've got to put on a show. Unless you're playing peak Barcelona, you've got to try to win. Do we all agree?"

Most people did. Vimsy mostly did. "Are we going to do a low block against Salford City?"

Salford were owned by a bunch of former Manchester United legends. The owners had pumped money into the club, and it now competed two divisions higher than us. We had drawn Salford in the FA Cup first round.

"Well, they're much better than us, so it's fair to be defensive. They'll push us back anyway, whatever we try to do. But we're at home, so we'll have a plan to score goals. I've, er . . . I've started watching their matches and . . ." I grinned. "I've got something in the oven. It's on low heat but . . . starting to smell nice. All I'm saying is that in football terms, we're allowed to do a low block against Salford but Southport aren't allowed to do it against us. Anyone who doesn't understand that, talk to Youngster on the way home." That sentence was deliberately vague. It could have meant they should ask him to explain it. Or it could have meant, talk to him as a punishment.

"Me?" he said, with his goofy smile making an appearance.

I was already past that joke. "When we do this low block, now, there will be this horrendous chasm in midfield and it will make it clear to everyone in this stadium what their manager tried to do. You got that? We are going to show this guy up. Do not pass the halfway line. Ideally, you'd stick by the penalty area. If you get the ball, belt it away as far as you can. Repeat until I tell you otherwise."

Now that I'd made him the official explainer, Youngster wanted to understand better himself. "What if someone puts it out for a throw-in, like you did against Kidderminster?"

"Walk towards the ball as slowly as you can. Throw the ball six inches. Jog back into position. All clear?" It was. "One more thing. While we're doing this, I don't want entertainment. No kick-ups. No overhead kicks. No triangles, overlaps, nutmegs. Get the ball and kick it hard. Anything else, I'll be pissed. Now get out there and stink the place up. You hear me?"

They walked out, not happy, not sad. They would obey. After all, I was their manager, and if I sometimes had weird ideas, that was because I was a handsome maverick tactical genius. I slapped my hands together, satisfied.

"Wait," said Livia, with a little frown. "You're angry . . . but you're not . . . but you *are*. I can't tell what's real."

"What's real is that I'm feeling frisky." Her eyebrows shot up. I laughed. "Not like that. Jackie's back, the women are going to the moon, and I feel unstoppable. Did you ever walk into a football stadium and feel like you owned it?"

"No. But you actually own a club."

"See," I said, thoughtfully. "I don't get that feeling there. With that club, I'm more like a consultant or something. Just helping out, doing a couple of side projects. We're all going down on Thursday, if you want to come."

She smiled. "I might."

"My calves are tight. Can you slap them like a karate kid?"

She tapped a treatment table. "Hop up."

I'd sent out a weakened team. After Ben Cavanagh's horror show against Kidderminster, I had no choice but to put Robbo (CA 38) in goal for a few games until Ben (CA 41) got his morale back up.

Then we had Trick, CA 31, the abysmal left back who at least gave balance to the side, and the overrated Gerald May (38) was back in at centre back. Youngster (40) got some minutes, as did Donny "D-Day" Dorigo, a fair player who was past his best but still just about had something to offer with his CA 34.

I'd rotated Sam Topps (56) out of the starting lineup, leaving Ryan Jack (61) and Raffi Brown (46) to roam the centre of the pitch. Ideally, I wouldn't need to use Sam today. It was going to be a long season, and he would play most of our matches.

Up front was Tony Hetherington, my second-best striker. He'd hit his CA limit of 44, but that was more than enough to score goals at this level.

That all gave us an average CA of 45.5, which showed how far we'd progressed as a team. The "strong" eleven I had picked against Southport at the end of the previous season had CA 41.

One invigorating massage later, Livia, the Brig, and I went down the tunnel and turned to our dugout. Livia looked up at the VIP section, where Jackie was sat with MD (short for Mike Dean, our managing director). MD was in heaven—the Three Amigos had re-formed! In a slightly different alignment, this time. Before, I had been very much the D'Artagnan of the group. Now, Jackie was the junior partner in the Three Maxeteers. And that's exactly how he wanted it. Less stress, fewer matches per season, and a group of very, very talented footballers to work with. He could build his management career, and his confidence, out of the spotlight. And, not that it affected his decision, I'm sure, he could get paid a full-time salary for three short evening training sessions and one match every other Sunday. Nice gig. I was beyond ecstatic to give it to him.

MD's ecstasy was slightly tempered by the startling news that I had bought a football team. His first question was how could I afford one on my five-hundred-pounds-a-week salary? And why had I done it? Did it mean I'd be leaving Chester, just as I'd started to get the car purring, reliable, and turning heads?

"BOOOO!"

Southport's manager was starting to crack. His name was Reece Killen and he looked like a bodybuilder. There was no question of his players refusing his orders. He would put traitors in a big blender with some yoghurt, kale, and protein powder and drink them for breakfast. His stubbornness was actually incredible—surely it was hard to stick the course amidst such fury.

He looked over at me, shooting daggers, blaming me for this debacle.

I very much wanted to get within earshot of him and give ten pounds to a nearby Southport fan. I'd say something like, "Your manager won't give you a refund, but you won't see any football tonight." Something like that. And that would cause an explosion with a chain reaction and I'd end up running around, laughing. But the Brig had asked me not to be provocative for a while. The more I kept myself out of trouble, the more he could devote his attention and energy to getting the person who had attacked me sent to prison.

And adding to the combustion was not the right move. Much better to do what I was doing (nothing) and let this play out as a contest between the manager, who thought defending for ninety minutes was his best chance of getting a point, and the fans, who wanted to be entertained.

Magnus smiled as he did a tiny head shake. "You're enjoying this."

"Aren't you?"

"No. It's excruciating." He laughed. "What are the chances you will crack before him?"

It was my turn to laugh. "What do you think?" I nodded towards the bench. "Have we got anything to read?"

"I've got some books in my bag," he said, turning to stare at it, like he had X-ray vision. "Er . . . *Gaslighting Recovery for Women. Owning Our Struggles. Your Brain on Art*, which, you know, is about neuroaesthetics. Obviously. Oh, and I got *The Science of Stuck*, just because everyone's talking about it."

"They are?"

"*My* friends are."

The title finally registered. *The Science of Stuck.* Henri was stuck at his current ability. So was Ryan Jack. And if there was one thing I was afraid of this season, it was that I would get stuck, too. So far in my recovery I'd eased back to CA 30, and my improvement was still rapid, but perceptibly slowing. If I was subject to the same limitations as my players, I'd get to CA 60 and stay there. "That one, please. Actually, you know what? You might be the perfect person to help me with something. Bit of an esoteric project. Sound fun?"

"More fun than watching two teams refuse to leave their halves."

"Ah, but you're wrong. Southport left their half. We didn't."

Magnus blinked. "You're actually proud of that."

"Course I am. It means they trust me. Oh! Look."

It looks like Southport will take a more adventurous approach.

"What?" said Magnus.

"Better sit down, if that isn't too bossy of me. Things are about to get unstuck."

I had two options. To react immediately and send my guys flying up the pitch, or to wait a fraction.

Waiting would allow Southport to come all the way to our penalty area and blitz us with shots and crosses. Risky. But I couldn't really imagine when I'd next use a low block in a real match. Possibly there would be times in the Salford City match. But after that? I sensed that this would be good experience for me and good practice for my players. We hadn't been doing a lot of serious defending recently. Southport, with their CA 38, weren't a major threat to us. The worst that could happen was that they'd fluke a goal and would then have legitimate reason to defend for their lives for the rest of the match.

Southport surrounded us, and the riled-up home crowd loved it. They cheered as the first shot of the match was struck. They oohed as a through ball was cut out. They applauded wildly as a series of crosses were headed away by my defenders.

What I couldn't quite tell was the mood of the Chester fans. I'd got them all worked up before the match by showing off the new women's manager, then I'd parked the bus and we literally hadn't left our half.

I smirked. Maybe I'd listen to the stupid fan podcast after this one.

Glenn Ryder, my dominant captain, headed away another cross.

Enough.

I took the shackles off, using the hotkeys to make Aff our playmaker, pass left, and focus on counter attacks.

Southport attacked, we took the ball from them, and four slick passes later Aff was driving forward on the left. Seeing Tony as his only option in the box, he drove, drove, and smacked a low shot diagonally towards the bottom right corner.

The keeper got his hands to it, but only spilled it into Tony's path. Open net, 1–0 Chester!

Reece Killen looked small, his arms hanging futile. After the match, I would savage him in the media, but why not get some extra digs in now? I turned and made eye contact with the Brig. "I'm feeling frisky."

"Please, sir," he said. He could handle the bodybuilder guy, but he wanted a quiet evening.

"Fine," I said, with a hint of petulance. If I wasn't allowed to dick around on the sidelines, my players would have to do it for me. I switched from a counter-attacking mentality to simply attacking. Normally, I'd have removed the playmaker and allowed everyone to make free choices, but some instinct made me set Ryan Jack as our on-pitch creator. Maybe it was because he was from the area. Maybe it was the sea air. Or maybe it was the way he was the best player on the pitch.

Whatever it was, I was right. He tore them apart.

Jack takes the ball under pressure and lays it off to Brown.

Brown passes wide and makes a forward run.

The ball comes back to Jack.

He sprays it left, first time, into the path of Aff.

Aff crosses low . . .

It's behind Hetherington . . .

But perfect for Raffi Brown!

He leans back and sidefoots it . . .

GOOOOAAAAALLLL!!!!

Brown timed his run to perfection.

Raffi, by the way, had added goals to his game in a big way. Late runs into the box, headers from set pieces, and composed finishes after fast counters. For example . . .

Robbo claims the cross easily. He rolls it left to Williams.

Down the line to Aff.

Aff is under pressure. He touches the ball back to Williams.

Square to Jack.

And a first-time pass over the halfway line finds Raffi Brown bursting forward!

The pass has bypassed the defence completely!

Now it's Brown rushing towards goal with only the keeper to beat . . .

GOOOAAAALLLL!!!!

It was never in doubt!

3–0 and Chester are rampant.

Some home fans are already leaving. The away fans are wishing them the best of luck as they depart.

At halftime, my players were laughing, joking, having a blast. I usually left a space for them to talk about their individual battles, discuss key opponents, and so on. This evening, there was none of that. There was no point. Southport were gone. Spent. We could do whatever we wanted.

I knew what the players would do—ease up. The game was won. No point wasting calories when we had another away trip on Saturday.

Wrong.

"Listen up," I said. "If you think I'm happy with three–nil, you're way off. We need to send a message. A message. Do you get me? Managers who think about low blocking us on their patch need to think what's worse: trying to compete against us and losing or trying to low block and getting humiliated during and after the match. Trick, Gerald, Youngster, good game, you're coming off. Sam, Henri, and I are going on. Anyone who eases up in the second half will not be considered for the Salford match."

Putting Sam and Henri on for the second half had the desired effect. I had them on the bench for emergencies, but my intention had been to give them the night off and the squad knew that. Bringing my big guns on with the game as good as won was quite a message. The players also knew from my changes that we'd be doing 2-6-2 for the second half, and that was as attacking as we could currently get. My threat would surely work—they were all desperate to play in the FA Cup match, doubly so if it was televised.

Glenn said, "How many goals is enough, boss?"

I thought about it. For some reason, I took the question very seriously. "Eleven," I said, nodding. "We can stop at eleven."

We didn't score eleven. We got to five soon enough and then the spark was gone. Five seemed to be the limit for the day, no matter how much I glared and pushed and cajoled.

I couldn't fault the players' effort or attitude. There was no on-pitch reason, no sporting reason, to keep playing at peak intensity. Sure, at the end of the season, goal difference could come into play, but that possibility was so distant, so abstract, it would never work as a motivational tool. Not until the end was in sight.

Missing the chance to really put a team to the sword—and get rid of this shitty manager—irked me for a couple of minutes, but I pretty quickly saw sense. There was no point raging about it. So I stood in the DM slot, sometimes mopping up half-hearted Southport attacks, but mostly thinking about Salford City and how we would play against them.

I switched places with Raffi; he went into the third centre back slot with me in central midfield. I kept walking ahead, into the central attacking midfielder (CAM) zone between the midfielders and strikers. I didn't intend to play there against Salford—my attacking skills were coming back much more slowly than the defensive—but I wanted to be surrounded by opponents. And the Southport manager did one good thing that match: He set a midfielder to mark me.

Surrounded by players and being man-marked, I made myself playmaker to make sure I got a lot of the ball and experimented with turns, half-turns, and one-touch layoffs. My question was, could I get the ball under pressure and make good use of it? Against Southport, yes. Very much so. The curse gave me a 10 out of 10 rating, as it had against Kidderminster. But against players of a much higher quality? I wasn't so sure.

Max, congratulations. Five–nil away from home. How do you feel?

I feel sorry for the two thousand six hundred and fifty fans who bought tickets, rearranged shifts, and got babysitters to come here and watch a sporting contest. I feel sorry for any dad who's brought his kid to his first-ever football match and seen one team curl up into a ball and play dead before the referee had even checked the nets and corner flags. It does me no good to see fans turned off the sport. I'll take the points, but I'd have preferred to lose four–three in an all-time classic with both sets of fans applauding their team off the pitch. That's the God's honest truth. Two thousand six hundred and fifty. Is that the biggest attendance of my career? I think it is, you know. And one guy denied them a spectacle. So I'm sympathetic to the fans and pretty angry at the person who did this to them. And to the directors who put that guy in a position of responsibility.

Is that why you didn't shake hands with Reece Killan at the end?

I'm not going to shake his hand knowing I'm going to come out here and slaughter him. Maybe he's a good guy, a good coach, I have no clue. All I know is he turned what could have been a fun night, a night of escapism for both sets of fans, into something pathetic and dispiriting. For what? To sneak a nil–nil? At what cost? Two thousand fans who'll think twice about coming to a Southport game again? Nah, it's shocking. It's cowardly.

But you played your part in that crazy first ten minutes. You didn't attack, either.

We're the away team. We were nearly relegated last year. When a match kicks off and the home team, in front of their highest attendance of the year, sets up against us like we're Brazil 1970 and they are Zaire, it's very confusing. I'm new to all this, Gary. I'm twenty-three. I don't have the experience to understand what's going on. What looks to me like open cowardice could easily be some highly sophisticated way of playing. I don't know, do I? I do know it's not my job to entertain Southport's fans. If I accidentally showed them how their manager had chosen to set up his team, that's coincidence.

Max, I think you might be teasing me a little bit here. I think you knew exactly what you were doing.

We've got something like sixteen away matches left this season. Maybe ten of those managers will think about going ultra-defensive against us. Now they know what will happen. We will copy them. Not a single interesting thing will happen in the match. As director of football here, if one of my managers put out a team like that, I'd sack them at halftime and take over myself. I'd offer refunds to all the fans who had to witness the shameful capitulation. But it'd probably be too late. Some fans who turned up will simply never come again no matter how many grovelling apologies I wrote. If there are any Southport fans reading this—hello, camera!—or watching, let me advise you to call Southport and ask for your money back. Gary is going to flash the phone number up on the screen now.

I don't know how to do that.

Ah, someone will have the number. Pass it around on social media. That wasn't acceptable. Get your money back.

Some people might say this is sour grapes because Kidderminster beat you with a defensive style.

No, that's not right, for many reasons. First, Kidderminster went toe-to-toe with us for an hour, and in that hour they outplayed us. Then they did a surprise switch in tactics which, no fake irony now, shocked me to my core. It was absolute genius. Perfect plan, perfectly executed. I have incredible respect for what Kidderminster did to us. And, by the way, their fans loved every minute of it. Everyone in the stadium loved that match and will talk about it for years. There's no comparison between that bravery, those warriors, that titanic contest, and tonight.

Who was your man of the match today?

Reece Killan. He was the star of the show. When people think of this match, they'll always think of him. This match is how he'll be remembered.

XP Balance: 2,799

Debt repaid: 2,480/3,000

While I took a shower, I thought about the rest of the season. If the interview did what I hoped, this Killan guy would get sacked and every other manager in the league would be wary about going ultra-defensive against us. Certainly in their home matches. We had another away game on Saturday; I was very interested to see how that guy would set his team up.

Meanwhile, playing the whole second half had really cut the amount of experience points I got. I got 4 XP per minute as the manager, and only 1 per minute as a player. I would need to give serious consideration to the number of minutes I played. I could play the last fifteen or twenty minutes every now and then, and maybe more if we were losing. Something like that.

Still, I was getting fitter and was moving—crawling—towards the 3,000 XP I needed to buy the Injuries perk. I had discount codes I could use in the shop, but saving ten percent on a 10,000-XP perk made more sense than saving ten percent on a much cheaper one.

I had decided to buy Injuries, then explore the Contracts section. If I could find out how much players from other teams were being paid, and how long their contracts were for, I'd be able to do all kinds of interesting things. After that, I was supposed to buy Wibwob, the 10,000-XP perk that it seemed would give me incredible tactical flexibility.

But I hadn't unlocked any attributes for ages. I really needed to see some progress there. Seeing one more attribute wouldn't make a massive difference to my performance as a manager, I didn't think, but on the other hand, the attributes were pretty fundamental. So . . . Injuries, Contracts, Attributes, Wibwob.

Quite a lot of XP needed for that lot, and that's if I didn't get sidetracked picking up monthly perks, which I would, because they were designed to be irresistible. I'd lost the XP I normally got from managing the women, although I planned to put the free time to good use.

One thing that would help get XP faster would be finally paying off my debt from when I bought God Save the King on credit. The curse was deducting ten percent from my income to pay down the debt, and the end was nearly in sight.

God Save the King allowed me to increase one attribute on one player every season. I didn't have a completely free choice, but one of the options was finishing. Last season, I'd used the perk to increase my client Ziggy's finishing from 16 to 17. Ziggy was doing okay down at FC United in the division below Chester. He'd played four times in the league and three times in various cups, scoring twice. Not amazing, but solid.

This season, I had planned to use the curse to boost Youngster, but he was improving steadily without extra help, so I'd started to think about using it on Henri Lyons—ironically another increase in finishing from 16 to 17. But then Henri's progress had stalled. Tomorrow he would go out on loan, and if his CA started to improve again, I would use the perk on him. If it didn't, if Henri had some kind of . . . block stopping him from getting better . . .

A block stopping him from getting past CA 58? When he had PA 90?

That would be a very low block.

"You okay, boss?"

"Huh?" I turned to see Raffi was showering next to me.

"You were laughing."

"Laughing at my own jokes." He tsked and got on with his scrubbing. "Six goals for you this season, isn't it?"

"I don't count. Take every game as it comes, Max."

"Maybe it's five."

"No, it's six." He grinned, showing all his teeth. Rare for him to be so demonstrative.

"People are taking notice," I said. "Scouts and stuff."

"Scouts?" he said, surprised.

"You just keep doing what you're doing," I said. "Good things are coming."

MD: Please do not initiate refunds at other clubs. Not at this club, either, but especially not other clubs. The Southport directors are not very happy with us right now.

Me: Okay, amigo. I pwomise.

Wednesday, October 25.

At training, there was an overwhelmingly good vibe. Physio Dean was by the side of the pitch, ignoring requests for massages, while he scrolled through social media. He was convinced, as we all were, that the Southport guy would be sacked as we trained.

"Where's Henri?" said Glenn, as we drilled side by side.

"He's on secondment," I said.

"What?"

"He's not training with us today."

"Oh. You gave him the day off?"

"No. He'll be working harder than he has for years."

"You're not going to tell me, is that it?"

I smiled. "There's a good chance I've done something very stupid. If that's the case, Henri and I will never speak of it. If it works, we'll let you know."

He looked into the middle distance. "Expect the unexpected. This place is a bit of a mind fuck, boss. There's always something mad happening. People like me need stability."

I bent to do some stretches. "You're doing great. You're more adaptable than you think."

There was no change in his expression, but I think he was pleased. "So Jackie's back. Got your Wednesday nights proper free again. You can go scouting or do some extra training or take your girl out."

"Absolutely," I said. "But not tonight. Tonight's all about the peaceful transition of power."

"Right," he said, not knowing what I was talking about.

"Tonight's the handover ceremony."

"Oh, I see."

"No," I said. "You don't."

Just then, Physio Dean jumped up and punched the air. To the tune of "Guantanamera," he sang, "Sacked in the morning! You're getting sacked in the morning. Sacked in the morn-ing!"

Glenn put his hands on his hips and stared. "You've done it again." He resumed his stretch. "Is that the end of the low blocks, then?"

"Far from it. There will be loads here in Chester. But away? Yeah. Let's see what Curzon do on Saturday. I think that'll tell us what we can expect."

"How do you get these ideas, though?"

I spoke a little more harshly than I wanted. "It's pretty simple. I imagine paying thirty quid to take my kids to see a football match. If they never want to go back, something's gone wrong."

Ryder nodded. We'd hit one of those weird little air pockets caused by my dual roles as player and manager. When someone hit those pockets, there was turbulence. He clicked his seatbelt back into place. "Yes, boss."

Before Jackie Reaper's first training session with Chester Women's first team, he checked the ladies were decent and went into the changing rooms at the sports complex. It was my instruction that he should say a few words to the women. Introduce himself to new players like Julie, outline his methodology, talk about his preferred formations, and answer questions.

I'd sent him a text saying I'd be late and he should get on with it.

Jill told me later that it was obvious Jackie had prepared well. He had lots of little notes on cards.

"Hi, ladies," he said, and that was as far as he got with his prepared remarks.

"Can I stop you there?" said Maddy. "Max hired an interpreter for Dani for today. Normally we do it by text message, but Max wanted a smooth introduction, so he's got a guy to come. Paid with his own money, he said. I think he's just in the toilet."

On cue, there was a flushing noise and an older guy, perhaps fifty, emerged. He didn't use the sink, but wandered out, admired the young women vaguely, and spotted Jackie. "You must be Reaper!" said the guy in a posh voice. He looked and dressed like an aristocrat who had fallen on hard times. He shook Jackie's hand, and Jackie reacted with horror as some liquid transferred onto his hand. "Now, then. Which is the deaf one? Oh, really? Splendid, splendid. Well?" he barked. "Let's get on with it! No slacking!"

Jackie stared at the interpreter with some distaste but composed himself. "Hi, ladies," he said, and glanced over. "Aren't you going to sign that?"

"What?" boomed the guy. He had the delivery of an olden-days board-treader. An act-OR. "No need, man. No need. Skip dessert, straight to the port, what!"

Jackie's jaw clenched and unclenched. He decided to rise above. "Me name's Jackie. Got scouted by Everton when I was a kid. Played striker at school, but they moved me to centre back." He was just warming to the tale, and the women were very interested, but Jackie couldn't help but look at the interpreter. He was making no effort to translate. "Are you gonna do your job?"

"What?" barked the guy.

"Are you going to interpret what I'm saying or what?"

"What on earth are you saying?" said the man, peering through rheumy eyes at the young whippersnapper. "I can't understand a bloody word."

"Is dat right?" said Jackie, a hint of menace in his eyes.

"Bloody foreigners," said the man, his cheeks flushing. "Come here, take our jobs, take our women. Can't even speak the bloody lingo! Brexit means Brexit!"

That was the moment Jackie hesitated. He looked around the room and some instinct made him focus on Dani. He pointed at her, and that was it. The women burst into laughter, and I emerged from the showers where I'd been listening. A few women, under the guise of texting Dani, had been filming the whole thing for me to watch again and again.

"Fucking hell, Max!" said Jackie, his entire head crimson.

I went over and gave him a hug and noted that his good-natured response to the prank had won him a lot of reputation points in the room.

When the euphoria died down a little, I spoke. "Jackie, this is Tom. He's an actor and, by the way, big fan of yours. He really, really didn't want to do this to you but fifty quid is fifty quid."

"I'm really sorry," said Tom, stretching out a hand. Jackie looked at it. Tom noticed. "Oh! It was hand sanitiser."

Jackie smelled his hand and sagged with relief. He shook Tom's hand. "You were bloody convincing." Dozens of tiny head shakes suggested he was mentally reliving the scene. "What would you have done if I hadn't said anything?"

"Fake sign language," said Tom. "Increasingly obvious until you confronted me."

"Should I do my speech or what?"

"No need," I said. "Everyone knows who you are. They know you're the new bosh. We can get out there."

Dani came forward and pulled me on the elbow. I stepped back and she looked at Jackie and signed.

"Sorry, Dani," he started, but Tom interrupted.

"She's asking if you can make her a better player."

"Oh, you really know sign language?"

"Of course."

As he replied, Jackie looked from Dani to Tom. "Look at her, not Tom," I said, which was the polite way but was harder than you'd think.

Jackie nodded and started again. "I'll make you a better player."

"Will we win the league?" asked Dani.

"If we beat Altrincham, yes."

Dani's next question came with lots of violent hand slaps. "Are we going to defend or are we going to attack?"

Jackie smiled. "Both. But most of the time we'll attack."

"I want to attack," said Dani. The sign for *attack* seemed to be one finger pointing up on one hand and the fingers of the other rushing in to cover it.

Jackie tried to do the sign himself. "Attack."

"Attack until we drop," said Dani.

Jackie grinned, and what he said next smashed away all doubts about his mental well-being. He was well and truly his old self. "My style is a little bit more *sophisticated* than Max's."

Dani grinned and gave me a traitorous look. She turned back to Jackie. "Show me."

I watched as Jackie led the women through their session. Simple drills, nothing complicated, but somehow the ball fizzed a little faster when Jackie was leading things. Somehow, there was more intensity, more concentration, and more output. Attributes and CA went green all over the place, like flash bulbs at a film premiere.

As soon as we'd agreed terms, his staff profile had appeared in the Chester Women menu. It stayed in place even though I was no longer the manager, and I remembered that it had appeared when I was director of football, not when I'd started officially managing them. The same numbers hovered above his head now.

JACKIE REAPER	
Adaptability	7
Coaching Goalkeepers	10
Coaching Outfield Players	20
Determination	7
Judging Player Ability	11
Judging Player Potential	14
Level of Discipline	11
Man Management	19
Motivating	15
Tactical Knowledge	15
Working with Youngsters	14
Coaching Style	Technique-based
Preferred Formation	3-5-2
Preferred Style	Attractive attacking
Other	n/a

His superpower, of course, was coaching, but he had enough going on to be a good manager, too. His high man management and motivating would pay off, as would his tactical knowledge. Fifteen. Did that feel high or low? We'd had interesting chats about football, and he certainly saw most of what I saw. But not quite everything.

Could Jackie Reaper bring these women all the way to the Women's Super League? I was pretty sure he could. I'd give him great talents, he'd train them up, and he'd make mostly good in-game decisions.

Yeah.

I smiled. Passing the baton felt awesome, and it made me even more ener-gised to find more Danis, more Maddys.

Their time was up, and a lot of happy young women were collecting their gear, about to head to the showers. I asked them to come over for a second. They gathered around me in a semicircle.

"Ladies. That was good, right? I know. I know. So, listen. I want you to know that I'm still here. I won't be at every match because I'll be out scouting. Checking out the opposition, stealing their good players. But I'm still here, the eye in the sky, making sure you're progressing, all that jazz. Jackie's your man-ager and you can trust him. He's, er . . . He's the guy who found me. Gave me my break. Believed in me the way I believe in you. All right? He's top. Have no doubts about that. Off you go."

They left, but Dani hung back. Tom provided a good opportunity for her to say some things to me without creating a digital record and without her parents checking what was said.

As always, she was blunt. "Who is a better manager? You or Jackie?"

"Me," I said. "And I'm a better scout. But he's a better coach. This is the perfect situation for you."

She considered that, then accepted it. "I want to sign a contract."

"Okay."

"And I want Ruth to be my agent."

"That's smart. You're going to be a big star."

She thought about that and signed with an excess of energy. "How did you know?"

She meant how had I seen it the first time I laid eyes on her, playing poorly in a pan-disability tournament in Crewe. I smiled. "Because I saw you could play like me." At first she nodded, but then the arrogance of the statement kicked in and she erupted into a whirlwind of flailing arms and dextrous fin-gers. Tom remained silent. "What did she say?"

"Er . . . I'll tell you after you pay me the hundred quid."

Thursday, October 26.

The convoy from Chester to West Didsbury and Chorlton AFC was sort of absurd, really.

Raffi led the way, and that made sense. He was going to have one of his private sessions with Cody, the second-best coach I knew. Raffi's wife, Shona, was in the car with him, and his dad was planning to come along. After train-ing, they'd have some family time.

The next car was the Brig's smooth Volvo, a real Rolls Royce of a car, con-taining said Brig and myself. I'd asked Pascal if he wanted to come and help me with my session, and he had said yes before I'd finished asking. Then I thought, if we're going to Manchester, Youngster might want to see his family, so he was tagging along, too.

Not far behind, I assumed, was MD. He was coming with two of the board members to check out the club I'd bought. The idea was to put their minds at ease about my commitment to Chester. Enough to get them to shut up about it, anyway.

Then there was a car with Vivek and his family. Vivek was a young PA–66 defender who didn't have much experience with football and that was holding back his development. The problem was that back home in Chester, I couldn't put him in the first team because he would one hundred percent cost us goals, and the under-eighteens were pretty terrible, so he wasn't learning a lot from the matches they played. The obvious solution—obvious to me—was to loan him to a club like West Didsbury and Chorlton. He would get minutes at exactly his level in a supportive environment, and if he messed up, the club's handsome, one-nation centrist owner would forgive him.

In yet another car were Livia and Jackie, and I would soon find out they had managed to get Henri in the car, though of course he would only travel in the passenger seat, after he had adjusted it to his liking.

From the other side of the country came Emma, and from just down the road, Ziggy.

A huge turnout for something of little consequence! But people were curious, and the more people said they were going, the more it turned into a whole thing.

When I got out of the car, I felt that unfamiliar sense of thrill and pride that came from the word *own*. I *owned* this place.

The giant floodlights shining down on us? I owned them. (I also owned the bills.)

The Ultras stand, with space for fifty hipsters? I owned it. (I also owned the cost of cleaning up the beer spilled after goals.)

The food huts, the changing rooms, the indoor spaces, and then—wonder of wonders—the pitch. I owned that. (I also owned a lawnmower.)

I tried to be ownerly. Suave and professional, but it was hard to stop smiling.

Some of the volunteers from West had come in to serve food and meet Emma and my various acquaintances. The main one was called Jane. She did a lot of fundraising, had the word *WEST* tattooed on her arm, and had two boys in the youth team. J.C., the men's first-team manager, was there. He was bubbly and enthusiastic and while his stats were low, he was open to the idea of helping Vivek's career get going.

I introduced Jane to Vivek's mum, J.C. to Vivek, MD to his West equivalent, and let them take care of each other. The area was bristling with hospitality freaks and organisers, and soon everyone was helping everyone take care of everyone.

Meanwhile, Raffi had half the pitch to himself for his session with Cody. I kept half an eye on it while I mingled and talked to the people who cared about my intentions for the club and, most importantly, for the young players in its charge.

I grabbed Ziggy and showed him the man of the moment. "Ziggy, this is Vivek."

"Viv," said Viv.

"Oh!" I said, pleased. Taking a nickname shouldn't have been a big deal, but it felt like one. "Lot of great players called Viv."

"Viv Anderson," he said.

"Who's been telling you about Viv Anderson?"

He pointed. "Raffi."

"Top lad."

"Viv Richards," said Ziggy, with a hummus taco primed and ready to be shoved in his gob.

"That's cricket," I said.

"Still a top player," he said, though it was hard to tell with his mouth so full. He wandered away to eat next to Jackie and Emma, and I got ready for my session.

Raffi's drills were pretty conventional.

Mine were pretty fucking weird.

First, Cody tied me with a long elastic rope. He gave Raffi the other end.

I had to touch a mannequin, step back, receive a pass from the "goalie," run away as Youngster sprinted towards me—the little shit was *fast!*—while Raffi held on to the elastic for dear life, and Pascal made a diagonal run.

If I could resist all the stresses and make all the calculations, I had to fire a forward pass into Pascal's path.

Trying to move and sprint and calculate while Raffi yanked my chain, almost literally, was pretty brutal.

After ten minutes I was wrecked, and during a break Henri came over.

"Max, I love your football club," he said, appearing about five feet directly above my head.

"It's not mine, I'm just the custodian etcetera, etcetera."

"What is this drill you are doing?"

"This is how we beat Salford City."

"Ah, yes, I see it now. The elastic represents the distorting effect of celebrity on a previously uncelebrated club."

"How was your training today?"

"Challenging. Strange. We need to talk, Max."

"Soon. Help me up."

He pulled me to my feet and Cody explained the next drill.

I would receive the ball with Youngster touch-tight to me. I would use one of three moves to get away from him, then fire an accurate long pass to Pascal. All the while, Raffi would be pulling me here and there with the elastic, a job he enjoyed far too much.

While I put my body through hell, my friends snacked, drank, and relaxed. A good time was had by all. Almost all.

The shower was cold. Not enough money for heating, even for the owner. But the company was warm, and even Raffi's dad pretended to like me.

"I'll be able to watch my boy on television," he said. "Wrapped up nice and warm. Perfect!"

"Are we on TV, then? That confirmed?"

"Yes," said MD. He was smiling, but stopped when he saw me react strangely. "Is that no good?"

"It's good. We get money, right? But it's going to make it harder to leave players out of the team. I'd drop myself to make space for someone, but . . ."

"But what?"

I sighed. "I have an idea of how we might win . . . but if it goes wrong, it could be especially embarrassing."

Friday, October 27.

Around 1 p.m., while I was checking videos of recent Curzon Ashton matches, I checked the Chester Men squad screen. Henri's CA had increased to 59.

I not only punched the air, but kung fu kicked it, too.

Saturday, October 28. Match 14 of 46: Curzon Ashton versus Chester.

As we approached 2 p.m., exactly an hour before kickoff, I felt a crazy amount of excitement. In a few minutes, I'd find out if my plan to take a sledgehammer to the low block option had worked. I felt like I'd done my part beautifully. I'd humiliated the manager who'd tried it, turned the fans against him, caused a civil war at the club, and Chester had won the match anyway. Oh, and the prick got himself well and truly sacked.

Surely, surely, no one would do it again?

Well, I was about to find out.

I didn't have a place where I could hide out like I did in the Deva. That was one big disadvantage—one of the only ones, really—of playing away. The options were uninspiring: wait in the dressing room, in the dugout, or on the pitch. Every option was far from private. I never did like opening my Christmas presents in front of others.

My mind raced through the other manager's options. If they played normally, there was a risk we would pass through their lines and run up the score. Defend, then. Keep our goal threat contained, try to score on a counter or from a set piece. Yes, absolutely. I was sure he'd be defensive. But *how* defensive? This guy was bang average in every way and had never had a unique or interesting thought. If *he* played normally, that would almost certainly be the default for the rest of the season. I was fairly sure of that. If he set up in a low block, it'd keep happening. Sixteen entertaining games of football, or sixteen absolute snorefests.

Come on, come on, I said to the clock.

"Mr. Best," said Youngster. "Are you okay?"

"Yes. Shush."

"I rarely see you nervous."

"I'm waiting to hear if I got planning permission for the large statue I want to erect. Of myself."

"On a Saturday?"

"Mate," I said, but then I burst out laughing. He'd distracted me enough. I stood up and went to the tactics board. "All right, guys. Team talk. You guys ready for this?" I scrunched my eyes up and clenched every muscle in my body. When I released, the feeling was moderately cathartic. "My information is that they'll be doing . . . a low block."

There was an outpouring of disbelief.

"What do you want us to do, boss?" said Glenn. "Copy them, stir up the home fans?"

I shook my head. Even I didn't have the stomach to do that sixteen times all over the north of England. Someone had said "You beat Max Best with a low block," and that was gospel now. We had to live with it for a few weeks, and then I'd very much sort it out in the January transfer window. "Just play normal. Normal rest defence. Normal overloads, overlaps. Mix the crosses, high and low. Be patient." I cleared my throat in a bid to mask my frustration, which of course only proved how frustrated I was. "This is our life now. Glenn, good news for you. Loads of clean sheets this season." A clean sheet is where you don't concede a goal.

"Yeah." He didn't look especially happy. None of us did.

Morale was high, though. We were fit. We would probably spend the next ninety minutes doing a glorified attack versus defence drill. And like Pascal had said, if we had thirty shots every game, we'd win nine times out of ten. The thought cheered me up. "Okay. Let's go plant our flag in their patch, yeah? Extra-loud victory music today. But you know what sound I really like? The home fans booing their players. Serenade me with that, lads, and you'll get a bonus."

"What's the bonus?" said Aff.

"A billion pounds each. I don't know, do I? I just thought of it."

"Boos?" said Ryan Jack.

"Yes, mate," I said, surprised by how dense he was being. He was normally razor sharp.

"No, Max. Booze. Booze for boos."

It took me a second, but then it clicked. "Yes!" I said, giving him a noisy high ten. "You give me boos, I'll give you booze. Boos today and next Saturday after the cup, we'll go out on the piss. My treat." I smiled as Trick's and D-Day's morale improved one level. Our morale advantage was unprecedented now. "Fuck these guys! Go and show them who's boss!"

HOME IS WHERE THE HURT IS

Curzon Ashton 0 Chester 2: Seals Third After Drab Affair

Chester went third in the table with a solid if uninspiring win over a woeful Curzon Ashton team. Two goals in quick succession saw the Blues race into pole position for the win, and they never had to get out of third gear to maintain their lead.

The first half saw the home team show no ambition, but they made it difficult for Max Best's men. At halftime, no changes were made in the playing staff or playing style, but one of Chester's attacks paid off, with Henri Lyons heading home from a Ryan Jack free kick. Curzon briefly showed some initiative, but their first real foray into the Chester half resulted in what is becoming a Chester hallmark: a fast, accurate, and deadly counterattack. The move was finished with aplomb by Raffi Brown.

Then came a bizarre cameo by player-manager Best, in which he seemed to reimagine himself as the second coming of Michel Platini, with disastrous results. Best, normally so controlled and composed, buzzed around like a drunk wasp, sprayed shots miles over the bar, hit crosses that nearly exited the stadium, and took one free kick that floated so slowly and softly into the arms of the goalkeeper that there was laughter in the press box when Best fell to his knees in disappointment.

All in all, a decent performance from the away side and most of the squad seem to be in good form for the massive FA Cup tie against moneybags Salford City next weekend.

During my post-match shower, I remembered that I had waited until after the 70th minute to go on the pitch so that I'd definitely have enough XP to buy the Injuries perk. I bought it there and then, and as I dried off, I checked out the sitch.

Buying the perk enriched the Injuries and Bans tab of a player profile. I looked at Henri's.

Injuries: None

Okay! That was the same info I got with the first five guys I looked at. But Glenn Ryder was talking to Physio Dean and they both had frowns on their faces.

Injuries: Potential foot injury

I wandered over. "What's the haps?"

"Guy stood on me at a corner," said my captain. "Twat."

Having a giant dude with spikes coming out of his shoes stand on your foot is just about as painful as it sounds, but as long as there was nothing broken, Glenn could play in the next game. "Dean. Full works. X-rays, MRIs, Rorschach tests."

"Rorschach tests on his metatarsals, Max?"

"You heard me. Get photos distributed to all the churches. I want people praying and laying on hands for this foot. I want, like, questions asked in the House of Parliament about this foot. This foot has to be ready to play next Saturday."

"I'm definitely in the team, then?" said the guy who was pretty much the first name on the team sheet. He'd never asked that before, even as a joke. I noticed that a few conversations near us had died down. People wanted clues to how I was thinking. If I wasn't careful, I could piss a lot of people off by excluding them from our televised FA Cup match.

I looked around before returning my attention to Ryder. "You're in if you're fit. I'm going to explain the whole kit and caboodle on Monday morning. There will be some unhappy people, and I'll need your help keeping their chins up. Do you know what I mean? We need to practice my weird idea instead of normal training, but standards can't slip. We've got Darlington soon."

"I'm with you, Max."

I looked around. The curse didn't say anything about Robbo's dodgy shoulder or Joe Anka's tight calves, so clearly they didn't meet the threshold of hurting enough for me to care about.

The only other potential issue was with Pascal. "Dude," I said, waving him over.

He hadn't been in the matchday squad, but he'd warmed up and kicked some balls around. He said he liked to get a feel for the stadium in case he ever played there in the future. He would note the pitch dimensions and how the wind blew and so on, along with tips on how to get the most out of the referee. Next time he played in that stadium or against that team or under that ref, he'd be even better prepared. "Yes, Max?"

"Anything you want to say to Dean?"

Pascal looked slightly panicked. He was never sure if I was pranking him or if there was some puddle of British culture he was about to splash into. "Happy birthday, Dean?"

"Why don't you tell us about your knee?" My new tab had said *Potential knee injury*, and I didn't like the sound of that. Knees were a lot more expensive than feet.

"Oh," he said, flexing it. "It's fine."

"Is it fine, mate?" I said, unimpressed.

"Well . . . I did feel a twinge."

"Report!" I barked. "Self-report! What the fuck!"

He turned red. "Sorry, Max, it's . . . it's nothing. I felt a twinge and then it was fine."

"Bullshit. Dean, can you pop in tomorrow and check it out?"

I had never asked him to work on Sunday before. This was serious. "Yes, Max."

"Thanks. Pascal, you'd better be fucking honest, right? No dicking around with this one. You are my tactical plan for Salford. Do you get me? So if you're going to pull up after five minutes, we're fucked. Like, we'll be a laughingstock nationwide. If you can't play, I'll come up with something else. But if you tell me you can and you can't . . ." I tried to think of a threat that expressed how angry I'd be without getting into overly violent imagery. The way I was squeezing my fists seemed pretty clear, though.

"Yes, Max. I promise."

I glared at him as he went off to his part of the bench. He sat and stared at his knee as though he'd never seen one before. "Boss?" said Glenn.

"Yep."

"I thought I heard a couple of boos at the end. Does that qualify for a piss-up?"

"Brig," I said, waving my assistant over. "Did you hear boos at the end?"

"No, sir."

"That's just these home fans lacking imagination. Their team was dire and we stuck to our task like champions." Having a post-match party was either stupid or necessary, depending on what happened in the match *after* the party. Squad morale had gone up when I'd mentioned it, and I didn't want to be a relentless taskmaster. The guys were doing everything I wanted, and a trip to Vegas, so to speak, could go a long way in terms of team bonding. "I was thinking this week might be ideal for a bit of a blowout. The cup match will be fucking agony for almost all the players; win or lose, they'll have earned a pint. Then on Tuesday, we're home to Tamworth. They're one of the worst teams in the league. I'll take a scrappy one–nil, there, and then we'll have high morale going into the Darlington game."

"Some players will overdo it, sir."

"This Monday morning, I'll outline the likely teams for the next two games. For example, Trick will start against Tamworth unless he drinks himself out of contention. And so on. Glenn, do you guys drink more or less when the WAGs are with you?"

He considered that for quite some time. "Less."

"Bingo."

"And you're paying, are you, sir?"

"I'll pay . . . the first such and such an amount. To be confirmed."

"There's nothing else you might need the money for in the near future?" said the Brig, watching me carefully.

"Can't think of anything. Can you?"

Of course he couldn't talk about our deal in public, so he said, "No, sir."

I tried to give him a cheeky grin, but it didn't come out right. Maybe it was the chat we'd had about dark mode. His eyes were cutting through me like a chainsaw. I could get scared or I could get practical. "If we were based in Manchester, we'd go to Stalybridge," I mused.

"What?" said Physio Dean.

"Staly Vegas, we call it. Good night out, there."

"Leave the planning to me, boss," said Ryder.

So I left him to it. I walked to my little spot of bench and got dressed. The Brig came over. "Would you like me to do the post-match interview, sir?"

"Yes, please." He started to walk away. "Wait." I got quieter. "Are you going to be monitoring my spending on an ongoing basis?"

Something of a twinkle came into his eyes. "No, sir. I was joking before."

"Huh. Today I learned jokes can be terrifying."

"One thing, sir. May I ask . . . why you played like that? In case it comes up in the interview."

While making sure we didn't let Curzon back into the game, I had played like hot garbage. "Sure. Some analyst at Salford will watch the footage of this and think I'm going to try to play CAM or right wing or something. And they'll see me playing dogshit and plan accordingly."

"So it's misdirection."

"Yes."

"I will say you played your best but had an off day. Something like that?"

I thought about it. My new perk came to mind. "Say I'm carrying a calf strain and tried to play through it but obviously it didn't go well and now I face a race against time to get fit enough to play in the cup, blah blah blah."

"Race against time. Got it."

"Actually, no, then people will stress about that the whole week. Just . . . pretend I played great. That will make Salford even more complacent. Say you thought I played with great dynamism and . . ."

"Thrust."

"Perfect. I'll watch the women tomorrow, by the way."

"Very good, sir. I'll pick you up."

Sunday, October 29.

Jackie Reaper's luck had turned in a big way. When he took over as the men's team manager, he had been catapulted into a stressful relegation battle with a series of tough away games. Now, as the women's team manager, his first match was at home to the worst team in the league, Ellesmere Port.

Their average CA was 16, and with Jackie playing an unexpected 4-5-1, ours was exactly 19. A few players had hit their CA caps already, but with the others progressing quickly under Jackie's coaching, we'd surely be the strongest team in the league from around January or February, depending on exactly how good Altrincham were.

A few postponements would be good, I thought to myself as I watched us quickly get a grip on the midfield. Like with the men's team, any matches that got moved to the end of the season would be ones we'd have a better chance of winning.

Ellesmere had a couple of players who would improve our squad, so I asked Jill to sound out their manager about a possible January transfer. Of course there were plenty of players I could get for free, but if I could sign a few tier-seven nobodies for a nominal fee, say two or three thousand pounds, then why not?

Jackie looked relaxed and confident, and his team played relaxed and confidently, and they eased to a 3–0 win marred only by Lucy hobbling off with a bad knock to the ankle. Later that evening, the curse told me it was strained ligaments and she'd be out for two weeks.

So . . . that was good to know, but Dean or Livia could have told me that. Did it benefit me to know it as soon as Dean did? Sometimes the curse seemed to come from an age before smartphones. Which it had.

The Injuries perk was probably most helpful in situations like Pascal's possible knee injury—if I could see those things, we wouldn't put him into a match and make it worse. Was that worth 3,000 XP? Probably. Long term. For the moment, I still had a fair amount of buyer's remorse.

More positively, Dean texted me that both Glenn and Pascal would be fit to play against Salford.

With the win in the bag, and another 180 XP in my pocket, I slipped away and followed Playdar to a field where a PA–55 ten-year-old right midfielder was doing outrageous things against his mates. I added his uniqueness to my collective.

Then it was back to Ruth's barn to watch video after video of Salford City, looking for something that would make me change my mind about the crazy tactical idea I had come up with one night when I'd eaten way too much cheese.

In the evening, Emma called and I explained my latest Maxterplan to her. She fell asleep before I got to the second slide.

Monday, October 30.

Both Salford and the club that bears its name had undergone remarkable transformations in recent times. Massive redevelopment centred around Salford Quays (at the end of the famous Manchester Ship Canal) led to the area being chosen for a major BBC office. The Quays are also the home of the Lowry Centre, where I had brought Emma to look at paintings of matchstick men going to watch the football, and the Imperial War Museum, where you could see another Lowry painting, this time of matchstick men going to work. Yeah, I don't understand that one, either. Still makes more sense than parading a horse around a football pitch, though.

Salford City, meanwhile, were bought by five legendary Manchester United players in 2014. These players were part of the "Class of '92," the group of young players who won the FA Youth Cup in 1992, progressed into the Man United first team, and dominated English football for years after. (David

Beckham, the sixth member of the Class of '92, invested in the club a few years later than the rest.)

The owners tracked their progress in a documentary—*that* sounds familiar—and Salford rose from tier eight to tier four. Last season, they'd made it to the playoffs, hinting they were one of the better teams in the division. I reckoned their best team would be around CA 90. Maybe even as high as CA 100. They would probably rotate the team to some extent, and they probably wouldn't come to Chester fully fired up, but still, they were almost certainly going to dick us.

"All right shut the eff up," I said, sweeping my eyes around the drab meeting room.

"Eff?" said Steve Alton.

"I'm trying to swear less," I said. My players and staff looked at me like I was crazy. "I'm going on telly, aren't I? I have to watch my Ps and Qs and not offend the wee 'uns."

"Can you say *wee*?" wondered Trick Williams, because that was his level as a human being. Getting rid of him in January would be better than a cup run.

"Let's get stuck in," I said. "It's going to be a long week. It's cup mania out there, but in here we have to be able to switch it on and off. Now is off. Later, get on your socials, hype it up, promise the moon. I want a full stadium."

"Boss," said Glenn. "Can we discuss something important first?"

"Yes," I said, getting slightly hot. "Let's talk about all the things that are more important than our televised FA Cup match against the team owned by David Beckham, Ryan Giggs, and Paul Scholes. Yeah, great."

He looked down, but decided it *was* important. "There's a rumour that Henri has been training with Tranmere Rovers."

"Well, that's crazy bonkers. Don't listen to mad internet things. You know all the footballers who turn into full nutjobs because they click on a flat Earth video and get lost in the algorithm. Do I need to stage an intervention before it's too late?"

"No. I think Henri is training with Tranmere because Henri told me he is training with Tranmere."

It was my turn to look down, and I got a rueful, sheepish kind of look on my face. "Fine. Henri's training with Tranmere. Great. Now you know. What's the problem?"

There was the mildest kind of uproar. People turning to each other, eyes popping, saying, "Did I hear that right?" and going "What the—?" Some guys flicking their wrists, a gesture meaning *holy sheeeet what*.

"So is he leaving?" said Tony Hetherington, my only other striker. I wasn't sure if he was excited because he'd get to play every game from now on or terrified because he'd have to play every game from now on.

"How do you get from there to there?" I said.

"He's training with Tranmere," said Tony, turning to look at Glenn for confirmation. Glenn nodded.

I brought my fingers to the bridge of my nose. "Everybody shut up. I've sent Henri to train with Tranmere. That's the end of the story. I've sent Henri to train with Tranmere and there's nothing more to say. That's the epilogue. You might say, hey that's a pretty boring and stupid way to end a story you need to work on your epilogues mate, and I'd say, yeah but that's the end so I don't know what to tell you. But that's *it*. He's training with them. He'll play for us on Saturday, as a sub probably, and he'll start against Tamworth and Darlington. Do I need to get the fixtures and read them all out? I don't get why you're reacting like this."

Glenn rubbed his fist against his cheek. "It's quite strange, Max. He plays for *us*. Why's he training with *them*?"

"What's strange about it? Look, I made a bet with the owner of Tranmere. He's a great guy, by the way. More money than sense, but I like that about him. Tranmere have those GPS vests, and we're doing an experiment. Today and Wednesday, they'll train as normal. Tuesday and Thursday they'll surround the training pitch with GoPro cameras. It's my hypothesis that Henri will train twenty percent harder on days when there's cameras around, and we'll be able to measure that thanks to the vest. All right? It's completely explainable. Explicable."

"But he was there last week," said Youngster.

"Holy eff!" I snapped. "Can we talk about effing Salford City? The biggest game of the season? Maybe? Do you think? I've already said I don't want him to leave and he doesn't want to leave. Effing wake up, lads! Are you going to walk out at three o'clock on Saturday, walk up to the nearest camera and start crying? Wailing and gnashing your teeth? Waah! Max did something I don't understand! That's more important to me than my career as a professional football playerrrrrr!" I stood with my hands on my hips for a moment, but the fake tantrum wasn't moving anyone. Ryder, in particular, looked like he would dig in for battle. I probably needed to tell them something close to the truth. "Look, I've had the fantastical, outlandish idea that training with different coaches with different tactical ideas, with a higher intensity, with better facilities, might help Henri. Might kick him up a level. Okay? The Tranmere owner is a mate. He thinks I'm bananas but he's letting me indulge my little daydream. He owes me a favour, which I've called in to get Henri sharper. Couple of weeks away from you lot might do him some good, don't you think? If you really, really need to hold his hand during training and swap bits of your packed lunches with him, let me know and I'll call him back."

Sam Topps had heard enough about Tranmere. "I'm ready to talk about the Salford match, boss."

"Thank you, Sam," I said, politely.

"Five thirty kickoff," said the Brig.

"Shit, right. We're on TV!" I beamed. "Guys! Guys! We're on TV! You excited? Ooh, Youngster, are you excited?"

"I feel that there is a wrong answer to this question. I will back my gut feeling and say no, I am not excited, even though in truth I am."

I nodded and pointed at him. "Be excited. You've earned this. But be proportional. This is not the best thing that's ever happened to us. This is going to be routine from now on. Cup runs, games being moved for the broadcasters, trips to Wembley. Enjoy it all, enjoy every minute, but don't come crying to me if you don't play this Saturday. This is the new normal. Got that?"

Sam Topps, the maniac, was in heaven. He loved it when I got intense like this. "Yes, boss."

"Quick word about us. When we're not freaking out trying to understand the interesting and creative decisions I make—and let's face it, modern psychology isn't advanced enough to help with that—we are a good team. We've got togetherness, heart, fitness, and sometimes a bit of quality, too. In this league, we are a menace. I effing resent the way teams are low blocking us, but in a way it's a compliment. They know if we play our best, we'll smash them. Right?

"Salford are a different proposition. They've got expensive players, okay manager, modern coaches, and with their celebrity owners, they're used to being televised. They had a bad start to the season, but recently they added a big, strong striker to be their focal point and since then their form has gone right up. It's a strong, fit team, good on the ball, and they've got a bit of a battering ram to bash through us if plan A doesn't work.

"So how do we beat them?

"We don't. It's impossible." I paused, waiting for some reaction, and got nothing. "Why is no one saying anything?"

"Because you've got a plan," said Aff, with a hint of excitement. Like Sam, he liked when I pushed him past what he thought was possible.

"Yeah, but when *I* say it's impossible, *you* say you have sometimes believed six impossible things before breakfast." *Nothing* from this bunch. Henri would have laughed. "Didn't we set that up? Sort of a call and response thing?" I walked over to my flipchart and brought it closer. The team stirred. The flipchart was proof I did have a plan. Even Vimsy shuffled from foot to foot, unable to contain his curiosity.

"Salford mostly play four-one-four-one, switching to four-three-three quite often. They like to get narrow and dominate the middle. That's important.

"Next, a quick lesson in pressing.

"Most of you think pressing means running fast at the guy who's got the ball, but that was twenty years ago. It's been refined and refined since then. I'm going to give you a crash course in modern pressing . . . in four slides.

"Slide one," I said, flipping to the first page of my presentation. I'd drawn a large black circle, representing a player, and a small black dot to show he had the ball. Four purple arrows showed the guy had complete freedom to move. "A world without pressing. This player can do whatever he wants with the ball. For now, let's focus on passing. He can pass in any direction."

I flipped to the second page. It showed the same scene, but now on the right of the black circle was a red circle, and the two purple arrows on that side were gone.

"One player comes to press from the right. What happens?"

Ben Cavanagh, keen to get back into my good books, spoke. "You can't pass to that side anymore."

"Right. So if you're coaching the team, what does this do? What's on the next slide? Turn to the person next to you and discuss it. Sorry, Pascal, but I'm going to ask people to snub you for this one." He smiled. He knew all this pressing stuff way better than me. German maternity wards were full of fluffy rabbit toys, wooden train sets, plastic things to smash, and *Pressing und Gegenpressing: Das Ist Der Hammer* by Ralf Rangnick. I let the guys chat for a minute. It was pretty interesting, really, watching them come at the question from all kinds of footballing angles, and all kinds of levels of intellectual curiosity. "Hit me."

Glenn went first. I think under Ian Evans he would have kept his mouth shut, but now he was willing to be seen to get the answer wrong. Progress. "Well . . . if you get another guy from the other side, you can block off all the passing lanes. Make him make a mistake."

"If you're willing to throw bodies at one player, yeah. If you can get them there in time. Good, thanks. Anyone else?"

Sam was our second most enthusiastic presser. "You slow down their attacks. Make them take another couple of passes and your defenders can get back into shape."

"Yeah, but the modern manager *wants* them to pass forward. Nice thinking, though. Pascal, tell us."

"You can control where their next pass will go."

I reached out to flip to the next page, but hesitated. This seemed like a good place to let them digest. "You can control where their next pass will go. Think through the implications." Watching people like Trick and D-Day try to think through action and reaction, cause and effect, was incredibly funny, but again, I wasn't allowed to laugh. "Okay." I turned to the third drawing. It had the same scene as before: the black circle being pressed by the red one. Down the page was another black circle, ready to receive the pass, but with another red circle storming towards him.

"I hate being pressed," said D-Day. "That picture gives me the willies."

"Me too. Coaches who do this stuff use words like *suffocation*. They want to suffocate the other team. Give them no space to breathe, no space to pass. It's pretty nightmarish."

"Are we going to learn to do this?" said Sam.

"Amazing question," I said. "By the time we get to League Two, yeah. I might not use it all the time, but we'll definitely have it in our locker. But today we only need to understand it and work out how to play against it."

"You're staying at Chester then?" said D-Day, and the two nearest players punched him in the upper arm while everyone else hurled insults at him. "It was a joke! I was joking!"

I laughed. "All right, settle down. Fucking hell, lads."

"No swearing, Mr. Best."

"Right. Right. So remember in the second picture the red circle came to press and we lost two passing arrows? I wanted to draw a kind of cone behind the red guy but I'm not a good enough artist. But does it make sense to you that behind the red circle there would be a sort of dead zone? A shadow into which the ball cannot be passed?" Lots of nods for that one. You couldn't pass through a solid object, and if you tried, you'd risk losing the ball in a very dangerous position.

I turned to my last, and biggest, sketch. Now the black circle with the ball was at the top of a rectangle representing the pitch. To the left of the pitch were four black circles, being pressed by five red ones. Beneath the red circle that was pressing the guy with the ball, I'd sketched a large grey rectangle and labelled it *cover shadow*.

"This cover shadow concept is really important to these top coaches. Basically, that's the zone where the ball carrier can't pass into. If the first presser gets there fast enough, the ball can't be played into this shadow. Got that?" Nods. "So the ball carrier is pretty much forced to play into *this* zone, but the red team can swarm into it, feeling pretty safe that there's no danger from the rest of the pitch."

"Max," said Vimsy, who was learning along with the players. "This cover shadow is only there for a few seconds, right? As soon as the ball is passed, it's gone."

"Yep, but it only takes five, six seconds for the reds to get the ball, or to set up the next situation where they get the ball."

"Your defence would be out of shape," he said.

"It's risky," I agreed. "But effective. In normal circumstances, we, Chester, wouldn't get a kick for ninety minutes. We wouldn't be able to exploit this space or any defenders who were out of position. Most teams at this level would panic, kick long and give the ball to Salford and they'd come right back at us. A weak team would have to defend for ninety minutes, get exhausted, and get smashed in the last twenty minutes. All right. Pascal, what's the solution to pressing?"

"Gegenpressing. Counter-pressing," he said, for the benefit of the others.

"We're not doing that today! We've only just learned what a cover shadow is. What's the other solution?"

The guy pushed his black hair across his forehead. "Other solution? Do you mean . . . technique?"

I smiled. "I do mean technique." I left another pause for the rest of the group to try to parse our words. "Guys. Imagine you run full speed at Messi. Is he worried about it? No, course not. Because you're shit, no offence, and he's Messi. Right? He's not going to lose control of the ball just because you come near him. He's got loads of options: nutmeg, use a skill, one-touch pass. There's no cover shadow against Messi. That's the power of technique. Now, *we* have a couple of midfielders who are way more press-resistant than this level—Ryan and Raffi. So that's handy. But what we really need is some kind of Messi-like figure. Some kind of technical super-genius. A wizard, perhaps."

"You mean you," said Carl Carlile.

"Oh, thank you very much," I said, smiling broadly, pretending to flush from surprise and pleasure. I fanned myself with my fingers. "Gosh. What a nice thing to say."

The guys were smiling and shaking their heads. I'd set it up and they'd fallen right into the trap. Carl, as the victim, felt he had to push back. "Boss, if you don't mind me saying . . . you weren't very Messi-like against Curzon." I looked at the Brig and Vimsy and smiled. They smiled back. "What?" said Carl.

"Mate, do you know how hard it was for me to play like that? That was deliberate. Imagine you're the manager of Salford. Are you going to man-mark the guy who has a boomerang for a foot? Anyway, I've only played the last parts of games. No chance they'll be expecting me to start, and at halftime when they reorganise . . . lol. Now, listen. I know my limitations. If I was doing my mystery winger shit, this conversation would be very different. I can't beat five men in one lightning-fast dribble. But I can beat the press, I can play medium-length passes with accuracy, and I can do it on repeat." I tapped the ball carrier black circle. "See . . . if this is me . . . then this . . ." I dragged my fingers across the cover shadow. "This doesn't exist. And you know what that means?"

"What?" said D-Day, who had a large collection of books but never got past the cover blurb.

"It means absolute fucking mayhem."

"Come on!" yelled Youngster, earning him affectionate pushes and back pats from the players nearest to him.

"I'm still thinking about my final lineup. This isn't a gambit to make you train well, by the way. But let me tell you what I'm leaning towards right now: four-five-one with me as the one. We're going to be under the cosh, so I'll mostly be playing as a DM. Basically a low block, working very, very hard to close down space, throwing bodies in front of shots, all that stuff you clowns love. Right? We need an absolutely immense defensive shift. But when we get interceptions, rebounds, whatever, you get that fucking ball to me. I don't care if I'm marked or surrounded. You can pass to Ryan or Raffi to get the ball to me. You with me?" They were. "Over on the wings, well, one will definitely be Pascal. He's absolutely essential. The other's Aff. That's how we get chances. I get on the ball, break clear of the press, slap the ball out to whoever's in the cover shadow. Right? Say it's Aff. Salford are all over the place at that point because they thought we'd play on the other side. So then it's a footrace between Aff and Pascal and their defenders. Raffi will steam forward and try to be an option for a cut back. But I'm imagining lots of balls played in front of the goalie for the other winger to get onto."

"What about Henri?" said Glenn.

"Sub. I'll see how I'm doing at halftime, but probably I'll have to come off and then as they're reacting to what we did in the first half, we'll totally change it. Go four-four-two or something unexpected." As I spoke, I remembered I hadn't used Triple Captain and Bench Boost in the FA Cup so far. "Second half, four-one-four-one, with Henri, Sam, and Youngster coming on. Look, I need to think that through, but I promise you, the subs are going to be as important as the starters. This will be a game of two halves. If we're ahead at halftime, anything can happen. Er . . . we need the first goal, I think. I don't think we can do this if they score first. But if we get the first, it's going to be epic. And if we get the first, the crowd are going to go mental. If we give them something to cheer, they'll be our twelfth man." I went through a mental checklist of all the points I wanted to cover. "Does everyone feel confident they understand the basic principle here? Salford think they're closing off the pitch, but we're going to play there anyway. Right? Lightning-fast breaks with their team all out of shape. Remember they like to move central? Yes? We're blitzing them down the wings. All right. So training this week is all going to be about these elements. I'll be working on beating the press and I'll need the goalies twice a day to work on my penalties. Aff and Pascal will be coordinating these fast breaks. Vimsy will be doing shuffle and slide drills for a four-one-five-oh low block. That's a new one, isn't it Vimsy mate?"

"New to me," he said.

"I might try something like playing Steve or Gerald in midfield, since we'll be defending so much. Spectrum's watching their set pieces, and he'll show us some clips on Wednesday, and we'll work on that. And every day we'll finish with an A-versus-B match where we set up like we're going to on Saturday and I can see what needs tweaking. I want you to think of this match as a heist. We're going in with a plan. Ice in our veins, execute, and we've got a serious chance. All good? That's it." I closed the flipchart, and, as always, found that nobody had moved.

Sam said, "How do you know all this?"

"This?" I said, tapping the flipchart. "I got this from a YouTube video. It popped up in my feed. You might want to stop watching your flat Earth videos and see what's going on in your industry."

He grinned. "I watch them sometimes. How did Arsenal beat Man City, things like that. It's this stuff, like what you've told us. But I can never really get my head round it. I mean, I know that I'm never going to be doing it." He got thoughtful. "But . . . now we *are* doing it."

I shook my head and got a mischievous grin. "We're not doing it. We're undoing it. That's much easier."

I invited myself to the digs for dinner, and of course Henri turned it into a whole thing. Charlotte had training, but all the other residents of Fawlty Maison sat around the dining table, eating a simple but delicious meat and two veg.

Henri tried to make me sit at the head of the table like some sort of Godfather, but it was his house, so I insisted he should sit there. We ended up leaving the seat empty, with Henri and I at the end, facing each other, with Youngster and Pascal to my left, then the Triplets.

"I hear you are creating some football without me," said Henri, veering towards sulk.

"I hear you've been telling the world our secrets," I replied, with equal snark. We eyed each other, then laughed at the same time. "Who first?"

"You. Tell me the plan for Salford."

I told him, finishing by saying that he wouldn't start, probably, and that he'd have to suffer and sacrifice in the second half and lead the boys home.

He thought about it. "You'll make the changes at halftime?"

"Mmm. I might play five minutes of the second half, just so they don't have time for complicated adjustments. If I'm absolutely wrecked, I'll do one minute or something."

"Good. Then I will replace you."

"I'll be making three changes at the same time, if all goes well. Three will replace three."

"I will replace *you*."

"What's the difference?" I laughed. This request was more batshit crazy than anything I had ever done.

"The difference is how it will be presented on the television. How it will be consumed by the collective unconscious."

He meant the camera would linger on my departure, meaning it would linger on his arrival. "Christ, you're vain. Fine. How about if I hug you like a brother and let the world know you're my special little pumpkin?"

"Yes, good. I like that. Now. A quick chat about your club. West Didsbury and Chorlton. Quite a mouthful. I assume you will rename it Best Didsbury and change the team colours."

"Changing the team colours would be an act of vandalism and show you don't care about history or community."

"Salford's new owners changed the colours."

"I know. Shows it's all about them and not the fans."

"What's *your* motivation?"

"Bit of fun, isn't it? And when Chester sack me, I'll have something to fall back on."

"How much did you pay?"

"I'll tell you later."

"Vivek will train there and play some matches. I see how that could aid his development."

"Hope so. We'll find out, won't we?"

"And will you be sending other players there?"

"No real plans, but it's an option. Guys like Benny and Tyson could get some game time. Michael, too, if he wanted."

"Me?" said the middle Triplet.

"Yeah. You, we could loan anywhere. Vivek's mum wouldn't let us send him somewhere rough, so West is perfect for him. In fact, I'd say we're the only club that could get him started. You're welcome to go and watch a match there and see what you think. We could send you for a month, and you'd play five or six games. Five times ninety minutes, see if it benefits you. At the least, it'd build your fitness."

He was frowning. "Do I have to?"

"Jesus, mate. No. If you're scared you wouldn't get in the first eleven there, then yeah, maybe it's not the right challenge for you." His brothers loved that, and I thought they would tease him about it until he came to me and said he'd had a think and wanted to try it. I turned to Henri. "Now tell me about Tranmere."

He talked about the training. Certain drills that Coach Colin liked. Some ideas the manager, James O'Rourke, was trying to implement for the next match. "And we play short-sided matches at the ends of most sessions. I am struggling to make an impact. Even Junior, who was my junior at Darlington, is sharper than me. Now, Max, let us be honest with one another." He stared at his empty plate. "I'll put away the dishes."

Andrew slapped Noah, who announced that he would do it.

"Thank you, Noah," said Henri. Noah moved with impressive rapidity—he didn't want to miss any of the football talk. "I understand your concept. You send me to train in a tougher group and it makes me tougher. I understand that. And I think if I stayed there for long enough, I would be able to compete better than how I am currently. But I think your plan is to send other players there, too?"

"I don't have *that* good a relationship with the manager and owner to do it like a factory process. But if I could, I would. For example, if I sell Youngster to . . . Everton . . . I could put as a condition that I can send five players to train with them for a month. Something like that. If the concept works, I can find opportunities."

"So you don't believe in our coaches."

"I do. To a certain point. But there's also the rest of the team, the opposition, the facilities. Everything will get better over time, but if I can send you to train at clubs who have already solved those problems . . . It's a loophole." I looked down the table and told a white lie. "Everyone here can improve beyond the current ability of Chester. It's my duty to look for ways to make sure that can happen."

Henri nodded. "I have been welcomed at Tranmere, even though everyone agrees it is strange. There's an assumption that I will sign for them in January. An assumption that I allowed to fester because it was easier. Also, I have played against some of the guys. They know I have something to offer. But if you sent Andrew, or Michael, to a similar club, even Tranmere, it might not go so smoothly. In fact, I'm sure it would be a disaster. You went to Darlington. You know how it can be for a new player. A new player who isn't even part of the club? Who blows into the house like a virus? The home cells, they enrage themselves. No, Max. I think . . . I think you need to reconsider this. It's a beautiful concept, but it doesn't survive contact with reality. You may loan players down, to your West, for example, but not up. That is my home truth, even if the truth hurts more at home."

I squeezed my eyes closed. Limits. Always limits. But since Jackie had returned, my mind had been fizzing with ideas. "People are scouting Raffi. How about if I let him train with one of those teams for a couple of weeks? They get a good look at him. I get a better player."

"And you sell him to that club?"

I made a noise. "Why would I? Highest bidder. It's on them if they assume I'd treat them differently. But that's a good scam, isn't it?"

Henri considered it. "Possibly. He *might* be accepted if his signing was presented as a fait accompli."

I got up and walked around. "What if I paid teams? There are higher-level teams with good coaches who are broke. Here's five grand, train five of my players for a month."

"Max," he said in a whiny voice. "The other players will snub them. Your employees will become depressed."

"I'm paying for a service," I said. "It's not just a favour to a mate. If someone bullies my guy, I'll be there with the Brig ten minutes later and we'll have a chat."

"You make enough enemies."

"You've made one great point," I said, stopping suddenly. "The culture of the receiving club needs to be right. *I* can loan players *up... to Chester*. The best West Didsbury players should come and train with us for a week. Imagine that. We can train them way past the rest of their division."

"What do Chester get from that arrangement?"

"They get me."

Henri smiled. "You shouldn't use Chester as your personal fiefdom. May I speak to you alone?" He stood and invited me to the patio, where we sat around a wooden fire and drank tea. I had peppermint.

After we'd fussed and got cosy and settled like a couple of senior citizens, Henri had a question. "How much did you pay for that football club?"

"A hundred grand."

"That's not much for a whole club."

"It's about a hundred thousand more than I should have paid. Those clubs don't make a profit. West was just about breaking even. If they paid staff, it'd go broke in weeks."

"I see. So what is your ambition?"

"Turn it into a talent factory. Use my abilities as a scout to dramatically improve the quality of the players—without losing the culture, of course, that's vital—and start making money from transfers. Plus, having good players means winning the league, getting a couple of promotions, going on cup runs. I don't see why they shouldn't get to the league below us in the next five years and compete with FC United. But there's no rush; I only need it so that if I absolutely had to, I'd be able to take ten grand a year out to repay the loan. Which seems pretty trivial, really. Same as here, if we are able to get the most out of the players, everything else will fall into place."

Henri shook his head. "Max, you have a mania for personal improvement."

"It seems so."

"Where does it come from? Your father?"

The fire crackled. "No."

Henri sipped his drink and looked up at what little could be seen of the night sky. "My father took great interest in my career when I was a phenom. He made me work harder and harder. He was never satisfied, though he followed my career with great interest. When it became clear I had been overrated and would never achieve great things, he lost that interest."

"Fuck. What did he want? For you to play for France? Anything less is shit? That's bonkers. Twenty guys play for France at a time. There's tons of incredible players who don't quite make it."

"I fell a long way short of that. I rose quickly and fell slowly. I thought I had found my level. The sixth tier of English football. Then I met you." He was quiet, and with anyone else I would have piped up to fill the awkward silence. "What was it you saw in me?"

"Movement. Composure, heading, intelligence."

"Scrapping?"

"That's always been your biggest weakness."

Henri inhaled, and it took a long time for the exhale to come. "My father wanted me to scrap. To make the defenders know they had been in a contest. To make them dread playing me."

"Your dad sounds like a shit coach," I said, and regretted it. "No offence."

"I do not take offence when you are honest. Truth is beauty. I . . . If I promise not to kick anyone, can I start the match on Saturday?"

"No, because that's not why you aren't playing. There's only one way to win, so we're doing that. You'll play the second half. Henri, mate, are you okay?"

"Being sent to another new club stirred up a lot of memories, Max. I've moved many times. The first four or five were upward. Villefrance to Bordeaux. Bordeaux to Lens. When I went home, the house was full of joy. Was it down or sideways, moving to England? Financially, it was very much up. Reading, when they had money, but my boots were cursed, I couldn't score, I was floundering, then the loans, the contracts signed and not renewed, down the slide. On my visits home, I would find that my father had been called away on 'urgent business,' or he would be civil but refuse to ask about football. My family home became a source of hurt. I moved to Corsica and became incredibly happy there. Corsica, where the goals came as easily as they ever had, then the strangest call. Darlington. Such a small club, such a cold town, but so seductive. They were desperate for me to sign." His eyes flickered towards me. "I want to be wanted, Max. It fills a need. I know it's pathetic to you."

I shrugged. "I'm too much a mess to judge you for that."

"What *would* you judge me for?"

"For scrapping when you should be dragging defenders out of position."

He looked up again. "*Merde.*" He adjusted the little blanket he wore over his lap. "I know. Put all the pressure on a single point. Use your talent in the most efficient way possible. That's very Max. Max for maximum. Maximum output. From your team. From your players. From your friends."

"I want what's best for you, if that's what you're saying. My friends are footballers, so . . . I try to help them in terms of football. Is that bad?"

"No."

I had the feeling he was on the verge of trying to tell me something, and he would if only I asked the right question, but I was way out of my depth. Someone like Henri would probably guess and be all sophisticated about it. "Is there something you want to tell me?"

He put his tea down and folded his hands. "Please don't give up on me." I was about to say something funny when I caught a shimmer of moisture reflecting on his eyeballs. I kept my stupid Manc gob shut. "You think I'm something . . . something that I am not. When you realise, you will share the disappointment of so many others."

I knew where I was now. The relief was exhilarating. "Have you ever heard of the sunk-cost fallacy?"

He blinked. "Of course."

"Well, I haven't. I'm going to keep investing in you until I get what I want."

"What is it you want?"

"I want to see peak Henri Lyons."

"He's not as good as you think."

"I know exactly how good you can be." I smiled, imagining the day I checked his profile and saw he was CA 90. "That'll be a good moment, when you get there. Do you want me to tell you when it happens? No, that'd be weird. That'd be like saying, 'It's all downhill from here.' Or would it? What would I want? Maybe I'd want to hear it. Hitting your peak's an achievement, and then after that the contest is how long you can stay at this level. Someone like Ryan Jack must have stayed at his peak for fucking years. I think I'd want that, if I were you."

He was shaking his head. "You think you can spot, what, the exact moment I can get no better?"

"To the minute."

He didn't blink for a long time. "I want that."

I touched all my fingers together and rested my chin in the first gap. "You're twenty-eight years and six months old. If we get promoted . . ." If we got promoted, that would theoretically unlock another twenty or so points in the CA he could get while at Chester. If he could get to CA 80 by the end of next season, he wouldn't be far off his PA of 90. Which he'd hit during our first League Two season, provided there were no unforeseen stumbling blocks along the way. And provided we got promoted every year. "You'll hit your absolute peak aged thirty years and six months. Give or take a few weeks. It'll be faster if I find a coach like Jackie."

"But you have a coach like Jackie. Jackie is a coach like Jackie."

"He's the manager of the women's team. Why would he coach the men's team?"

"Because you've got everyone doing everything."

"I'm not going to push him. We've only just got him back. If he volunteers, holy shit, wow. That'll be a red-letter day. But I won't ask. I do have a couple of scams lined up where he'll *want* to volunteer, but right now I feel bad for even thinking of them. He's allowed to be happy, right? He's allowed to have a go at being a manager." I laughed. "He's like a nepo baby who wants to be taken seriously as an artist or something. He's desperate for me to see beyond his gorgeous bald head. Nah, I'm working on the assumption he won't coach the men. I don't need someone as good as him, anyway. Don't need the grin, the humour, the man management, the tactical ideas. Just need the coaching. I hope to find it. In the meantime, it's mad schemes and plans, Henri, that you will go along with willingly, because *you* are not going to give up on you."

He breathed out, slightly shakily at first, but then with confidence. "Agreed."

"Come into the light for a minute." We went back inside. "I learned a shamanic trick while on a mountaintop. Tell me if you feel anything."

While I kept a close eye on him, I used God Save the King to increase his finishing by one point. Annoyingly, his CA increased, too, which distracted me from his face. That said, I felt sure he didn't flinch or show any visible sign of anything having changed.

"I didn't feel it," he said.

"Probably for the best," I said. He gave me a strange look and wandered off to the kitchen. I double checked the information the squad screen was giving me. Increasing his finishing had bumped him from CA 59 to CA 61.

I stood there with my mind very slightly blown. Of course I'd realised there was a connection between attribute growth and CA growth, but I wasn't sure I'd ever seen it play out so obviously one to one. PA was a limit to how much all the other attributes could improve. I'd suspected that already, with some level of certainty, but now a new and interesting thought occurred to me: If Henri's PA was maxed out and I increased his finishing, his PA would have to improve. Right?

It didn't seem like I would ever use this loophole, but for the first time I saw a way to increase someone's PA. Another rule I could bend! And if similar perks ever became available, I might be able to go from bending the rule . . . to breaking it.

"Shall we return to the fire?"

"Absolutely."

Most of that week, I had horrible, oppressive dreams. Themes of suffocation, strangulation, confinement. By day we worked on my tactical idea and refined it. I worked on evading the press and took penalties against the keepers until I thought I had my new technique down pat. There was an air of quiet optimism, of determination. Around the town, growing excitement as the big day neared.

On Tuesday night, I went scouting at one of Chester's five-a-side places and found a couple of half-decent squad fillers. Sent Jackie a fifteen-year-old PA–20 forward, just in case. But I was stopped every two minutes for selfies. It didn't help the feeling of claustrophobia.

So the next three nights, I drove to Manchester and Stockport and watched five-a-side, adding XP and finding a few prospects for West. It wasn't an easy sell, getting them to go for a trial at a tier-nine side they'd never heard of, but I didn't need to sell it. I just needed the guys to go down and watch a match. They'd get sucked in, and if they didn't, there were plenty of fish in the sea.

Going home eased my dreams at first, but on Friday night, the foul mood came back with a vengeance.

XP balance: 501

Debt repaid: 2,558/3,000

West Didsbury and Chorlton first team average CA: 10

FA Cup first round: Chester versus Salford City.
I named the 4-5-1 that I had planned, but one thing Secretary Joe had pointed out when I'd told him my plans over a quick coffee was that I'd be able to name *nine* subs and use *five* (instead of five and three). What a luxury! Especially considering anyone who came on would be benefitting from Bench Boost. It was also amazing in terms of keeping players happy and motivated. Everyone except Michael Harrison and Angles (our goalie coach) got named and would be able to dream of getting onto the pitch.

Salford would play 4-1-4-1. They'd rested a few players, but they had their key striker and DM in the starting lineup. Their average CA of 98 was alarming. The players were far more talented than their recent performances would have suggested. The Class of '92 might have changed the kit and badge—vandalism—but they were investing.

Our fans were streaming in. The stadium wasn't sold out, which disappointed me, but the ticket people thought we'd get close to 4,000. The biggest crowd of my playing or managing career. If we got them going . . .

The BBC had been in the stadium putting up cameras and whatnot. They'd kicked poor Boggy out of his little room, and generally strode around like they owned the place, making demands, upsetting the regulars. I supposed that would happen more and more as we rose up the leagues, but it was still fucking annoying. Didn't make me want to play nice with the broadcasters, although I had it in the back of my mind that if we were media friendly, we'd get picked for more of these games in the future.

The players prepared as close to normal as possible, though the nerves, excitement, and tension weren't helped by the late kickoff. The extra two and a half hours of waiting and dreaming and dreading was sapping their mental energy. They'd been giving it large on their socials through the week, but now they were raw with nerves. Their mistakes would be broadcast live to millions. But if they scored . . . The Brig and Vimsy seemed to have decided to let the lads enjoy it, let them vent their tension with extra silliness and banter and bombast.

I went along with it; I didn't want the lads freezing before the match. They'd switch on when the match kicked off . . . probably.

The only real difference for me was that I popped up to the director's box to show my face to the Weavers—Emma was in Chester kit with a West beanie; she always knew how to put a smile on my face—plus various Cheshire bigwigs, Chester board members, and sponsors. Then it was down pitchside to talk to the BBC guys. The BBC guys turned out to be an attractive blonde called Carly.

Max Best, you're the manager of Chester Football Club.

Yes. Yes, I am.

There's a fantastic atmosphere building.

One of the first things I did was turn the pre-match music off. I want to hear the fans, not Ed Sheeran.

What are you doing today?

Do you mean what formation?

Yes.

That's pretty personal. You should take me to dinner before you start asking things like that.

You might be a bit young for me.

I'm getting older every day. It's one of my superpowers.

You've been doing a lot of 3-5-2 recently. Will we see that today?

Do I have to tell you that? Is that part of the deal? It seems weird. Tell me what Salford are doing and I'll tell you my plans.

They're doing 4-3-3.

No, they're doing 4-1-4-1. Watkins as DM, Johnstone as the striker. Looks like they've put their reserve fullbacks in for today. The guy's got to rotate his squad but we might be able to do something with that.

You're optimistic, then.

No, we are going to get absolutely thrashed. This morning we were on social media reminding fans that we've got slots for player sponsorships. For two hundred pounds we'll write your name next to Magnus Evergreen or Steve Alton in the match programme. That's the level we operate at, Carly. We're a fan-owned club. No billionaires in the shadows behind famous players. We don't even have a nutritionist. I saw my backup goalie eating a Mars bar this morning. (Other chocolates are available.) No, this is going to be one-sided. Dull as dishwater. I've told the lads if they get a shot on target, I'll take them to Disneyland. Not the real one. I mean Flamingo Land in Scarborough. They've got flamingos. And land.

You've named yourself in the starting lineup, but you've only played twenty minutes here or there. Do you think you can play the whole ninety minutes?

Nah, that's politics. The board want me to play today so that I'll be cup tied. They want me to stay here and they think if I can't play for another team in the cup this season I'm less likely to be snapped up. I'll probably potter around for ten, fifteen minutes, try to make some new friends. Maybe I'll ask Watkins if he wants to swap shirts with me. Get first dibs on that, know what I mean? Then, yeah, let one of the proper players do the rest of the game.

Max Best, thank you very much and good luck.
Yep.

I went into the dressing room to rouse the troops. What they needed, of course, was to stop thinking about the magic of the cup and what it'd be like to score a famous goal and what it'd be like to get annihilated on TV.

"Guys," I said, in a quiet, calm voice. It took much longer than normal, but the group settled down. I nodded as I looked at them. Average morale 6.1 (compared to Salford's 4.6); average CA 46. The lineup was a bit strange—we were nominally a 4-5-1 but the striker was me and I would play as a DM. I had Gerald May, the defender, playing in central midfield. "Henri, how you feeling?"

His time at Tranmere had been incredible. With harder, higher-level training, plus the bonus he got from God Save the King, he had added four points of CA in two weeks and was now my best player with CA 62. He was on the bench. "Good, Max," he said, apparently in earnest.

"Amazing. We know the plan. Low block, defend for our lives, earn the right to play. Now, I know you're all a bit hyper, so it's time to get back into heist mode. Remember the heist? Ice in our veins. Clarity of thought. For that reason, I am going to read you a poem. This will, I'm sure, get you in the right frame of mind. Everyone ready?"

This got some smiles. I was being weird because they needed me to be weird. "Ready, boss," said Glenn.

"Top. Here we go." I cleared my throat and read from my phone. "A centipede was happy quite, until a frog in fun . . . said, 'Pray, which leg comes after which?' . . . This raised her mind to such a pitch, she lay distracted in the ditch, considering how to run."

Tony Hetherington was the first to react, which was a good omen in case any balls bounced near him in the penalty box. He slapped his thigh and got up. "You're mad, you are! You're absolutely crackers."

"It's about not overthinking things," I said. "It's another way of saying let it happen."

"Crackers."

It was smiles all round. Job done.

We were as ready as we were ever going to be.

"If you're just joining us, Salford City, owned by David Beckham, Ryan Giggs, and the rest of the Class of '92, have come to non-league Chester City for this first-round FA Cup match."

"Chester FC, Clive."

"That's right, Andy. I always make that mistake. And some are saying Chester manager Max Best has made a mistake. His star striker, Henri Lyons, is only on the bench today. What do you make of that?"

"It's a strange one, Clive. Must be a bit of tension in the camp because looking at the team here, Chester don't have a natural striker. They'll need a target man if they're going to relieve the pressure Salford put them under. It's a bit of inexperience from the young manager. They think highly of him round these parts, but I'm surprised to see a non-league team playing a big game like this without a target man. Teams need an out ball. I just hope that decision doesn't hurt them."

"Nearing kickoff here at a boisterous Deva Stadium. Let's see if this game produces a diva, and if the fat lady will be singing at the final whistle."

Triple Captain.

Bench Boost.

Salford to kick off. I lined up in the striker position, but as Salford knocked the ball around, I took a few steps back.

They came at us like lightning. Fast, athletic, technical, zipping the ball around for thirty demotivating seconds. When they finally hit a loose pass, our throw-in looked like a minefield. Carl Carlile looked around, saw danger everywhere, and threw the ball down the line towards Pascal. There followed one of the most unequal physical contests in the history of football, and the reds (formerly the tangerines) were back in possession, back in our half, and we settled into our low block.

A couple of midfielders exchanged passes, and I saw where the ball would go. I moved towards it, expecting to take it off the toes of the receiver. But by the time I got there, he'd burst past me. He played the ball wide left, a cross came in, and Johnstone headed the ball powerfully down and in.

One minute, one goal. At this rate, we'd set all kinds of unwanted records.

We were too stunned to get mad, or scream at each other, or whatever. I stood there, head empty, when Ryan gave me a little push towards the halfway line. As the "striker," it was my job to restart the match. At least I'd get a kick of the ball.

I passed to Ryan, who zipped it to Aff, who played it back to Magnus. He played it to Ryan, who passed to Raffi. I went on a curving run outside him. He dabbed the ball into my path, and I was instantly dumped on my arse by Watkins, the quality defensive midfielder I had a bit of a manager crush on.

Salford, a goal ahead and confident we were shit, passed the ball around for a while, not too bothered about attacking. They would do a professional job, taking the heat out of the match, quieting the crowd, winning by expending as little energy as possible.

They passed around the defence for a while, forcing me to go and pretend to press them so that they'd pass forward. When they did, they broke through our lines with ease, and six, seven, eight passes were zipped around on bewildering diagonals, ending in a shot that went just wide. Robbo in goal got nowhere near it.

Robbo took the goal kick to Carlile, who passed it to me even though I had an opponent close by. That was very much the plan. I received the ball, feinted to pass back to the keeper, burst the other way. My move took the guy by surprise, but he flung out an arm, grabbed my shirt, and stopped me moving.

The ref blew for a free kick, then jogged away. I frowned. Didn't he realise I was just about to launch a counter?

There followed two minutes of living beyond our means, straining every sinew and finding we were slower, smaller, shitter. Salford had chances. Peppered our penalty area with crosses, through balls, even some intricate build-up play. Even with all our players defending in a low block, they got our fullbacks isolated, dribbled past, hit endless crosses and pull backs.

And when we survived and tried to pass out, they smothered us. Got hundreds of players into the area around the ball, stopping us from breaking out. Twice more I got the ball, somehow got my legs working, got past my opponent, and was fouled. Both times, the referee blew for a foul and walked away.

I followed him. "Is that it?"

"What?"

"That's our break. We're on the attack. That's three times we've been shut down by fouls."

"So?"

"So that's a yellow card. Three yellows."

"Get lost, yellow card." He turned away, laughing.

I saw red.

The suffocation was happening. From Salford, fairly, pressing us into inescapable corners and traps, unfairly, with snide fouls and gamesmanship, from the ref, who was still reffing like it was the 1990s, from the TV guys who I knew would be slaughtering me, from the board who only understood 4-4-2, the fans, from every player who'd bought into this plan. What was that phrase? Home is where the heart is. Nah. I thought of Henri's dad covering his house with shadow. Losing this wouldn't mean a thing if we were in Salford. But we were in Chester. Home is where the hurt is.

CA 100 versus CA 50, and the bigger team could foul at will. Still, I'd expected some of that. Why was I playing so shit? Smasho and Nice One had warned me: When you step up a level, it takes time to adjust. Well, if it took me twenty minutes to get up to speed here, we'd be 8–0 down with fourteen completed passes. We should have played 4-4-2 and taken our chances. Conventional, boring, but that's how you did a giant killing. That's how you beat a better team.

Salford attacked while I stood, stock still, having something of a meltdown. The ball zipped around—so fast! so accurate!—until May, showing his worth by being a large obstacle where we needed one, got in the way of an attempted chip (bit early for Salford to be dicking around to *that* extent) and suddenly I was on the ball. I exploded past a guy and was ready for his shirt grab. I smashed my elbow in the direction of his hand, made contact, was blessedly free, and suddenly the pitch was open before me. I sprinted, accelerated, but the rest of the players had stopped.

The referee had given a foul. Against *me*.

I wandered back, head in hands, unable to understand what I was seeing. The Salford guy was on the floor, clutching his wrist.

"Calm down, Best," said the ref, as he showed me a yellow card. The first yellow card of my career.

"Hang on. I get fouled but I get booked. That's what's happening here, is it?"

"One more and you're off."

The "injured" guy went off the pitch for treatment, and my team lined up to defend the free kick. Not me. I stood in the middle of nowhere, blood boiling so intensely I'd soon lose all my body's water.

The cross was sent in—too soft, too slow, rubbish—and May was there, heading clear. I sprinted, gathered the ball, and hared to the left side of the pitch. Salford guys were sprinting back. My instinct was to run down the line, all the way into the penalty box, and shoot. But those days weren't back, not yet. I feinted as though I'd do just that, then tapped the ball once, backward, once more, to the side, opening my body for a massive diagonal pass to Pascal on the far side.

A Salford guy took me out.

Free kick. I got part of the way to my feet, watching, waiting for the inevitable yellow card. When it didn't come, my fury reached new heights. I glared at the ref, eyes bulging, veins throbbing, and finally reached a level of anger so pure it was like flying a plane through turbulent clouds and coming out to the absolute peace and serenity above.

From this new state, I heard the fans to my left. They were almost as angry as me. I gestured, demanded more noise. They obliged, spitting bile at the pitch. Salford might not have been intimidated, but the ref was.

Aff appeared next to me. "Pass," I said. He touched the ball, and I faced up the nearest Salford guy, the same one who had just fouled me. I moved towards him. There was no match, no wider contest. There couldn't be. Not with the ref so clueless. With a sudden drop of the shoulder, I bolted forward, but cut back to the side of the pitch so I'd only be in contest with this one guy. I cut in and out, waited, waited for his weight to settle, then bam! Double dribble, like the old days. It didn't need to be very elegant, and holy shit, it wasn't, but it achieved my aim. I got past the guy and surprise surprise, he fouled me.

The crowd went mental. Absolutely mental. I sat on my arse, watching as the referee went up to the guy, had a word with him, touched him on the shoulder, all paternal and shit, and walked away. No extra punishment.

I flopped to my back. A little bit theatrical, you might say, but it helped in working the fans up. For as long as we were in the contest, they'd go apeshit every time we didn't get a decision, every time the ref showed bias to Salford.

But so what? We had one way to play, and our opponents could stop it at no cost. Even if the ref finally gave a couple of yellow cards, someone else would foul me. They would take it in turns, never risking a red card. I suppose I should have been pleased to be considered worthy of rotational fouling. I lay there, panting, beads of sweat forming all over as my exertions caught up with me, thinking about the £41,000 in prize money we'd never see, about the tantalising prospect of another league match being postponed in my season-long Maxterplan. I thought about how I could make as many beautiful plans as I wanted, but if the other team cheated, were *allowed* to cheat, there was nothing much I could do about it.

Aff bent and lifted me up. "Come on, boss. Keep going, yeah?"

"Yeah," I mumbled. I didn't mean it.

"Still one–nil here, but Salford's early dominance has faded away somewhat."

"That's right, Clive, Chester have dug in well, but they aren't offering anything going forward. They need a big man up top. I want to see Henri Lyons come on. He's a great player for this level."

"Come on for his manager, maybe. Best has spent most of the first twenty minutes here scowling and getting into heated discussions with his opponents and the referee. He's got to be careful or he'll be sent off."

"He's a very frustrated young man out there. Whatever he's tried to do with this lineup, it hasn't worked. If I'm on the bench there, I'm telling him to change it. Go four-four-two, play direct, give your defenders a breather now and then."

"Funny you should mention that. There's some movement around the home team dugout. What's this? It looks like . . . they're dancing?"

"I wouldn't call that dancing, Clive. Swaying, maybe."

"Swaying. Perhaps we shouldn't laugh. Could be for a local charity or something. But they're all up there, waving their arms around."

"I think we're allowed to laugh. Look at Best."

"Look at his face! Just look at his face! Max Best's smile is lighting up this stadium. What on earth was that all about?"

"Watch out, here come Salford."

After the little scene on the left, we'd had a spell of possession. Ryan to Raffi, Raffi to Pascal, who had been virtually anonymous, back to Ryan, and he, Aff, and Magnus had played keep-ball. Salford had put a lot of energy into all their pressing, and seemed happy to let us have the ball in a harmless position.

Finally, after a little break in which I allowed my rage-o-meter to come down to "toddler who can't remember why he's mad," I showed for the ball, turned, beat a man, tried to get past a second, and was barged off the ball. Fairly, I suppose, but the fans reacted like the guy had flicked ninja stars at my ankles.

I slapped the turf in frustration—at myself, this time. I put my hands on my hips and started to give serious consideration to subbing myself off. When I looked over at the bench, I saw Vimsy, the Brig, Henri, Dean, and Youngster side by side, doing the air dancer hand movements we'd used in the early days of 4-1-4-1 Let It Happen. They were telling me to stick to the plan. That they still believed in me. That I needed to stop trying to make things happen, and . . . you know the rest.

It was the Brig that made me laugh. That serious face, those arms ready to switch to dark mode in an instant, waving around live on TV.

I took a few breaths as I walked back towards goal. Salford were attacking down our right. The winger got himself a bit of space, crossed, and just before Johnstone nodded it home, Robbo was there, plucking the ball from the air like lifting a cat from a tree.

I put my hand up, and Robbo slingshotted the ball to me. I took a touch. Watkins was the nearest defender, and he came from the left of the pitch, creating a massive cover shadow there. The rest of the Salford team moved right, where they would swamp Pascal, Ryan, or whomever I passed to.

One . . . more . . . step . . . Watkins was nearly on me, so I lifted my leg like I'd play a long pass to the right. He reacted instinctively by moving his body weight in that direction. I smashed the ball, twisting my foot at the last second, nutmegging him. The ball zipped thirty yards, right into the path of Aff. There was no one near him. He raced forward, and now Salford were in full panic mode. They streamed back, just about catching Aff, but Pascal was the fastest player on the pitch. Aff fired a long diagonal pass, too far in front of the goalkeeper for him to come. Still, he took a few steps towards it, realised he was in no-man's land, and could only dive despairingly as Pascal side-footed the ball into the unguarded net.

One–all, and the stadium erupted. Limbs everywhere, noise, passion, emotion. Pascal celebrated wildly, sliding on his knees to the corner flag even though we'd agreed never to do that because it wrecked your ligaments. The rest of the lads zoomed over and crashed into him, which we'd also banned.

I knelt and took the opportunity to make some calculations. The match stats were as expected: terrible ratings for me and for Gerald May. Pascal had been on 4 out of 10, but one kick later he was up to 8. Robbo and Ryder were defending like the old pros they were: both had eight. More important than the ratings was how well everyone was doing their job, and I found myself nodding. Very well.

This plan worked. Whether they knew it or not, Salford's greatest strength, their ability to press us, squeeze us, suffocate us, was their biggest weakness.

It reminded me of the famous scene from the BBC's *Planet Earth* series. A bunch of snakes grabbed a little gecko dude, but more and more snakes came to join the party, squeezing and squeezing, not realising the little dude had already slipped away. They were strangling themselves.

I looked over at my bench. They were delirious.

The emotion of the situation threatened to overwhelm me. I gritted my teeth and stretched my hamstrings. When my guys walked back to our half, I snapped at them. "Come on! Back to work."

Salford kicked off and, stung by our equaliser, immediately surged forward. Their clever midfielders played a few passes to each other, but with supernatural timing I stopped jogging sideways, burst ahead, intercepted, and I was away. In seconds, I was at the centre circle. I dropped a shoulder left, went right, had Pascal running right, Aff left, and felt Raffi coming up behind. I calculated the next six passes in the blink of an eye, passed right just as a defender slid in. Another guy out of the way! Change the calculation! Pascal threatened to go right, but cut the ball back to me. I hit it first time, full of side spin so Aff wouldn't have to break stride. He cut it square, and Raffi thrashed it into the back of the net.

The stadium shook. It was Salford's turn to look stunned.

"Scenes here in the northwest! Little Chester are on course for one of the biggest cupsets of the year. If you want to kill a giant, they don't get much bigger than a team owned by David Beckham!"

"It's extraordinary, Clive. I can't believe what I'm seeing. It was all Salford for fifteen minutes and now Chester are bossing the game."

"Salford look scared to commit bodies forward."

"And with good reason! Every time Chester break, they look deadly. Pascal Bochum is a revelation. Such a bright player!"

"Chester's plan looks obvious now, though for a long time it seemed like a muddled mess. How will Salford respond?"

"Their old heads will put their foot on the ball, slow things down. Let this frenzy fade away, stamp their quality on the game."

"Let's see. There's Watkins now, and he turns and plays it back to his goalie. You called it, Andy. There's *one* calm head out there."

It looks like Salford have adopted a more cautious approach.

I got goosebumps when the message came through. Attack! But no. They *wanted* us to spread out so *they* could counter *us*. Felt like a trap. I kept things as they were, even if that meant a quiet five minutes when the bubbling intensity of the cauldron died down. That was five minutes where I could let my mind and body rest.

It looks like Salford have adopted a more attacking stance.

Here they came! Another push. They'd added another body to the rest defence, though. Less threat from their attacks, but more solidity against our counters. It didn't bother me. If we got into their cover shadow, we'd create mayhem. Aff, Pascal, and I had great decision-making, most of the time, and if you had the defenders facing their own goal, everything got much easier. The hard part was breaking through the initial press.

"Salford pushing hard to get back into this match now. They've got a corner. It's fired in towards their dangerman Johnstone. It's punched away. Best competes for it—the crowd rises to their feet in anticipation of a counter!—but Watkins comes away with it, passes left. They've been dangerous down that side. Cross comes in. Nodded away. There's a scramble. Shot! Blocked by Ryder. Shot! Blocked by Alton. Shot—no! Passed wide. Great composure. Here comes Solent, pulled back, another block! Solent again. GOAL! It's there. He's done it! Heroic defending by Chester, but they couldn't clear their lines. It's two–all!"

"Argh, that's devastating for the non-league team. It'll be one-way traffic from here. Game over, I'm afraid."

"Approaching halftime, Chester still just about in this game. At two–all, who'll be the happier manager?"

"Oh, that's tough. Salford's will be pleased to have got over that scare, but he'll be upset at how his players lost the plot for those ten minutes."

"Salford attacking down the right. Dubhlainn, the Irishman, is there covering—and he comes away with the ball! He's really a good player."

"Two-way player, Clive. Like gold dust."

"No chance for a quick counter this time. Jack on the ball. He's a lovely player, isn't he?"

"He is. You can see he's played at a high level. Lovely passing range."

"Short pass this time, though. Lays it off to Best. First time to Brown. First time to Best. They're like a pinball machine!"

"Trying to get under the Salford players' skin. I've got to say, you don't see football like this at non-league very often. There's a swagger about this group. I'll have to come and watch Chester."

"They're making some new fans, I think. The ball's played wide. Carlile hasn't gone forward much. Neither has May. They get some rare passes in. What's this now? Salford are pushing up, squeezing the space—"

"Kick-ups!"

"Best is doing keepy-uppies on the left of midfield. That's not going to be to everyone's taste. He's challenged now—OH! WHAT A PASS! Max Best has volleyed that, diagonally—he's, he's—it's Bochum on the end of it. The keeper's come storming out. What's he—OH! He's wiped Bochum out! Bochum headed the ball over the keeper—Best's pass—bounced up—what's?"

"Red card!"

"The red card comes out! The keeper's off! Salford are down to ten men!"

"That was absolutely magnificent from Best. He annoyed you, he annoyed me, he annoyed Salford. They lost concentration, and Bochum made that run. The pass, though, left-footed volley, fifty yards, bouncing in Bochum's path. He's only a little fella but he can still use his head! He nodded it over the keeper, then it's a simple case of running round and a tap-in. I've got to say, this Chester team are winning me over. They're outclassed but they've got heart. They've got imagination."

"And now they've got a free kick in a dangerous position. Salford are replacing Solent with their reserve goalkeeper. Down to ten men. This is some game."

"Salford are reeling. Ryan Jack standing over the free kick. It's just outside the penalty area. Is it too close for a shot?"

"You'd have thought so. A few yards back would be ideal."

"Well, finally ready for the free kick. What's next in this extraordinary contest? Ryan steps forward, but it's a sideways pass to Best. He shapes to shoot—we know he can hit them—but he helps it on to the left. Dubhlainn is one on one with his marker. Takes him on—that's brilliant—to the byline, crosses, no, he cuts back, oh and he's taken down!"

"Penalty."

"Yes! The ref's given it! And a yellow card for the right back. Some irony there. Chester couldn't buy one at the start of the half, now there are cards flying everywhere. Penalty to Chester! Salford are furious."

"Best to take it."

"He did say Chester might get joy against the reserve fullbacks . . . Oh, there's some gamesmanship from the new goalkeeper there. He's scuffing up the penalty spot, knocked the ball out of Best's hand. The game hasn't been played in the best spirit, but that's disappointing."

"That's poor. That's really poor. But if he puts Best off, he'll think it was worth it."

"Very long delay here. What do you think, Andy? Will he score?"

"He'll blast it top-right. That's his move."

"Let's see if Salford have done as much homework as you. The crowd hush. The referee is telling players to stay out of the box. Now Best has gone forward. He's giving the goalkeeper a piece of his mind."

"Ah, there's no need for this. Come on."

"Best re-spots the ball. High drama. Waits for the whistle. Steps forward . . ."

Justified flashback cliffhanger!

In book 4, chapter 6, The Art of Phwoar, I took a trip down to "Lahndan," where I watched Brentford beat Fulham. Playing that day was Ivan Toney, and I commented on his masterful penalty technique. You forgot the scene, and so did I, until I realised I would play a match with no strikers. Henri was my first-choice penalty taker, Tony my second. One or the other had played every minute of every game this season.

So who would take our penalties, if we got one, against Salford? Ryan Jack, perhaps. But first, I wanted to try something out. I couldn't do my unstoppable blast-the-ball-so-high-so-hard-no-keeper-could-ever-save-it thing. But maybe I could do the Ivan Toney method. After all, it was about mind games and anticipation more than technique or power.

I practiced and practiced, and thought I had got to grips with the method . . .

The Salford players jostled me, got in my face, talked shit about me and my hair, my skills, the fact that I was a manbaby. The goalie knocked the ball out of my hands, scuffed up the penalty spot.

The ref, of course, bottled it. Did nothing.

I needed a cool head for this penalty—it could be a £40,000 kick. All I had to do was stay calm.

So when the dust had settled and it was nearly time to shoot, I walked up to the goalie and jabbed him in the chest.

"You classless prick. This is *my* house, and if you disrespect it, you're gonna find yourself in a *world* of hurt. You fucking hear me?"

"Get fucked," he said, but he was raging. Desperate to make this save. Hopping around, bursting with energy, ready to spring to his feet and roar with triumph. I thought about pointing to one side of the goal to get into his head even more, but that hadn't gone well in testing.

I stood two steps from the ball. Everything would be compressed into fractions of movements.

The whistle went.

The first stride, slow, slow, eyes focused on the right of the goal.

The goalie on his toes, bouncing, then tense, ready to explode either left or right. Good balance, this prick had.

Into the second stride, slowing even further. The slowness was absolutely messing with the guy's head. He was used to opponents striking hard shots and this was messing up his timing something rotten. The tiniest glance left and his entire body was electrified, ready to go, but then my eyes were right again.

My foot was near the ball now, about to make contact. The shot would be slow, but the goalie had to choose, had to dive.

Eyes wide as saucers, he committed. Right!

I rolled the ball, very, very slowly, to the left.

My first goal for Chester happened at one mile an hour.

The slowness of the drama somehow led to an even greater release when it came. I jogged past the goalie, making sure he saw I was giving him a Maxy two-thumbs, and then—fuck him—it was all about the fans. Giving them something back for all their support. A cocky, smiling trot along the touchline, soaking up the adulation, suggesting I couldn't hear what they were offering, then a shortcut across the corner flag and over to the main stand, where I stood in front of the away dugout, arms aloft, face pointing straight up.

Then hugs for my staff, big drink of water, and, fists clenched, back onto the pitch.

This job wasn't done.

Salford kicked off, and the ref blew for halftime.

Okay, so it was done for now.

There was some aggro in the tunnel. Some people didn't like certain things that had happened. Who gave a shit? I invited the Salford manager to do one (translation: feel free to leave the area), went into the dressing room, and flopped onto a treatment table.

Dean was there in a flash, asking me what was up. "Legs. Headache."

He massaged one leg, Magnus the other, and Livia did her ASMR thing on my neck and head. For a while I fretted about how like a pandered prince I must look, but then I relaxed into it, and my head started to clear.

What to do?

I hadn't for a minute thought we'd get one of their guys sent off. What would happen now? They would still slap us on talent alone. We could do insanely good counters for as long as I played. What was in my tank? Ten minutes? Fifteen?

And Bench Boost. I could bring on five guys who would all play out of their skin.

Henri had to come on. So from 4-5-1 to 4-4-2, with me dropping back to be the DM. But that was just 4-1-4-1. Why not do that? Why not get Youngster on? No, it was too early for him.

My head started swimming again. I couldn't remember a harder decision. There were so many variables, so many options, so much at stake. No doubt the TV guys would be replaying incidents from the first half, poring over them in slow motion, discussing them in minute detail. My mind drifted that way, too, thinking about the rough start, the jersey pulls—no! *Focus on the future.*

"Henri. Brig. Vimsy. Glenn. Sam."

They came and stood around the massage table. The Brig kneeled like a knight before his king. "You called, your majesty?"

His joke was pitch perfect. The others crouched or kneeled, too. All smiles. "How long can you stay kneeling like that at your age?"

"Long enough to receive my instructions, oh great one."

"Someone get the Brig a bean bag," I tried to yell, but it hurt my head. "Right. We've got a man advantage. I want to stay on the pitch a bit longer, but I want to get Henri on. Are you good to skip that scene you were fantasising about?"

"Yes, Max. I will sneak on at halftime and not get the reception I deserve. Of course."

"Who's coming off?" said Sam.

"Yeah. Here's where it gets tricky. Henri for Gerald makes sense. Call it four-four-two with me as the second striker, but doing whatever I want. Do that for five minutes, see what they cooked up during the break."

"Their manager is roasting them," said Livia, delighted. She'd moved to the other side to give my brain trust a better view of the side of my head.

"I want to get Sam and Youngster on, soon as poss. Four-one-four-one, but that means taking Raffi or Ryan off, and they're killing it. Three-five-two means no Youngster. Four-one-four-one right now means no Pascal, and he's our biggest threat today."

"What's our best chance of winning?" said Vimsy.

I was silent for a while, and the only sound from our corner was the oily squelch as my aching muscles were cared for. "Stay as we are till we see what they're planning. Then probably four-one-four-one or a switch to three-five-two."

"So Sam has to wait," said Henri. "And so do I. It's simple."

"Come on, boss," said Sam. "Don't worry about hurting my feelings. Win first, worry about the rest later."

I exhaled. "Right. Right." Something loosened in the calf Magnus was working on. "Magnus, thanks. Get yourself a break. Second half's going to hurt."

Salford made a few tweaks at halftime—passing and marking instructions, certain players told not to make forward runs, small stuff. As far as I could tell, they would mostly keep playing the way they had.

The match restarted and I realised instantly that I was running on fumes. That spongey, bouncy energy I'd had in the first half was all gone. What, then? Swap me and May for Henri and Youngster? Already?

Salford attacked, we low blocked it, and Magnus fizzed the ball to me. I one-touched it back to him, moved towards the left touchline for the return pass. He fizzed it again and I made a show of turning to the inside of the pitch, then spun around to the right. The guy who'd come to press me was left floundering, and once again the entire gamut of possibilities was open to me. I dribbled almost lazily, and as a defender came sliding for the tackle, I dabbed the ball left-footed, just a few feet forward, past the slide, for Aff to collect. I tracked him, and suddenly we were bearing down on the penalty area. The nearest defender didn't know whether he should go to the ball or cover me. He chose Aff, who stopped and turned full circle. The first poor decision we'd made on one of these counters.

But Aff, now on his right foot, had seen something I hadn't. He hit a soft cross into the penalty box, where Raffi took it on his chest, took one stride forward, and stuck the ball low into the corner before a defender could recover.

Four–two! I joined the celebrations on that one, not going quite as ballistic as my team, and came to a decision. "Gerald," I said.

"Is it time?"

"Yeah. How did you like being a midfield general?"

"I didn't mind it." He was all smiles. Four passes in the match, four headers, 4 out of 10, four goals for the team.

I sent him first, with Youngster coming on to great applause. Then Henri replaced me, and there was a standing ovation. That's why Henri wanted to be the one I swapped for. Nothing to do with being shown on TV a few more seconds. It was so he could pretend the applause was for him!

Livia handed me my hoodie and some marathon paste, and I sat in the dugout for a couple of minutes while my heart rate recovered. "My massage didn't do much," complained Dean. "Ten minutes of rubs to get a minute more from you. Bad ratio."

"I'll be able to play on Tuesday, though, won't I?"

"Not if you get wasted tonight. Which you've earned."

I lapsed into silence, watching as Salford went defensive for a few minutes while they digested my changes. Our average CA was 47.8 now, but we had two Bench Boosted guys on the pitch. Could we keep hold of our two-goal lead?

I glanced at the rest of the bench and had an absolutely mad idea. What if I brought Ben Cavanagh on? His CA was three points higher than Robbo's, and he'd be Boosted. If I could get a super keeper for one match only, this was it! But the risk was enormous. If it went wrong, his confidence would be back in the mud, maybe permanently. I had to take a long-term view of his career. Maybe I would have done it if the TV cameras hadn't been there.

Henri was looking sharp. Youngster was gliding around nice and smooth. The drained feeling was replaced with cautious excitement. We could do this . . .

I got up and took stock of the stadium. Now that I was off the pitch, I could really appreciate the noise. It was amazing. It washed around in fits and starts, circular, sometimes vertical, drowning out the away fans then being drowned out by them. The competition between the sets of spectators was keeping ours on their toes. Keeping them hungry. I looked around to see if Crackers was enjoying this, and saw, in the stands, all kinds of things.

There, to the left, Jackie Reaper, next to Jill, their profiles above their heads. Farther left, a pocket of scouts. Just behind me, more scouts. And over to the right—I couldn't believe my eyes—

"Come on!" screamed Vimsy.

I snapped my head round and saw the ref had given a free kick over on the Salford left. Their winger was a fucking menace! This situation didn't feel good. They'd pushed a lot of bodies forward . . .

"Fantastic finish from Johnstone! He had defenders all around him, but he rose highest and headed home! Salford are back in this one! Four–three. Wow!"

I shook my head. Johnstone was a Goliath, and I wanted one. I texted MD, saying as much.

Then I looked over to my right, half expecting the guy would have gone. But no. He was there, staring at me, absolutely blank in that way Scandinavian detectives are on those TV shows.

Folke Wester. And next to him, *his* profile not showing but easily recognisable, was Jonathan Hurts, the league's most expensive player.

The Darlington manager (and his star left back) had, what, left his match early to come and watch this one? No, they'd played last night. I should have expected him here.

What did him being here change? I'd shown more of my hand than I'd planned. Shown more of my tricks than was ideal. The penalty would get him hot under the collar. He'd have to plan for me starting, not just coming on at the end. But I still hadn't headed the ball since I'd started playing again. He'd have noted that, that was for sure.

What else did I want him to think? That I was reckless. That given half a chance, I'd throw caution to the wind.

Suddenly, the path ahead hit me in the face, fully formed. A formation I hadn't used in ages.

"Subs," I said, urgently.

"Who?" said Vimsy.

"Ryan and Raffi off, Tony and Joe on."

"Tony and Joe?"

"Yes, mate." While a bemused Vimsy got those changes ready, I went over to Sam. "I messed up, mate. Couldn't make it work. I'll make it up to you."

He tracked the changes. "What . . . four-four-two diamond? Are you sure?"

"Not really," I said, unable to stop smiling. Showing pleasure was definitely the wrong vibe. All of Sam's family would be at home, watching, expecting him to come on their telly like a real player.

"You've got one sub left," he said.

"You want to play CAM for the last five minutes?"

"Yes I want to play CAM for the last five minutes. Unless that costs us the match."

"Let's see how this goes. It might blow up. It'll probably blow up. It's madness."

"And once again the pattern of the game returns to attack versus defence, with Salford very much in the ascendency. They're doing all the pushing."

"Chester look good on the break, though. They're going more direct, and Bochum is trying to get to the loose balls. It could pay off."

"Ball hit long. Johnstone wins it. Knock down. Hit wide to the right back. He can hit a good cross. Not this time, though. It goes all the way to the left. Bad tackle there! Yellow for Carlile."

"Lot of tired legs in that defence, Clive."

"Yes, I think that might cost them late on. Or now. Here comes the cross— oh, disaster! It's in! It bobbled around, it pinballed. Who stuck it in? Salford don't care, they've grabbed the ball. Want to get on with it. They don't want a replay."

Four–all, and the gulf in quality was finally starting to tell. Salford were still fit and fresh, but our starters were really flagging. The diamond experiment hadn't worked—Youngster hadn't been able to beat the press like I had. He could defend, indeed, he had more interceptions and tackles than I had, but that burst of creativity to get the ball into that cover shadow was lacking.

"Sam, it's nearly time," I said. I would go 4-4-2 and hope Sam's energy would make a difference.

I bit my nails as Salford came at us yet again. Carl was walking a tightrope against the left winger; one more mistimed tackle and he was done. But the guy was a fighter. He never, ever quit, and now he won a duel. He played a tired pass to Youngster—so tired he mishit it completely.

Incredibly, this shit pass, this abomination of technique, utterly bamboozled the guy who was pressing Youngster, and he went the wrong way. Youngster, his tactical brain working a mile a minute, simply tucked the ball inside to his left foot, pushed forward, sorted his feet out, and scampered away.

The next phase was utterly bizarre. It looked like someone had glued chess pieces onto a clear piece of plastic, and when you moved one, you moved them all.

As Youngster ran forward two yards, so Henri and Tony ran two yards, and the defenders ran two yards. Youngster ran two more yards, and everyone else ran two more yards. And this continued for no less than forty yards, almost box to box, and suddenly someone had to do something. A defender left the line, moving to the ball. Youngster toe-poked it forward to Henri. He touched it first time to Tony, who touched it back. Henri had the chance to win the match! I was gripping Sam and he was gripping me. What would happen? The tension was unreal. I bobbed my head forward as though I'd slotted the ball under the goalie. But Henri still hadn't shot yet. *Why not, you DICK?*

Suddenly, the fans behind that goal fell silent, hands on their heads, despairing, and a hush went round the rest of the stadium. Only when Henri's arms rose, as Tony, Youngster, and Pascal converged on him, did we realise what had happened. He'd sat the keeper down and dinked it over him, calm as you like, in front of the away fans.

The manner of the goal didn't interest me as I ran around in a circle like the stupidest hamster.

"Sam! Get on there," I demanded. "Think of the lowest block you've ever seen, then get fucking lower!"

When the dust settled, I heard the new song the fans had spent months perfecting. To the tune of Bob Marley:

"We're gonna be iron! Like a lion! Henry Lion!"

Henri locked onto it, cocked his head, and an ear-to-ear grin took over his face. He waved at them to sing louder, and they tried, but they were already at max.

I braced myself for the final, desperate bombardment from Salford. Five more minutes of nonstop pressure.

But it didn't come.

They were finished, and as the crowd whistled and booed, demanding the referee blow for full time, as Robbo watched a feeble long shot fly over the bar, he suddenly raised his hands, a gesture copied by a handful of other players. All my starters fell from exhaustion. Some of the Salford players collapsed, too, and a couple were in tears. A mini pitch invasion happened over to my right, the joyous fans contained by the stewards and police, and our hospitality person broke my no-music rule, blasting Bob Marley's *"Iron Lion Zion"* so that we could better serenade the match winner.

Chester 5, Moneybags Salford 4.

Getting knocked out of the FA Cup by a non-league team. *That had to* hurt.

3

SCURRILOUS

**Football glossary: *Judas. A player who betrays his team.
See: Sol Campbell leaving Tottenham to join Arsenal.
See also: Luis Figo, Ashley Cole, Mo Johnston.***

I had to do my post-match interview before my shower, before I'd calmed down, so my emotions were all over the place (elation, aggression, salesmanship, blind loyalty) and my responses were a weird mix of charming and snarky, patient and intense.

The shower was more like an ice bath and I was in urgent need of warming up. Two options: Emma or alcohol. *Por que no los dos?*

"Captain," I said. "Where are we going?"

"Somewhere close," said Glenn. "What's our booze budget?"

"Five hundred English pounds," I said, bold and brash, and instantly regretted it. That was a week's wages. Three hundred would have been fine!

"Reckon that'll go a long way," he said, pulling his jacket on. "Since drinks are free."

"What?"

He looked around. I was the last to get showered and dressed. Even Henri had cut his ablutions short. Glenn nodded. "All good, lads? Best behaviour now!"

Seemed like the plan was to leave our gear in the changing rooms and come back to get it. That was optimistic. In a few hours, most of these players would have drunk themselves into next week—in some cases, literally.

"This way, Max," someone said. My thoughts were a bit hazy and insubstantial, and the lads seemed to have learned not to let me make decisions after matches. From being the focal point, the leader, the decision-maker, I had switched roles into being the meekest little sheep. One sheep, many shepherds. One more moment to tug on the heartstrings. One more surge of sentimentality for the group. One more reason to run through a brick wall for them.

I followed the conga line through the bowels of the stadium towards the car park—had they booked some minivans?—up and down some stairs, and there we were outside the Blues Bar. I hadn't been back since my attack. As soon as I stopped at the boundary, I found the Brig to my right and Henri to my left, hands under my arms, guiding me through the doors.

A huge cheer erupted from the fans. There must have been a hundred and fifty in there. (I later learned loads had been turned away to make space for the players and WAGs.) D-Day and Trick raced to the bar, keen to get started on their binge. Steve and Robbo did, too, but on the other side. They colonised a section and started pouring pints. They looked pretty good at it.

Emma appeared out of nowhere and wrapped her arms around me. She tried to pull away, but I held her there. "What?" she whispered.

"I'm bloody freezing," I said, and she stayed snuggled into me so long I closed my eyes and nearly drifted away.

"My dad wants to congratulate you." She looked around—he'd been swallowed by the seething mass of bodies.

"Oh," I said. "Better do it soon. We're about to embark on an epic session. It's going to be despicable."

"Didn't Glenn tell you?"

"No," I said, and it struck me for the first time how odd it was to choose the Blues Bar. The fans wouldn't mind us getting wasted, unless we lost on Tuesday. Then this very public session would come back to bite us on the arse.

"Glenn," called Emma, and my captain came over. He handed me a pint. I took a sip, and the pleasure was unreal.

"Okay, confession time," said Glenn. "We love the idea of a midseason blowout, Max, we really do. But we had a chat and decided we'd rather win the league."

"What? We can do both."

"No. No, we can't. We're doing a two-drink maximum so we'll be ready to play on Tuesday. You, though. You can get blottoed."

"Wait, no. I thought it through."

"Max, you're not in charge of events. That's my job. There's always a week in December when the Saturday match gets postponed. We'll do it then."

I had questions. Lots of questions. But Gerald May grabbed his fellow centre back and whispered something urgent. They went away, leaving me with my thoughts, and with my girlfriend. "What a group," I said.

"Yeah yeah yeah," she said. "They've realised they're riding a wonder horse and don't want to mess it up. Now come find my dad. I want to show off."

I worked the room a little bit—was forced to work the room, more accurately—making my way to Sebastian and Rachel Weaver. The latter was still visibly flushed with excitement from the match and was on her second G and T. The former was extremely gracious and said something along the lines of how he'd misjudged non-league football. I nodded and went "uh-huh," but it was clear something was going on. Some news spreading round the room, not so much among the fans, but the senior players.

"Something's up," I said. "Have they done the draw for the next round already?"

"No, it's tomorrow," said Emma, which warmed me even better than the beer. I gave her a kiss—our first in front of her parents, I guessed—but then the music in the room cut off and someone tapped a microphone.

Over on the raised platform in the corner, where bands sometimes played little gigs, Glenn Ryder was looking sombre. "Max? Where's Max? Can you and Emma come over here, please? MD, you'd better come, too."

Me, Emma, and MD? WTF?

Glenn made me stand to his left. I leaned against the wall, frowning. Emma was next to him, and MD was behind her. Still on the platform, still visible, but not part of the immediate scene. Not one of the presenters. And that, I realised, is what it looked like. A TV show. The rest of the first team crowded round the front of the platform in a semi-circle, with the sponsors next, and then the mass of fans. The only ones who hadn't come over were those still queuing for drinks. When the drinks arrived, so did the fans. It was clear that something portentous was about to go down.

"Hi, everyone. I'm Glenn." Big cheer. "Max has asked me to come up here and apologise for shipping four goals." Big laugh, and I relaxed. Whatever this was, it was fun. "Personally, I blame the defensive midfielder. He went missing." Laughs mostly from the players—the fans had seen me lining up as striker and that was where they assumed I'd played. "Okay, don't want to interrupt the celebrations for too long, but I thought it might be interesting to hear what Max said in his post-match interview."

I stopped smiling and stopped leaning. *Oh, shit.* MD's eyes locked onto mine with impressive speed. I tried to smile but it ended up being one of those things where you bite your bottom lip and your upper lip curls away.

"Emma, can you act the role of the hot blonde reporter?" He handed her a second microphone.

"I can try," she said, with a delicate giggle.

"I'll be Max. Hang on. Let me get my Manchester face on." He did something like Jamie Tartt from Ted Lasso: pretty, smug, vacant. The first traitor detected! "Here we go."

Emma spoke in her best BBC reporter voice for a while, but eventually reverted to her natural Geordie. She read the question from the transcript on Glenn's phone. "Max Best, you've led your team to a famous victory. How do you feel?"

Glenn didn't even try to do a Manc accent. He read what I *allegedly* had said. "Yeah, fine." Massive cheer from the fans for this.

"Great win but there was an incident in the first half where you could have been sent off."

"What? Ah, no, they changed the rules from when you played, Carly. That thing where the guy grabs me and tries to rip my shirt all the way off? We do that in private now and sell the feed on a special website. Seven ninety-nine and you can use the offer code *ooh that's spicy* for ten percent off your first month."

Had I really said that on TV in front of an audience of millions? Emma giggled for quite a while. "Max, were you flirting with that blonde reporter live on the telly?" I shook my head and there were laughs. She rolled her eyes theatrically and continued. "So you don't think it was a red card?"

"Yes, clear red. Pascal was through on goal and the keeper wiped him out."

"I meant the one where you elbowed the guy who was grabbing you."

"I think the referee gave a yellow card."

"But do you think it should have been red?"

"Do I think the yellow should have been red? Wait, this came up in my Science GCSEs. It's something to do with prisms, right? Refraction or something. It's hard to think about light waves and all that when you're being manhandled by a lot of beefy boys. As you know better than me, Carly."

"Max," said Emma, disapprovingly. Back in character, she said, "What did you think of the referee?"

Glenn smiled, shaking his head as he read my reply. His smile wouldn't quite die down, making it hard for him to read it in the right tone. He took a breath and attacked it. "I thought the referee was great. He handled the game well and showed that he has a crystal-clear understanding of modern football. I'd say he has nothing to improve, and do you know something? I feel pretty sure he would agree with me."

The laughter was quite pleasing, I have to say. Even MD, who was trying to look stern, couldn't help but shake his head and let one out every few seconds. I wondered why he was there and got a slightly uneasy feeling about it. What had I said?

"Can you tell us about your penalty?"

"Yep. So as you can imagine, with the occasion and the pressure and the importance of the prize money for a small club like us, I was a bag of nerves."

Glenn held the phone up to Emma, who hadn't expected it so soon. "Oh! Er . . . You didn't look nervous. Wait, probably . . . You didn't *look* nervous."

"Inside I was a big old bag of worms. Very anxious. And do you know what I did? I said a little prayer. I asked Jesus if he wouldn't mind awfully making the goalkeeper just, like, fall over or something. And do you know what?" Glenn couldn't continue—the laughter was almost as loud as the goal celebrations had been. Finally, finally, he felt he'd be heard if he spoke. "And do you know what? He just fell over. Just like that." Henri was wiping away tears. Trick and D-Day, with half a pint left in their plastic glasses, were red. Youngster was no less amused, but he wagged a finger at me anyway, for blasphemy or whatever.

"There was a bit of afters?" Emma frowned. Off mic, but still very audible, she said, "What does that mean?"

"It means your boyfriend dumped the goalie on his arse then let him know about it," explained Glenn. "Shit, I lost the place. Here we go, bit of afters. Er . . . Max speaking again. That goalie is a big talent with great character and temperament and I'm sure he'll have a long career in whichever industry he tries his hand at next."

"Max!" complained Emma, but Glenn was showing her the next question. "Raffi Brown was very impressive today." Big cheer from the Blues Bar, and the man himself was sent up to the platform. He was holding little baby Serina in his arms. She was fast asleep even though we were being super loud.

"Scouts are always coming here asking me about Raffi Brown. Raffi, Raffi, what about Raffi? And I always tell them Raffi's terrible." Raffi looked at me with surprise and perhaps a flash of anger. The crowd's buzz died down. "He isn't two-footed, he can't go box-to-box, he isn't a Rolls Royce player who should be playing at a higher level, and he wouldn't grace the midfield of teams such as Everton, Bournemouth, or Leicester City. So stop scouting him."

Raffi smiled, accepted the round of applause my one-star review generated, and retook his place in the mass.

"Tell us more about Pascal Bochum," read Emma, and there were more cheers and the little guy got up onto the platform. He looked very, very ready to be assessed the way Raffi had.

Ryder put his hand on the forward's shoulder. "Pascal Bochum is too small to play at this level or any level. Pascal Bochum does not know how to move into space, how to combine with other players, how to use his gifts for the benefit of the team, and is not a player who has earned the respect of every player and coach at this club. He's not for sale, don't ask, next."

"Bad boy! Bad boy!" came the cry from about twenty people, almost immediately rising to include everyone in the room, save perhaps the Weavers and sponsors. "Whatcha gonna do? Whatcha gonna do when he's running through?" The chant was followed by the usual round of applause the fans gave themselves when they were pleased with their own work.

Emma cleared her throat and gave Pascal an arm rub as he departed, smiling but weepy. "You're through to the next round. Who do you want?"

"Pierluigi Collina or Uriah Rennie," said Glenn, and about half the audience laughed. I'd named the two most respected, most famous former referees.

"I meant which team."

"I absolutely do not give a wotsit," Glenn said I said. "But do not choose us to be on TV again." MD was suddenly seven feet tall, all the hairs on his head seeming to stand on end. Glenn continued. "And if you do, you'll need to treat my employees with more respect."

"Me?"

"All of you. Your engineers and sound men and all that. We have a guy, Mr. Marsh, who commentates on every match, and I've heard that you kicked him out of his room and were sniffy and demanding, and you've basically been bossing my staff around for days. There's no amount of money you can pay me that will give you the right to annoy, disrupt, and demean my employees. If you want a second date, Carly, someone with a corner office will get in touch with the employees whose weeks have been ruined and they'll explain what went wrong."

Emma said, "Max Best, thank you very much," but no one could hear it over the cheers and applause. A very drunk man was yelling "Don't mess with Chesters!"

I went over to take Glenn's microphone; he was nearest. I divided my attention between MD and the semi-circle in front of me. "Maybe I should say something here. I know the TV money is good and all, but we're not moving *Seals Live* again. Not while I'm in charge." I waited for a response from MD. He was looking at me like I was the Joker in the Batman movie, setting fire to an enormous pile of cash. "The thing is," I started solemnly. "The thing is . . ." I turned the volume up from three to eight. "Nobody puts Boggy in the corner!" From eight to ten, pointing at the crowd, I added, "Boggy Boggy Boggy!"

The crowd knew what to say, and they knew to point back. "Oi oi oi!"

"Boggy Boggy Boggy!"

"Oi oi oi!"

"Boggy!"

"Oi!"

"Boggy!"

"Oi!"

"Boggy Boggy Boggy!"

"Oi oi oi!"

And so our media guy became the first in the world to get his own chant. The music came back on, and the party kicked into high gear.

MD came up to me a moment later and suggested that I had cost the club fifty grand. The same fifty grand that could have bought us a new striker. He was seriously unhappy.

I didn't flinch. "In this world, it's just us." The unhappiness continued, so I repeated Chester's motto to him. "Our City, Our Community, Our Club." I kept staring at him until he took in a little breath. I saw the exact moment he deleted fifty grand from the imaginary ledger in his head; he nodded. Still not happy, but I chose to believe that on some level, he knew I was right. I tapped him on the upper arm. "What we're selling can't be bought." In my mind's eye I opened the glossy catalogue of the antiseptic, anti-fan, anti-football fare being served up by almost every club higher than us in the English pyramid. "They'll be back. On our terms."

The team, incredibly, stuck to the two-drink limit. Something like half didn't imbibe a single drop of alcohol. Trick and D-Day had their two pints and went home. I was a billion percent sure they were leaving to continue boozing away from prying eyes, but no. They went to sleep. They really wanted to start on Tuesday night!

On Sunday morning, I woke up, brushed my teeth, went back to bed, and snuggled close to Emma, suggestively. She didn't have a midweek match, though, and she hadn't felt much need for restraint, so she'd been knocking back all kinds of cocktails and shots at the club's expense.

While I waited for her to stir, I went through my curse screens and nearly leapt out of bed.

Something had changed. Finally!

Your Reputation in England: Very Poor

Your World Reputation: Unknown

Ha! Whoo! I existed! At last.

Something told me it had to do with Manager Points. I'd long since suspected that Manager Points weren't something I could spend like Experience Points. My MP went up when I drew or won, sometimes by baffling amounts, but all in all it seemed to be a numerical value for how good a job I was doing. Winning against Salford had earned me around 1,400 MP, taking my total to 2,050, way ahead of Folke Wester and everyone else in the National League North. Pep Guardiola got more than my season's total by winning one

Champions League match, so I was extremely aware of how unimportant my results were in the grand scheme of things.

But it was progress!

We were getting somewhere!

Also, the monthly perk dropped. It was like it had been waiting for me to get the big cup match out of the way before landing.

November Special Offer

New perk available for the month of November: Parasight

Cost: 3,000 XP

Effects: Whenever player or staff profiles are displayed, Parasight will also reveal any agents in the area, their employer (if applicable), and the total transfer value of the AUM (assets under management) of the agent or their agency.

I mean, wow. It would take some grinding to get the XP, and it would delay the Contracts perk and Wibwob and all the rest, but this seemed absolutely essential. Imagine seeing all the rival managers, scouts, *and* agents who were at a match. That could be really fucking useful.

And the assets under management thing was intriguing. If I met an agent with only one player, I would learn what the curse thought that player's transfer value was. That could be a very useful data point in the lower leagues where a lot of agents only had a few clients. I assumed as we rose through the ranks I'd end up mostly dealing with giant companies, so it'd be impossible to learn anything about individual players from the aggregated data. But take, for example, Harry Kane. His agent was his brother, and I reckoned Harry was his only client. If I got in a stadium with him, I'd know Kane's transfer value, as assessed by the curse.

Would that be useful? No clue. But I wanted it. God dammit, imps! If their goal was to get me back watching Premier League matches on my nights off, they'd absolutely nailed this one.

On Monday morning after training, I had two visitors.

The first was Michael Harrison. He was the only member of the squad who didn't get named on the subs bench against Salford. He was a bit down about it, which was crazy, really. He was nowhere near ready for action, but he had been training with the guys for a while and he felt he was starting to find his feet.

He asked if I was punishing him for not wanting to go to West Didsbury. I didn't like that and got a bit hot. All I wanted was for him to improve faster and I was willing to try anything, and I let him know in no uncertain terms that I didn't appreciate him doubting my motivations.

He cooled down first and said if it would help him, he'd go. I told him that I would never send someone with a bratty attitude to West because it was fucking top there and I didn't want ungrateful guys stinking the place up with their inflated sense of entitlement.

The Brig smoothed things over and after restating our positions to us—which was really calming because it made us realise we wanted the same thing—we agreed Michael would probably go to West in January for a month, with the option to extend it for the rest of the season if the experience was good for him.

Then Sam came in. During the Salford match he'd been all team first, don't worry about me, boss. But in the cold light of day, he wanted to talk about his status. Why had I picked Raffi over him? Why hadn't he been the first sub to come on? And so on. I took him through my tactical thoughts for the entire match, told him what I thought of him, that I needed him, but that sometimes the tactic picked the team. He knew that, he said, but he'd never been at a club that rotated the team before. He understood it, he respected it, but . . . he wanted to be first pick.

He was at CA 57 out of 60, making him one of the top three players in my squad. I felt like I knew him well enough to say the right thing. But me being me, I decided to do the opposite.

"Okay, Sam. I'll pick you first, no matter the situation, no matter the scenario. And I'll never sub you off either, no matter how badly you're playing or what the team needs. You know what? I've got a little tent I don't use. Let's put that in the centre circle and you can fucking live there. I'll get you a little mailbox."

Sam sat there, rubbing his forehead, amused but frustrated. I waited for him to say something, but the Brig intervened. He moved over from the back of the office, where he normally hung out while I did my admin. "Sam. Watch this." He turned to me. "We've had a transfer bid for Sam, sir. Fifty thousand pounds."

My reaction was instant. "Fifty? This January? Forget it."

"They've raised the bid, sir. A hundred thousand pounds."

"Shit," I said, not really enjoying this role-play. It was an agonising decision. I could replace Sam easily enough, but only with a guy who was CA 30 and would take a year or two to get to Sam's level. "I mean, I can't turn that down, that covers the budget shortfall and keeps the club solvent, but holy shit. We're not winning the league anymore." I played out the ramifications in my head. "I'd have to switch formations. Andrew's a year away from being ready. I don't want to play CM. Nah, mate. Don't like this. Don't like this at all. No deal."

The Brig gave Sam a brisk nod, and the midfielder shuffled to the door, looking a bit perplexed, but with his morale a level higher than when he'd arrived.

In the afternoon, Secretary Joe called to tell me the FA were looking into the incident where I'd tried to free myself from the unwanted, sweaty attentions of that Salford player. Joe, the traitor, called it "the one where you elbowed that guy and nearly broke his wrist."

"What does looking into it mean?"

"You might get a ban. Three-match ban, most likely."

"I thought you couldn't relitigate a ref's decision?"

"He's saying the yellow card was for kicking the ball away."

"Will it stop me playing against Darlington?"

"No."

The following three matches were ones we should win without me needing to step onto the pitch. So, whatever. It'd help me save up XP for Parasight. "Call the FA, tell them I said they're a bunch of twats, then hang up."

He sighed and told me he'd keep me informed.

On Monday night, the draw for the second round was made. We were away to Walsall.

They were mid-table in League Two, a few places above Salford City, but I was sure Walsall had a weaker team. Still, they would be way better than us, and without my perks giving us a boost and without our rabid fans intimidating the referee, it'd be tough. Really tough.

Walsall had decent attendances, 5,500 on average, but looking at their history in the FA Cup second round, we could expect something like 4,000. We would split the gate receipts, getting forty-five percent of the income each, but it wasn't going to be a cash bonanza. And, with all due respect to Walsall, it didn't seem like we'd be in the top ten picks to be shown on TV.

(Incidentally, for the first time I wished I had the Finances perk. I wasn't sure exactly how much we'd made from the Salford tie. MD was back to being distant with me.)

Getting Walsall was frustrating because there were plenty of teams in the draw we could have beaten quite handily or had a good go at, and if we got to the third round, away at Tottenham perhaps, we could have made millions.

Ah, well. That's football. At least it would mean another postponement of a league match. One more game being played at the end of the season when we'd be much stronger. We *would* be much stronger, right? The Brig's role-play had helped Sam but had put me on edge. Could we keep all our players in January? I needed to have backup plans in place in case we suddenly lost key players. People I could bring in, even ten minutes before the deadline.

I took my director of football glasses off and looked at the League Two table again. There in the middle were Walsall. Three places below but rising quickly were Salford. And just a couple of places above the relegation zone . . . Tranmere.

I sighed. How long would Mateo stick with James?

And, being honest, how long *should* he stick with James?

Tuesday, November 7. Match 15 of 46: Chester versus Tamworth.

Tamworth came to our gaff. Average CA 38, playing in red. They were known as The Lambs.

Yeah, lambs to the *slaughter*.

(That's terrible. Cut that.)

On the footage I saw, Tamworth played 4-3-3 at home—quite attractive football with tricky forwards—and 4-4-2 away. It was a very sensible blend of trying to put on a show for your home fans while picking up some points on your travels. Good manager, good team, seemed like a club with its head screwed on.

But we'd been blasting teams left and right and had just hit five past a League Two side, so out came the low block. And for once, I was relieved.

We were hungover. Mostly from the incredible noise and intensity we'd experienced a few days before, but also from having a pint or two. It was shocking how much you could see the alcohol messing with people's legs, their coordination, their decision-making, three days later.

Naming the lineup was hard. I really wanted to leave Glenn, Ryan, and Aff out of the eleven. They needed a break (and I wanted them fresh for Saturday's Darlington game), while D-Day, Joe, and Trick needed to start. It was hard to balance all the factors, and in the end I took a risk on 3-5-2 with Ben Cavanagh back in goal for the first time since his meltdown against Kidderminster, Trick Williams playing the Aff role, D-Day as a second striker, and Joe right mid. The biggest gamble was throwing Andrew Harrison into midfield. He was CA 12, but he could run around, tackle, and pass the ball to someone good. Against a low block, he'd be fine. I had to start Ryan Jack, but I tweaked his instructions so he wouldn't have to run around or press.

I made Sam Topps captain for the day even though I suspected his influence wasn't that high, and he nearly burst with pride. His morale shot to Superb.

So with an average CA of 41.5, we set about our business, with the stadium eerily quiet. The fans had a hangover, too.

We moved the ball around quite well, but the last pass always went astray. D-Day overcomplicated things—he really wanted to be the match winner. The only saving grace was that Tamworth's manager didn't realise how weak our team was and didn't come at us.

After fifteen minutes, Ryan Jack went down with an injury. The curse told me it was his knee, which gave me all kinds of stress. So I had to throw Raffi on; no break for him.

Fortunately, Raffi scored from a corner to put us 1–0 up, and the guys passed the ball around for the rest of the game, taking some potshots every now and then but basically saving their collective energy. I thought about going on for the last ten minutes, but I really, really wanted to save myself for Darlington. I swapped Henri for Tony, and really couldn't have done any more in terms of freshening up the lineup while still making sure we were favourites to win.

Tamworth came at us in the last five minutes, but I went men behind ball (ugh) and Ben didn't have a shot to save in the whole match. He caught some crosses and made some good clearances. I hoped the evening would get his season back on track.

Okay, three points, not a memorable game, but I'd learned a lesson: no more mid-season parties.

The win left us in a pretty decent position, all things considered. The top four teams were winning most of their matches, but the early season pace couldn't last. One thing was sure: We'd leap ahead of Darlington if we beat them.

	TEAM	P	W	D	L	F	A	GD	PTS
1	Kidderminster	16	11	5	0	32	9	23	38
2	Darlington	16	10	5	1	25	14	11	35
3	Chester	15	11	1	3	39	15	24	34
4	York	16	8	6	2	26	17	9	30

There wasn't much time to enjoy the win, though. While I was in the shower, the countdown on the bomb hit zero and it exploded. My phone started popping off and didn't stop for days.

The scurrilous article Emma had been dreading finally arrived on some shitty website not worth suing. The biggest surprise was the ecosystem of content that had been pre-developed around the article. TikToks, YouTubes, all kinds of social media stuff, hashtags, memes. This wasn't just an article—it was a massive, coordinated campaign that came at me in waves.

Impressive, really.

But it all started with wave one: the article. And looking at the identity of the co-writer, I knew I had found my first proper traitor of the season. Bingo was the local sports reporter and he had come across as a cool guy. I'd given him an exclusive interview with Miss Fox and her class.

The main author, of course, was the Australian prick who had scammed Emma into dishing the dirt on me. I refuse to dignify him by using his real name.

Bigger than Judas
by Cameron Sandpaper and Bingo Williams
reprinted without permission

Scarborough, Monday 2nd January, 2023. Max Best poses in front of the Darlington supporters, hands clasped together in fake prayer. Someone takes a photo, adds the words *Bigger than Jesus*, and a meme is born.

Many Darlo fans remember Max Best's time at the club fondly. One recent poll named him second in a list of the team's best ever players. But our investigations have led us to a different conclusion. The gospel truth is that Max Best derailed Darlo's push for promotion, did for David Cutter, and left behind a deluge of devastation.

"It started before we ever even saw him," said one of our many sources, most of whom wish to be anonymous for fear of reprisals from Best, whose temper is notorious. "He had some kind of relationship with the receptionist at the training ground. She was only about sixteen, but she'd do anything for him. She was at his beck and call, like she was afraid of saying no."

Another insider said, "He turned up on Remembrance Day so that he could act all sombre in front of Cutter. He's sharp like that. Got a sharp eye for a shortcut. He [Best] acted all sad during the two-minute silence and Cutter lapped it up. We saw right through it but what can you say?"

What can you say, indeed? Once he'd softened the manager up with crocodile tears, it was time to insinuate himself into the team.

"He gets himself invited to join our training session, which was really annoying because we had important games coming up. Of course, he's a decent player but he can't resist having a dig. He says "ah this is too easy let's make it more fun" to show us up, like. Very disruptive and annoying, but he realises he's gone too far and tries to laugh it off. Doesn't really work on us, but Cutter is only seeing the goals and free kicks so now we've got this brat training with us, and playing, too. We couldn't believe it."

Also unbelievable was Best's attitude behind the scenes. One senior player, vastly experienced, told us just how bad it got. "He refused to sign the code of conduct. Like he was above all that. Teams need rules that everyone agrees to. Best said no and was frankly obscene in the dressing room when we brought it up. Then he comes in late, trains on his own, does whatever he wants. It wasn't long before the young players were running riot."

His on-pitch output made up for it, though, surely? Another source remembered the early matches. "There were certain people he didn't want to play with, so he set about making them look like fools. He'd pretend their passes were no good, even though us on the pitch all saw they were just fine, and he'd thrash passes just far enough ahead of a striker so he couldn't quite get there. It was crazy. Look at those highlights again and you'll see there are two or three players Best never, ever passes to, and one striker who scored a ton of goals that season never got an assist from Best. And Cutter fell for the trick and the striker got dropped."

The more people we talked to, the more we realised how deep Best's poison had sunk. "One day I went to training and a few lads snubbed me. I didn't get it at first, but I realised Best was forming his own little clique and splitting mates apart. He wanted us all fighting each other. Before he came, we were one big happy family."

It wasn't only naive young receptionists Best had inappropriate relationships with. "He spent a few nights at the digs, and within minutes he was tapping up the youth team's star player." Tapping up is the unethical, and illegal, practice of talking to under-contract players without permission of their clubs.

"What would bother me if I was a Darlington fan," said Brad Rymarquis, a prominent agent with good connections to the club, "is how blatant it is. No sooner is he in charge of a club than he's poaching Darlo's best young players. For free. And those lads who went to Tranmere for cheap? Best was behind that. I'm not sure how it benefits him, but he was behind it, mark my words. Tranmere never had a scout up here. Never."

Surely the tapping up was a sign Best had his eye on the exit door as soon as he'd arrived. "He had his eye on a manager gig somewhere. He was always meeting people from Chester or Telford. We thought he was playing them off against each other and it was so obvious to us we couldn't believe how easily they were falling for it. He never gave two hoots about Darlo or the fans here. It was just a stepping stone, and while he was here, why not pick up a few impressionable youngsters? Because that's the sick thing about him—he doesn't mind if he's stealing players for his next team or for his agency. He'll make money coming and going."

Agency? A player on the fringes of the first team said, "When he came he said he was representing Henri Lyons, the guy who'd slagged the town off. Best was trying to get him to Chester so he could skim his ten percent, but what we later learned was that David Cutter wanted to reintegrate Lyons, and Best lied to Lyons about it so he could get paid. Lied to his client! He doesn't care about anyone but himself. When I see them laughing and joking these days it makes me sick. Lyons was a difficult guy to understand but I really think his heart's in the right place and the way he doesn't realise Best is taking the pee out of him . . . It makes me sick, it does."

So Lyons could have stayed in Darlington? We came up with an impeccable source. Someone incredibly close to Best. Close but, like Best, ever ready to betray. Over coffee, she dropped bombshell after bombshell. She offered to buy me something stronger; she was *thirsty*. Her story was enough for me. It made Best look even more twisted than we originally thought.

"Max had a plan to play until the end of January and leave after the evening match. He would cancel his contract right there in the changing room and ten minutes later, Chester would register him. Yep, right there in the changing room after a match, he would leave the club without telling anyone. He had it all worked out. Henri was part of the plan but not party to the plan. Max knew Darlington wouldn't let Henri go to the same National League North club as him because they'd be too dangerous together. So he got Henri out and then he would follow later. But something went awry with the schedule that ruined the concept, so he left near the start of the month."

He left, in fact, after his Bigger than Jesus moment, but we'll get back to that. What about Henri Lyons?

"Max arranged everything, then told Henri. Henri thought it was crazy and told him not to do it. He said it was disrespectful and all that kind of thing. He was really insistent on doing right by Darlington, but Max didn't care. He wanted to leave."

Get paid and leave. For not only would Best be extracting money from his new client, he was also on a hefty goal bonus. Another insider with knowledge of the club's finances said, "Best was on silly money for goals, so he was shooting from everywhere. He'd have ten shots a game because that was cash money to him. Didn't seem to bother him if other players were in a better position. He was costing the club so much money they were having to make cutbacks, but it didn't stop him. Cutter tolerated it because he thought Best would sign a contract and the club would get some money when they sold him, but Best strung him along and we never got a penny. I know for a fact in the back office they call him The Leech, which is ironic because the building staff call him The Lech. Short for lecherous."

But surely a young man doesn't sign for his first professional club and immediately plot his exit? One player's girlfriend was more than happy to offer confirmation. "He was planning it from the start. We bumped into him the day after a match, and he was really unkind and unfriendly. His girlfriend said he spent the whole morning reading about himself online, which is typical of the man, really, and when I tried to be nice and set up a dinner, just being friendly, like, Best says great let's do it in February. His girlfriend tried to hide a laugh—she's as two-faced as him; they're made for each other—and I didn't think much of it until later. He knew he'd be gone in February, even then. It was shocking when I realised he was planning to betray us the whole time he was there. It shook me up. How can you be so cruel?"

There was already a startlingly clear pattern of behaviour, if only one person had seen the whole picture. But Best was sly enough to limit how much damage he caused in front of any one person or group. One of the young players tried to raise the alarm and was ignored. "He came into our school lessons whenever he wanted. I was, like, trying to get an education and that. Because football's a short career and it's, you know, precarious. So when Best came in we'd all groan because it was like, mate, I've got exams next week."

But why was he there? "He fancied our teacher. I mean, to be fair, she was well fit, but he could have done that at breaks and stuff. But maybe he did it in class time so's his psycho girlfriend wouldn't find out. She was his stalker or something, I heard. But I got a bad grade, and I think that's as much Best's fault as mine, in the end."

Yet another source confirms much of the above, and adds to it. Incredibly, Best became even bolder over time. "Oh, I could tell you stories about that man that'd curl your toes. Did you know he took Henri Lyons to Chester and they played a whole match in secret? A trial with Darlington's record signing as the star of the show. What if he'd got injured there? There's a reason people don't do things like that. The fallout could have been enormous, not that Best would give a toss. Then he himself went on a secret trial at Sheffield Wednesday, and the only reason he isn't playing there now is that he didn't like the way someone was talking to him, and he shot his mouth off, the way he always does. Except at Wednesday he didn't have a couple of goals to his name, right? So they binned him off right away, as Darlo should have done the first time he skipped training."

Skipped training? "Yeah. Used the old sick mum excuse. She was sick any-time he needed a morning off. Oh, and he did a runner during a match, sulking after he got subbed off, and he said he'd gone to see his mum. It's horrible, really, because she really is sick but he never goes to see her."

But it was near the end where Best's ego was spinning wildest out of control. "He wanted to take a penalty in his last game, so he demands the ball. Cutter's said that Blondie is on pens, but Best is going mental. He says he wants the ball or Blondie will wake up in a ditch somewhere. It was sick. Then he scores and goes off to do his Bigger than Jesus stuff. Which is really not on, especially not at Darlo with its Quaker roots. There's disrespect, there's extreme disrespect, then below that there's Max Best. They say those who the gods love die young, and that's how I knew he'd survive his attack. He'll live a long time, that prick."

Which brings us to perhaps the single most shocking part of the story. The events of halftime against Kettering. With his team losing 2–0, with two players and the manager sent off, Max Best committed the ultimate crime in sports.

He refused to play.

"We had to beg him not to do anything stupid," says one player who was there. "He was already getting undressed. Ready to flounce just when we needed him. He'd taken so much from the club, disrupted everything, made everything into chaos, the way he does. And now we needed a bit of something, and he said, nah, I'm not doing this. I'm too good for this. We had to plead with him. His mate Junior asked Best if he'd play if we let him do the tactics. You know, like you'd do with a kid. Go to the dentist and I'll buy you a new toy. At the time we were all pumped full of adrenaline and everything that happens in a match seems normal, but later when I thought about it, I thought it was sad. Pathetic, you know? But it also made me angry. He wants to be a manager? Fine. But he's not the manager. He needs to shut the eff up and play like the rest of us."

Another witness was less equivocal. "It was mutiny. Plain and simple. He cost us the league that night. It was never the same in the dressing room. That was the night Max Best got David Cutter sacked, and I'll never forgive him for that."

This weekend, one year to the day that Best darkened Darlo's doorstep, he'll be back with his bimbo and his French "friend." He will get a good reception from the home fans, those that only know him as a flying winger thrilling them with his on-pitch antics.

But there will be no such love from his former teammates, coaches, or backroom staff. They know all too well what Max Best did. For them, Best resembles a biblical character whose name starts with J. And they don't mean Jesus.

That night and all through the next day, as the article and the reaction videos and the reaction-to-the-reaction videos went viral in two English towns and almost nowhere else, I got urgent texts. Dozens of urgent texts. From Emma, from Henri, MD, Longstaff, Miss Fox, and many, many more. All were close variations on the same theme:

We need to talk.

4

GOALS AND GHOSTS

Football glossary: *To ghost in. To appear out of nowhere,
like a ghost, with a perfectly timed run into the penalty area.
He ghosted in at the far post.*

Saturday, November 11. Match 1 of 1: Darlington versus Chester.
One hour before kickoff.

The dressing room was ghostly quiet. Almost silent. No claps, slaps, shouts. No come ons, no big game today boys, no make sure you fucking want its.

Instead of talking, I scribbled names on the tactics board. Robbo in goal. Re-energised by being dropped and put back in the starting eleven, he'd been training like a demon. His CA had crept up to 40, which, given that he was thirty-four years old, really seemed like turning back the clock. He watched as my marker formed the shapes of his name. No reaction. He was as affected by the mood as everyone else.

The back four were Magnus, Glenn, Gerald, and Carl. The half-American right back was on CA 52 now. He was very close to catching Glenn and becoming our best defender.

Youngster would roam the lines between defence and attack. Today he looked very young. Very callow. As one of the most sensitive members of the squad, he was quite affected by the Judas article and what had come after. This match would be a big test for him.

In midfield, from left to right, Aff, Raffi, D-Day, and Joe Anka.

Up front, Henri.

I wrote out the subs. Ben, who had put his recent tribulations mostly behind him, had improved to CA 43. Steve Alton, who had moved past Gerald May in CA; Sam Topps; me; and Tony.

As soon as I wrote the last name, Trick Williams stood and threw down his shinpads. "What about me?" he hissed, because even if he was angry, it would have been unthinkable to shout into that void of sound.

I clicked the lid back on the marker, then shook my head.

He put his fingers to his nose, fussed in his bag to get his wallet, and went out, slamming the door behind him.

Another sign of our very obvious dysfunction. Our very public disunity.

The article, it seemed, had done its job.

Transcript from Seals Live, 3:00 p.m.

Boggy: And we're off! Darlington get things going, kicking from left to right in their black and white kits. If you're just joining us, Chester coach Spectrum is back with us for this big game. Top of the table clash.

Spectrum: Hi.

Boggy: The atmosphere is febrile.

Spectrum: What does that mean?

Boggy: Noisy.

Spectrum: Oh, yes. The home fans are well up for this one. The team, too. Very fast start from them. Playing high balls forward. Direct.

Boggy: As we talked about before kickoff, that's probably because they let the grass grow long. Trying to make it hard for Chester to play their usual passing game. And they've overwatered the pitch for the same reason. It's all very underhand these days, isn't it?

Spectrum: I'm trying not to think about it. It's all making me very, very angry.

Boggy: Long balls being hit towards the Chester penalty area, but so far the back four are coping. Youngster trying to mop things up, but he's struggling with this pitch. It's been less than sixty seconds here and he's already played two wayward passes.

Spectrum: Not sure he'll have played on a pitch like this. He'll adapt.

Boggy: Cross swung in from Hurts, the seventy-thousand-pound left back. Headed away by May, not very far, ball played back to Hurts, another cross, another half clearance, my goodness is it going to be like this the whole match? Now Chester get some control. Raffi Brown holds off a challenge, finds D-Day. He tries an ambitious pass out to Anka, but it's easily cleared by Hurts. What do you make of this team selection? Ryan Jack is injured, but no Sam Topps?

Spectrum: I can't really work it out. Of course, it could be . . . you know. Fallout. From all the stuff that's been happening.

Boggy: [pained groan]

Five minutes in and Darlington were well on top. They were bullying us in midfield especially. Tough tackles, yes, but also quick to the ball. Aggressive, powerful, and the crowd loved it.

I spared a few seconds to tune into the vibe. It was hard to tell how much they had been turned against me and how much they were using any excuse to force a win. They knew they had the best team in the league, on paper, and had invested heavily in a bid to get out of the division. And they knew we were the biggest threat.

If they could beat us today, we would have lost to each of the top three teams, and teams that win the league don't do that.

Yeah, fair to say the home fans would have been up for it anyway, but the article had pushed some of them over the edge into nastiness.

The left midfielder they had bought, Dicks, had one of those long throws. He hurled it in now, all the way to the penalty spot. There was a bit of chaos, and Captain Caveman leapt and headed into the net.

The noise was intense. On another day I'd have found it intimidating, but today it passed right through me, touching nothing. They were ghouls; I was a ghost.

As the initial celebrations died down, a chant rose up.

"Sacked in the morning! You're getting sacked in the morning!"

I tried to pick out MD in the director's box. How close was he to firing me? I didn't see him, but I did see one of my players wandering around the stand like a lost soul. I knew who he was looking for. I knew it all too well.

Boggy: Twenty minutes gone here in Darlington and the Blackwell Meadows stadium is bouncing. It's one–nil to Darlington, and it has been pretty one-way traffic so far this half. Darlington started ferociously, an absolute maelstrom of long balls and crosses, and when Chester have broken forward, player-manager Folke Wester has snuffed out the danger. So far, Henri Lyons has been a virtual passenger. This is where I get nervous about him lashing out.

Spectrum: Doesn't seem much danger of that today. Like a lot of the players, he's subdued. They aren't even talking to each other. Have you seen it? Glenn Ryder is organising his defence, but that's it.

Boggy: Isn't it very Sunday League to want your players to gee each other up and shout?

Spectrum: Not really, but even if it is, we normally do it and today we're not. I don't like seeing us . . . not be us.

Boggy: D-Day has been ineffective, but I must say he has worked hard.

Spectrum: Very hard. He's playing like someone who was told he'd get the first half and to leave everything out there.

Boggy: Mmm. So maybe Sam Topps will come on second half. Maybe he has a slight knock.

Spectrum: Oh. Look. He's coming on . . . *now*. What?

Boggy: You're not impressed with Best's decisions today.

Spectrum: If there's ever a match where you could understand that his mind wasn't sharp and clear, it'd be this one. Right? All the drama. It's shocking how much it has affected the rest of the team, though. I think we might have to write today off and sort of rebuild.

Boggy: That's the end of Donny Dorigo's shift. Little twenty-minute cameo from him, there. Lots of industry, no end product. No handshake from Best as he leaves the pitch. No words spoken from the bench. It's like the *Mary Celeste*. A ghost ship. Oh, I don't like this. We've gone from riding the wave of the cup run to this, all because of one horrible, scurrilous little piece of vicious . . . *trash*.

Spectrum: Come on, Boggy. It'll be all right.

Boggy: Reports of an incident with Trick Williams in the dressing room. Players not talking to each other. Team spirit gone. Strange decisions. Being battered by Darlington. The manager standing there, arms folded, not moving. His every move since joining put under the microscope, examined and reexamined. Are we witnessing the end of the Max Best era?

Triple Captain looked like it was working. Glenn Ryder had shrugged off the early setback of the goal and was leading by example. When he played like this, he was enormous. He wasn't quite at the Christian Fierce level of physicality and mental strength, but he was close enough for my purposes. To Glenn's left, Magnus was winning his duels. To his right, May was struggling manfully against Blondie. Blondie had a big CA advantage, but May was just about keeping him under wraps. Just about. And on the right, Carl was up against one of Darlington's two big-money signings. Dicks, the left midfielder, was on 6 out of 10, which showed that Carl was winning those battles.

Hurts versus Anka was not an equal battle, though. Hurts was a seriously good player and was on 9 out of 10, which was massive for a left back who hadn't scored or assisted. I'd known he would be a pain point and there was nothing I could do about it.

Bench Boost was working, too. When Sam had jogged onto the pitch, it was like he was gliding. Changing direction as easily as Pac-Man dodges ghosts. And in the first couple of minutes of being on, Pac-Sam ran around gobbling up balls and burping them to Raffi.

It would be an exaggeration to say putting on a Bench Boosted midfielder turned the tide in our favour, but the difference was stark. The contest evened out. We were snapping into tackles the way Darlington had been doing. We won midfield duels in a way we hadn't before. Suddenly, the Aff-Raffi-Sam line became the dominant factor in the match. They didn't have things all their own way, but the more they outperformed their rivals, the more Henri got into the match, which pulled Darlington backwards, and the more they were pulled back, the more Youngster had the breathing space to think his way into the contest.

Around the twenty-five-minute mark, I noticed that the crowd were far, far less noisy. I hadn't known what to expect in terms of reception, and the whole day was made even weirder because, just as things were getting spicy, we had a one-minute silence to honour those who fought and died in our many wars. Sneaking the stuff about me abusing Remembrance Day into the article made sense, because when the referee blew to end the silence, there was what felt like genuine, deafening anger, aimed at me, for disrespecting the memories of the fallen. Then a spine-tingling roar, urging the home team to start fast.

Now, though, their team's early energy and verve was fading. They had come out throwing haymakers and one had landed, but one wasn't enough. The team knew that, Folke Wester knew that, and the fans knew that.

We got our first jab through the defences.

Nice interception from Youngster. He plays a simple pass to Evergreen.

It's played forward to Aff. He turns and finds Brown is in support.

Brown moves across the pitch and fizzes a pass to Anka.

Played first time back inside to Topps.

Topps touches it to Brown, who looks up.

Glorious curling pass out to Aff. He's motoring forward.

He tries to pick out Lyons.

Great pass!

First-time shot!

Good block from Caveman.

He really had to stretch there.

I nodded. Yes. Good. Let it happen.

Words and phrases from the article swirled around me like smoke. *Judas, leech, mutiny.* I looked up, exasperated with myself, fixed my jaw, and concentrated.

The racket from the home fans bumped up a level as they attacked, but suddenly my whole body started tingling, and as the ball was played to Blondie's feet the hairs on my neck went haywire.

Strong tackle from Ryder. He meant that one!

The ball pops out to Youngster.

Great one-touch pass to Anka!

He's got some space for the first time in the match.

He looks for a cross but decides to keep going.

All the way to the byline.

He cuts the ball back . . .

Lyons cocks his leg, ready for the volley . . .

But the ball's blocked!

It seemed to come off the defender's hand.

The Chester players are demanding a penalty.

And the referee has given it!

The assistant referee had a perfect view of the incident.

It looks like Lyons will take the spot kick against his former team.

Ah. Right. About that.

Boggy: Huge excitement here at Blackwell Meadows where Chester have a penalty. Chester have a penalty to draw level! Spectrum, be honest with me now, something weird is going on, we can all see that, but this doesn't look like a team that have given up.

Spectrum: No, they don't. They weathered the storm, and now they're giving some back.

Boggy: Bit of a delay here while the usual gamesmanship goes on. Referees are far too lenient with these players who try to put the penalty taker off. It's cheating, plain and simple.

Spectrum: Oh my God.

Boggy: What? What?

Spectrum: Max is going to take the penalty.

Boggy: But he's not even— Oh! Chester are making a substitution.

Spectrum: Max, no. What are you doing?

Boggy: Youngster is leaving the pitch. Just as he was coming into his own! That's a shame. But Max wants to take the penalty, it seems. There's absolute bedlam here. No one can believe what they're seeing. Folke Wester looks like he's seen a ghost. Best has used two substitutions in the first half. The second, to bring himself on to take a penalty. Will he sub off after he takes it?

Spectrum: I don't know what's real anymore.

Boggy: I'll tell you what, no one is trying to put *him* off. It's a straight contest between Best and Larkin. Oh, my nerves. Everyone in the stadium is grabbing the person next to them. This is unreal. Unreal.

Folke Wester had been planning for this day since the start of the season. Like me, he'd realised this would be a massive, massive moment. Possibly the pivotal day for both teams. Winning would be a statement, would boost one set of players and fans. Losing would be a disaster, would demoralise and demotivate the other.

His manager stats were the same as when I'd last seen them: discipline 18, motivating 20, man management 8. A banshee. Ruling by fear. Not a good coach, not much of a tactical brain. His playing stats had decreased slightly: His pace had dropped one point to 6. His positioning was still 20, he had heading 16, tackling 14, and his stamina of 11 wouldn't be tested if he stuck to the confines of his defensive midfield role.

He was, in truth, a formidable presence in that part of the pitch, but we didn't normally attack through the middle.

Wester had grown his grass long and come to watch me play. He'd studied his tapes, noting that I tended to play the last half an hour. He had a plan A that would be something like what Kidderminster did to us. He had a plan B in case I played from the start, as I'd done against Salford.

He'd dropped his dirty bomb, spreading toxicity, hate, and bile.

And I had absolutely no doubt he'd been studying my new penalty technique in great detail. He would have a plan to counter it.

But he just didn't get it. He couldn't conceive of the ways *I'd* been preparing for this match. He didn't have the imagination to think beyond me starting and finishing the game. What if I played the *middle*?

There was no question he had instructed someone to go in hard—real hard—as soon as I stepped onto the pitch. But again, lack of imagination. Who could have dreamed I'd be so arrogant and selfish as to bring myself on to take a first-half penalty? They could still try to kick me out of the game, but only after I'd scored.

The referee pointed to the goal line, ordering the keeper to step back.

In goal was Paul Larkin. Smokes, the first-choice goalie, was out with a minor finger injury. It didn't matter too much in terms of this match, but if I humiliated Larkin, it would make Wester blame him for their defeat and would cause the kind of division Wester had been hoping to create in Chester.

While the ref tried to make himself the centre of attention by walking along the edge of the penalty area pointing at players, I had a look at some faces in the stand to my left. There were plenty of people who believed what they'd been told this week. They were all kinds of mad at me. There were a fair few, I thought, who were unsure.

Paul Larkin took a step behind the goal and picked up his water bottle. Someone had taped notes on it. How to save an Henri Lyons penalty. How to save a Max Best penalty. I wondered if they had bothered doing one for Tony Hetherington? Probably.

The whole thing was almost certainly theatre. There was no way to stop what I did. Put simply, I made the keeper dive, then kicked the other way. If I kept my cool, it was virtually foolproof. I would only miss if I was, for example, blazing with fury about an article that Wester had funded.

The free hit button was flashing. How tempting was that? This goal could change the entire course of our season. Could change the entire course of my career. Could be the goal that propelled me to the Premier League. I pushed the button away.

The referee was ready now. Paul Larkin was ready. He looked confident. He had a plan.

I twitched and the stadium hushed. A few stray shouts could be heard. They were not very nice.

I took a step to the right. Then another step.
Paul Larkin did not look very confident.
No more shouts came.

Boggy: Here we go. Oh, what? Best is moving away. No, he's—he's what? He's going to take the kick with his left. What's he playing at?

Spectrum: Oh, Christ.

Boggy: This is it. Best, left-footed, steps, goalie moves, no, the ball—it's in!

Spectrum: [guttural scream]

Boggy: Best scores! He's scored! With his first touch of the match. He—what did he do? His new technique. He's . . . he's . . . what's he done?

Spectrum: Come on! [off-mic] No, I won't be quiet. Get bent.

Boggy: Spectrum, did you get a good look?

Spectrum: Yes! The keeper had instructions, right? He'd been told which way to dive. But that was right-footed. So when Max changed his feet, Larkin was in two minds. Does he do what he was told? Or the opposite? So, Max, he's about to kick, and the goalie, he's about to dive one way, thinks better of it, and when Max makes contact, the goalie just falls to one knee. Max has done him all ends up. Oh my God, the adrenaline. What a rush. The balls to do that. Fuck me.

Boggy: Language, Spectrum. I have to say, there was absolutely no response from any of the Chester players. No celebrations. When the ball went in, the away fans went crazy, but the players, they turned their backs and walked back to their half. And nothing from Best, either. So it's one–all, but . . . I don't know. I don't know what's happening.

Spectrum: The next five minutes will tell us.

I scored and told myself not to look at the Darlington players. But I couldn't help but walk past Folke Wester, even if it wasn't exactly on my way. He was tall, slim, powerful, good-looking. But under the light-brown hair, above the dashing, sensual lips, were the eyes of a true psychopath. This guy was vindictive, unremorseful, and exploitative. He was smart, too. Smart enough to plagiarise my tactical ideas.

But he'd made a lot of mistakes recently, and he was about to make another one.

I walked past, saying nothing. Three-quarters of the stadium had fallen silent, but now a spark of life came back as they tried to encourage their team to get back in the game.

I took up the DM position and looked around. Darlo's average CA had crept up since I'd seen them in training, and they were now on CA 53. With Smokes in goal, they might have been 54. The best team in the division, on paper. Far ahead of our average CA of 48, plus they had home advantage, plus whatever deleterious effects their media assault had engendered.

They should have been hyped. Super motivated. Confident to the point of arrogance.

So why did they look terrified?

Boggy: It's, er . . . It's Chester in the ascendency here at Blackwell Meadows. Sam Topps is absolutely bossing this game. Is that right?

Spectrum: Yes. This is the best I've ever seen him. He's unbelievable. I know people laugh at me for being a kiss-arse, but it's not Sam, it's Max.

Boggy: What's he doing? What does an expert see when he watches this?

Spectrum: He's giving a masterclass in the position. Youngster was doing okay, making interceptions, taking the pressure off. But here, there's no pressure. There's zilch. Darlington can't get through.

Boggy: But what's he doing?

Spectrum: It's his positioning. He's in the right place for every second ball. Quick one-touch passes up to midfield and the break is on. The front five are playing with all that freedom now because the back five are so solid.

Boggy: There's a lot of long balls still from Darlington.

Spectrum: That's my only doubt about Max in that role. He's not going for headers. He hasn't headed a football since his, you know, and Darlington are trying to target him with high balls.

Boggy: It's not working, though.

Spectrum: [laughing] No. Gerald or Glenn are swapping places with him when the high balls come. Watch and you'll see Best drops to centre back, May goes to DM, wins the header, or not, and they switch back again. It's so smooth it took me all this time to notice.

Boggy: That doesn't seem like a team that's, well, as dysfunctional as it looks.

Spectrum: [musing] No. But when did they practise this?

Boggy: In training.

Spectrum: After the article came out, Max trained with the women.

Boggy: Oh. Oh dear.

Boggy: Coming to the end of a very strange half. Forty-four minutes on the clock, and I'm sure there'll be a minute or two added on for the substitutions and penalties, and a couple of stoppages where Chester players were hurt by hard tackles. Still this aerial bombardment, still Best has nothing to do with it. Darlington's number ten wins that header, there's danger here, Ryder is isolated, and Best comes out of nowhere! He raced in front of the striker, Blondie, and let it go out for a goal kick. Blondie gave him a push, trying to wind him up, but there was zero reaction from Best or from anyone.

Spectrum: That's incredible recovery speed. He could play as a centre back, you know.

Boggy: Not if he won't head the ball.

Spectrum: That's true. Maybe he could be a sweeper.

Boggy: Can you have sweepers in the modern game?

Spectrum: I wouldn't have thought so, but Max talks about it sometimes. It wouldn't surprise me if he tried it once.

Boggy: Robbo takes the kick short. We've adapted well to this long grass. Such a base tactic, that. Really poor. We're moving it around the backline. It's played to Best—ooh, he dodged a savage tackle there.

Spectrum: They can't get near him.

Boggy: They keep trying, though. It only takes one. Ball's out on the left with Aff. Chester pushing up the pitch. Comes to Best. He brings them back again. This is the thing they do where they make space?

Spectrum: That's right.

Boggy: It's awfully stressful, you know.

Spectrum: I'll tell him you want him to stop.

Boggy: Ball's clipped forward to Raffi Brown. He's quietly been having a good game. Not put a foot wrong, has he?

Spectrum: They've been trying to provoke him with snide kicks and elbows and all that. They've picked the wrong guy.

Boggy: Who's the right guy to try to wind up?

Spectrum: I would have said Max, but . . . not today.

Boggy: He's back on the ball again. Darlington are chasing shadows. Wester is screaming at everyone to get back into shape. Best with a simple pass—no! He's on the move. Here we go. Goosebumps! Best's dribbling. He's surging to the centre circle. Going right for Folke Wester! This is the duel we were all waiting for, player-manager against player-manager. Has it ever happened before? Not that I can remember. Best . . . what will he do?

Spectrum: Nutmeg.

Boggy: He's slowed down, looks like he's ready to get cheeky. Oh! Big pass out wide. Darlington were just coming for him, but the pass . . . and Aff's surging ahead. He's isolated. No support. He doesn't need it. Cross comes in . . .

Folke Wester was there, in my path. I shifted my weight to the right and surged ahead, towards Jonathan Hurts in the left back slot. Could I bring Folke all the way out of the centre? This was his one chance to get up close and personal himself.

Wester followed, tracked me, and I felt a full-body thrill. The Bench Boost had smashed me past my limits, past my current ability, and I was playing with something like the pace, skill, and power I'd had before my murder.

I could do whatever I wanted. Nutmeg the bastard, double-dribble, do it again. I could score from long range. I could pop the ball on my forehead and run twenty metres.

Snippets from the article slid across my vision like subtitles in a movie. Emma, my mum, Miss Fox.

The ice-cold rage returned, and I slowed down. I clipped the ball to Aff, and stopped. Folke turned, surprised, and tracked back towards the space between his centre backs. Hurts tucked in to protect the far post.

With their aggro off me, I sprinted.

Aff had no choice but to attack the line and whip in a cross. Fortunately, he'd been brought up on his home pitches doing nothing but that. Long before he learned to slap, he had mastered the art of crossing at the end of a long sprint.

He was aiming, I think, for Henri, but Henri had gone to the near post.

He had gone to the near post because I was arrowing into his usual hunting ground.

The cross, holy shit, the cross was beautiful. You can't understand how gorgeous it was. The height, the curve, the speed, it was sublime. I like a nice team move. I love me a dinked finish, a chip, a volley, a no-look backheel nutmeg, but there's something about a perfect cross that sends me into raptures.

I leapt, crashed into Jonathan Hurts, met the cross full between the eyes, and powered the ball down at the goal line, where Paul Larkin could do nothing more than fall backwards, slowly, a sandwich board toppling at the first breath of the coming hurricane.

The surge of joy was almost overwhelming. The need to run to the fans, to cheer, to pump my fists, to shout, was almost irresistible. Two seconds of a snarling, contorted mouth, of fingers curled into cat claws, of crunched abs, and I remembered my purpose. I got a grip, wiped my face clean of emotion, and walked back to my slot. Ready to go again.

Boggy: Stunning! Stunning from Aff. Sensational from Chester. What a goal! What a headed goal! Best ghosted in at the far post, leapt high, and left Hurts in a heap, left the goalie on his backside, again. Darlington are shattered; Chester are leading two–one. Chester are beating Darlington in their home patch. Chester are making a huge title charge here. But . . . a header! And no celebrations again. It's surreal. Spectrum, explain it to me.

Spectrum: I can't. What I heard was that the men trained as normal. Normal stuff, Wednesday to Friday. Best was separate, but whatever this is, this vow of silence thing, that must have happened today.

Boggy: Oh, God. Something else happened today? Something we haven't heard about yet?

Ninety minutes before kickoff.

The team bus was making good time along the A1M. I went to the driver and asked him to pull in at Barton services. He suggested he didn't really want to, and I suggested he did, he just didn't know it yet. He gave me a funny look, but he turned in and parked.

The place was an absolute mess of concrete and seemed to be a dumping ground for anything and everything, as long as it was ugly as sin. The driver opened the doors, I got off, and I heard the Brig command the players to follow.

A minute later, the guys were assembled around me in a semi-circle.

I'd barely spoken a word to them since the article had come out.

My jaw, as it had been for days, was tight. I tried to loosen it. "Guys," I said, but it came out gruff and angry. I counted to five and tried again. "Guys. You know what the deal is today. The stakes. And you know I never ask you for anything. Only to train like lions, play like kings, and do your community work like legends. It's really not much. Well, today I'm asking you to do something for me.

"You know what this is all about. People slagging me off, trying to get personal, trying to get me angry so I make mistakes. Trying to turn us against each other, blah blah blah.

"Now, listen. I talk shit about you all the time, and you shrug it off. I say you've hit a shit pass or aren't training hard enough or you're late or your haircut's bad for the brand. Doesn't bother you, why would it? But if I ever said anything about your girlfriend. Your wife. Your mum." They bristled, just imagining it. "Right? They crossed the line. They knew they were crossing the line. That was the whole point of it.

"Since Tuesday night I've had people begging me to respond, pleading with me to do an interview, get my side out there. And I said no, I'll do my talking on the pitch. I'm going to put on a show, lads. A real treat. You've seen some of it before, but they haven't. I promise you this: There will be a lot of regrets in that town by half past five.

"Now, what I'm asking—not really asking, actually, demanding—is that you don't say a fucking word in there. We don't talk. Nothing more than the essentials. As soon as we get back on that bus, it's mouths shut until we're back here going the other way, home sweet home. We're going to play football, smash them out of the title race, and leave. Leave the talking to me, you hear me? And by the way, I won't *be* talking. I'm not talking to the media. Not in there. The club will pay the fine, and if they don't want to, I'll pay it.

"Don't celebrate goals. I'm fucking serious. I told you not to knee slide and you keep fucking doing it. I told you not to jump on each other's backs and you keep fucking doing it. But I swear to God, if you celebrate in there today, I will savage you. If you're chatting and laughing at corner kicks, you'll be training with the kids on Monday. If you start fucking swapping shirts with those pricks, holy Christ, I will end your careers."

The lockjaw was back. I counted to ten.

"People are going to talk about this for years. The day they wiped the smirk off Max Best's face." I nodded a few times. Let's see how they like me without the grin. Dark mode. "At the end of the season, we'll parade all our trophies round, shove them in their faces. We'll smile, then. I promise you that."

Donny Dorigo had a death wish, because even as I blazed with fury, he smirked and spoke. "So you're staying, then?"

There was a horrified silence, but as I glared at him, I realised what he'd done. He'd taken the edge off, just enough. My face softened, not quite into a smile, and I blinked. "Mate," I said, affectionately, and the group exhaled. But then I frowned. "I need you in midfield today. You know the plan. I need to trust you today, Donny."

He took a few steps forward and reached out his hand. "You can count on me." I clasped it. He nodded. "They shouldn't have brought your girls into it. That was low." He nodded some more. "No talking. No celebrations. What is it, though?"

"What do you mean?"

"Like, we're some kind of . . . ghost army? Silent assassins?"

I put my arm around his shoulder while I pondered his words. "I don't know what it is. But it's what I want."

Boggy: Oh, nearly! Great play from Brown, but Anka couldn't quite control it. Here come Darlington. Hurts. Long ball—and Best with a towering header! I can't believe what I'm seeing, but it very much seems to be the case that the Chester manager has been pretending he can't head the ball . . . for months! It boggles the mind. There's the halftime whistle. Two–one to Chester in a bizarre, incredible match. Don't go anywhere!

Spectrum: Neither are Chester.

Boggy: What? Oh. The Chester players are . . . What are they doing? Sort of milling around, ten yards from the side of the pitch.

Spectrum: They're waiting for the Darlington lot to clear out. Don't want any aggro. It's very telling they're expecting some dirty tricks in the tunnel. Very telling, indeed. Sums this place up. [off mic] Yeah, you heard me! You know full well what I mean. Shut up. Shut uuuup!

Boggy: Spectrum's made a friend with a local so-called reporter. On the pitch, still no one's saying anything to anyone. Very, very strange indeed. Okay, well, we'll be back in fifteen.

When the tunnel was as clear as it was going to get, I nodded and the Brig led us through. Vimsy was stationed in the middle of the pack, with the subs at the end. Whatever Darlington had planned, our precautions put paid to.

We got to our places and sat in near silence while we drank and ate marathon paste. There were a few whispers with players asking each other to pass a bottle or to mention a problem they were having on the pitch. Dean and Livia were checking on Joe and Henri.

Next door, we heard the demented ranting and raving of Folke Wester. He was giving it the full hairdryer treatment, and poor Paul Larkin seemed to be bearing the brunt. It didn't affect me. I was a ghost. Still on Earth for one purpose only. To haunt those who had hurt me and mine, to turn their dreams into nightmares.

The absolute pleasure of being on the pitch and being something like my former self washed over me, and I found myself smiling. The speed, the purity of thought, the ability to think something and expect it to come off. Memories of a hospital bed, of weeping because I couldn't feel my toes, and now this. Not quite God mode, but good enough for the National League North. Ghost mode.

I closed my eyes and imagined what I'd do in the second half. Go crazy on the nutmegs? What about an overhead kick? Nah, too flashy. I didn't want to entertain these fans. I wanted to smite them.

"Excuse me," came an unfamiliar voice. Someone from Darlington. A match steward. I tensed. Was this part of the attack? "Mr. Best? Your girlfriend is here. She's asking if she can come and see you." The guy grinned. "I said it wasn't the best time an' all, but she doesn't seem to know much about football."

I frowned. "Let her in," I said, and thought back to this morning's text exchange.

Emma: I want to come today.

Me: No.

The door pushed open a little and an Emma-sized woman came in.

I got to my feet. "Miss Fox," I said. All movement in the dressing room ceased. At the time, I thought everyone was wondering if I had a secret second girlfriend, but later I realised they knew she was from the article, even though it had named almost nobody, including Emma. I introduced her anyway. "Everyone, this is Miss Fox. She teaches English here."

"And business studies," she said, which in retrospect was absolutely wild. I suppose she was nervous. She looked around, uncertainly, at all the people staring at her. I thought her gaze lingered on the Brig a fraction longer than on anyone else.

"This is Chester Football Club. The man about to kick you out is the Brig."

Again, she looked at my assistant manager, and again, the *sizzling* chemistry. But Miss Fox wasn't there to flirt. "Mr. Best. Max," she said, inhaling. "I'm sorry to barge in on you like this but you wouldn't take my calls. I want to tell you to your face that I had nothing to do with that horrible man or his horrible article."

"I know," I said softly.

"Oh."

I gave her a tiny smile, even though it broke the whole *ghost avenger army of assassins* vibe. "I'll return your call some time I'm less busy, if that's okay."

"Yes, of course. I mean . . . But the boys. None of the boys said what it said. You know they loved your interruptions. They all thought the world of you."

"What about Bingo?"

She looked down. "He got laid off. Cutbacks. He's scrambling around for whatever work he can get." She rubbed her arm. "It's no excuse, but . . ."

"Are you in trouble?" It hadn't occurred to me that other people might be affected by the article, which is one of my many failings as a person, but someone had idly wondered if the teacher would get in trouble for letting me barge in all the time.

"Nothing I can't handle," she said, chin up, and a ripple of admiration spread through my squad.

"Miss Fox," I said.

"Faulkes," she said, speaking directly to the Brig.

"You can't just barge into my classroom whenever you want. You're distracting my boys."

"Oh," she said, recognising the way I'd turned the tables. She smiled. "*He's* going to kick me out, is he?"

"John Smith," I said, "slap her on the arse, say 'there's a good girl,' and don't let her back in."

The Brig didn't move, so Miss Fox raised an eyebrow and said, "Well, John Smith?"

The Brig gestured towards the door and he closed it behind her. When he came back, we saw something unbelievable. He was blushing.

"Go on," I said, gesturing that he should follow her.

"What about not saying anything inside the stadium, sir?"

"Go and chat her up, you dick," I said.

He looked down and gruffly cleared his throat. "I'm, er, in a relationship, sir."

"What? Oh. Fine." The scene was over, so I instantly fell back into the ghost assassin mindset.

"I thought you knew," he said from behind me, but I was back at the tactics board, sliding magnets around.

With Aff at left back and Magnus in midfield, we could bring Tony on and play 4-3-3, with me dropping back to DM, making it a 4-1-3-2. I really liked the look of that. Showing good formations in front of Folke Wester was maybe not the best idea, though. What else? Could do 3-5-2 with me as second striker moving back to CAM to face up to Wester. Or swap Joe for Tony and I could go right midfield. I couldn't do all my mystery winger stuff, but I'd be able to do some of it, thanks to the Bench Boost. And just the fear of having me there would probably make their talented left-sided players go defensive.

Henri appeared at my side—stealthy as fuck!—and I glanced at him. He looked like he was in agony. I checked his profile in a brief panic, but it was all good. "What?"

"It's not fair," he whispered. "You make us stay quiet. Then in comes a goddess and you kick her out in an instant, and the Brig blushes and the revelation that he is dating. Maaaax, please. We need to vent. Give us two minutes."

"You can have two hours."

He groaned. "On the bus home, yes?"

"Yes."

"Fine. You are banned from my house. For two days."

"Fair. Now get your game face on."

"*Oui*, Max. Oh, and Max?"

"Hmm?"

"Good header."

On Wednesday morning, I hadn't gone to training. At nine o'clock, I was knocking on Livia's front door. She was at work, of course.

The door opened, and a bleary-eyed Liverpudlian peered round it. "Fucking hell, Max."

"Are you awake?"

"No," he lied. "What do you want?"

"I want private coaching."

He scratched his chin. "Is this about Darlington?"

"Yes."

More scratching. He didn't think to invite me in. "What do you want?"

"Headers."

"Headers?" he said, confused. "I would, but . . ."

"But you don't want to overwork yourself. You're easing back in."

"Yeah."

"That's fine. I'll train with the girls. Or rather, they'll train with me. Twenty minutes getting on the end of crosses and doing clearances, twenty minutes beating the press, twenty minutes something I'll think about when you say yes."

"And on Friday? You shouldn't overdo it the day before."

"Today and tomorrow if you can manage that, and then you can have Friday off. Someone else will train the women."

"If I say yes, can I go back to bed?"

"Yes."

"Then yes."

Wednesday had been good, but the Thursday session was better. I brought Aff, Joe, Ben, and a bunch of kids, and the first-team guys fired crosses for me to head at goal. It was, in fact, my dream session, because I was sort of tricking Jackie into coaching three players from the men's team. A single session led by Jackie made at least one attribute go green on each of them.

I wondered what it was doing for me. In his first Beth Head master class, Jackie barely had to glance at Youngster to make him go from CA 1 to CA 2. Youngster was a high-potential kid, but I was almost certainly PA 200. Two sessions with Jackie had probably added five points to my CA, given the low starting point.

What was I now? 35? 40?

If I was CA 40 and had the Bench Boost, could I perform like a CA-50 player? We'd find out soon enough.

We left the dressing room a minute early, to avoid aggro, and I made the lads line up in our half in a 3-5-2 formation. A coach spotted it, and when a steaming Wester sprinted out of the tunnel, the coach buttonholed him.

He and his staff then had a blazing row, which resulted in Wester smashing his fist into his palm as he laid out some very, very clear instructions.

By my own rules, I wasn't allowed to laugh.

Wester was so stunned by my change that he fell into a low block. And so I really did change to 3-5-2, since he was so afraid of it.

For a couple of minutes, we passed the ball around aimlessly. I followed the referee so that Darlington would think twice before elbowing me or kicking me off the ball, as they had been trying to do the whole time I'd been on.

Suddenly, Wester realised he'd been tricked in some way and screamed for his players to revert to the plan. I instantly switched back to 4-1-4-1, and the moment he realised I'd somehow done that wordlessly led to another face of fury.

Darlington came at us hard, then, but they had been hyped up at halftime, ready to come out with all guns blazing. The little delay while Wester tried to understand what I was doing cost them the chance to use all that pent-up motivation.

We swatted away their attacks with ease, and slowly rebuilt the momentum we'd had at the end of the first half.

I still had one more sub I could bring on: either Steve Alton in defence or Tony in attack. I wanted to wait until at least the seventieth minute, though, and probably the eightieth. A Bench-Boosted Tony still wasn't as good as an Henri. A boosted Steve was probably way better than a May, but if I used him too early and we got an injury, we'd be down to ten men.

There was nothing strategic for me to think about for a good half hour, then, so I concentrated on doing my job.

And every time I lost concentration and thought about going on a silly dribble, doing a flashy nutmeg, or trying a shot from the halfway line, the article flashed in front of me, and I was all the way back in the fucking zone.

I ran around, cleaning up, tidying, putting opponents in little boxes and marking them "sorted" and "for the bin."

I headed balls away, I did one-touch deflections to bypass pressure, I played simple passes and sprinted to be an option for a third pass.

The home crowd, by now, were quiet. There were times I thought I could hear Boggy and Spectrum doing their match commentary, especially during our attacks. For example, the time we got a free kick about thirty yards from goal. This time I treated myself to a cheeky shot on goal, and a very slightly indulgent use of the Free Hit perk. After all, I'd spent two times ten minutes practising under Jackie's watchful eye. If I'd been free kicks 20 in the past, and recovered to, say, free kicks 5 . . . A couple of free kick "lessons" from Jackie (which was simply him standing near me and grunting), plus Bench Boost, plus Free Hit. Could I imagine I was free kicks 10, for one shot?

Boggy: Raffi Brown still hobbling around. That was a nasty one.

Spectrum: They're a vicious bunch, these. Cowards all over the place. [off mic] I'll say what I want.

Boggy: You're just winding him up. But now, it looks like Best will take the kick. It's to the right of the penalty area, about ten yards outside the box. Good angle for a far post cross, and indeed lots of bodies going there. The centre backs are up. Lyons and Brown are there. Aff lurking left; he'll compete for any scraps. Up steps Best. Oh! He's hit the crossbar.

Spectrum: Wow.

Boggy: That was some strike.

Spectrum: Pure. Oh my God, Boggy. Are we getting Max back? If he's back, this league is over. Yeah, even this prick next to me knows that. He's leaving! Yeah, leave, you knob!

Boggy: [quietly] He's just plugging his laptop in. Do you want to swap seats?

Spectrum: [quietly] No. I'm not scared of him.

Boggy: He's much bigger than you.

Spectrum: Head in the game, mate. Head in the game. [very loud] Come on, Chester!

An hour gone, and Darlington's spirits were sinking. The fans had known which way the wind was blowing as soon as I'd scored the penalty, but the players had kept chatting away, talking shit, trying anything to get under our skin, but our inhuman lack of response, the way we were robotically dismantling them, had drawn their sting and now was sapping their morale.

They had begun the match with fairly high morale: 4.9 on average, which was high for a non–Max Best–led team. Their fast start had brought that up to 5.5, but it had been steadily falling back to its starting point. With me on the scene, the decline had continued, and now was at 4.2.

The stadium was so quiet (apart from the Chester mob, those beautiful drunken louts) that I heard Wester call out the change he wanted to make at the next break. So I smashed men behind ball, set myself as playmaker, and we passed the ball around our penalty area for over a minute. It made no sense except to mess with Wester's head. I saw him staring at me, eyes wide with amazement. He realised I'd heard what he was planning and had gone defensive. Somehow, I was afraid of what was going to happen!

We finally lost the ball, it went out of play, and the change was made. Glynn, one of the main sources for the article, one of the few whose words hadn't been distorted or outright invented, was coming on to demonstrate his insipid brand of midfield scheming.

I wanted nothing more than to meet him on the field of battle, a nice old 50–50 tackle in the centre circle. We'd both go in hard and we'd see who was still able to walk at the end of it.

In fact, I found myself hunched up, fists clenched, moving out of my zone towards him. He noticed and his morale instantly plummeted. Scenting blood, I bared my teeth and calculated the next fifteen passes, getting into position for when it would happen. Getting in position for when he'd get the ball at a time when I could get *him*.

Here comes Best with his bimbo. The sad thing is, his mum really is sick.

The words assaulted me, smacked me in the back of the head, left me dead and dying in a ditch.

Thirteen, fourteen. I burst out of my body, a whole new one forming just in front of me. At Usain Bolt speeds, I homed in on Glynn. He felt me coming, and bravely turned, shielding the ball, and he tried to lay it off while cringing at the pain that was coming.

I stepped around the meaningless worm, latched onto his pass, and now the counter was on. I was past Wester before he knew what was happening. Caveman and Shrek both came at me, leaving Henri free, if only I could get the ball to him.

Get the ball to him? Are you joking?

I scooped the ball up and over, on a nice diagonal so he could bounce the ball across the keeper. Raffi Brown stormed past me, doing what I should have done, hunting the follow-up.

Henri shot left-footed, and it smashed off the right-hand post. Larkin had frozen, but now he got his feet moving, and hurled himself bravely in front of Raffi, blocking the shot with his face. It came right to me.

Time slowed.

I saw everything.

Raffi moving left, getting out of my way.

Henri moving towards the far post, arms raised. I could clip it to him and he would nod home.

He wouldn't be offside, either, because Caveman and Shrek were running to the goal line to act as an extra pair of goalies.

The act of tackling me would fall to Wester, coming from my left, or Hurts, from my right.

Good defence from a good team. But it was a mistake to think they could stop me, just as it had been a mistake to try to anger me, just as it had been a mistake to try to play football against us. They should have low blocked and scrapped for a 0–0. They were the best team in the league on paper, but as I'd learned from Ian Evans in one of his favourite phrases, football isn't played on paper.

The ball rolled into that magical space between foot and leg, the front of the ankle joint, the place I'd always been able to make a ball spin for fun, even before the curse. It hit me just there in my personal sweet spot, began its new journey, and I turned and walked away, walked back towards the halfway line, waiting for the noise from the away fans that would confirm what I already knew.

Boggy: Brown with the rebound—he has to score! No! Comes to Best. He chips. It goes up, spinning, dips, oh! Oh, that's genius. That's perfect.

Spectrum: Ahhhh!

Boggy: Incredible! Three–one Chester!

Spectrum: Perfect hat trick.

Boggy: What?

Spectrum: Left foot, right foot, header. Perfect hat trick.

Boggy: You're right. But how did he do that? There were men closing him down, men on the line.

Spectrum: Don't ask me. I only coach humans.

The match was done now. Darlington fans were streaming out. Those who remained were pale as sheets. Their players were going through the motions. I wanted to sub myself off, mostly because I expected a leg-breaking tackle from Hurts or Dicks, but if I went off, Wester might have been able to rally his troops.

So I switched to 4-5-1 with me as the striker and Henri in midfield, men behind ball. See out the match with no more drama, no more entertainment, and no more injuries.

I went to the middle of the Darlington half, walking from side to side. They didn't have a fucking clue what I was doing, but Wester kept enough men back just in case I somehow launched a counterattack from this massively offside position. When Hurts went forward, I raced into his spot and waved for the ball. Wester brought him back instantly. By doing that, I was able to keep enough bodies out of our half so that Darlington's attacks lacked the numbers to break down our low block.

The clock crawled to ninety, the referee allowed three minutes for stoppages—there hadn't been many, and at the final whistle, while Folke Wester fled with his 6 out of 10 match rating and his zero points, my players formed a vague circle around Glenn. I wandered over, sent them to the referee, silent handshakes, they returned, I waited twenty seconds for absolutely no reason other than to be weird, then sent them to the away fans. Claps over head, saluting the support, calm acknowledgement of the songs and chants.

While they were gone, some Darlington players tried to shake my hand, offered to swap shirts, tried to chat. I blanked them, and when they were insistent, walked away.

Finally, my players came back, created a barrier between me and the world, and we crossed the pitch, intending to shower and leave, silent as the grave. There wouldn't be much traffic; most of the home fans had long gone.

"Max," called a voice I knew. I stopped, and so did my team. They left a gap.

I looked up and saw the old driver and kit man who was one of the good guys at Darlington. He'd got my boots all cleaned up as a leaving present. "Pat," I said. He looked ten years older than when I'd seen him last. I wished the curse would show me his injuries. I had a deep suspicion about why he looked so shit.

"Well played, lad. I want to shake your hand," he said.

I shook my head. "That won't be good for your career. Better to leave it."

"You let me worry about my career. Come on, now."

I shook his hand, and it was like he had released my leg from a bear trap. In that moment of humanity, I cast Bravery Boost on myself. "Are you all right, mate? You don't look well."

"Ah, I'm seeing a specialist. It's treatable, he says. You don't mind me."

"Jesus. There's some perspective, right? We're out here kicking a ball around like it's important. Listen. You call me if you need anything."

"Ah, no. No need for that. I'll still be here when you come back."

"Pat. We're not coming back. We're getting promoted."

"We could come up in the playoffs."

I thought about explaining to him that I would sooner let Kidderminster win the league, drop to second, and smash the playoffs just to make sure Darlington finished the season with nothing . . . but nah. I didn't quite have that level of spite in me. Not quite as much poison as had been written about. Plus it was Remembrance Day, and these old boys made me sentimental with their shuffling walks and artless dignity. "If we do come back, we'll have a cup of tea together, yeah? Just like the old days."

"The old days, he says. What does a kid like you know about the old days?"

I looked around the stadium that used to be my home. "I know you don't get them back."

The bus driver pulled into the same service station, and we got out just as before.

"Guys," I said, with the hint of a smile playing around my lips. "Thank you very much. You were my . . ." I tried to think what they were.

"Avenging angels," said Youngster.

"What's that?"

"Twelve angels who punish wrongdoers."

"Fuck, that'd be a good TV show. Wouldn't it? Twelve angels, is it?" I looked around. "Well, we're more than twelve. Everyone played their part today. That was beautiful. Amazing. Just like in my dreams. Seriously, I owe you one. Oh, here's my ride."

With impeccable timing, a very fancy car—a Rolls Royce Phantom or some such—pulled up and Sebastian Weaver got out. He came over. "Did you win?"

"Yep."

"Well?"

"Pretty comprehensive, I'd say."

"Good. Fuck 'em."

My players were smiling. "Some of you know Emma's dad. If you don't mind, I'm off to Newcastle to have some lovely family time. Sunday in Newcastle. I'm sure there's lots to do."

I was joking, and Sebastian did a tiny head shake. "Monday, too."

"What?"

"Emma told me she'd disown me if I didn't let her off work. So we're kidnapping you. I hear that's all the rage at Chester Football Club." That was a good line. Lots of chuckles and little jeers as the lads mocked each other for their performance at the preseason boot camp.

"All right, lads. Tell you what, how about you take Monday off?"

"No, thanks," said Glenn.

Henri added to the thought. "We have Buxton at home on Tuesday night, Max."

"Fuck me, this league is relentless," I laughed.

"*I'll* have Monday off," said D-Day, to more jeers.

"Guys, get on the bus. Turn the music up. Find out who the Brig is . . ." *Porking* didn't seem appropriate. "Find out who the Brig is *courting*. Enjoy tomorrow. See you on Tuesday. All right, get fucked."

They started filing back onto the bus, but D-Day came over and asked if I had a minute. Sebastian went back to the car to give us some privacy. "Max, er . . . Trick didn't come back with us. He asked me to take care of his stuff. It's just . . . I know you don't get on with him, but he's a mate, and . . . he was just as mad about the article as me, like. I don't know what got into him today. He's not a bad guy, honest, it's just—"

I put my hand on his arm, and it was like pushing the off button. "Do you know the way I'm all like *team team team* and *it's just us* and all that stuff?"

"Yeah."

"Do you believe it?"

"Sometimes. Not . . . Sometimes."

"Do you believe I believe it?"

"Honestly? Not the way you say you do."

I smiled. "Trick's fine. Trust me. Leave him alone for a while, and hopefully in a couple of months he'll be able to tell you a helluva story." I patted him on the chest. "Good shift today. Love it."

"Er . . . good penalty, boss." Our first bust-up had been when he'd tried a cool penalty and fluffed it.

"It was, wasn't it?" I said, smug as a bug in a rug.

Then with one half-full backpack, I was spirited away to Newcastle for what had turned into an incredible luxury: a two-day midseason holiday.

Audacious single-chapter epilogue.

Trick Williams knocked on my office door. "You wanted to see me, boss?"

"Yes, close that, have a seat."

"Hello, Mr. MD. Mr. Brig."

"Relax, Trick. You're not in trouble. Tell him, Brig."

"You're not in trouble."

"Oh." He didn't believe us.

"Right, let's get down to brass tacks. You've read this article thing?"

"No. I mean, yes."

"Did you," I said, sternly, "at any point enjoy it?"

"No," he said, shaking his head.

"Max," complained MD, with a slight smile.

I held my hands up. "Sorry, Trick, that was a joke. I couldn't resist. It's fine if you enjoyed it. Thing is," I said, getting up and going to the window. The window where Ian Evans and I had once done battle. The fight that could be said to have started my journey to Darlington. "Thing is, if Ian Evans hadn't seen immediately that I was a total dick, I would have started my career in Chester. And that article and all the events that the guy twisted round, it would have all been about Chester. Do you know what I mean?"

"I guess," he said, but he didn't know what the conversation could possibly be about, so he wasn't really listening. Only when he knew what it was about could he relax and process it. But that processing could happen later.

"I'm not going to defend my actions or try to put my spin on things," I started, but Trick surprised me.

"You don't have to," he said.

"What do you mean?" said MD, holding up a hand to forestall my question.

Trick nodded a few times. "I mean most of it was pure garbage. You show them up in training? Like, er . . . no. You're miles better than us but you've never done that. You refused to play? Just doesn't sound like you. Right?"

"Right," said MD, softly.

"So those two lads from Tranmere, er . . . Junior and Barkley. They came to training yesterday. Wanted to see you, but you weren't there. Anyway, Henri stops training, we all go into the meeting room. Junior tells us some stuff, like how it really went down at halftime in that match. He goes, 'Everyone's saying let's keep it tight and Max is like fuck that, let's go for the win.' Sorry, boss, but that's just obviously what really happened. Know what I mean?"

I nodded.

"And Bark said you never tapped him up because you promised Cutter you wouldn't, and you told him to stay at Darlington for a couple of years and fight for his place, and Cutter threw Pascal at you, which we knew anyway. Oh, and he said how you made their lessons fun when you interrupted and they were doing, like, fake interviews with you and all that." Trick was smiling, obviously remembering how Bark had told the story. It made me smile, too. "Plus we already knew loads of it was pure lies, like when you brought Henri for his trial. That wasn't you, that was Ian Evans. You had Henri doing free headers from crosses and shit. Evans turned it into a match. And the bit where it said you wouldn't follow team discipline. I mean, that does sound like you. Like, try and fine me, bro. I remember that day Glenn was kicking Henri and you lifted him up and pushed him twenty yards like it was nothing. Junior cleared it up, though."

"Excuse me," said MD. "What did Junior tell you?"

Trick looked at me, and I nodded. He told MD and the Brig about how I'd ripped up the list of fines and punishments, squashed the paper into balls, and given myself a little extra bulk in the underpants department. MD was soon cry-laughing, and I nearly joined in when Trick said something I never knew before.

"So after that, the captain, when there's a new guy and he gives him the fines list," Trick paused, struggling to breathe, "it's laminated."

We lost it.

Four guys, in a room, laughing. Big laughs, my first since reading the article. I retook my seat.

"Okay, Trick, amazing. Thanks for that. I needed that. But all I wanted to say was, I'm not going to defend myself but it did make me think about the way I act. You know? How could it not? And I *am* a bit schemey. A bit plotty. And that's where people misunderstand me, or I help them to misunderstand me. Now, I've been plotting around you." He instantly became wary. I held a hand up. "Hear me out. It's not that bad."

"It's not a bad *plot*," said the Brig, emphasising the negativity of the word.

I shook my head. Not helpful. "Let's just establish a few things we can all agree on. Starting points. Say yes to show you agree with me. First one. You and I are never going to be superfriends."

"Yes," he agreed.

"I think your sense of humour is," I waved my hand around, looking for the right words, "crude and exclusionary. You think it's standard in the football business and why should you change?"

"Yes."

This was going great. "Top. You are thirty-three."

"Yes."

"You'll be thirty-four next year."

"Yes."

"Chester will be in the National League next year."

"Hope so."

"That one's a yes, mate. Thirty-four-year-old Trick Williams will struggle in the National League."

"No," he said.

I smiled. "I say yes. And that means you're not likely to get a contract here, and I doubt you were expecting one anyway."

Quietly: "Yes."

"That's where my plots come in. You read about this Bradley Rymarquis dude in that Judas article. He hates me. At one time I thought he might have— No, I shouldn't say that out loud. Anyway, he hates me and he's always looking for ways to put the boot in. You with me?"

"I think so."

"Now, I wouldn't mind if you left the club in January. When I'm feeling gloomy, I sometimes picture you shaking everyone's hand before getting in your car and driving off to your new manager." I smiled, and Trick pushed his teeth together and sort of smiled back. "And surely you'd like to get back to a proper dressing room where they tell all those jokes you like and where you can laugh at people like me."

"Max," said MD.

"No, it's all right," said Trick, adjusting on his chair. "I think I get where this is going. Go on, boss."

I leaned closer. "I've had MD in every director's box for weeks, right, bragging about how we're going to win the league and we're top and the only thing that worries him, he reveals, after a scotch gets him indiscreet, is my secret fears that you'll leave in January because we don't have left backs in the eighteens, we only have Magnus, who's no good going forward, and you're also my cover for Aff. In short, you're kinda secretly the key to our whole campaign."

He was annoyed now. "Which is a load of crap."

I looked right into his soul. "No, mate. Not a load of crap. It's basically true. You and I both know I'd switch to three-five-two or something if you left, but if you leave in January, I *will* have to find a replacement. It'll be some kid, probably, so I might save on wages and maybe get someone who can grow into the position and all that. But you're good going forward, you're very consistent, and if you do end up staying, I'll be absolutely fine with that. It looks like a load of low blocks from now on, so Magnus being more solid defensively isn't an issue. You're a better fit for my system. But you're thirty-three. If we can cook up a scam to get you a good contract somewhere else, let's go for it."

"With this agent guy?"

"Yeah. That's the joke—he's a good agent. He'll find someone who will take you, on a good wage, maybe an eighteen-month deal, and he'll work extra hard for you, all to piss me off. And when the ink's dry, you and I will be able to have a good laugh about it. It's win-win, isn't it? One of my team gets a great deal, bit of financial security. I free up some wages and a slot for a kid. I get my enemy working for *my* players." I beamed. "I fucking love it. Oh, and you get things, too."

Trick thought about it. He looked at the other two men. "Is this legit?"

MD nodded. "He got me involved a while back. He mentioned you getting a tasty deal out of it. That's good for us. Helps us persuade players to come here, doesn't it? From here, if you're a young gun you get a transfer to a big team, and if you're, ah, aging gracefully, we still increase your market value. It's a good story for us to tell."

Trick moved his eyes one chair along. The Brig said, "I don't actually see any friction between you and Max. As far as I can tell and from what I've seen, you're a model professional." He shrugged. "Using his enemies to get yourself a nice, juicy contract." He grinned. "Why not?"

"What would I have to do?"

I pointed to the flipchart across from my desk, where I'd written out the team and subs for the Darlington match. "If you're with me, I'll cross out your name. Obviously I'd love you on the bench in case Aff gets injured, but there are ways I can do without a left-footer. I have a vision for how the match will go, and you won't come on, anyway. I probably won't even use my third sub. Anyway, when I name the team, you make a big scene, flounce out. You storm around until you find Rymarquis. You tell him you're sick of me, you loved that Judas article, if he gets you a move you'll dish the dirt on me. Something like that. He might do it because he knows I need you without the dirt stuff. The Brig has suggested I remove myself from the plotting at this point and let him take over. Which . . . He's probably right. Mine have a habit of blowing up in my face while biting me on the arse, which is really something."

"And then I'm out of the team?"

"Fuck no. Until you move, you're more in the team than ever. We're going to run up your stats. Get you some goals and assists. You're really proving your worth to prospective new employers!" I laughed, then got serious. "Thing is, though, if it all works out and you get a new club in January, we have to try to get you back here for the last game of the season."

"What for?" he said, with a deep, worried crease on his forehead.

"For the fucking league winner's party, you dick. For your medal. What the fuck do you think?"

We waited while Trick's brain cells fired. It didn't take long.

He got up, went to the flipchart, and crossed his name out. He turned back to us with a massive grin on his face. "I'm in."

"Great. You'll talk to the Brig. All right? Oh, and Trick?"

He looked worried. My voice had gone stern again. Very stern. "Yes, boss?"

"Put the lid back on the marker." I leaned back, satisfied. "We're not made of money."

SERVED

We arrived at Casa Weaver in the suburbs of Newcastle and Emma ran down the drive to hug me, to check I was in one piece. She'd find and count the bruises later, but right then, I felt unbreakable. Her dad gave us a minute.

"You did it," she said.

"We did it. *We* did it. The lads were immense. Massive. Unstoppable."

"I wanted to go."

"It's over. Finito. Let's move on. You and me. We'll enjoy this weekend, yeah? Two days, like real people. But I want a proper break."

"In the summer?"

"No. Soon."

"Oh."

I knew what she was thinking: that I was talking shit. Managers didn't have midseason breaks. I squeezed her. "Somewhere cheap, though. When's the last time you slept in a tent?"

Dinner was Emma, her parents (Sebastian and Rachel), Gemma, and a friend of Rachel's. She was called Agnes and nobody explained exactly who she was. Fortunately, my imagination provided the entire story, and I felt no need to check it.

Agnes and Rachel had gone to school together and were sort of friends in the not-really-friends-but-somehow-always-thrown-together sense. They'd had daughters around the same time and that had repointed the ever-crumbling brickwork of their relationship so it would last another decade. Now their daughters were all grown up, and Agnes's girl—Jennifer, probably—had got engaged to a dentist. Or . . . some kind of influencer. No, a dentist. And since Rachel knew I'd be coming, she had invited Agnes. Any one of my many titles beat dentist, right? Unless you needed a root canal, in which case no amount of Manager of the Month awards would impress you.

So yeah. Agnes was a weird choice of sixth guest because no one at the table seemed to like her all that much.

At first, the match against my former club was the only topic of conversation, which was odd since I had no interest in joining in. I only opened my mouth to shovel up soup. The others were telling Agnes about the Judas article and the ensuing hundred hours of drama, with Gemma seeming *very* well informed about MD's thoughts and feelings. She piled in on my decision not to respond in the media. I wondered if those were *her* thoughts, or MD's. What was going on *there*?

Interesting as it was, I let it wash over me. The whole thing was ancient history and if I had my way I would think about it one more time, on the last day of the season, and then never again.

"I watched you play," said this Agnes person, and after a long silence I realised she was talking to me.

"On the BBC?" I said, coming back into the room like a languid ghost.

"That's right. Rachel said you'd be on before *Strictly Come Dancing*. My husband came in and asked what the matter with me was. Said I'd never sat for a football game my whole life and maybes I was a bit old to be starting. I said it's young Emma's friend playing, and he said oh right, and he sat with me. Not long in, he's shaking his head and he says, 'I hope it isn't that one.' Meaning you. Found you a bit theatrical. A bit much."

"Is he a Newcastle United fan?"

"He is, yeah."

"What a shame to disappoint such a paragon of virtue."

Agnes understood this to be a rebuke of some sort, but it was delivered with such handsomeness that she took it well. "Course, he doesn't abide much by all the falling over and rolling around and complaining to the referee. He's a rugby man first and foremost."

"Max is amazing at rugby," snapped Emma, and I was filled with such instant warmth that I was on my feet, behind her chair, wrapping her in my arms before I knew what I was doing. I nuzzled my cheek against hers, let our fingers intertwine.

"He liked the little fella," said Agnes, trying to get back in our good books, even though she didn't know what she'd done wrong.

"Pascal. We like him too. Don't we, bebs?"

Emma relaxed into me. "Max doesn't much care what people think about him. He *says*. But he loves it when you say nice things about his players."

"I care what *you* think," I said, reluctant to let go. "We're playing against South Shields soon. That's up here somewhere, isn't it, Agnes? I'll get you free tickets if you want to see us live."

"Oh, lovely," said the dentist's future mother-in-law, may God have mercy on his soul. We both knew she would never mention the tickets again.

"So you won today," said Rachel, quietly ecstatic with my performance so far. "What does that mean?"

Without moving away from Emma, I said, "Means we're second behind Kidderminster. Four points behind."

"Oh, I'm so sorry," said Agnes.

I smiled. "It's actually really good." She was such a noob there was no point talking about games in hand or goal difference or my theories about a late-season charge. "We're on course to win the league by fifteen points or so, I reckon. It was a good day."

"Almost perfect," said Sebastian, and it took me a second to realise what he was saying.

I kissed Emma's hand as a presage to returning to my seat. "Right. The team I own lost. Got knocked out of the FA Vase."

"The what?" said Emma.

"The cup."

"The FA Cup?"

"No, it's a cup called the Vase."

"The trophy is a vase?"

"No, there are three cups. The Trophy is a different cup to the Vase."

Emma jabbed her spoon handle into the table. "Max."

I smiled again and made my way back to my chair. "It's simple. There are three cup tournaments for different levels of team. Everyone can enter the FA Cup, but really it's for the big teams. Who are the big ones around here? Sunderland and Middlesbrough, isn't it? Then there's the FA Trophy. That's what Chester play in. It's for the biggest fish of the small fish. We're playing in that next Saturday. *My* team, West Didsbury, play in the FA Vase. It's for tiny teams. Tadpoles and smaller. Now, what's fun is that the Trophy and Vase play their finals on the same day. So next year, if Chester and West get to the final, I'll be guest of honour in both games. At Wembley Stadium. I wonder if I'll get two different VIP boxes? I'll need two girlfriends."

"Sorry," said Agnes. "You own a team?"

"Yep."

"The team I watched? You're a player and the manager and the owner?"

"No, I own a different team. They're not on TV. The best player is called Spurgeon. That's his *first* name."

"Oh."

"Clubs should be owned by the fans," said Sebastian. We'd been all mates in the car but now it was back to taking sly digs at each other in front of the ladies. He was fucking rubbish at it.

"Good job I'm a fan, then. Emma is, too. Aren't you, babes? Hummus! Hummus hummus!"

She didn't join in. "Tell us about the match."

"Yeah," I said. "They started strong. Then we sorted them out. Lesson learned. Nuff said."

"Not nuff said! You've barely said anything."

"Please, Max," said Gemma. "Ems was so upset this whole week. I know you're satisfied, but we want to share that feeling. D'you know? All we know is what was on social media."

"Don't believe what you read there. That's sort of the point of the whole thing, right?"

Gemma tilted her head. "I'm talking about Chester's official accounts."

I tried to suppress a grin. "What . . . What did we write?" I hadn't authorised anything, and I'd told Spectrum very, very clearly not to post anything that I hadn't okayed. Too many teams got into trouble from their socials. Napoli were going to lose their hundred-million-Euro star striker because some pyromaniac in *their* back office—a Napoli fan!—had posted on the club's official accounts mocking him for missing a penalty. My solution was to post almost nothing, ever, and, yeah, do our talking on the pitch.

Gemma smiled at me. I was starting to like those wide, Julia Roberts lips. As happened more and more, I wondered what would have happened if I'd met her without Emma. Could we have . . . ? No, I wasn't thinking straight. It was lack of carbs after the match. I needed some pasta in me, is all.

While I reached for the bread, Gemma showed me the latest post from Chester's account.

ChesterFC: Chat shit get banged.

My lips stretched Roberts-wide of their own accord, and I looked up at the spotlights, deeply amused and just a little proud. But I'd have to remind Spectrum of the rules. I didn't want this shit getting out of control. If he did it again, I'd revoke his password privileges.

"Maaaaxxx," whined Emma. "I heard the match on *Seals Live* but Boggy goes hypersonic every time you get the ball. Normally Spectrum explains things but today he was too busy fighting. Tell us about it from your point of view."

"I came, I saw," I said, and returned to pumping soup into my uncultured gob.

"What? What's the last bit?"

"I came, I saw. The rest goes unspoken."

"Does it fuck," said Emma.

"Emma!" complained her mum.

"Maybe," said Sebastian, "there's a match report you could read, love."

I snapped my fingers. "Great idea."

Emma whipped out her phone. I reminded her of the name of the local paper and reporter. Her eyes popped when she struck gold right away. "It's there. Whoa. The match report is called *Revenge Is a Dish Best Served Goaled.*"

"I'm sorry, what?" I said.

"*Revenge Is a Dish Best Served Goaled.*"

My jaw had dropped open. "No no no." I stood and walked around their dining room, hands on my head. "But . . . but that's genius. That's incredible. Best served. Do you get it? Revenge is a dish that *Max Best* served . . . in this match. Best is me. Not an adjective. Goaled instead of cold. Best, me, served his revenge with goals. That's what it means."

"Yes, it's clever," said Gemma.

"It's not *clever*," I said. "Clever is a pine marten that mugs me off every night but only when I'm alone in the barn. Bastard knows not to mess with Emma's sleep or she'll rip the roof off to get to him. No, that headline isn't clever, it's fucking *world-shattering.*"

"Who wrote it?" said Rachel, with a strange glint in her eye.

"Max's reporter friend Gary. Shush while I read it," said Emma. I skimmed off my soup while Emma skimmed the article in that lawyerly way of hers. Then came the frown. "Very strange match report. It . . . it doesn't say the name of the other team. Doesn't say when the goals were scored, what the attendance was. It's all about how 'the home team' are a bunch of liars and cheats and they got what was coming to them."

"Send me the link," said Gemma.

"Listen to this," said Emma, bringing her phone closer to her face like she couldn't believe her eyes. "'As punishment for throwing their own employee under the bus, Best scored a penalty.' Employee? Who's that, Max?"

"Do you remember there was a weird bit at the beginning of the Judas piece—Judas piece? Is that a pun?—about a receptionist?" Emma nodded. "They made it seem like I had her under hypnosis or some crazy shit," I explained to Agnes. "She was just a girl who had a tiny crush on me and they made it into a big deal. Horrible. She doesn't exactly work for the club, but she basically does."

Emma nodded and continued reading, "'As punishment for bringing his mother into their tissue of lies, Best scored a cowering header.'"

"Towering header," I corrected.

"Right. Towering. 'As punishment for insulting his beautiful girlfriend, Best scored a beautiful third goal.'" She closed her eyes. "I've never been called beautiful in a newspaper before. Does that make it official?" She looked back at her screen. "'The revenge continued as Chester's white-hot fury melted away the low tactics of the opposition, so that soon the home team even lacked the chops to *cheat*, and their abject, pigeon-hearted efforts in the last twenty minutes were played in front of three empty stands. The home fans had scurried from the stadium, as timid as their players, having been taught a harsh lesson in football, truth, and justice.'" She blinked. "It's all like this. Is this real? Listen to this for an ending: 'Winners in silence take their bows, losers in disgrace send in the cows.'"

"What the what?" said Gemma.

I mopped up the last of the soup with a bit of bread. "They let the grass grow long to try to stop us playing. You get used to it, but you have to force every pass. It builds up fatigue in your muscles, makes it more likely you'll get injured. It sounds like gibberish to you but that's a deadly line. Their fans will take it as a slap to the face. I can imagine a lot of Send in the Cows t-shirts being sold, for example from the website sendinthecows dot co dot uk, which was registered earlier today."

"They grew the grass?" said Rachel, and she looked proper angry.

"Yeah," I said.

"Send in the cows, my God." Emma didn't know what to make of it all. "Pigeon-hearted efforts? That's mean to pigeons."

I looked at her father and raised an eyebrow. He squashed his lips together.

"What's going on?" said Rachel.

"Nothing, dear."

"Emma, what time was that article published?"

"What? Er . . . about twenty minutes ago, it says."

"Huh."

"What?"

But Rachel remained silent, leaving it for her daughter to put all the clues together. "Max! You've *read* this. But how could you have read it if it was just published?"

"He wrote it," said Gemma, giving me a sly look. I couldn't quite keep my poker face on.

Emma blinked and after a few seconds, folded her arms. "Oh! Are you joking, now? Are you *joking*? All that stuff you told me about not responding, not replying, and you've done it. You said you wouldn't lash out, but you've written a whole newspaper article!"

I swallowed my last piece of soupy bread. "That wasn't me. That was Gary Beswick."

Sebastian picked up his wine. "Max wrote it in the car. Or I should say he read it aloud in the car. He'd written most of it beforehand. Before the match, even. Like he knew exactly how the match would go."

"Witchcraft," said Emma, uncrossing her arms so she could cross her fingers in front of her face.

Sebastian was nodding. "It's one of the craziest things I've ever witnessed, and I once watched a drunk try to unlock what he thought was the front door of his house but was, in fact, a postbox."

I shrugged. "It was pretty obvious how the match was going to go. I made some notes, sure, some ideas for phrases. An option for the title, perhaps. When it came time to craft it, your dad chipped in. We had a bit of a bicker when he insisted I should use *obfuscate* instead of *blur*. And he was adamant about pigeon-hearted. I let him have that one, even though I didn't really believe in it. I like pigeons. People who don't like pigeons don't understand pigeons. Pigeons are unbelievable. Now, if you'd said magpie-hearted . . ." This was another dig. The nickname for Newcastle was The Magpies.

Emma read through it again and pointed out the obvious. "But Max, though. This doesn't address the Judas thing. What about the fans? The sponsors? The parents of the young players? You need to reassure them."

I shook my head. "People who need to know, know. Anyone who believes shit with no proof can do one. I've said this twenty times. You can't fight lies with the truth. But, look, I had a think and decided I'm going on that podcast. The one with the guy you wanted to sue. I'll set some ground rules. They're not allowed to say the D-word, things like that. I'll let them raise one or two points about all this Judas stuff. But I want to respond my way. Positive. When they go low, we go high. The future's bright, the future's Chester. The best revenge is scoring a perfect hat trick. The best revenge is living well. Take your pick."

Long silence in the room while Rachel and Agnes brought our mains. Nice cut of meat, some veg. No doubt they'd asked Gemma what footballers ate and so we were getting the Henri Lyons version.

"So we won," said Emma, thoughtfully. "Justice was served. The truth is out there, sort of. You've messed up his plans by reacting in the most Max way, which is to do the opposite of what people expect. And what? He's getting sacked and we don't need to think about him again?"

"Depends what happens in January. They *are* the best team on paper. I smashed them pretty good today so that could send them into a tailspin, but it's poss they'll recover. I can't imagine they'll give him more budget for transfers but it's a crazy old world."

"So what happens next?"

"Next we beat Buxton on Tuesday. Then the FA Trophy, which as you know is different from the FA Cup and the FA Vase. Then we've got two very tricky league games." I rubbed my hands through my hair. "It just keeps coming. I've got three major problems." I bit my thumbnail for a while. "One. Teams who all-out defend against us. It only needs a few to get away with it to cost us the league. Two. I can't get the staff I need. Three. I've hit a plateau in my recovery. It's all so relentless, games every three days, it's hard to rest, it's hard to think. At some point I need a break. A proper one, where I can really switch off."

"Then have one," said Rachel.

"It's not that easy. Football managers don't go on holiday midseason."

"That's right," agreed Sebastian. "It's not done. It'd be the end of his career if he popped off to France for a winter break while his team kept playing."

"Hmm, that's not what I'm worried about," I said. "I'd *go* on a break. Don't really give a shit if people like it or not. I need a break, end of discussion. The problem is, who'd do the matches when I was away?"

"John Smith," said Emma. "Your *assistant manager.*"

"No."

"Jackie."

"Too soon."

"Vimsy."

"No."

"So what are you thinking?"

Sebastian was offering me more wine, but one glass was enough of a treat. I took my glass to the tap and rinsed it out so I wouldn't be tempted to drink more. I leaned against the sink and smiled. "The problem is we're tier six so anyone good will want a job at a bigger club. We don't have anything to offer that they can't get somewhere much higher up, where they'd get much more money and get to work with better players. So why would someone good drop down loads of divisions? It's impossible." I made my way back to the table and started cutting up my piece of beef. It cut smooth. "That's where my mind was at. But then . . . Then I had the craziest fucking idea."

The next day, Emma took fifteen minutes in the morning to stitch my hat trick to the end of the inspirational tekkers recovery video. She wanted to end on the towering header because her dad told her that was the best goal, but I gently insisted she should end with the spinning chip, because the degree of difficulty was much higher and because it was thematically closer to the kick-ups I'd been trying to do in Tenerife.

She chose the music, posted it on her socials, and then we went to look at fancy suits until I got bored, which was quite soon after we entered the shop.

In the next couple of weeks I went grinding, centring my efforts around Manchester so I could pop into West to check on Vivek, hang out with Ziggy, and see my mum. Obviously. (You don't believe everything you read, do you?)

I also made time for extra sessions with Cody Chambers, but they were disappointing. I was having to fight incredibly hard to gain tiny improvements in my skills. I was starting to feel stuck.

And it wasn't just a feeling—I had some hard data to prove it.

I'd been making steady progress with the Airofit breathing trainer, increasing my lung capacity from 3.3 to 3.8 litres in next to no time. But in the six weeks since, I'd only improved to 4.1 litres and the number wouldn't budge even though I used the trainer twice a day.

One of the problems was my playing style. I did a little bit of everything. If there was, indeed, a cap on my CA, then not only had I hit that cap, but I'd hit it with a jack-of-all-trades build. High on passing and technique, with below-average ratings in heading, free kicks, stamina, and so on. I could function as a quality DM for the level, but if I wanted my flair, skills, and long shots back, I'd have to find a training loophole or buy a perk that would let me use Bench Boost in every match.

I very much doubted the curse would make the mistake of offering that.

It was on one of my trips to Manchester that the three-match ban for "serious foul play" dropped, I simply shrugged. Whatever.

A reduction in my playing time was not necessarily a bad thing. It meant that getting the XP needed to buy Parasight would be easy if I went to enough high-level matches, and fortunately I was able to get into a couple of Women's Super League games at the Death Star in Mordor.

Yeah, getting experience points was a lot easier than finding talented staff willing to drop down a few levels . . .

Monday, November 27.

J: Hello and welcome to a very special—and probably very long—episode of *Deva Victrix*. I'm J, your host (solo) and with me in this very fancy studio is the last guest we ever thought we'd get. Max Best is here!

Max: Yep.

J: We've also got Chester's managing director, who we used to know as MD MD.

MD: Hello, everyone, and may I take this opportunity to say how pleased I am to be here.

J: You got your name cut in half. You're just MD now.

MD: That was Max, I think.

Max: Communication is abbreviation.

J: We've also got the men's first-team assistant manager, John Smith, AKA the Brig.

Brig: Good afternoon.

J: Max, what's going on? What are we doing?

Max: You've got that sore throat still? We'll do most of the talking. How about that?

J: Sounds like the right way round. The listeners get enough of me. I'm sure they'd rather hear your voice.

Max: Er . . . the basics. You guys went tonto after a recent match in the northeast.

J: The Darlington game. [long pause] Oh, sorry. The D-word game. The recent match in the northeast. Right. Right.

Max: You went tonto, full thirty-six-hour bender, ran down your immune systems, and caught that mega-flu that's going round. Knocked you right out, didn't it? You've not podded since. So about then, I said I wanted to come on. Reduced my fee from six thousand pounds to zero.

J: Ha.

Max: Don't laugh at that. I'm taking the piss.

J: I mean, yeah. I know.

Brig: What's that story?

Max: When I started here, they invited me on, and I said I'd do it for six grand. Obviously a joke but they took it seriously like all—

MD: Max.

Max: Ugh. Now, the idea of talking to all three of you muppets at once was, just, nah. No thanks. So I thought, let's do it my way. And this is my way, isn't it?

J: Tell the listeners.

Max: Probably I'll be the one giving the orders, I reckon. So your normal setup is dire. Three drunks in a pub. It's garbage. I get you can't bung three grand on top microphones and all that, but it's like one of you headbutts the mic once per minute, one of you rubs it with a cheese grater for an hour. I've never been able to listen to more than three minutes of your show, even the episodes where you were slandering me.

J: Wait—

Max: So I've asked Boggy to let us use his space from his day job. What is this, Cheshire Old But Gold one-oh-six point nine? It's nice, isn't it? Holy shit, take your hand away from the microphone. Are you serious right now? Do not touch it. Oh my God.

J: Yeah, it's just, yeah. Habit.

Max: Proper studio, check. Good audio, check. Superstar guest, check. B-lister sidekicks, check. Boggy himself is in that booth doing whatever. This will be the greatest podcast in history. There are three guys on your show normally. I call you Huey, Louie, and Dewey.

J: Which one am I?

Max: Louie. The one who hates me.

J: I don't.

Max: Sorry, something's in my pocket, here. Annoying me. Can you hold that a second?

J: Sure.

Max: You got served.

J: I . . . what?

Max: Tell the listeners what's in your hand.

J: Er . . . envelope. It's got the name of a company on. Weaver, Weaver . . . oh shit.

Max: Open it.

J: I don't want to.

Max: You have to. It's the law.

J: No . . . [paper crackling] Oh God, oh fuck, oh shit. Wait . . . What's this?

Max: What?

J: It's blank. It's just a piece of blank A4.

Max: Oh. Guess I'm not suing you then.

J: Oh, fuck! I'm sweating. Why would you do that?

Max: That's a prank, bro. I'm getting revenge on people spreading lies about me. I'm not interested in suing fans of the club, but just so we're clear, call me a grifter again and I'll have your house.

J: I didn't. I won't. I mean—

Max: That could be a good business model. Move from club to club, some guy chats shit about me, gets banged in court. Rinse and repeat. Rinse and repeat, that's a good line, isn't it? Because rinse means "extract all money from." All right. That was satisfying. So, listen, J. Top tip. If you slander someone, don't record it and voluntarily upload it to millions of servers worldwide. Those episodes are still online. You need to take them down. Today. Do not post this until you delete those episodes. Boggy, don't give him the files.

MD: He's right, J. It's bad for the club. You can't suggest financial misdealings when we're trying to get new sponsors and build the brand, you just can't. And it's really unfair to Max. Really unfair.

J: Holy fuck.

Max: You need a minute?

J: I saw my life flash in front of my eyes.

MD: You're a season ticket holder, aren't you?

J: Yeah. Since I was fifteen.

Max: Did you ever see Smasho and Nice One?

J: No, missed them.

Max: Oh.

MD: Which stand?

J: The McNally with my mates. Getting a bit long in the tooth for it now, but going to the main stand is . . . it's like you're officially old, now, isn't it? We're all clinging on to the McNally for as long as poss.

MD: I grew up on the McNally, myself, but soon as I got a good job moved to the main. I was a bit pompous back then.

J: Turned out all right for you, though, didn't it? Watching from the box and all that. Nice and warm.

MD: I wish I'd stayed a few more years, let my hair down.

J: Can't see you ending up in the firm, scrapping against Wrexham's lot.

Max: Guys, you can do a hooligan episode any time. Let's talk about me.

MD: [tutting]

Max: We're eleven minutes in, there's been one half-decent prank but no actual content. People want podcasts to get to the meat. We're still doing the stupid introductions! For the listeners, I chose J from the three hosts because he's the one who doesn't like me. You can't say I'm here for an easy ride. We're going to talk about the matches that this podcast missed. Then we'll assess the state of the squad. And we'll finish by talking about the short-term future of the club, in which I will hint at some shocking developments that will appal everyone in this room except for the Brig.

MD: What?

Max: Let's clear that up. Brig, why are you here?

Brig: I thought the fans might like to hear from me.

Max: No, you thought you'd come, say almost nothing, and when someone like J says, "*Why does that guy never talk to the fans*," you can say you went on *Deva Victrix*.

Brig: You understand me very well, sir.

Max: And MD, why are you here?

MD: Same as John, really. But also because you insisted. I thought I might keep you out of trouble.

Max: Good luck with that. J, you were at the match against my former club. Is that right?

J: Yes. That was amazing.

Max: So you saw the way we didn't celebrate the goals and all that. We were so focused on playing. Just play, nothing else.

J: It was so strange. We were trying to find the word to describe it. Best we came up with was *controlled.*

Max: Okay, that'll do. It was a very controlled performance. These players, though, they're like mustangs. Wild ponies, the lot of them. They want to roam and frolic and flick their hair. What's the word for the thing where they rise up on their hind legs and swish their hair around? I squashed them into little pens for one match only. A couple of days later we played Buxton. Were you there?

J: Yeah.

Max: Don't come to matches when you've got an infectious disease, mate. Jesus Christ. We've got players out sick. Is that because of you?

MD: Max.

Max: I wasn't sure what was going to happen against Buxton. What sort of hangover would the players have? Like . . . you can tie a mustang to a wheel and make him . . . plough? . . . corn? But that's, er, you could break his spirit or something. The lads, though, they weren't sulky or anything, not in the slightest. I have to say they were right there with me against my former club, and then they let loose against Buxton.

Brig: I did suggest it would happen that way, sir.

Max: You did. But it could have gone the other way.

Brig: It could. That's true. And pigs might fly south for winter.

J: We won six–nil. It was never in doubt.

Max: It *was* in doubt. Everything comes with a cost. You can bully or bribe a player into running twice as far on Monday, but then he can't even walk on Tuesday. You've got to be thoughtful. Six–nil was amazing. I would have been happy with a scrappy one–nil. Buxton were unlucky because they had a couple of players out and we got an early goal, but wow. The lads were ready to go. All I had to do was point to the pitch and off they went.

J: I heard you don't do much screaming and shouting anyway.

Max: What's the point? These guys aren't babies. Most of them were with Ian Evans. They know about duels and all that. They come ready to play. My job's to tell them how to win, not how to thump their chests. If they don't perform, I'll let them know.

J: We had great performances from Trick and D-Day.

Max: Yep. Anyone want to say anything more about Buxton?

MD: I'd like to say, as a fan, that it's amazing you want to whizz past that game. We're not used to winning six–nil around here. In other seasons, it'd be our best result. J, this is what it's like working with Max. He'll rave about a two–nil loss and be absolutely unmoved by scoring six. He doesn't think about football like you or I.

J: That's why I'm glad we're doing this. It's good to know what's going on at the top of the club.

MD: What are you doing?

Max: I'm thinking if there's a way I can connect the Buxton game to the things I need to say at the end.

MD: What things?

Max: [sigh] We're not at the ennnd. This should come in the "next steps" bit. Here's a sneak preview. I have three challenges. Three problems I need to solve to keep this club on an upward trajectory. Okay? Three things. Ah, I've got it. Ahem. So, J. MD. You know that Buxton match? The players were fit and fresh, they'd hyped themselves up, they wanted to release all that tension, they wanted to celebrate goals and run around and do knee slides and all that?

MD: Yeeeees?

Max: Well, I didn't need to be there that day, did I? I had a two-day break with my girlfriend, but I could have spent the whole week away if someone had done the Tuesday game. Bearing in mind I woke up from a coma and have been working seven days a week since. The Buxton match would have gone the same, if, for example, I was in a tent in Scotland reading comics.

MD: Maybe we should talk about this off-air.

Max: There's nothing to talk about. This is me telling you I'm not going to stand there for forty-six matches every season. No way. So we need a solution for that. And I've found one.

MD: What is it? Who is it?

Max: I'm not saying today. Today's about reminding everyone of how awesome I am and how all my decisions turn good in the end.

MD: John, do you know about this? What he's planning?

Brig: I do. I'm sure there will be some, er . . . puzzlement, but the only person who should be offended is me, and I'm not. The club will benefit.

Max: Ah, this is going well now. I can feel it. Buxton, six–nil. Bosh. Up next, Lancaster City in the FA Trophy. Semi-pro team at home. Potential banana skin, but I felt I could rotate the team in a big way. Ben back in goal, Trick and D-Day starting again, Andrew Harrison in midfield. Tony up front. Really trying to rest players like Aff and Glenn, who are going to play most games.

J: It was a fairly subdued day. Kind of a comfortable win where you don't push the boat out.

Max: I want to go full throttle every game, I really do, but we have to be realistic. The squad is small and players *will* conserve energy.

J: Oh, I meant it as a compliment. It's like MD said. We haven't had that feeling for a long time. Two–nil up and they're not coming back. That's . . .

MD: Relaxing.

Max: We have good control at the moment. I'm happy with how that feels.

J: The Lancaster manager was serving a seven-match stadium ban.

Max: Right. I forgot about that. It didn't help them, but realistically . . . didn't make a difference. See? He could have had a week off. Enjoyed himself. I hear Devon is nice this time of year.

J: There were some people saying the manager was dressed as the mascot and he was giving them instructions from inside the suit.

Max: I mean, obviously that's exactly what happened.

MD: Max, don't say things like that. The official position of Chester Football Club is that we didn't see the manager inside the stadium and as far as we know, Lancaster were in full compliance with all FA rules and regulations.

Max: Lancaster don't even *have* a mascot. And you don't bring your enormous owl mascot to away games!

Brig: It was a frog.

J: Did you tell the ref or anything?

Max: No. It was funny. Then we had two nail-biting matches against Alfreton and South Shields.

J: Hang on. We've missed something.

Max: The Cheshire Cup?

J: Your ban.

Max: Ban. It's clever, really. You give me a three-match ban, but the press release says I'll miss the FA Cup second round. But when you look at it, the third match of my ban is the Cheshire Cup. So we've got to decide if I risk playing in the FA Cup or not. If I play and we win and someone turns round and says, nope, invalid player, you're outta here . . . It's no good progressing if they kick you out of the competition.

J: Why don't you check?

MD: We've checked. We hear different things every time.

Max: They're winding us up. Sending us round in circles. The Cheshire lot say the Cheshire Cup counts as a serious game, but the national FA keep repeating that the third match of my ban is the Walsall game. Trust me, it's a four-match ban disguised as three. I'm not going to risk it. Nah . . . If someone wants me to stop playing but can't be too overt about it, this kind of thing is the way to do it. It is literally fiendish.

J: So you're definitely not playing against Walsall?

Max: [sigh] No. Not that it matters. I'm dogshit.

J: What?

Max: Never mind. Where was I? Okay, we're on a winning run. Seven wins in a row in all competitions. Not bad, right? Then we go to Alfreton and it's a totally different team to what I was expecting. That was a shock because I'd played against them in my first full match for my former club and they were weak. That was in the FA Trophy, and I knew they'd rested some first teamers. Then over the summer they changed managers, and he brought some of his favourites in. They're good now! Big turnaround over there. They still played —four-five-one—our scout confirmed that much—and they made it hard for us in midfield. We were a bit off the pace, bit sluggish.

J: Did something go wrong? Could you have changed the tactics?

Max: Tactics were fine. We had sixteen shots and they had eight, something like that. We lacked a bit of spark, is all, and they did us on set pieces and held firm.

J: Gutting.

Max: Yeah, don't like losing but overall I was pleased. Two things. One, sometimes you have those games. So, okay, you play bad but you're still on top. I'm quite happy to see that. It's not like we had players on four out of ten, looking lost, doing stupid things. No, it was fine. Sometimes fine isn't enough, and that's where you credit the opposition. And that's the second thing. Seeing Alfreton that good I think will really help us this season. They'll take points against the other challengers, too. Kidderminster still have to go there. Anything you want to ask about Alfreton?

J: What would you do differently if you could replay it?

Max: Honestly, nothing.

Brig: The illnesses and injuries were disruptive.

Max: We had eleven players and five subs. It's my job to do something with them. Of course it's easier if you've got your whole squad but Alfy had injuries and suspensions, too. The way we set up was our best chance of winning. Sometimes there's a bad bounce, the ref doesn't see someone pinning your goalie, something like that. It was a good game and the better team on the day won. Absolutely no problem with that.

J: We'd have won if you hadn't been suspended.

Max: I'm not sure about that. I don't think it would have made much difference.

J: It would.

Brig: He isn't fishing for compliments.

Max: We need to win matches where I'm not available.

MD: We *do*.

Max: I started to get the feeling some players and fans think I'll come off the bench like a genie and do all kinds of mystical shit. I can't do that. There are twenty-one other guys in the first-team squad. Every one of them needs to be thinking and acting like a match winner.

MD: A lot of players are scoring and assisting.

Max: I'm talking about a game like Alfreton where it's all okay but someone thinks, shit, *it's my turn* and gives me a nine out of ten performance. That's the next level for this team, but we can talk about that in a minute. There's one more match to mention. South Shields. Another match where I got to spend a couple of days up in sunny Newcastle.

J: You played four-two-four away from home. There was a lot of chat about that. People calling you naïve.

Max: We were two–nil up at halftime. Our collapse had been coming for days. That would have happened with any formation.

Brig: Max wasn't happy with the performance after our second goal went in. There was shouting.

Max: Didn't work, though, did it? Shields scored two quick goals, and it took us half an hour to get our heads right. It's so annoying sometimes. That's why I always want us to attack. Two goals isn't enough. Score a third. Done that? Great. Three isn't enough. Keep going.

J: So that was a mentality thing, not a tactics thing?

Max: Tactics thing? I switched to four-four-two as soon as I saw they'd checked out. The tactics are mint, mate. That one was the mentality, yeah. I told them South Shields were good. Didn't I, Brig?

Brig: You did.

Max: But they wouldn't have it. Newly promoted side, struggling. Yeah, it's been a step up for them, but they're really good. They have some quality play-ers, I can promise you that. Halftime, I was fuming. Fuming. We did a tag team of shouting. Me, the Brig, and Vimsy. Couldn't get through. It was one of those days I'd have subbed off the entire team if I could.

J: At two–nil up?

Max: The score doesn't matter. You don't throw your standards to the floor like it's a dirty towel. Okay, maybe if it's four–nil and the other team want to go home, fine. I don't like it, but fine. Two–nil against a hungry team? That's moronic. I was fuming. It's still making me mad now. It's good I couldn't play that one because there would have been punches thrown.

J: If I was a player, I don't think I'd ever know where I stood with you.

Max: I think it's clear. There's a match where you try your best and it doesn't quite click. No problem. There's a match where you're playing great but you do your own thing. Veto. Problem. Do as you're told. There's a match where you're playing great and you choose to stop. Big problem. What's your day job?

J: I'm a mason.

Max: Mmm. Looks easy, but it's not, right?

J: Yeah. Everyone always tries fixing their own walls after a storm. How hard can it be? It's just bricks. Then they call me.

Max: You know when you've done well, and you know when you've half-arsed a job. Right?

J: I never half-arse a job.

Brig: His customers are never disappointed.

All except Max: [laughter]

Max: What's happening?

MD: It's a masonry joke.

Max: No more jokes that I don't understand. But if you ever did half-arse a job and I said, hey, this isn't good enough, you'd bluster and defend yourself but you'd know I was right. You've got to realise that I know *exactly* what my players can do, what they *should* be doing, and whether they're *doing* it or not. That to me is as clear and obvious as when some idiot puts a brick in sideways.

J: All the bricks go in sideways.

Max: I should sue you for that joke.

MD: We won that match in the end, however. Which made it six wins out of seven since the Kidderminster game, with two cup wins in that period, too. It's really impressive, Max.

Max: I like that we're getting wins against top seven sides. We're ahead of where I thought we'd be. Okay that's the reviews of our recent matches. Let's take a break, have a cup of tea, and when we come back I'll reassure you about the state of the club and then scare you about what's coming. Good?

J: Just talking to Boggy there reminded me of something the fans loved. You had a bit of a run-in with the BBC.

Max: I don't like that framing. I love the BBC. Forget whether you think they're left or right. Imagine this country without it. This is a third-world country with two world-class organisations, the Premier League and the BBC. I've been reading about this show they did. *Ghostwatch*. Did you all see that?

MD: I remember it. I was fifteen. I didn't watch it. I read about it and thought it sounded naff. I regretted it—people talked about it for days.

J: What was it?

MD: It was a ghost story, but with famous presenters and broadcast as though it was all live and happening. People were really scared.

Max: There was a scene early on when they were in the so-called haunted house. They were in the girl's bedroom where the ghost was most often seen. The presenters were chatting away saying oh well, there's nothing there now. Except the ghost is right there in front of the curtains. You, the viewer at home, can see it but no one in the show is reacting to it. That's genius. They scared the shit out of the whole country, and they got five hundred thousand complaints.

Brig: Five hundred thousand?

Max: I know, right? I'm obsessed by the whole thing. What other country could do that? You need a national broadcaster willing to do something loads of people are going to hate. You need great actors who can switch from serious to jokey, credulous to sceptical. You need great writers, actors, technology, and people who value television as an art form. We're so lucky.

MD: I'm not sure you should take your inspiration from a show that made a lot of people unhappy enough to phone and complain.

Max: If everyone likes what you're doing, you're doing it wrong.

J: Do you believe that?

Max: I have to. If we don't keep pedalling, we'll fall off the bike.

J: So you want people to complain about you?

Max: It's more that if I do what needs to be done, there will be complaints. There were complaints about Pascal. For example, from you, J.

J: I'm happy to say I was wrong.

Max: There were complaints about Youngster.

J: I'll hold my hands up.

Max: People have complained about the Brig, about turning the music off in the stadium, about using Magnus so much, about the Triplets, about me spending time on the women's team, about not playing a striker against Salford. It's just endless. If I did something that made everyone instantly happy, I think I wouldn't be able to sleep. I'm not trying to piss you off but if you are pissed off, that seems like a good sign. Someone might look at things you've said, J, and think the secret of life is doing the opposite.

MD: Max.

J: I'd love to offer a defence against that . . .

Max: I think I was saying I loved the BBC. Seriously, without the beeb this country would be uninhabitable. What I said about them wasn't political, it was wipe your shoes before you come in my house, know what I mean?

J: Nobody puts Boggy in the corner. We love it when you say things like that; it shows you get the club. But you don't do it often enough. You're aloof.

Max: I'm *busy*.

MD: I was interested in my reaction, if I can get pompous again. My first thought was about the money. The financial future of the club.

Max: Which is right, mate. You've got to do that.

MD: Right, but as J says, it shows you get the club. So how am I opposed to that?

Max: I should be more diplomatic.

MD: I didn't like being on the wrong side of the argument. My first thought should have been for Boggy.

J: So are we still in the BBC's bad books?

MD: No. We weren't the only small club with grievances about the TV companies. Max opened the floodgates and a lot of club directors added their voices. A lot of accusations of rudeness and staff feeling belittled. I got a call from a lady at the BBC. She clarified that many of the workers are contractors and she would remind them in no uncertain terms that they were guests at clubs.

Max: She didn't like being called a dick when she hadn't done anything wrong.

J: She hired dicks.

Max: That's true.

MD: She wanted to interview Boggy and do a little piece on him that they'd show before the next round. A peace offering, you might call it.

Max: But Boggy turned them down. Didn't you? He's nodding. I think he's sex on legs but he's camera shy. So it was a storm in a teacup and a good result all round.

Boggy: They're not showing Chester so it makes no sense to have a piece about me before the match they do show.

Max: [whispering] Did you know Boggy could talk?

J: [whispering] No. [normal] Were you disappointed not to be picked for the live coverage? We're the giant killers. We must have been close.

Max: Would you have picked us? It's not a glamour tie, let's be honest.

J: Especially if you're not playing.

Max: I might wear something glamorous.

J: Your clobber is really bad.

Brig: [cough]

Max: In my former club all the kids were asking their mums for the Max Best hoodies, and the mums were ecstatic because they're dirt cheap. So I kind of got stuck dressing like this.

J: Really?

Max: Yeah. I don't mind. It's one less decision to make. If you're rich enough to laugh at me for how I dress, good for you. If your kid rushes to the cheapest thing in the shop and says, "Daddy, can I have this?" I mean . . . you're welcome. Shit clobber? It's not something you can hurt me with. Clobber, trims, drips, who cares? Well, I care about trims. Some of the haircuts in this place are genuinely disgusting. That said, it has been suggested that if I look a bit sexier against Walsall that could help us attract more TV deals in future. I had a look at some fancy suits but I'm undecided so far.

J: We won't be live, though.

Max: No but they still film it all. They show the highlights. Okay, I think I wanted to talk about the state of the club.

J: Okay, okay. But hold on. While we're still doing the past. By far the most common questions we got were about the article from your former team.

Max: Right.

J: You don't want . . .

Max: I'm kind of done with that. I was done with it before it even happened. What's the, like, number one question?

J: Just, sort of, which bits are true? I know you don't want to talk about it. I think I understand that. Everything I've heard says the whole thing was a tissue of lies. So why defend yourself? I get it. But . . . it's really the most asked question from the listeners.

Max: Ask me one specific question and I'll see how I feel about it.

J: Let me get . . .

Max: Don't touch that microphone.

J: You work with people mentioned in the article, like Henri, and, like, what do they think about it all? Not, like, is it real because obviously it isn't but does it affect your relationships?

Max: I think it brought some of us closer together. I'd already told Henri everything. I'd told MD almost everything. MD, right, I was all ready for him to tell me off or whatever, but he was clever. He flips it round. He says, we're here if you need us. If you need someone to talk to, we'll organise it.

J: Like a therapist?

Max: I guess. That's what you meant, right?

MD: Yes.

Max: So he's being all kind and supportive, and that makes me want to tell him point by point my side of it. He's damned clever sometimes. If he has time to think about something, he's great. Anyway, it was immediately clear I didn't need to worry about being sacked or anything like that. And we could have a proper chat about how the sponsors would react, or the parents of youth team players or whatever. He wanted me to do something like this right away, but I wasn't into it. Do my talking on the pitch, and by the way, what do *their* sponsors think? What do *their* youth team players think? Because who's looking out for their careers? Seems to be me more than anyone working at *that* football club. Right? That's how a parent could read that article. Yeah, my former club shot themselves in the foot big time, because there are tons of people in football who are fucking pissed. Like, proper pissed. The owner of Tranmere wants to withhold payment of the transfer fees until the club issue an apology. A protracted, public legal battle? That is terrifying for them.

MD: Will he really hold back the money?

Max: He doesn't like being mugged off by some lowlife worms. So the worm king better be looking over his shoulder because how can the club apologise until they've sacked him and thrown him under the bus? Oh! I'll say one way the article was effective. The entire thing had one main goal, and that's to make sure I would never manage that team. And believe me, mission accomplished.

MD: We hope you'll stay *here*, Max.

Max: Until we lose five games in a row. Then you'll have binned me off before the final whistle has finished peeping.

MD: Come on.

Max: I'm just saying. I know exactly how safe my position is.

J: Hang on, Max. I don't want to change the topic just yet. Tell us how you felt when you read the article.

Max: [blowing air through cheeks] First read through I was thinking, *is that it?* We knew something like that was coming, because people told me they'd been tricked into talking by a worm. I read it again and that time was sort of mathematical. Like, false, false, false, true but spun, false, true and it makes me look good, and so on.

J: What was true but made you look good?

Max: Me asking for training to be harder. I mean, come on. Standards. The third time I read it was more from an outsider's point of view. Like, what's my girlfriend going to think? What's MD going to think? The worst part was about the receptionist. She used to blush when I went in and that is the entire story. I've had those little crushes myself, so I know what it's like. I kept wondering if her friends were teasing her about it, stuff like that. And I kept wondering how that detail even got included. Like, I remember the first conversation we ever had. I said, "Hi, I'm Max, I'm here to see David Cutter." And she said, "I'll get him for you." And that was by far the most we ever spoke. So some player, some worm, must have talked to her and she's gone "Oh what's Max like?" or something like that and he's realised. He's got jealous and remembered it. It's so pathetic. But then for the club to read the text and say, yeah, let's throw her under the bus to make Max look bad . . .

MD: The official position of Chester Football Club is that we don't know of any definitive link between the authorship of the article and the football club in question.

Brig: It shows the character of the two men involved. Max goes to war for Boggy, risking future TV money, because he can't abide people treating his staff with anything less than total respect. The other person offers up a young girl as red meat.

J: I'm getting the sense that behind the scenes, there wasn't much criticism of Max for all this.

MD: Criticism of what? The only thing I didn't like was the manner in which he thought to come to Chester, late on transfer deadline day, out of the blue, so to speak. It's not a very nice thought but it's a thought he had when he was not being treated well there, and in the end it didn't come close to happening.

Max: See, this is boring. I'm so bored. This is a rubbish conversation. I knew I should have batted away all those questions. It's not about if I made mistakes or if I could have done things better. It's about moving forward. It's about what's next. If at any point you decide you don't like what I've done, fine. Sack me. Just spare me the mind-numbing forensic analysis of every word in every sentence, holy shit.

MD: See what I have to work with? He's not afraid of being sacked. That's supposed to be my main weapon against him.

J: He knows you won't sack him.

Max: Lose five games and I'll be out the door. We all know that. But it doesn't worry me. I look at all these defensive managers clinging onto their jobs by their fingernails. Maybe I shouldn't be so harsh because they're living their dream and they'd do anything for one more day. But I'm not afraid of losing my job in the normal sense, no. Imagine I was free to focus on playing. I'd be earning silly money in no time. Sack me today, I could be on five grand a week before we hit December.

J: Or you'd go to the club you bought.

Max: What? Be serious. That's a hobby. That place is a retirement home for elderly squirrels.

J: When that news came out it was one of those "excuse me what" moments.

MD: I know the feeling.

Max: If you want to come down one day, I'll give you a tour and you can film it and all that. You should forget it exists. I hadn't planned for any crossover with Chester, but I couldn't shake the idea that it was a great place for one of our young players to get some match experience.

MD: It is perfect for that. If Max didn't own the club, I wouldn't have thought twice about the proposal.

Max: The state of Chester. The youth teams are doing well. We've got two groups who are really strong.

J: People are starting to sit up and take notice of the under-twelves.

Max: Mate, they are mint. The women's team are obviously having a good go at their league. You can get the main man to come and talk about it in detail. *Jackie . . . is at the wheel, tell me how good . . . does it feel?*

J: That's a Man United song.

Max: I know. I keep trying to make the lyrics fit Chester. One day. Hey, what's the latest with the Man United takeover?

MD: Nothing much is happening. The Qataris dropped out and the billionaire from Manchester is in pole position. According to reports, he'll buy a minority stake but he'll run the football side.

Max: It's so strange. I mean, I *saw* him there. He was involved with the Qataris.

MD: Who?

Max: Huh? What? Nothing. And the Saudi Pro League? That's still a thing, right?

J: I suppose. Probably buy loads of players in January again. I don't really keep track of it.

Max: Yeah. Billions swilling around all over the place. When we've got some of that money, I want to switch the boys to being, like, one group per year. So we'll have elevens, twelves, thirteens, and so on. We'll need more coaches, obviously. And physios. I'm overworking them as it is. Then at least two girls' sides. Under-eighteens as a platform for the first team. And . . . under-sixteens? Not sure. Three would be great. Jackie can choose. Depends if they get promoted. What I'm saying is, things are great, but nowhere near right.

J: Sounds ambitious.

Max: No, it's basic. Okay, so the men's first team. We've got two good goalies, Robbo and Ben. Ben's good but I want a lot more from him. I think he doesn't realise how good he can be.

J: Can we talk about rotation? Everyone says it's bad. You should have a first-choice goalkeeper. Everyone says that.

Max: Nah. So that's the goalies. The defence is good. Steve Alton was a good signing. Very happy with him. Very happy with Carl's progress. Vimsy's got them playing as a unit. I need someone else in the rotation, though. I'm under budget on the wages. Did you know that? I want another coach and two signings. I think one has to be a defender.

J: I didn't expect transfer talk.

MD: Me neither.

J: People always love sending in questions about transfers.

Max: It might have to be a loan signing. I don't like doing loans, but we *need* cover. Centre back who can cover at fullback, ideally.

J: Why don't you like loans?

Max: We're developing someone else's players.

J: But if it gets us wins . . .

Max: Yeah. But we should have caught Vivek when he was twelve. If we had, he'd be getting first-team minutes already. And because I've been training twice a day, I haven't been scouting as much. See what I mean? There's a cost to everything. I think I was right to work on myself to the extent I did because there are games when I can help the team. But I remember last January thinking we really need to build up the eighteens, and it hasn't happened.

MD: For obvious reasons. No one's mad at you.

Max: I'm just giving the fans an idea of the trade-offs.

J: You need to delegate more.

Max: Yeah. Remember you said that. Boggy, clip that bit out and send it to me so that when I start delegating more, he can't get mad at me.

J: I'm suddenly very nervous.

Max: Yeah. We got Jackie in, by the way, call that delegation if you want, except he's better than me. And we got a scout. She's part time but we're building up to taking her on full time.

MD: She's one of the parents Max got into a fight with on his first day here.

Max: It wasn't a fight. It was a polite disagreement. It always stuck with me how switched on she was. She's really helping me now. I'd love to send her around non-league looking for players but for now I've got her scouting our next opponents. She's so good. Okay. Goalies good. Defence good but one addition, please.

J: Are you talking to MD, there?

Max: No because he always says there's no money. If I wanted to bring in another defender I'd go on a fan podcast, get them excited about the idea, and let them pressure him.

MD: [sigh]

J: Have you got anyone in mind?

Max: As a defender to come in? There are names but I'll look into that more in December. Closer to the transfer window, our phones will start ringing. We need to be nimble. Ready to move. Moving onto the midfield. That's our greatest strength, I think. Ryan was a great signing. Aff and Sam are absolutely killing it in training.

J: Why is that?

Max: What do you mean?

J: What's changed in training to make them so much better?

Max: Nothing in particular. We do a few things slightly different—we'll put Trick, Aff, and Raffi in one drill so they get used to playing with each other. Really trying to get our partnerships and triangles going. It's more work for Vimsy but those on-pitch partnerships are one thing I insist on. No, I'd say most of the improvement is about mindset and giving them breaks. If I tell Aff he's not playing on Saturday, he can train hard for four days and still end the week fresher than before. Do you know what I mean? I told them my priority was training and they're into it.

J: And Raffi's really kicked on.

Max: Did you know we had a bid for him? Some cheeky twats faxed us a transfer bid. My first one as a manager. I'd have framed it if it didn't make me sick.

J: How much was it?

Max: Like, five percent of what he's worth. Really annoying. I'm going to smash that team when I'm back to full fitness. Cheeky twats.

J: You looked back to full fitness against your former team.

Max: Nah. That was anger. That was a one-off. I'm stuck. I've hit a wall.

J: Don't be so hard on yourself. You nearly died.

Max: It's not that. I'm . . . just stuck. I don't need to play every game, and don't really like playing DM anyway. I could go most of the season without playing, I reckon. But I like the idea that I can come on and inject some pace and purpose and all that. Or if some team is really cheaty, I can go on and punish them. But then I need to be a lot better than I am. Like, genuinely, I wouldn't pick myself for right midfield. We've got Joe and D-Day who offer something different, crossing or dribbling. I can't do either.

J: It'll come back. Don't rush it.

Max: I might have to get weird with it. We'll see. Right, so, the midfield is pretty good.

J: Hang on. Can we talk about this transfer bid for Raffi?

MD: No.

Max: Yes. What's your question?

J: Well, how much would you accept?

Max: We're not selling this January. There's no amount of money that could make me part with any players.

MD: Raffi has a release clause that Max put into his deal.

J: See, that's weird, isn't it? Sorry, Max, but that's weird.

Max: I wasn't the manager then. You knew I was Raffi's agent when you offered me the job. It's a bit late to say it's weird.

J: No, I get that but if there's a deal that's good for you but bad for the club, or good for Raffi but bad for you, or whatever. It's a mess.

Max: Our interests are aligned. In summer a club will pay his release clause, and his career will kick onto the next level. Him leaving this January would be bad for him long term.

J: If he moves this January you'll get some more cash. You, personally.

Max: If there's a club that makes an offer where I think, hey, this could be good for him, I'll consider it. The next question is, is that transfer fee enough for Chester? If those two things are right, there could be a deal. But he's got to play. He's got to develop. I think six more months here is the best thing for him.

I'd like a new car. I'd like to take my girlfriend on holiday. But when it comes to Raffi, my priority is Raffi. If we give him everything he needs to grow as a player, the money will come to everyone, won't it?

Brig: The conflict would be if a club offered an amount of money that made MD want to bite their hand off, but that Max felt was far short of the level.

J: How much?

Brig: [sound of pen on paper] MD?

MD: God, yes. I'd take that in a heartbeat.

Brig: Max?

Max: No. No chance.

MD: Are you kidding?

Max: That's half price. You know that.

J: How much is it? What does it say?

Brig: That's classified. The amusing thing is, they are both right. It's an amount of money that would very much help the club. But if the club is patient, it will get the amount Max wants.

MD: You don't know that.

Brig: Max knows best.

J: Can you say what the release clause is, maybe? That'd be good to know.

MD: Your call, Max.

Max: What's your advice?

MD: I think you can say it, but we'll never get that much.

Max: It's eight hundred thousand.

J: [low whistle] For a non-league player? That's . . . optimistic.

Max: Have you seen Raffi play?

J: But . . . How much was Jamie Vardy?

MD: A million. But that was ten years ago. A million then is like two million now. Eight hundred isn't . . . completely out of the question.

Max: Eight hundred grand is nothing for a player of Raffi's potential. In the summer, we'll get that, or as close as makes no odds.

MD: Or we'll get nothing if he leaves the following summer.

J: [pause] Maybe take the money?

MD: Don't say that. You can't *tell* him what to do. He's stubborn.

J: Oh. What about Henri? He's still on a month-to-month deal, right?

Max: The idea there was to explore our options and see what was best for him. I, as a friend, wanted him to go to League Two.

J: To Tranmere.

Max: To anyone. He's at a stage where he needs to be playing at that level. But he loves it here. He loves the football, the fans, the city, and he wants to stay. People in football undervalue happiness. He's happy. So I've been thinking, can we get to a level where it's fair that he stays here? And I think we can. So he wants to stay and he'll help us get there. It's perfect.

J: So why doesn't he sign a contract?

Max: He doesn't need one. If I say he can stay, he can stay, and if he says he'll stay, then he'll stay. As it happens, we decided it'll be better for him in terms of insurance and work permits and all that if he signs something. So we're looking at a two-year deal.

MD: What?

Max: Oh, sorry, J. This is subject to approval from MD.

MD: I'm delighted, of course I am. He's a wonderful player and a great person. But why didn't you tell us?

Max: I forgot. What's the hurry? Everyone needs to relax. Jeez.

J: Bit of a podcast exclusive! I'm made up, me. He's brilliant, he is. Brilliant.

Max: And Tony's a good backup slash second striker. But we are short in the forward lines. Aren't we, MD?

MD: Oh, God. You've set this up. Got us all happy about Henri and now you're going to ask for money.

Max: You know this one. We talked about it.

MD: Oh, him. Yes, we've been exploring an option in the forward areas of the pitch. But as I told Max, it's too expensive. We've made a ridiculous offer and we've been turned down. It's not going to happen, Max.

J: Who is it?

Max: Sorry, bro, can't name names. Let's just say I have an idea for a signing that will shock a lot of people. We'd have to overpay, big time, but it'd be worth it.

J: Have we got a transfer budget?

Max: Not really, but the TV money will help. If we beat Walsall, yeah, I'll be able to bring in three players no problem. But if not, do you want me spending to make sure we win the title?

J: Yes.

Boggy: Yes!

MD: Max, don't do this.

Max: Okay, this player would be epic. But I promised we wouldn't have to do another Boost the Budget. Things are on the up financially, but it'd be strange to blow a load of money on a certain player and then say, lads, lend us a fiver.

J: Win us the league and we won't mind. Seriously.

Max: Listen, what happened when I was in hospital was really special for me. You lot pulled together, didn't you? You did something. You raised loads of money when inflation was running wild and your bills were going mental. I know for a fact some fans went without heating so they could send money to the club. No, it's not that easy. The player I want would be an extravagance like you couldn't believe.

J: I don't know who it is, but I want him. Do it, MD!

MD: When Max mentioned the player, I thought he was joking. It's the least Max player of all time. But the more I think about it, the more I can't stop thinking about it. I like a lot of things about our manager, but I think my favourite is that he's not stuck to some abstract philosophy. I see you getting excited. Max, can you put a stop to this, please? You know the numbers don't work.

Max: I'm not ready to give up yet. I had an idea. I told you that I had three problems, J. One is solved by that player. I mean, it's that simple. MD is right to worry about the money but if we're flexible . . . Okay. That's the first team. We need two more players in January. MD, do you agree with that?

MD: Based on the fixture list, yes.

Max: J, do you have any questions about the team?

J: Trick Williams.

Max: Good player. Having a bit of a purple patch. I think he could have a big December.

J: I wasn't at the games, but some people said you played him left wing and Aff at left back.

Max: They're both flexible players. Sometimes we try things.

J: And you get on well with him.

Max: I get on with him about as well as I get on with you, J.

J: I know I said some things I shouldn't have, but—

Max: Near the beginning of the season, few matches in, I said to Trick, "Look. You're off the levels you were showing last season. Sort it out." I'm sure it's not nice to hear that, and it's worse if it's coming from a weirdo teen-man. But two weeks later, he was back on it. Do you know what I mean? There are players I get on with more naturally who aren't back to their best, and it's nearly Christmas. Do I sit next to Trick on the team bus swapping Panini stickers? No. Do we go on long walks looking for four-leaf clovers and putting daisy chains in each other's hair? Not very often. So what? He's a consistent player who does what I say.

J: You like consistency and obedience.

Max: Course I do.

J: What's your management style?

Max: Oh, shit. Er . . . I'm making it up as I go along. I'm just trying to do it how I'd want it done. Yeah, bit of fun, few laughs, but you've got to graft. And they've got to improve. All of them. I try to make it so that players are allowed to ask questions and give ideas. Henri likes that, and the other players have learned it's all right to say they don't understand or don't know what to do and whatever. Like, there's twenty of us in that room, so someone has an idea. Know what I mean?

J: Not really.

Max: And I look at other managers and they're ranting and raving trying to hype their players up. Okay, but we're running riot in the middle of the pitch and it's your job to notice that. Basically, what I'm saying is I do my main job and that's putting players in the right positions and telling them what I want them to do. If I then make some mistakes about how I talk to them or forget that they've got wives and families and all that, we can sort that out pretty calmly.

J: You forget they have wives?

Max: We train Monday morning. Near the end I have a genius idea and I'm like, "Top, come in tomorrow afternoon so we can practice." Someone— Glenn, normally—sighs and says, "Great, Max, are you going to book us a new hospital appointment?" And I'm like oh, right, real life. Fine. You know, if we were losing matches that kind of thing would fester, but because they know I'm good at the main thing, they tolerate some other stuff. I mean, all they have to do is remind me and that's the end of it. It's not like I'm making promises to players about days off and changing my mind at the last minute like other managers do. And we *do* extra training, it's just a case of planning it. We can't be as spontaneous as if everyone was twenty-three and had complete control of their timetable. Brig, what do you think about my management style?

Brig: They will write books about it.

Max: Who? Comedians?

Brig: You get better every day, sir.

Max: Hmm. Next topic! The future. Let's say our goal is to win the league this year.

J: Is it?

Max: Yes. What could stop us doing that? At the moment, we're in good shape. We're second, three points behind Kiddies with a game in hand.

J: And a massive goal difference.

Max: That's not going to come into it. If we're level with any team, we'll smash them on goal difference. And if we get this player I want . . .

J: Right, you've really hyped me up about that. But that was deliberate, wasn't it? So you can get the money.

Max: Yep. You'll agree it's a good signing, but you'll baulk at the cost. There are, I think, three crazy things I want to do this season. Three things you'll lose your minds over. One will be that deal, if we can arrange it. The other club is absolutely not interested, as MD said, and what we've offered is already bonkers. There's a number where they have to go with it. Can you stomach it? I'm sort of softening you up, I'll admit. Ten years from now I'm pretty sure you'll think wow, that was fun. But when you hear the numbers, holy shit. That's your money. I know that.

J: And the other two things?

Max: [pause] Three crazy solutions to three serious problems. One can be solved with cash. That's the player. The other two need some imagination. I'm not sure which one will wind you up the most.

MD: I don't like the turn this podcast has taken.

J: You don't know about this?

MD: No.

Max: The thing is, do you trust me or not? Do you think I'm doing a good job? I only know one way to do it, and that's my way. Is it insane? No. It's totally logical. To me. But anyway, I can't do it the way you would do it, or the way Boggy would do it. Because that to me would be wrong. So one of the two things, you won't like it, but you need to get over that as quickly as possible.

J: But what is it?

Max: It's . . . a new member of staff. I can't say more because I haven't got it sewn up yet. I think it could be a Jackie Reaper–level signing, and it will be such a massive relief for me as a person. Just in terms of my schedule, my peace of mind. We absolutely need this person, and I think it will happen.

J: But we won't like it?

Max: MD won't like it for about three seconds and then he'll see the upside. Probably. You'll need longer. Remember to breathe. It'll all be okay.

J: And the third thing?

Max: Yeah. That'll infuriate you. I can imagine you'll never be as angry about anything as you are about that. But I have to do it. For me and for the club.

J: When's this bomb going to drop?

Max: It's not a bomb. It might look like a bomb, but it's really a rainbow. The thing is, one of the reasons I wanted to do this podcast was because it all ties in. If you think I'm a parasite and a villain, you're going to spin everything I ever do into the worst possible light. If you can step back and think, *This looks selfish, but I can see how this benefits Chester long-term*, then we'll be all right.

MD: I'm worried.

Max: Check this out. Kidderminster play three of the top six in December. If they win them all, fair play. But they're going to drop a few points somewhere, and then we'll be number one for Christmas.

J: Christmas number one.

Max: Possibly Boxing Day number one, but you know what I mean. Everything I've done so far has been all right, hasn't it? I've taken some big swings. Pascal, Youngster, Magnus. Different formations, rotating the goalies, fake Jackies, real Jackies. Cup runs, new sponsors. I think I've earned a bit of leeway to get a bit weird. Don't you?

J: [long pause] Max Best, thanks for coming on *Deva Victrix*. I enjoyed it; let's do it again sometime.

ASSISTS

Football glossary: *Assist. The pass that leads to a goal.*

From Chester Online, *Monday, November 27*
It's Sandra Who?
Confusion and Questions as Chester Unveil Second Assistant Manager

Chester FC have announced the identity of their new assistant manager—and it's a woman. Sandra Lane, 36, had previously been working with girls' teams in the Manchester City academy system.

At a press conference held this evening, an unusually happy and talkative Max Best believed he had secured a coup. "Sandra is three things: She's top. She's class. And she's mint. Getting her to leave one of the most desirable positions in world football was not easy, but in the end she found the idea of working with me irresistible. I am buzzing. Absolutely buzzing. I feel like I just signed Messi. No pressure on Sandra, but she's better than Messi. No, that's crazy; cut that. She's better than Pep. Ah, no, cut that, too. She's better than two hundred other coaches, I can say that for sure."

When asked about the challenges of working with men, Best laughed. "I think you're coming at this from totally the wrong angle. She doesn't have to prove herself to this mob. They have to prove themselves to her. We employ three people who have worked for a Premier League club. Sandra Lane is one of them. If I was one of the players—and guess what, I am—I'd be buzzing. She's an elite coach. I think she can help me get closer to my old levels and that's worth the wages alone. She's also great on tactics. Oh, man! I feel like going hang gliding or something. Where's the nearest aerodrome?"

"I'm very happy to be here," said Miss Lane. "Max challenged me to step outside my comfort zone and I'm really looking forward to getting started. I was unsure at first, I must confess, but he wouldn't give up. Frankly I haven't been pursued this hard since I was an extra in a zombie movie."

Initial reaction on OhNo!, formerly known as Twitter, was positive.

A user named Cliff Daps wrote: "Getting a coach from Man City is like buying land where you know there's going to be a new tram line. It's so clever it almost shouldn't be allowed."

Chester coach Spectrum was quick to add his thoughts. "Max has done it again! Such a positive development. How on Earth has he managed that?"

Well-known fan J, who hosts a popular Seals podcast, wrote, "Absolutely bonkers but you know what? I say give her a chance. He's obviously planning to let her manage a couple of matches so he can take a break, and if we want to win the league, we have to back the team extra hard those days. It's as simple as that, really."

Not everyone was so keen. There were plenty of confused faces outside the Liverpool FC shop in Chester.

"It's awfully strange," said Regina Dwight, 57. "I thought they had that army fella as assistant. He's awfully handsome. What's his role now?"

"How much are they paying her?" grumbled Eric Bishop, 55. "Man City wages in the sixth tier? He'll be the ruin of us all, that man. Mind you, if she can remind Youngster of the way he's supposed to be passing, she'll be well worth the dough."

"More Max Best chaos," said John Stephens, 53. "He's had a couple of weeks where everything's been smooth sailing, so now he wants to muddy the waters. He's always up to something. He's like a naughty toddler. If it's too quiet in the other room, you have to go and check on him. How can you have two assistant managers?"

Max Best himself appeared surprised when the question was put to him. "Of course I need two assistant managers. John Smith manages my assistance, and Sandra assists me by managing. What's the confusion?"

Time will tell if this latest move is fruitful or folly.

Tuesday, November 28.

We got the lads into the meeting room before training, along with the physios and coaches. MD popped in for the big moment. Jackie had dragged himself out of bed before 11:15 (when *Bargain Hunt* starts on BBC One) for the first time in months, which says everything about the level of interest.

The guys sat on the cheap plastic chairs very much like schoolboys, with the staff leaning on the wall to the right. Jackie took a position to the left, near the front. Sandra hovered nervously and awkwardly behind me. Where would she end up in this little jigsaw puzzle of ours? Probably where Jackie was, I reckoned. From there, she'd be able to chime in on football matters, but wouldn't be the focus.

"Okay, shut your gobs," I said. "We're here to meet our newest member of staff. Everyone paying attention? I've got us a class gerbil. He's called Nibbles. Midfielders, I want you to get together and organise yourselves so that you feed him every day. Strikers, change the water. Defenders, you clean the tray. Goalies, bedtime stories."

"What's a gerbil?" said Pascal.

Magnus spoke. "It's a cute little pet often used in schools to teach children about caring for animals. Max is making a joke about how we have a new teacher."

I gave him a Maxy two-finger guns. Some memory threatened to come into focus. To Sandra I said, "You were a teacher, right?"

"Yes," she croaked, and I was reminded of how nerve-wracking these situations could be. I was also reminded of how little interest I'd shown in her other than what she could do on and around a football pitch.

"Okay, playtime's over. Let's get serious. I've hired Sandra. She's a top coach and I am very, very smug that I've been able to pull this off. And let's cut the crap—if I came here saying I'd nabbed one of Man City's coaches and his name was Sandro, you'd all be buzzing. Wouldn't you?" That hit home. "Good. Here's the plan. She's going to settle in. Take it slow. She has to get to know you as players, so *there's* a solid fifteen minutes of hard graft. Then she wants to get to know you as people. And some of you have . . . Henri, what was that phrase?"

"Rich inner lives."

"Right. Some of you have rich inner lives. Some of you have bankrupt inner lives, but that's fine. She'll get to know you, you'll get to know her, and boom, you'll realise our season just got afterburners. What I'd like, I suppose, is for everyone to be supportive, especially in the first weeks while Sandra's moving house and there's this media interest. Be chill. Relax. Come with an open mind."

"Can we ask questions?" said Glenn.

"In a bit. Here's why I've been, what did you say, *pursuing*? Here's why I've been courting Sandra. She's an elite technical coach. She's a floating tactical megabrain of Max Bestian proportions. And she's brave."

Jackie spoke up. "I was Max's assistant when we played against Sandra's team and I remember thinking, I want someone to look at me the way Max looks at Sandra."

Sandra looked down—I don't think she was used to this lavish praise. "Mate," I said to Jackie. "I'm doing a team meeting for the men. The manager of the women's team shouldn't be talking."

"We're the same level in the hierarchy," he said.

"We're the same level when I'm the men's manager, but I'm also above you when I'm DoF, and below you when I'm a player. That means I *envelop* you."

Jackie simply kept smiling. "Okay, Max."

"I'm just saying that I don't go round interrupting *your* team meetings."

"No, no. You'd never do dat." Some chuckles from the lads.

"Sandra. Couple of words?"

She cleared her throat. "Hi, everyone." She inhaled. "I'm dead nervous. This is weird." There were chuckles up and down the room. Me and Jackie fake-bickering with each other had helped everyone relax. "As you know, I've been coaching at City. Really enjoyed it. Done my badges up to UEFA A. All with the girls, of course. I've never coached men." She gave the room a worried look.

I laughed. "Am I the only one who thinks that's an advantage? If you can manage twenty teenage girls, you can cope with these guys. They're a load of gerbils. What about your background?"

"Well, I'm from Manchester." Her eyes flickered, wondering if being from the world's greatest city would perhaps not go down well. The players didn't have time to react, though, because I burst into applause and Youngster, Raffi, and the two Triplets followed. "Okay. Ha. As Max guessed, I taught Sports and Exercise Science in college. Um . . . I'm single—it's complicated—I like dogs, Netflix, beach holidays. Er . . . look, I just like football." She thought it was a lame finish, but it was fucking perfect. Right in the top corner.

"Max?" said Glenn.

"Go for it."

"I'm asking all the questions from the group so you don't get mad at anyone in particular."

"Oh, much better that I get mad at *everyone*. Yeah."

"Sandra, what do you want us to call you?"

"Sandra?" she said.

"Like, we call Max boss or gaffer. The Brig calls him sir. Some of the lads were thinking we could call you *Miss* but we don't . . ."

"Miss? Like in school?" She had a quick think. "Why not?"

"What's the difference between you and the Brig?"

"That's a question for me, I think." I pointed. "Brig's fitness, conditioning, standards. Sandra's football. Technical stuff. Passing, formations. If you have a question about beating the press, Sandra. If you need someone to scream in your face from five inches away, Brig. All good?" I switched to an annoyingly sarcastic voice. "Now, if you have any special boy problems that you don't feel comfortable talking to a woman about, you can talk to the Brig or Vimsy. All right?"

Glenn ignored the last part. "How did you meet Max?"

"I was coaching the under-sixteens. On Friday nights we used to play seven-a-side indoors. We did passing drills, movement. The score wasn't that important; it was all about player development and getting experience against real people in real situations. One day, Max turns up. He was . . . courting . . . one of the players from Manchester Metropolitan University."

"Whoa! You don't know that."

"You were," said Youngster.

Argh. I forgot he was there at that time. I shrugged. "I was merely inter-ested in women's football. I might have spent more time with one of the women than the rest, but that's because she was the organiser and, I have to say, quite knowledgeable about the growth of the sport and its standout characters. It's a big leap to infer any sort of relationship from that."

"You kissed her full on the mouth in front of everyone," said Jackie, the traitor.

"That was before kissing women full on the mouth without consent was considered bad. Can we please get on with the story?"

Sandra nodded. "Max was there to watch his girlfriend, sitting on the benches at the back, and suddenly he's on his feet, managing the team. It hap-pens sometimes. A guy gets it into his head he's the next Pep Guardiola and it's only women so how hard could it be?" She shook her head with a wry smile. "It was different with Max. It was like there were invisible tendrils all over the pitch. Our moves stopped working. It was strange."

"Wait," said Steve Alton. "He just made himself the manager from one second to the next? Bossing them around?"

"Yeah. The referee complained. Said he couldn't manage because he hadn't filled in the forms, so he said he was the nutritionist."

"Max was telling them the best place to get pork," said Trick, which a lot of people found very funny. The intensity of my glare meant Trick was the first to stop laughing.

Sandra didn't know Trick was the 1970s reborn. I planned to spend plenty of time telling her about the squad and wondered if I should start with Trick to get an unpleasant task out of the way, or save him till last like a treat. For now, she continued her tale. "We played twice, and the second match was the only defeat we ever had. Four–nil. Their goalie scored twice but it looked *meant*. They battered us on counters. That's when I met Max. And Jackie, though Jackie wasn't jumping around singing songs about himself. A couple of weeks later Max appeared at a City match on crutches, battered and bruised, high on painkillers, and he did my halftime team talk and tried to give me a player for my team. I haven't been able to get rid of him ever since. And now I'm here."

"Let me tell you a couple of things from those times," I said. "As I said, Sandra was a brave manager. Fearless. She played with no centre backs for a few minutes in response to one of my changes. It's easier with rolling subs but she made more in-game changes than any manager I've played against, and she spotted my changes fast. Her players improved noticeably in the weeks between our two games. Those attributes alone would get her in this room. But what I liked most was that when we won, she got the match ball and gave it to our goalkeeper, and instead of shouting at me about my dirty tricks, she thanked me for pushing her players and giving them a wake-up call. She's got the perfect mentality: train hard, play hard, win and lose with class. When I'm throwing tantrums and refusing to shake hands with twats, Sandra will be representing Chester with grace and dignity."

Pascal put his hand up. "What's your favourite formation?"

"Four-two-three-one," said Sandra. "Switching to four-two-two-two." Pascal and Youngster looked at each other and their eyebrows shot up. They were biiiig fans of that answer, the nerds.

"We won't be using a double pivot," I said, before they got too excited. Football hipsters often called defensive midfielders "pivots" because they were the point that all the passing moves went through. "We have two DMs who can do the job of, well, two DMs. So we only need one."

"We do?" said Sandra, wondering which players could do the job of two.

"Youngster. Or me."

"I've seen Youngster play. There are times he could use support."

"That's just because he's learning. He *can* do it on his own."

"What if he goes forward to join an attack? We're left with nothing."

"So? Either an opponent tracks him, so they have one fewer in their transition, or he's left to roam, in which case we have a high-probability chance of a goal."

"It's very risky."

"No risk no fun."

"Pep likes a double pivot."

"Pep is a hack."

"You promised to stop bad-mouthing City."

"Seriously, though. I would smash him at non-league level."

"Sorry, Miss," said Trick. Invoking the name of His Holiness Pep G the First had made him realise exactly how far Sandra had dropped. "Why have you come here?"

"Er . . . Max persuaded me." She scratched her head. "I'm not sure how." Good laugh on that. "Charlotte said I'd love it."

"I'll do this one," I said, and something in my tone made everyone prepare for an extended rant. "There are ninety-two teams in the football league, and at least ninety are owned by what we might call penis people. The weird thing about penis people is that they get scared when they meet someone who doesn't have one. They like to appoint managers who have dangly bits. There are precisely two female managers whose achievements in the women's game are so enormous that I think they'd get jobs managing a men's team at a pretty big club. Sandra would have no chance. Zero. She wouldn't even get an interview. It's nice being part of the Man City industrial complex, but if you're ambitious, how far can you go? She'd have to be unbelievable to end up as the women's team manager. You with me? Now check this out. Loophoooole. The loophole is me. Me? I don't give a shit who you are. If you can improve my players, I'll drive to Manchester three times a week for a month to sell you on my vision. What I've offered Sandra is the chance to manage some games. As it happens, I desperately need a break, so I'm more than happy. And to be honest, there are plenty of matches now where the fake Jackies could stand on the sideline and get wins on their CV. And what if we've got a big match coming up and I want to scout that team? If they're in this division, we almost always play on the same days so I can't. Well, now that Sandra's here, I can. By the end of next season, Sandra will have been the manager for ten wins in men's football. That's ten more than any other woman in this country. With that on her CV, she'll be the first name that comes up when there's *any* managerial vacancy in the Women's Super League, and I can imagine there will be a few progressive clubs who'd consider her for the men's team. You with me?"

"You'll only give her the easy matches, then?" said Glenn.

"No. She's mint. She's miles above any other manager in this league—er, one exception—and there isn't a single doubt in my mind that she'll be able to step in. Holy shit, guys, it's such a relief to me. Such a relief. So that's the deal. Do you get it? She's going to coach the shit out of you, help you achieve your goals. And in return, we're all, collectively, going to help Sandra achieve her goals."

"Sir," said the Brig. I checked the time. We needed to get onto the training pitch.

"Okay, that's it. Any other questions you have you can write them down and put them in the nearest bin. Just get the fuck on with it. One thing, though. In the next weeks we'll be playing the usual four-one-four-one and three-five-two in matches, but I've got a new formation for you to work on in training. Four-four-one. Henri, I need you to train like a support striker. Lots of sideways movements, making triangles with the left and right mids. Okay, get changed and out on pitch one in five. Big game tonight!"

They filed out, with a few of the men coming over to shake Sandra's hand or fist bump her. When the last players had gone, MD came over. "Four-four-one, Max?"

"Yep."

"That's er . . . that formation's Pep approved, is it?"

Sandra smiled. "The only thing I don't understand is why none of the players commented on it."

Jackie gave her a pat on the back. "Because it's a madhouse. Welcome to Chester."

I watched as Vimsy, the Brig, and Jude took training. I asked Sandra to supervise. It was only a light session because we had a match that evening, but it was good to see that her attributes hadn't changed when she'd been put in charge of men. I had thought there was a slight, tiny possibility that the curse would reassess her skills based on working with penis people instead of women. But nope, she was who she was and that meant my pool of potential employees was double any other manager's.

SANDRA LANE	
Adaptability	4
Coaching Goalkeepers	5
Coaching Outfield Players	17
Determination	14
Judging Player Ability	8
Judging Player Potential	8
Level of Discipline	13
Man Management	15
Motivating	12
Tactical Knowledge	18
Working with Youngsters	18
Coaching Style	Technique-based
Preferred Formation	4-2-3-1
Preferred Style	Attractive attacking
Other	Likes her players to close down the opposition

Her coaching outfield players score was really high—surely high enough to raise our ceiling and to be a kick up the arse to Youngster, Pascal, and the Triplets. And her tactics score had given me confidence that she'd be able to run matches without me. Would I have given her the men's team job if I was sticking to being a director of football? I mean, I'd have preferred Jackie, but she was a legitimate contender. She wouldn't do well in a club where she had to make decisions about transfers, but with me giving her talented players, she'd smash it.

She'd agreed to come cheap—£500 a week for the rest of this season, which would double next year. The Brig's salary would at least double, too, and I planned to double my own salary. That was all needed, especially my bit, but I was already mentally burning next year's increased tier-five budget. Hopefully

Sandra would improve the squad the way I expected and we'd be able to nail down promotion, start selling players, and get their replacements up to speed.

There was the small issue of the twin-assistants thing. Even as I watched, Sandra stepped forward to offer some instruction, but then stopped herself and looked to the Brig for permission. That particular moment of awkwardness was met with good-natured smiles, but I'd have to keep an eye on it. Make sure they were both happy and both doing what they were best at.

As happy as *I* was, anxiety was starting to bubble up. The better I kept my end of the deal and gave Sandra an impressive CV, the sooner she'd get poached by a bigger club and I'd be back to square one. I knew I shouldn't worry about it, but I also knew that I should.

She'd only been at the club for ten minutes and I was thinking about how I could possibly replace her.

Cheshire Senior Cup second round: Cheadle Town versus Chester.

We had been drawn to play away in Cheadle, which was pretty funny, really. Cheadle is right next to Didsbury, and Cheadle Town actually played in the same division as West.

"Basically a home game for us, isn't it?" I told Sandra on the team bus.

"I guess," she said, trying to smile. She was really nervous. It struck me, then. Did I have another Jackie situation on my hands? Would every super coach I hired flame out in some way?

I gave her some space while I thought about some other things. The Brig had asked me for £3,000 in cash. I took it to mean things were moving apace in the manhunt. Great.

We'd had another bid for Raffi Brown. Second bid from the same team. I'd instructed Secretary Joe not to reply to the offer of £50,000, but I supposed he must have done, in secret, because they came back offering £70,000. Seventy grand for a player of that quality? Maddening. Four hundred K was the minimum, and that would only be a consideration if I wasn't his agent. But I was. I'd talked to him and he assured me he was happy at Chester and happy for me to keep thinking about his long-term career. So there. Stick your seventy grand where the sun shineth not.

I checked the job vacancies screen. Ten of the seventy-two managers in the EFL—the three leagues below the Premier League—had been sacked and not yet replaced. Ten clubs looking for managers! Some good clubs there, too. I noted, unhappily, that James O'Rourke at Tranmere was listed as "slightly insecure." I couldn't really blame Mateo—Tranmere were flirting with relegation. I just hoped James got a full season. He'd never had a full season as a manager. After all he'd done for me when I was recovering, I sincerely wished him the best.

This game against Cheadle, then. It'd be a cakewalk. Pretty boring, really. But it would feature one enormous personal milestone: I would pay off my God Save the King debt at last!

With all the matches I'd been managing, plus using free Sundays to watch Man City women (and seduce Sandra), plus the women's teams from Blackburn and Sheffield United, I'd smashed past the 3,000 I needed to buy Parasight. Now I'd be able to see agents like I could see players and coaches, and the ten percent being siphoned off my XP income would soon be a thing of the past.

XP balance: 1,180

Debt repaid: 2,966/3,000

Thinking about XP made me think of the ways in which I had an unfair advantage over Sandra. This match would be a good chance to review those, while teaching her about the players and what I wanted from her when I was away.

The match kicked off and I repeated what I'd told her in front of the Brig, but with more detail. When the Brig was my on-pitch assistant, I could do all kinds of crazy shit, like control players telepathically, and he wouldn't notice. Sandra would, which meant I had to explain my thought processes more and cook up a plausible explanation about why players were switching positions so fluidly. I felt the benefits of her coaching plus getting pushback on my ideas outweighed the infinitesimal risk she'd think I was actually telepathic.

"Okay, Cheadle Town. Pretty much as weak a team as you're ever going to be involved with." Average CA 8.

"Except the Met Heads."

"Relatively speaking, the Met Heads were much closer to your girls. Okay, so we're doing four-one-four-one. I lied when I told that lot it was the best formation for this match. I'd have done three-five-two if I wanted to run up the score."

"You wanted me to get familiar with it."

"Right. Keep an eye on Youngster. He sets our tempo. I divide players— mentally; this is private—into bronze, silver, gold, and platinum. This lineup today is really weak, but it's still about as strong as Chester when I started." Our average CA for the day was 40.8. "I'm pretty proud of that."

"I was impressed by training. They work hard."

"I told them I was judging them more on what they did in training than in matches. Ben's in goal. He had a bad match but he's back in contention for the number one jersey. He and Robbo are both silvers, but Ben can go platinum."

"I might write this down. Don't worry, I'll be subtle."

She got her notebook and made some squiggles. "Okay," I said, scanning our back four. "Trick is a low bronze. He's got a decent left foot but obviously I'm looking to upgrade there in a big way. We have a good left back but he's sixteen. When you're settled I might let him train with the first team. See what you think. See what we can do to fast track him."

"Okay."

"Centre backs. Steve Alton is a low silver. Gerald May is a high bronze. Right back today is an experiment. Andrew Harrison's a midfielder but I reckon he could play right back in more games like these. It lets me rest Carl and will be a bit of a shock to Andrew's system. I learned from you that giving minutes is crucial for development."

She smiled, then returned to her notebook. "Carl's gold? Silver?"

"Gold. He's almost as good as Glenn now. I reckon we focus on this eleven so you don't get overwhelmed. DM today is Magnus. Silver. Seems to improve slowly but surely. I don't know his limit. He's a strange one. In midfield we've got D-Day left, Pascal right. Both high bronze. Pascal you know has a high ceiling. We've got to give him minutes to develop without wasting him on shitty pitches. Let me worry about when he plays. I think I know what I'm doing there. There's Ryan. He's class. Platinum. I'll give him the first half. Sam's gold."

"Only gold?"

"Yep. High gold. He's near his limit but he's fantastic. You'll love working with him."

"And Tony's up front on his own." She added a sceptical twist to her tone. Tony lacked any outstanding qualities.

"He's silver. Perfectly fine for this season."

She nodded as she finished her notetaking. "Five bronze, four silver, one gold, one platinum."

We watched in silence for a while. Ryan was running the game, making it look like a different sport to most of the other players. He was spraying passes out to Pascal, who was giving the defence kittens with his speed.

After D-Day dribbled past his marker and crossed for Tony to score our first goal, I checked if Sandra had any questions about my rankings. "Not now. I think I broadly see the outline. Ryan's platinum for sure. You know them better than me. I think if you gave me your ratings for the whole squad that'd be very helpful if you get sick and I have to do it on my own."

"Sure. We'll have a chat before Walsall. After you've worked with them for a few days. Let's talk formations. At the moment we can easily switch between seven."

"Seven?"

"I know, it's shit."

"It's more than we do."

"Yeah, well. We can't always win on talent; we have to get funky. We've got four-four-two and diamond, plus four-two-four. We don't use those too much, but as you know, we will if we get the new striker in."

"Goliath."

"Right. It's going to be a big shock for you."

"I don't know. I'm almost excited by it. Charlotte was saying you and Jackie are maniacs about technique, passing, just like a real club."

"She said that?"

"Yeah. No offence."

"None taken. It's just the phrasing was unexpected."

"But to knock it long to a big man." Sandra laughed. "It's like you're on non-league safari, Max."

"We still need to agree to terms with the club and the player. But we won't be knocking it long. No chance. If anything, we're getting *more* sophisticated.

Okay, we've also got four-three-three, but we don't use that because Aff is our best player."

"Aff? Not Henri? Ryan?"

"You'll see. He's incredible. He makes everything work. He's number one for assists, which is amazing if you think Ryan takes all the set pieces. The last three options are about dominating midfield. There's four-five-one. I'm thinking about that for the Walsall game. But mostly we use either four-one-four-one with overloads down the sides, or three-five-two if we're not expecting much from the opposition."

She made notes of the seven. "It's pretty good. You must have worked hard."

I thought of the months of grinding. Watching Sunday League while sipping from a thermos. Kebabs with no onions. "Yeah. But changing from one to another could be the difference in a match. Right? And from game to game, it lets me use the whole of the squad. I've very slightly squashed their tendency to think that minutes on the pitch is the only measure of their self-esteem, and they can all see what I'm doing when I name the teams, but still, they want to play. Is it the same with the girls?"

"Oh, yeah. Totally. Tears and tantrums if they're not starting."

"Did you ever drop the Butcher of Burnage?"

"Not often. You know, she was shocked the first time you called her that. Upset, I think. Now she loves it."

I smiled. "She's great. You're going to help me get her to Chester, right?"

"Nope."

"Ah!" I said, pointing up as though I'd solved a crime. "You want her still there for when you're the Man City boss. I get it . . . I get it."

At halftime, we were 2–0 up. I did a semi-serious team talk, mostly for Sandra's benefit. Not that she needed it for her own skills, but to show a sort of model of what I thought should happen at halftime. As well as calmly talking to the players, I asked the Brig and Vimsy if they had any thoughts, and asked Dean to report on players who'd got knocks in the first half.

It was very Jean-Luc Picard in Star Trek, and there were some puzzled faces from people who were used to me being more Willy Wonka.

"Sandra," I said, to finish. "If you wish, you can nominate a player and choose either Vimsy or the Brig to scream in their face. Some players find it very motivational."

"Er . . . not today. Everyone's playing well."

She'd mentioned it casually, and I barely noticed she'd said it. But morale went up!

"Captain," I said.

Sam Topps got to his feet and yelled, "Come on!"

I suggested to Sandra that she might want to make observations for ten, twenty minutes, and she could suggest the first substitutions. While she concentrated, I watched her in my peripheral vision. The curse told me she was perhaps not as good as Jackie, but she was better than most. Giving her and Jackie two similar teams in the same division would have been fascinating. Jackie would very slightly outpace her in terms of coaching, but she'd pick up more wins through in-game management.

But they were both limited. They were both human.

A little over a year ago, I'd been bitten by a radioactive spider and now I could do all sorts of superhuman things. I'd suggested to Old Nick that I wanted the powers of a top manager and had even named Sandra's very own Pep as a point of comparison. Where did I stand?

My very first power was the ability to see player profiles. This had been bolstered every time I'd bought an attributes perk. Sandra could definitively tell if someone was better at heading than someone else, and she could have a good stab at filling in numbers like finishing or positioning. But having them all instantly appear and be reliable was staggering. There had been matches where I'd been able to leverage information about a player I'd never seen before to turn draws into wins. I had no doubt Pep would be able to do something similar, acting on instinct alone, and he had access to as many data analysts as he wanted. The data would come from scouts and data companies from all over the world. I was limited to what I could see with my own eyes. Advantage Pep.

I had the advantage, however, when it came to making tactical tweaks. While Pep seemed able to make drastic changes mid-half, I could do it at the speed of thought. Like most managers, Sandra would normally need to wait for an injury break or halftime if she wanted to do something significant. The curse also told me when opposing managers changed things. Today, against Cheadle, it was a basic 4-4-2 all the way through, but my perfect knowledge of my opponent's tactical instructions had saved me from disaster on many occasions.

Super Scout. It let me see how good players were and how good they could be. Incredible. It had led me to Ziggy, Raffi, and dozens more. Now Raffi was a £70,000 player, according to the market, and Ziggy was earning a living wage from the sport. Sandra had no such skills. Pep was good at spotting elite players who would fit into his system. It was rare that he made a bad buy. Still, I wouldn't swap my skills for any team of analysts.

"Why don't you let Aff take corners? He should be amazing."

"His delivery is too slow. He likes to chip to the near post. It winds me up. I like arrows into the six-yard box."

"Huh."

"Feel free to test it in training. If you can get Aff to put some pace on the ball, great."

Sandra tapped this into her phone. Why it didn't go into the notebook along with everything else was a puzzle for another detective.

What had come next from the perk shop?

Fantasy Football had been another monthly perk, priced so as to keep me grinding. But it had paid off big time. I never would have beaten Man City or Salford without the Triple Captain and Bench Boost perks, and the Free Hit had probably given me three or four extra goals in my time as manager. Buying the perk that extended the use of Fantasy Football from once per season to once per competition per season was another buy I was very happy with. Sandra had nothing of the sort. Pep? Maybe he could lift his players for a certain match against Liverpool or Arsenal, but he couldn't, for example, make his superstars run like crazy against Salford City. He almost certainly wouldn't *want* to, but that wasn't the point. The point was I *could*. And as I got more mature and experienced, maybe I could lift my players for key games, too.

"Andrew's blowing. We should sub him off."

"Go for it."

I watched with interest as she made the change and it happened on the tactics screen. I'd had a vague worry the curse wouldn't let my assistants change anything. It was much better this way. Maybe I could even get her to tweak the team in ways I couldn't. I'd have to use it carefully, but . . . But that was a thought for another day.

"Why are they playing high balls for Tony?"

"Panic. Habit. I'm hoping the more we train technique, the more they'll play simple passes as their default."

"They're just giving the ball away." Her face was set. Hard. I'd seen this look before, when the Met Heads were turning her world upside down.

I smiled. By raging and cajoling, I'd been able to greatly reduce the frequency of these aimless, almost cowardly punts, but there were still so, so many. But now I had an ally on the training ground. If there's one thing City didn't do it was kick a high ball to a short striker.

God Save the King had been expensive. 3,000 XP for a boost to one attribute for one player every season. I'd used it on Ziggy last season, and Henri this. In retrospect, I'd have been better off unlocking two more attributes, but at the same time I knew if I had the option to double the use, I'd pay double the price. Especially now that I better understood the relationship between attributes and CA. I could use the perk to turn CA 98 players into CA 100 ones. Probably . . . Sandra and Pep were fantastic at turning PA into CA, but they couldn't create PA like I thought I could.

Anyway, improving players with one click was fun. Fun was underrated.

"What's Youngster doing?"

"He's lost concentration. Normally Glenn spots it and yells at him. Sam will do it in a minute."

"Can I tell him?"

"Yes."

Sandra did just that. Youngster's eyes boggled and he spent the next thirty seconds checking his position and glancing at her.

"If he's playing DM, he needs to be able to concentrate for ninety minutes."

"I agree. So does he. But it's his first full season. If he stops improving, we can push him hard. Tell you what, though, if he shoots from outside the box you can go absolutely tonto."

"Bad, is he?"

I closed my eyes. "I think it might be my least favourite thing in the world."

One monthly perk I'd skipped had been Shocktober. It had offered me loads of pun-based advantages, especially against stronger teams. I was right not to buy it, but if there was ever a more serious, less complicated version I'd be interested. Such a perk would be useless for Pep, since his team would always have the higher reputation in any match. Me? I would spend most of my career managing the underdog, and the more we progressed, the bigger the underdog we'd be.

"I thought the other bench always tried to rile us up."

"I think they don't know what to do with you. Yelling at women doesn't fit their version of masculinity."

"Oh." She stood like a teapot. "Is that good or bad?"

"I don't care. Your job is to ignore it and make sure everyone else is ignoring it. Come down hard on anyone who retaliates or gets involved."

"Clear the bench, you said. That's funny. In baseball, it means the opposite of what you want."

Clear the Bench would be a good name for a perk. What would that involve? I blinked the thought away. I was in the middle of analysing my actual purchases, not dreaming up imaginary ones.

Some perks had given me more info in my match overview. Match Stats showed things like how many shots each team had taken. Fine, but nowhere near as cool as getting the match ratings. If you didn't pay one thousand percent attention, you might not notice that a player on the far side of the pitch was putting in a 5 out of 10 performance. Seeing the match ratings let me fix my weaknesses while exploiting those of my rival managers. Sandra and Pep had to do this by their personal feelings, which would sometimes be wrong.

Not always, though. She'd been frustrated by Andrew Harrison's shift at right back, and he was on 5 out of 10. She tried her best to hide her annoyance at Tony, who had been on 5 before his goal. I thought about asking her to rate the players at the end of the game to see how well they matched what the curse thought, but it seemed a bit cold. I'd try to be more subtle about it.

She said, "This system would work much better with someone like Michail Antonio as the lone striker."

Antonio was a very powerful, hard-working player who specialised in winning duels and holding the ball up. "He started in non-league. Did you know that?"

"I didn't."

"From non-league to winning West Ham's first trophy in forty-odd years. My ears prick up every time I hear about a Premier League player who started in non-league."

"I bet." She looked at me. "I notice you've changed the subject."

I shrugged. "We've got what we've got. When we play well, we get to the byline and do cut backs. All Tony has to do is kick the ball two yards in a straight line, and he's absolutely capable of doing that."

"I know this will be frustrating sometimes." She nodded to herself. "I have to learn patience."

I'd unlocked the History tab on a player profile. That showed me a summary of the player's career, such as which team they'd played for, how many yellow cards, their average rating, and so on, but so far I only had the data from the previous season. It would be very cool when it was fully unlocked, but that whole thing was quite far down my wish list. I felt that this perk chain would prove most useful when trying to recruit players. Being able to quote their stats from past seasons would make it seem like I'd been tracking them for years. Flatter them. Pep didn't need such a perk—players wanted to play for him.

Staff Search was a database of every coach, physio, and assistant I'd ever met. It was pretty top. A couple of times a week, I scanned through to check if anyone had lost their jobs—coaches were often sacked along with the manager who had brought them in. Pep had his own retinue that he took with him from club to club.

"Sandra, how do you really feel about having the same title as the Brig?"

She pulled a face. "I like him but it's a football club. I'm the football assistant. *Primus inter pares.*"

I pulled a face of my own. I'd had no choice but to give the pair of them the assistant manager title. First because the Brig's salary was so huge, then because Sandra wouldn't drop so far to be a mere coach. Two assistants was one too many, even in my distorted reality field. What was that phrase someone had taught me? Nothing odd will do long. At some point, I'd have to find a way to normalise having two senior employees who needed senior titles. Get rid of the weirdness. "First among equals. That's me, though. I need you both."

"What do we do if there's a dispute? Like if we're disagreeing on what training a player needs."

"Do what's best for the player."

"What's best is what I think." She shook her head. "Why's he here, anyway? Charlotte said Henri said he could make a killing . . . oh. Bad phrase. He could, you know, get rich as a mercenary."

"He could. I'm not a hundred percent sure why he's staying. I think he's got the same mania as you and me. We'd call it improving players. He'd call it improving young men. It's not what he's used to, but I think he's realising here he's got the best part of his old job without the . . . dark mode bits. The three of us want the same thing. I don't mind if you disagree from time to time. I'll think about the hierarchy and get that a bit more serious. I didn't really expect you to come. Sort of didn't let myself believe it was happening." I thought about the amateurish way I'd gone about checking her profile and convincing her to leave her golden cage. "How does Pep find new coaches?"

"Women's youth team matches, mostly. Don't worry, you're doing it right."

I smiled. Having a cocky edge would serve her well. Well, whatever Pep was doing seemed to be working for him, but I preferred my version—cold, hard facts.

The Injuries perk helped me keep track of what injuries my players had. I found it most useful during matches. It would say something like "suspected knee injury" and if it was possible I'd whip them right off the pitch. I felt I was getting fewer serious injuries than other teams in the league because of that. If it cost me a few points here or there in specific matches, it would pay off in the aggregate. And injured players were fucking miserable to be around. They were bad for morale.

Which brings us to Morale. Seeing that a particular player was happy or sad was pretty amazing, especially to a self-absorbed prick like me. By keeping an eye on moods, I could try to intervene to give a boost, or put a generally happy team on the pitch. Pep's teams were so good and the system so robotic that morale seemed less important, but given equally talented squads, morale could be an area where I'd outperform him.

And getting that squad was made slightly easier by having bought Playdar. It led me to talented players who were currently playing football, including back-garden kickabouts with their mates. I'd found a few good players with it, and since Jackie had taken the women's team off my hands, I'd been using it a bit more often. Sandra and Pep would only be able to find new players from within the world of football, but for them, that would be enough. As managers, they wouldn't need to worry about budgets the way I did.

And that was it. The budget. Money solved all kinds of problems for top managers. Money meant worldwide scouting and data analysis, meant being able to attract any coach you wanted, buy any player. At some clubs, the manager could buy two new right backs every summer until he found the right one.

Yeah, I thought, as I looked at Sandra again. I was on my way to becoming a top manager, but it wasn't clear I'd ever be able to bridge the gap between myself and managers who had billions of dollars behind them.

As we scored our third goal against Cheadle, I resolved not to worry about it too much. For now, I needed to focus on bridging the gap between Chester and Walsall.

"What do you think?" I said.

She scanned her notes. "I think you're underrating Trick. I think Andrew will never be a right back. I think D-Day is the personification of why City discourage players from dribbling—he'll drive me mad, the way he gives the ball away. I think Pascal is clever and I think Youngster is doing the work of one player." She looked at me. I was smiling. "What?"

"This is going to be fun."

Saturday, December 2.

Winning our FA Cup match against Salford had achieved three main things. First, it had pushed a tricky midwinter match against Gloucester back to some currently undetermined later point in the season. The Maxterplan in action.

Second, we'd got over forty grand in prize money, which was fast being spent on buying cast-off equipment from other clubs and gyms. (We now had a pretty decent amount of boxing gear; I had been getting pretty good on the speed balls before my progress got capped.) We had spent about five grand buying new, top-of-the-line goalkeeper swag, such as a little machine that spat table tennis balls at them to hone their reflexes. I'd have played with it but didn't want, as yet, to get my goalie skills back.

Finally, getting to the second round was very much the fulfilment of my promise to go on a cup run.

And the fans were loving it. Outside the Deva stadium were hundreds of them, waiting to board the coaches that would take them two hours to the midlands. Burly builders getting wasted from minute one, burlesque dancers, building society managers. Shy accountants, dog food tasters, colour experts, computer hackers. Politically left, right, and disinterested, marmite lovers, marmite haters, Max Best fans, Max Best sceptics.

The only thing they had in common, the only reason most of them would ever have occasion to talk to one another, was the local football team.

One coach was full and ready to depart.

"Just waiting for one more passenger," said the driver on his microphone. "I think that's him now."

Many curious heads turned—this was a break from the norm. How would the driver recognise one passenger in particular? As they looked, the answer revealed itself. Half the passengers started chanting, "Brig! Brig! Brig!"

The coach doors opened and the Brig climbed on board. The cheers were ear-splitting. He gestured that the passengers might want to reduce the volume by ninety-eight percent or so.

A guy who had been sitting on the front of the coach stood up. He was wearing a Chester baseball cap, sunglasses, and what was now plainly a false beard. He took the three items off.

"Best! Best! Best!" Almost everyone whipped out their phones and filmed me.

I took the handheld microphone sometimes used for bus tours of scenic Cheshire. "Good morning, ladies and gentlemen, welcome to Chester Golden Chariots, also known as Bobs Cars, note the lack of apostrophe which does *not* bother me. Bobs Cars, the *only* way to travel. Today's maximum cruising speed will be some seventy mph and with good headwinds we should arrive in glorious Mykonos in approximately thirty hours." I pretended to receive information from the Brig. "Ah, that's next week. Today it's two hours to sunny, er, Walsall. Which is in Birmingham, according to the internet. Please be careful if you go to a fish and chip shop. They have different words for everything. What we'd call a chip barm, they call a chip muffin." There was uproar. "What?"

"It's called a chip bap!" yelled one idiot.

"Sorry," I said. "It is the official position of Chester Football Club that chips served in a bun is called a chip barm. Isn't that right, Brig?"

I thrust the microphone in his direction. "Chip butty," he said, and winked at one of the female passengers.

"Is anyone here for the first time?"

A pair of hands went up. A couple wearing Chester kit, scarves, and bobble hats. "We are!"

"All right. If you're one of us, you get on the bus. I know you'll all make these dudes feel welcome. Make a right old fuss of them." I looked around. "I just wanted to thank you for your support," I said. "Sometimes the match is so intense I tune you out so I can focus and make good decisions. Especially if I'm playing. But the other guys hear you, and the opposition do, too, I promise you that. Oh," I smiled. "The referee, too. Not that we try to influence the refs." Good laughs. "It's going to be really hard today but we're going there to give our best and to represent the club in a good way. Getting to the third round could put millions in the bank, and my players are complete media whores, I've learned. They all dream of being on TV. So believe me, we're motivated. We're going for the win today." Big cheer. "And the Brig and I are going to travel with you until I start to feel that maybe it was a mistake." Another cheer.

On cue, the driver pulled away, drove thirty yards, and stopped. He opened the doors.

I grabbed the mic. "Okay, that was enough. See you at the match!"

We got out and walked to the Brig's car. I got in the back, because we'd pick Sandra up.

"Was that good, sir?"

"I think so. They'll share it on their socials. Talk about it. It'll be one of those things they bring up when I'm on a losing streak. 'Yeah, we lost today, but remember when he sat on our bus in disguise? He gets the club. We've got to give him time to turn things around!' You know, stuff like that."

"And perhaps these good memories will become useful when you, ah, take your break."

"Exactly."

FA Cup second round: Walsall versus Chester.

We arrived with a much larger contingent than normal. Being able to name nine subs and use five meant there was lots of anticipation. For some players, this would be the highest-profile match of their careers so far. For someone like Trick, it could be as good as it ever got. His last hurrah in the Cup.

And for one player, it was a bewildering and shocking opportunity to get some first-team experience.

I was "suspended" and Gerald May had picked up a slight back strain, so instead of naming two goalkeepers on the bench, I'd brought fifteen-year-old Benny to Friday's training and named him as the final sub today.

His dad, Nice One, had made his name and cemented his legend by taking Chester on two famous cup runs. I'd made sure the TV guys knew the story because they would for sure point their cameras at Benny in the warm-up and they'd play up that angle in the highlights package. Like father, like son?

I had no doubt Nice One had been a very good player—based on the crappy footage I'd seen, I wouldn't have been surprised if he was CA 100 or more. The internet said he'd had a season with twenty-six assists, which seemed like an accounting error. Benny had PA 40, so realistically he didn't have much of a future at the club, but I felt pretty good about giving him this moment. Especially because the fans were loving it. MD had texted, telling me his phone started blowing up when the news broke.

Benny. Good kid with good finishing. I couldn't put him on the pitch; Walsall were a very good League Two team, very solid, lots of rugged men who knew their business. They'd eat him alive. No, just being on the bench would make his year.

The lineup, then, was 3-5-2 with Ben, hopefully back to being my first-choice keeper; Glenn, Carl, Magnus; Aff, Raffi, Ryan, Sam, Joe; Henri and Tony. Average CA 51.1.

Sandra stood next to me as I filled in the team sheet. "No bronze, four silver, five gold, two platinum."

"That's right. This is our strongest team."

"And we still expect Walsall to play four-four-one-one."

"Yes. They're not resting their first teamers; they'll put out their strongest lineup. They really want to win this."

"What's your special secret trick for this one?"

I smiled. "When the Met Heads beat you, we spent three weeks plotting it. When Kidderminster beat us, they did the same. Three weeks! Their directors told MD. We've had three *days* to prepare for this one. No tricks up my sleeve, I'm afraid. We'll do our best and take the wins where we can. One win would be if the media pick up the Benny story. Another would be if they notice how sexy I look today. Either or both will help us get picked for the TV matches next season." I smoothed down the front of my expensive (for me) new suit. "What do you think?"

She looked me up and down. "If you'd worn that instead of your hoodie, I'd have come here a lot sooner." She fidgeted with my tie and took a step back. After another long look, she nodded. "But if you're really trying to get the TV companies back, maybe don't tell them off live on their own broadcast. But . . . hmm."

"What?"

"I thought you'd send me out to do the interviews."

"Oh. I wasn't planning to. Do you want to?"

"God, no. I just thought maybe it was good for the club's image if, you know. A woman. For the sponsors. Media attention."

I frowned and looked down at myself. "*This* is for the sponsors. Look at me. I'm pure eye candy."

She smiled and nodded. "All right, Max. You ready for the team talk?"

"Yeah. I'm going to read from a Wikipedia entry about the worst television shows ever made. Henri's going to love it. Wait till you hear about *The Briefcase*." That old, familiar look. Was I joking, or . . . ? "By which I mean to say I'll remind them of Walsall's strengths and weaknesses that we talked about yesterday morning and get the lads hyped without overloading them with information."

After doing just that, I took Benny, Pascal, and Robbo aside. "Benny, how are you feeling?"

"Great, Max! It's amazing."

"Yeah. It's just that you look pretty stressed. I was wondering if this was maybe a bit too soon for you. Maybe all this was a bit unfair."

"No! I'm ready. I'm ready to play."

His attempt to look fierce was extremely funny. "All right. But you're not going to play. You know that, right?"

He rubbed the back of his neck. "I mean, yeah."

"But you need to be *ready* to play. This is all about the experience, yeah? About learning the standards. And there's no better role model than Pascal. You follow him and do what he does. Right?"

Benny's head bobbed up and down several hundred times. If I'd met him in a bank, I'd have assumed he was off his tits on cocaine. "Right. Right."

"And if Pascal gets on the pitch, you do what Robbo tells you."

"Like what, boss?" said my goalie.

"Send him for warm-ups and whatnot. Point out weaknesses in their goalie and defenders. Get him ready to come on."

"Even though he won't."

"Right."

I don't think Robbo was terribly happy at losing his place again, but he shrugged. "You're the boss, boss."

I went around the dressing room checking on morale, looking at the tactics board, and talking to Sandra, the Brig, Dean, and Vimsy. There was nothing left to do. The truth was we had very little hope of winning and there was zip I could do about it. The best thing I could do for the team was to act natural, act chill, and the best thing I could do for the club was to look good and seed a story the media could pick up on. But there was no fire inside me. We would lose with a whimper, and it was my job to put a brave face on it.

The bell rang and the dressing room cleared out, leaving just me and the Brig. "Sir? You're not yourself."

"I had to inhibit. Be a good role model for Sandra. She isn't going to tell wild, irrelevant stories before matches."

"Are you still thinking about *The Briefcase*? You shouldn't go down internet rabbit holes late at night."

"I can't help it. They gave poor people a hundred thousand dollars and then said, yeah but there's this other family who needs the money more than you. So you could clear your family's debt but be seen as heartless, or you could stay poor but make viewers think you were a good person. Whoever came up with the concept needs to be locked up." The Brig was the wrong audience for this. Maybe Henri at halftime. "Do you like my suit?"

"I do. But there's something else. What's troubling you?"

I checked the room was really clear but lowered my voice anyway. "This has two–nil to Walsall written all over it. I don't see how we win unless we get some spectacular piece of luck."

"Perhaps this will prove to be your lucky suit, sir."

"I doubt it. Things are going great but days like these are never not going to blow."

Walsall's average CA was 80, which was a lot less than Salford City's. But Walsall's manager was clearly extracting the maximum from his players and that was one reason I was dubious about our chances. They had a good defence, solid midfield, and a powerful forward. They even had a central attacking midfielder, a true number 10, operating as the conduit between midfield and attack. If I had a better left back, I would have used 4-1-4-1 and let Youngster deal with the CAM.

But I had Trick. So it was 3-5-2, let our best lineup battle theirs, and may the best team win.

The best team started winning pretty much as soon as the whistle blew.

I found myself looking around the boxy stadium with its red seats and one oversized stand. We'd brought around 800 fans and they were making a decent racket over there. The home fans didn't seem very enthusiastic about the match. There wasn't much history between the teams, Birmingham had very little to do with Chester, and there wasn't a lot of jeopardy. If we hadn't beaten Salford, the attendance might have been 500 fewer.

I sighed and settled into my spot, trying not to let my depression show on my face.

It couldn't all be wins and knee slides and glory and chanting. There would be days like this, and plenty of them, where we were simply out-matched. If it had been a league game, I'd have concentrated furiously so we could beat them in the return match, but by the time we got to play Walsall as division rivals, sixty or seventy percent of the players would be different—on both teams.

So I spent some of the first half talking to Sandra about the players. She told me what she'd picked up in training and I either agreed or suggested something else for her to look out for (a polite way of telling her she was wrong). I said I had developed a weird connection with the group so I could make formation changes pretty easily but that she'd need to work on that.

Then she got interesting.

"You know you do easy sessions the day before a match?"

"Yes."

"Cutting edge teams don't do that. They go hard all the time."

My neck nearly snapped from turning. "What?"

"Yeah. Brighton, for example. Every session's a session."

Brighton were ripping up the Premier League on a fraction of the bud-get of other teams. They were amazing. "But if we can do that, players will improve faster."

"Yep."

"Shit." I paced around, thinking things through. "What about overload-ing? Red zones?"

"The way you rotate the team, you could do it. Ideally, we'd have proper fitness data. GPS trackers and all that."

I paced around some more. "I think . . . we have to start next season. I can't stress their bodies halfway through with a massive change like that. Right?"

She shrugged. "I mean, probably. But you could move set pieces to Friday afternoons and get an extra session in during the week."

"Can you do it so that . . . the extra session is initially easy and very slowly add to the intensity over the course of, like, months?"

"Piece of piss," she said.

For the first time that day, the quality of my smile matched the quality of my suit. "If you're giving me higher-quality sessions and *more* of them, remind me to double your salary next season."

At halftime, Walsall were leading 1–0 and we hadn't really troubled them. We'd battled hard to turn our 5 out of 10s into 6 out of 10s, and we hadn't been embarrassed. But we hadn't been able to get much goal threat going.

I gave a non-demented team talk aimed at negating Walsall's CAM. I also swapped Henri and Tony so we could ping high balls to the left where Henri might win some headers that Aff could get on the end of. It was pretty caveman stuff, really, and I actually felt embarrassed saying it in front of Sandra. But it was my job to try to find some point of advantage and that was all I could think of.

In the first minute of the second half, Carl fired a hopeful ball long in Henri's direction and a Walsall centre back headed it away. So that was that.

I shook my head while I blew air from my cheeks.

"Sandra. Manager chat."

My new assistant snapped her notebook closed and came over. I pretended to point at certain areas of the pitch while I asked for her thoughts about the latest developments in the Premier League. The Man United manager had seemed amazing at first, but this season things had unravelled very quickly, and the team had no passion or discernible way of playing. "That's the takeover," she said. "The uncertainty. You've got chaos here but it's all in your wake, isn't it? The players are following you. At United, there's a vacuum at the top and the players are sensitive to it. Also," she felt she needed to add, "United are shit."

"Hmm. What about Burnley? I went to see them in the Championship, and they were slapping teams morning, noon, and night. The manager looked like the next big thing, but they've lost every home game."

"It's a huge step from the Championship to the Premier League. He's trying to play like City with Burnley players. And he refuses to compromise his principles, so they keep getting smashed."

"What would you do?"

"I'd be pragmatic until I had the players to play my style. What about you?"

"I think I would, too. But I can't help but admire the guy. He's going to get himself sacked but . . . it's amazing."

She swept her eye across the pitch. "I think we should switch to four-one-four-one and see if we can't get some control of the ball."

I hadn't told her I knew we'd lose. "That's right, but . . ." I nodded to the bench. "If we've only got one striker, I can't bring Benny on."

"Benny? You told me you wouldn't use him."

"I told *him* I wouldn't use him. Now I'm thinking giving him five minutes at the end is the way we turn this loss into a win and move on with our season."

"Because of his dad."

"Right. The fans will love it. It'll show I'm keeping my promise to care about the youth team. Show I'm serious about giving these guys chances. It'll energise the whole youth system, not that it needs it, and it'll keep the fans warm on that long trek home."

"It's only two hours."

"Unless we score soon, I'm going to do it. He won't be nervous because I told him he wouldn't play."

"Ah, right. I see."

"He'll run around like a headless chicken and that'll be funny. That'll keep *me* warm on the long trek home. Anyway," I said, lowering my voice, "it's personal. My Chester story began with him. If I can't win, if I can't optimise or maximise, I'm going to keep the promises I made to myself. That's never steered me wrong." Now it was my turn to be surprised by *her* smile. "What?"

"That's how you beat me."

"What do you mean?"

"Nothing. Get your head in the game, Best. I'm not giving up just yet." She jabbed her finger at the pitch. "If *they're* still fighting, so am I." She took a couple of paces forward. "Joe! Wake up! Get tighter on that! Ryan! Tony was open! Drop a pass behind! Get them turning. Come on, boys!"

Sandra's burst of instructions got us further into the game but then we got dicked on a counterattack. It was weird to see. I couldn't remember the last time we'd conceded to a fast break.

I sighed and made a raft of subs, giving some minutes and the chance to be on the highlights to Trick, Pascal, Youngster, and Steve. Even though we'd lost Aff, our average CA only fell a few points, to 48.5. Still, we were closer to being half of Walsall's level, and my next change would be to replace Tony, CA 44, with Benny, CA 8. We'd basically be playing with ten men at that point. I mean, literally. Ten men and a boy.

Walsall made a bunch of changes, too, and that excited me very slightly. There was a big drop in quality from the first eleven to the subs, which partly explained why they weren't pulling up any trees in League Two. Still, though, it'd take a miracle for us to get anything.

We kept plugging away, though, and with Trick and Pascal fresh on the wings, we actually got a couple of decent moves going.

But Walsall recovered, shut us down, and that was that.

With the clock on eighty-five, I called Benny over and while I talked to him, I swapped him and Tony on the tactics screen. I would have taken Henri off, but the next match was a week away so there was no point resting him. Behind Benny, Vimsy was getting the board ready.

"Did your dad ever tell you about how he played in the FA Cup?"

"All the time," said Benny. I think he was trying to roll his eyes, but it didn't work. Here, now, he was buzzing. If he'd ever failed to understand what his dad had accomplished, this experience had brought it home.

"Great. So now you'll be able to tell your own kids."

"What do you mean?"

I turned him around and showed him his squad number was being displayed on the board. "Stay near Henri. Look for flick-ons. Keep your shots low." I pushed him and he stumbled, dumbstruck, to the side of the pitch. Tony was waiting for him. They exchanged a high ten and I gave Tony one, too. Before I let him take his seat behind me, I mumbled in his ear. "One for the fans, mate."

"Yeah," he said, too tired to think of something more apt. His smile told me how much he approved. He'd made his debut once and he'd been around the club long enough to know all about Nice One and the son who was following in his footsteps, if slightly higher up the pitch.

When Benny's name was read out, the Chester fans reacted with a moment of stunned silence followed by a massive roar.

The roar saturated Benny with more energy than a human being could hold—he ran around like a feathered domesticated animal whose body ended at the neck. He sprinted to the right, then to the left, and then he needed a breather. Absolutely hilarious. I couldn't help but turn and grin at my support staff.

When the match clock struck eighty-nine and the chance of a comeback was less than zero, the Chester fans pumped up the volume. A song was dusted off from the olden days, starting with the dads in the crowd. It was derived from the football staple "Nice One, Cyril" and for the first time, I had an inkling of how Benny's old man got his weird nickname. It didn't take long for the young'uns in the crowd to learn the lyrics—most had grown up hearing them and the memories came back in a rush of nostalgia.

Nice One, Smasho
Nice one, son
Nice One, Smasho
Let's have another one!

My smile was starting to hurt now. I looked at the bench again, wondering who would have been around the last time those songs had been heard in a cup match. Vimsy? He wasn't a Chester guy. Dean? Far too young. No, this was a moment for the real Chester old guard. The MDs and the sponsors. The granddads. I'd have to listen to *Seals Live*. Boggy would be in heaven.

On the pitch, Henri won a header—finally! The ball whizzed towards goal and Benny was on it like a flash. Young, nimble, eager, he zoomed towards it . . . Could he? He couldn't, could he?

A defender casually jogged towards Benny's line of attack and the teenager crashed into him, landing with his limbs all over the place. Bit of a harsh lesson in standards, that. I felt Vimsy nodding behind me, appreciating the defender's mastery of his position.

The ball was collected by the other centre back, who touched the ball to the right back. He had Trick haring towards him, so he played it straight back to the previous guy, who lazily dabbed it back to the goalie.

But Benny had one thing going for him: He was too inexperienced to realise he'd had his arse handed to him by a wise old hand. What he knew best was the simple virtue of running flat out almost all the time. So he redirected his latest sprint from the centre back to the goalie. Only when the goalie shaped to pass the ball to the fullback did Benny give it up as a lost cause. He put the brakes on and turned, wondering if he should press the fullback. It seemed wrong—Trick was there. So what was he supposed to do?

The goalkeeper thought better of playing the short pass and decided to whack the ball to the halfway line.

For some mad reason, the ball didn't ever get more than three inches off the turf. It flew straight and true, as though a line drawn by an analyst in the studio, at Benny's heel. It hit the heel, bounced back the way it came, and went into the net while the goalkeeper fell to his back and covered his face.

Henri jumped for joy, and he and Trick ran to Benny, arms aloft, ready to celebrate the kid's first-ever professional goal. But Benny, now that he'd worked out what had happened, ran into the goal, retrieved the ball, and dodged his elderly teammates on his way back to the halfway line. He put the ball on the centre spot, squeaked "Come on!" and was ready to go, pacing up and down like a de-aged version of me. A panther, a caged tiger released and out for blood, a cold-hearted assassin, calculations complete and ready to execute.

"Oh my God," I said.

"What?" said Sandra.

The board went up. There would be four minutes of injury time. Our fans had gone berserk—full savage, threatening to shake the stadium apart with their dancing and screaming and shouting.

"We can do this," I whispered, and after a second, I was in full flow. On the touchline, screaming at my players to attack. Oh, what I would have given to push a defender forward. I set the entire team to make forward runs and made them all press.

Walsall, despite being well-coached and full of experienced, disciplined players, were shaken. They couldn't keep the ball. Pascal showed why he considered pressing to be his superpower. He terrorised his fullback, the left mid, and even the left-sided centre back. They hoofed the ball long when they saw him coming. In the middle, Ryan Jack had rolled back the years, Youngster was full of running, and Raffi Brown looked ten feet tall.

Headed clear by Ryder.

Jack picks up the loose ball. He chips forward to Brown.

Brown has options! He chooses right.

Bochum steadies himself and fires a low cross.

Lyons is there!

He slides and lifts the ball over the keeper . . .

. . .

But it's saved! Incredible reflexes. The goalie has made up for his previous error.

That wasn't true. We were only having these chances because of the goalie's mistake.

Williams receives the ball with his back to goal. He looks for support.

He lays it off to Brown. Brown finds Youngster.

Youngster plays it simply for Jack to run onto.

His first-time pass makes the defence turn.

Bochum is running onto it . . .

But the defender slides in.

Throw-in to Chester.

The defenders are all going forward.

Cavanagh looks to his manager, asking permission to go forward. He's told to stay.

Carlile's throw reaches the penalty box.

Alton flicks it on . . .

And there's mayhem! Pinball in the Walsall area.

Benny falls over. Was he fouled?

The ball is cleared.

One last chance for Chester.

Williams gathers, hits a quick cross. It's headed out as far as Jack.

He chips it forward—more chaos!

The ball somehow falls to Brown. He hits the post!

No, it was saved. The keeper got a hand to it.

Corner to Chester. Surely the last chance of the game.

Score and they'll earn a replay at home.

Yeah, and I'd be able to play in it. That would be something.

Ben was waving at me again. Should he go up for the corner? Well, why the fuck not? He wanted it—he was almost on the halfway line. He sprinted forward.

Ryan Jack with the corner.

All eyes on him.

The referee stops him from taking it. He wants a word about some jostling around the Walsall keeper.

Now he's ready.

The corner's hit—hard and fast.

Cavanagh rises highest.

A thumping header!

But it's saved!

Chester's goalkeeper has a header pushed over the bar by his Walsall counterpart!

And that's the final whistle.

Walsall survive a late scare to progress to the third round.

I rushed onto the pitch, headed straight to the penalty area where almost all my players were slumped. They'd worked their arses off and had got no reward for it. But I was buzzing. I was thrilled.

I embraced Ben—he'd kept us in the game in the first half when Walsall had been coming at us from all angles. The curse rated him 9 out of 10 and that was before he'd nearly scored the equaliser.

Then I picked out a few others. Henri had worked tirelessly to create space for others. Ryder and Carlile had stretched themselves trying to keep a lid on much better players. The midfield had been dominated but not overrun. And Benny! I gave him a hug. The little brat was pretending to be devastated we'd lost because that's what he thought Max Best would want.

I waved the team over to me and led them towards the Chester fans. They clapped and cheered and when we took a few steps back and pushed Benny forward, they hit maximum volume.

Now, finally, the debutant allowed himself to smile and laugh.

Good times. But something was missing. I called Livia and asked her to hand the phone to Sandra.

"Where are you?" I demanded.

"You said you wanted me to be statesmanlike and do all the handshakes with the other team when you forgot or refused."

"Fuck that. Get over here."

By the time she crossed the pitch to where we were, someone had spotted Nice One and forced him to cross the advertising hoarding onto the pitch, where he stood arm in arm with his son as the fans and players sang his song.

Nice One, Benny
Nice one, son
Nice One, Benny
Let's have another one!

Maybe I should have let Sandra do the post-match interviews. I was drunk on football.

Max, you nearly got back into the match there at the end.
Nearly, yeah.
You needed a slice of luck.

Whoa, whoa, whoa. You think because we're a non-league team, we don't know how to score goals? Mate, we don't have eighty-million-pound sex pests on our team, but we know how to stand still while a goalkeeper fires the ball at us from eight yards away. We can do the basics. There's no luck about that.

What were you thinking when your goalkeeper went up for the corner?

I was thinking, gosh, I hope he scores. [Attractive toothy laughter.]

What did you make of your team's performance?

I'm ecstatic. I can't believe it, really. I think this is the first time I've been surprised by them like this. I know what they can do and when they do it, I'm happy. But to compete with Walsall like that for so long, stay in the game, and then to yeah, get a lucky bounce and really try to hammer that opportunity . . . it's so good. That's pure character, that. I didn't do anything. A few of our good results, yeah, not to be smug about it but they're because I was clever or had a plan or something. Today was all about them. I didn't think we could do that. That's blown my socks off.

What did you say at halftime?

I was trying to talk about this TV show I've been reading about, but no one was interested. I'll have to find a subreddit or something. That one's even too niche for Henri.

Young Benny made quite an impact and there were great scenes at the end with his father.

Yeah his dad was really kind to me when I first came to Chester. It's just a mad story, what happened today. Mad. It's totally messed with my head. Years from now I'll be talking to you saying, "Oh you were there the day we beat Walsall," and you'll be like, "No, Max, you lost," and I won't be able to process it. It feels so much like a win. I wouldn't swap this for a win. No chance.

There's a big prize for the winners. A third-round tie against a big team.

I wouldn't swap it. Walsall's next game might be Tottenham away and good luck to them. They'll make millions. Our next game is against Swindon Supermarine, and we'll make a cash loss on the day. We'll get to the levels we want, but in the meantime, I wouldn't swap places with Walsall's manager. I wouldn't swap places with anyone.

After I'd done my media duties, I stared at my experience point counter.

XP balance: 2,226

No debt! And managing against a tier-four team had been giving me *eight* XP per minute, and unlike against Salford I hadn't ruined it by playing half the match. This haul was enough for me to buy the December perk, but it wasn't the time to think about that. No, this was the time to stare into space with a vaguely happy smile, idly humming the "Nice One, Benny" song. The Brig came to rescue me. "Ready to go, sir. We need to stop off at the dressing room."

I fell into step beside him. "Top. Where's Sandra?"

"She wants to go on the team bus."

"Sick of me blabbing on?"

"The difference in the level of detail when you talk to her and when you talk to me is striking. I'm grateful you simplify things for me. But no. She said it's two more hours where she can get to know the players."

I shook my head. "I've struck gold there."

"Platinum, sir."

Huh. Had I ever spoken about my player ranking system with the Brig? I thought I hadn't, but perhaps I had. Or perhaps he'd overheard us or decoded Sandra's squiggly handwriting. I rubbed my face. I was suddenly very, very tired. "All right. The plan. A week of top training. Win in the FA Trophy, win a few league matches, Christmas number one."

"And then a break." He pushed a door open and held it for me.

"And then a break." The Brig was smiling as I passed him. I realised we were back in the dressing room. He *had* mentioned that, but it was the expression on his face that puzzled me most. "What?"

"I got you something." He tapped an expensive-looking travel bag.

I took it and carefully unzipped it—I didn't want to break it and have to pay a thousand quid for a new one. I reached in and pulled out one of my shit hoodies. One of the ones the Brig hated so much. "Mate," I said. I had a whole outfit in there, right down to my most comfortable trainers. It was like he'd poured me a whisky and fetched my slippers. "What's this all about?"

"One simply wishes to remind you who your best assistant is." He tried to keep a poker face. "Actually, it was Emma's idea. You might say she gets the pre-assist on this one."

"The two assistants thing *is* weird," I said, as I loosened my tie. "In the summer I think we'll relabel you head of performance or something like that. How does that sound?"

He fake-coughed with his hand covering his mouth. "I have seen at other clubs there is a more suitable title."

"Oh?"

"Director of high performance."

"Absurd. I love it. You're hired."

"Very good, sir."

THE TWELVE DAYS OF CHRISTMAX, PART 1

i.

On the first day of Christmas, the cosmos gave to me . . . a perk to drive me crazy.

Sunday, December 3. Match 6 of 22: Chester Women versus Litherland Remyca Women.

I took a break from scouting bigger teams and went to check in on our women. Jackie had set them up in his favoured 3-5-2, no surprises there, and no surprises that the ladies had surged ahead in CA. Charlotte, for example, was loving being our star midfielder and loving Jackie's sessions. She'd exploded to a CA of 35, far ahead of everyone else. Dani had improved to 28, which was pleasing. But six of our core squad had hit their limits. I planned to address that in January with a few well-chosen transfers.

Since taking over, Jackie had been doing well, except for a 5—0 loss to Leeds in the FA Cup, which no one could blame him for. I was sure I'd have lost by more. Other results had gone well, and I was sure we were already the second-best team in the league. The only matches of interest would be those against league leaders Altrincham, who'd won all their games, and our return against Wythenshawe.

I went to stand near Sandra, who had come as a fan of Charlotte and Kisi (CA 19, substitute). Henri spotted me from behind what looked like three scarves and made a beeline. He pulled one of the scarves down. "Max. I have been thinking of some ways I might help the team."

"Oh, have you?"

"Yes. I would like to discuss certain drills that Sandra might want to include in our sessions."

"No. It's her day off. Try tomorrow."

Sandra smiled. "It's okay, Max. I'm always happy to talk to our support striker."

Henri poked his tongue into his cheek, then realised he was being teased. "You refer to Max's plan to sign," he sighed, "a player he berated us for even mentioning. He threw such a tantrum as to make me shudder to even *think* the name Goliath. Did you hear about the balloon?"

"No," I said. "And she won't."

Sandra raised her eyebrows and led Henri away by the elbow. "Let's go over there so he doesn't try to paint over the truth."

I shook my head. The story of how I'd downplayed Goliath's abilities by using a helium balloon to mimic him *could* go down badly. I'd need to get ahead of it and tell him the truth—that it was intended to get my players to concentrate on their own jobs.

I turned to my latest dilemma: the monthly perk.

December Special Offer

New perk available for the month of December: The Panopticon

Cost: 2,000 XP

Effects: Permanently adds perks to the perk shop. Purchasing these supplementary perks will add tranches of squad data to the manager screen, ultimately allowing a manager to oversee all players registered with the club. Each squad (e.g., various age groups) must be purchased separately. New perks will appear in the system store when new age groups or club-linked squads are created. For example, one perk will add a squad page for the men's reserves (if applicable), another will add a squad page for the women's under-eighteens (if applicable), another will add a page for any newly created disability teams.

For once, the curse was trying to explain itself, but I struggled to get it clear in my mind. When the light-bulb moment finally arrived, I realised I had no choice but to buy it. I'd be able to add all the age groups to my screens, and thus track every player in the Chester system. Currently, I had the men's and women's first teams and nothing else. If I bought this perk, then bought the men's under-eighteens, I'd be able to track Vivek and Kian just like I could track Henri and Raffi. In Vivek's case, that would mean not having to drive to Manchester to see how he was getting on.

As I added youth teams for the women, and more age groups for the boys, I'd be able to get them in my screens, too.

I quickly checked what a *panopticon* was, and wished I hadn't. It was a very sinister (to me) concept for a prison where inmates can be viewed but can't view the jailor. A prison of the mind. Lots of the monthly perks had been copy-pasted from my own brain, but this one had Old Nick's fingerprints all over it. The name was diabolically perfect. It made me feel queasy about buying it, but not to the point that I would let the chance slip.

Attractive as the perk was, it was really time to get stuck into the Contracts section of the player profiles. Knowing how much other teams were paying their players would be incredibly useful, and I needed it as soon as poss because I'd have to rescout everyone I was interested in, ideally before the January window closed.

So, yeah. Nick wanted me to grind, and he'd got his wish. I mentally cancelled a couple of nights out with Henri and Emma, and replaced them with trips to watch games.

I bought the Panopticon perk, mentally sighed as the perk shop filled up with 2,000 XP purchases for the various age groups and the Chester Knights, and looked around for something to cheer me up.

On the pitch, Dani—wearing gloves, outrageous—shaped to do a one-two, but simply drifted past the defender without passing.

I smiled.

That was one of mine.

ii.

On the second day of Christmas, the cosmos gave to me . . . a call-up to England C.

Monday, December 4.

Secretary Joe never interrupted training, or one of our meetings, or a team talk. He thought of himself—wrongly, in my opinion—as less important than the players, and the idea of entering the inner sanctum of the dressing room would never even occur to him.

So when he ran-walked to me while we were doing one of Sandra's complicated passing drills, nearly being bundled over by retreating defenders and hit by multiple balls, I knew it had to be something big.

I waved at Sandra and she blew her whistle. Everyone stopped, many guys with heads in their hands. She was pushing us, all right.

Joe told me the headline.

"Everyone in," I said, and Vimsy shouted it out. Soon I was stood with my arm around Joe facing a semi-circle of inquisitive faces. "Got some news."

I gave Joe a little shake. "Oh. Me?"

"Yes, you."

"Um." He held up a little piece of paper like he was Neville Chamberlain. "We got an international call-up!"

"You're joking," said Joe Anka. Everyone was looking round, wondering who was good enough to have been chosen to represent their country. "Is it Pascal? Germany have a shit team these days."

"Not *that* shit," said Raffi, who immediately hugged his mate to show it was a joke.

"Magnus, where are you *from*?" said Steve Alton.

"I am eligible to represent nations from three continents," he said.

Secretary Joe pointed. "It's Raffi."

There was a fairly lengthy silence. "But he's English," said Sam. "Or is it for Jamaica? Your dad's from there, right?"

Raffi was utterly bemused. "I suppose I could play for both. But . . . not from the National League North. What's going on, Joe? This a prank?"

"No!" said the secretary. "It's England C."

Lots of the players went, "Oh!", but there were plenty who were even *more* confused.

"I've heard of England," said Pascal. "I've even heard of England B. In the past, the B team was used as a sort of reserve for the main England team. But I have never heard of England C."

"Me neither," I confessed.

Secretary Joe blinked. What kind of football genius had never heard of England C? "It represents England at non-league level. It's the best players from non-league, Max. I'm surprised you never got a call-up, though it only plays once or twice a year."

I frowned, wondering about the timing. I'd played a few games for my former club and then been prevented from playing for months. I shook my head. This wasn't about me. "So . . . all these scouts. Some were from *England*." That wasn't right, though—the scout profiles I'd seen at games had never said anything of the sort. "But . . . they were all from clubs."

Joe nodded. "The England C manager has a network of mates who work for clubs. They tell him who's good, who to look at, parallel to doing their own jobs. Raffi might be the only player from this league. I'm sure the rest will be from the National League."

"Fuck me." I scratched my eyebrow. This was mental. "Let's just roll with it! Round of applause for the England international!"

Raffi looked embarrassed and when the applause got a bit quieter, said, "Maaax . . . let's train."

"Yeah, good call, good call." I rubbed my chin and pretended to get serious before launching into a version of "It's Coming Home." "Maybe we could tweak the drill to three lions on his shirt! Serina Brown not screaming!"

Raffi had to stand there while we all, including Henri and Pascal, sang England songs at him. He finally burst out laughing and accepted a big, big hug from me, then from Glenn, and then everyone wanted a go.

While the man of the moment wasn't looking, I asked the Brig to whizz off and buy an England shirt with Brown and the number 8 on the back. We'd make him wear it in training.

"Joe, when's the match?"

He looked at his paper. "Nineteenth of December. It's a Tuesday."

"At Wembley?"

"Moss Lane."

"Where's that?"

Again the look. How did I know super advanced things but not the basics? "That's Altrincham, Max."

"Right, I've been there!" I got the attention of the group again. "Lads! Hands up who wants to go to . . . wait for it . . . Manchester! To watch our mate play for his country? Yeah, that's what I thought. Joe, get us a hundred tickets and three coaches. Glenn, can you get stuck into this? Help with the planning? Sandra, are you coming?"

"Any excuse to go back to Manchester."

I tilted my head. "Have you had girls called up to England?"

Her eyes flickered towards the big group that was around Raffi. They were listening intently. "Might not be a good time to talk about it."

"Go on."

"Loads, Max. Like, half the girls you met got international call-ups."

I nodded. I understood why she didn't want to discuss it there: It could make Raffi's achievement seem small. But I didn't agree. "Well, Raffi's my first." I closed my eyes and imagined what it'd be like. Running out wearing full England kit, in Manchester, his home city, in a stadium that shared its name with his dad. "And you never forget your first."

iii.

On the third day of Christmas, the cosmos gave to me . . . a seasonal gift from Bonnie.

Wednesday, December 6.

I'd planned to go to watch Sheffield United versus Liverpool in the evening to get some red-hot Premier League XP, but instead, well . . .

It started in the morning. At exactly quarter past eleven, Jackie called me.

"Max. Can we meet quickly over lunch?"

"Maybe. Just tell me something first. You woke up to watch *Bargain Hunt* and you found an urgent email, so you called me right away. Right? Right?"

He seemed confused. "I've been up since eight."

"Hmm." That didn't fit my theory. Which meant . . . which meant he was lying. "Hmm."

"I'll be in your office at twelve."

He hung up.

Hmm.

Jackie seemed pretty fresh-faced and alert. Maybe he *had* been up since eight, as he claimed. I looked around my office, which was still festooned with pictures of Jackie Reaper the player. I didn't have much ego when it came to decorations, but perhaps I'd hang up a Raffi Brown England shirt. That'd always bring a smile to my face.

"Er . . . what are we doing?" I had suddenly realised I didn't know why I was there. In my head it was to solve the mystery of whether Jackie woke up after eleven. Not that I cared if he did—I just wanted to prove my theory.

"Waiting for Bonnie."

"Bonnie?" I said, astonished. "What about?"

"No clue. But she's been building up to this for ages, I could tell. She's been *almost* talking to me since about a week after I came back. Almost. But for whatever reason, today's the day."

"She wants to leave. She wants me to sack you. She wants to play striker. She . . . what could it be?"

There was no point guessing. I never would have got there in a million years.

She came in and we sat around the chess board where it was a lot more casual. After some chit chat, she embarked on her narrative journey, not making eye contact with me except for the occasional glance to see if she could tell what I was thinking.

"We're from Carlisle. You know, up by Scotland."

"I know Carlisle," I said. Mum had said I often played as Carlisle United when I played Champion Manager. "It's the same latitude as Mexico City."

Her eyes popped open. "Is it?"

"No, I made that up to sound smart."

Her face crumpled into an annoyed laugh. "Please, Max. This is hard for me."

"Oh. Soz."

She nodded and regathered herself. She took a breath. "We had to move. Ended up in Blackpool. That was all right for six months or so, but we had to move again. Chester. We keep moving south."

"We?" said Jackie.

"My family. My mum." She inhaled. "And my sisters."

"They're all kleptomaniacs," I said. "That's why you have to keep moving."

Bonnie laughed far more than the joke deserved and that's when I realised just how nervous she was. "No, it's . . . It's football."

"What?" I said, laughing from amazement.

"Sorry, can we get a cup of tea?"

I pulled a face at Jackie. "Get her a tea, you dick!"

"We could go to a coffee shop," he suggested. "Max's treat."

"No, let's stay here. Private is good. There's that little kitchen thing, right? For the credit card people."

"Fuck that," I said. "Whatever this is, it's a VIP situation. What do you think, Jackie?"

"I reckon so."

"Let's go get a proper brew. Yeah?"

I led them upstairs and got buzzed into the top floor of the credit card place. I'd been in a couple of times to talk to my new superfriend and next season's main sponsor, Agatha. Her gorgeous PA had better things to do than make me and two randos tea and coffee, but she did it anyway, and even offered to let us use a meeting room.

"Oh, no, they're much too fancy. I wouldn't feel comfortable in there," said Bonnie, and that melted the PA's heart in a big way.

"You get yourself in there and you let me know when you want a refill. Maybe you could pose for some selfies one day. Loads of us in here are big fans of yours."

Bonnie was taken aback that the woman knew who she was, but Bonnie was the captain of the women's team and with her large frame was extremely distinctive.

So we settled into the plush seats and admired the view. Cheshire in winter, with a light drizzle and glowing grey clouds. Idyllic.

"Max," said Jackie, looking back at the PA's desk. "I'll give you one thing. You have a way with beautiful women. The more perfect they look, the smoother you are."

"I'm not smooth. I'm normal. They're just people. It'd be a crying shame to deny them my jokes just because they have good cheekbones." I scoffed and added, "Anyway, you do all right, too, mate. How many times have I seen a coach come to our dugout to scream abuse at us, only to see Livia and back away, struck dumb?" I took a sip of my tea. "The way to a man's heart is by making a cuppa just how he likes it. Fortunately, Emma is a sorceress. She even makes Typhoo taste good." I stood and looked down. The view of the pitches was amazing. "Have you ever been to the Nou Camp or the Bernabéu?"

"Both."

"I bet the views are like this. You pay a hundred Euros and the players look like ants." When I went, would I be so far from the pitch the player profiles wouldn't even kick in? Surely I'd see them from anywhere inside a stadium? Surely?

Jackie went to the window. "Ah, Max. This is nothing. This is like the middle section. Now imagine another one up there." He pointed. "Another thirty thousand people. You thinking of playing in Spain? Managing? Real Madrid?"

I scoffed again. "Where's the challenge in that?" I remembered we were supposed to be listening to Bonnie and retook my seat. She was giving me a very curious look. "How's your coffee?"

"It's amazing. I think . . . I think it's the best coffee I've ever had."

I nodded towards the PA. "She's a genius working with top-of-the-line materials. Like me managing Real Madrid."

Another unreadable expression crossed Bonnie's face. She put her cup down and covered herself with both hands. I frowned at Jackie and he frowned back. Bonnie recovered. "I'm twenty-five. My next sister is twenty-three. Then there's a twenty-one-year-old. Dad's out of the picture, permanently. He left after the youngest was born and you can imagine mum thought that was that."

"Right," I said, confused about where this could go.

"Then a few years later, mum's preggers again."

"Different dad?" said Jackie.

"Oh, hell yeah!" said Bonnie. "She never said who it was. We never met him. One-night stand, I think. Oh, God. Can't believe I'm telling you this."

"You don't have to," I said, mixing elements of sympathy and annoyance.

"So, you've probably guessed the rest."

I laughed. "I have not. I don't have the first fucking clue what's going on. But I'm enjoying your company."

Bonnie cleared her throat. "It's, er . . . It's my youngest sister. Angel. She's fifteen now."

Time felt like it stopped. She'd been blabbing about Angel when I wanted her to sign a contract. "Angel is a person?"

"What else?"

"Could be an *angel*," I said, and I got *two* weird looks that time.

Bonnie bit her bottom lip. It almost seemed like she was close to tears. "What happens is, Angel joins a football team. Six months later, we have to leave. I don't want to leave Chester, but I can't keep her away anymore. If it doesn't work now, this time, then . . . then she might accept it's never going to happen. But . . . She saw your Harry Styles video and lost her mind. She saw you coaching Dani. She believes you gave me a contract for *me* and not as a way to get to *her*."

That pissed me off. "And you don't?"

"No, Max, I do. I do. But I have to protect her. That's my job. Isn't it, Jackie?"

"Course it is," he said, even though he knew as much about the situation as me, which was almost nothing.

"I don't want to have more conversations about why I do things," I said. "That's all I fucking get."

Jackie tutted, but Bonnie reached out to touch my hand. "I know. I know. We all know. I'm here because you're a good person." She sighed. "And because I can't hold Angel back anymore. Not since you appointed Sandra. That was . . . You didn't know it, but that was dynamite."

I kept my mouth shut, so as not to get worked up into a self-righteous, self-pitying state.

Bonnie continued. "Let me just . . . Right, so . . . So Angel is a striker."

"How old is she, exactly?" said Jackie.

"She's fifteen. Nearly sixteen. February fourteenth. Obviously." I checked with Jackie—he didn't know what was so obvious about that date and Bonnie never explained it. To me, angels collocated more with Christmas than Valentine's Day. "She's a striker, and a good one. Very good. Too good."

"Too good?" said Jackie. He was taking up the slack left by my dip in mood.

"Like scoring a hundred goals in one season."

"A hundred?"

"She got to ninety-nine in the third from last game, decided it was a cool amount, and refused to play the next game. She changed her mind and played the first minute of the last match."

"Where she scored right away."

"Exactly."

Jackie was smiling. "Are you telling me there's a hundred-goals-a-season striker in your family, and you're only just now thinking to tell me about it?"

Bonnie rubbed her hands, one over the other in an endless circle. "Yes. But it's not that simple."

He considered that. "The reason you have to keep moving. That one-night-stand guy. He's bad news."

"No. It's not that. I mean, he might be. Mum's not the best judge of character, right? No, it's . . ." Bonnie took a big inhalation of breath and let some of it out. "I know it's hard to believe about my sister, but . . . She's beautiful. Absolutely stunning."

I waited for the next part. It didn't come. "So?"

Bonnie turned to me. "So men lose their minds over her! Especially when she plays football. Stalkers, creeps, maniacs, madmen. She attracts every stark-raving lunatic for miles around. Three months in, we've got three restraining orders. Four months, we're staying with friends. Five months, the road outside is full of plain clothes police. Six months, we've had enough and leg it."

I finished my tea and stared at Bonnie. She was in earnest. I tried not to smile. "You're telling us . . . you've been reluctant to let us take a look at your sister because she scores so many goals we'd want to sign her, and she's so irresistible that every man who lays eyes on her will instantly turn into a stalker?"

"Max," complained Jackie.

"I just want to know what the conversation is," I snapped.

"That's the long and the short of it, I suppose," said Bonnie.

Confusing. She was serious but she *couldn't* be serious. "So what do you want? You want us to not sign her? We've been not signing her every day since you joined the club. We're doing great at that."

She gave me another exasperated smile. "You should sign her. But no media. Don't put her on posters. Sign her as a player and don't do the rest. Dani signed with Ruth's agency. Angel can sign with her, too. Ruth will understand. Maybe a few sponsors who understand Angel won't be available like a normal player. One photoshoot, boom, that's it. It's really hard, Max. She knows she needs to be protected but she loves the attention. She can't get enough of it. And we understand she could make a lot of money, but it's not worth it if she winds up dead in a ditch. But you and Jackie, you're as good as it's going to get. And Ruth and the Brig. It's all, like," she stopped. "It's her only chance to do what she loves most."

Her words hung in the air.

"Bonnie," I said. "I like you. I think you're amazing. I'm glad you told us this and it's obvious that it's been hard for you. So if what I say next is, like, accidentally offensive, I'm truly sorry. But your team is going all the way to the top. I'm looking for players who can cut it in the Championship and the WSL. Scoring a few goals in primary school doesn't impress me much. There's no way she's as good as you think. And I believe you when you say she's good-looking and you've had bad luck with crazies, but there's loads of good-looking people." I thought about her story. "Maybe not in *Carlisle* . . ."

Bonnie did that thing where your eyes and cheeks go big and then deflate. "If I bring her to training tonight, will you be there?"

Jackie was out on the pitch setting up little cones, being assisted by Jude and Jill. I was vaguely surprised to see Jude there, but it turned out he wanted to learn at the feet of the master and tried to join Jackie's sessions as often as he could.

On a little row of cheap but amazingly comfortable camping chairs, which looked like super-soft versions of the famous Hollywood director's chair, sat me, the Brig, Ruth, and Bonnie. The latter was too nervous to join the session. Ruth was intrigued. If Bonnie was right, she would get a new client, a superstar, and doing a good job would mean making as . . . *little?* money from her as possible.

I was beyond relaxed, for two reasons. First, there was no chance that in *football* terms this Angel was worth *any* level of hassle. And second, women always massively overrated the objective attractiveness of their friends and family. Which was sweet and heart-warming, but I'd learned to totally discount their opinions. I'd also learned the hard way not to trust any photos, ever. Nah, this would all take ten seconds and then I planned to whip Ruth, the Brig, and maybe even Bonnie and her plain, talentless sister out to dinner. Nando's, maybe?

The women emerged from the dressing room in dribs and drabs. Dani, Maddy, and Kisi in one little chicken wing. Charlotte, Pippa, and Julie McKay in a squirt of piri piri sauce.

"Was that your stomach?" said Ruth.

"I think there are moles here," I said, raising a foot as though looking for a hole in the soil. The noise happened again. "Fine. I forgot to have lunch. Got distracted, didn't I, Bonnie?"

"Sorry, Max."

"No, I'm sorry if I sounded dismissive. Of course it's awful to have to keep moving around. It's just the main thing is the security fears, right? And we've got the Brig to help us. Help you. See, now that he's around I've kind of gone from worrying all the time to thinking oh holy shit." I was up on my feet before I had time to think what a bad look it was.

A girl in a beanie and gloves had jogged out onto the pitch, after Mo but before Robyn. Her player profile told me her name. Angel.

ANGEL		
Born 14.2.08	(Age 15)	English
Acceleration 12		
	Handling 1	Stamina 5
	Heading 9	Strength 4
		Tackling 4
	Jumping 5	Teamwork 5
Bravery 5		Technique 5
	Pace 10	preferred foot R
	Passing 4	
Dribbling 5	Positioning 2	
Finishing 20		
CA 5	PA 155	
Striker		

Even from a distance it was obvious she was attractive, but that wasn't what I was responding to. Along with a lot of mediocre numbers—CA 5, teamwork 5, tackling 4—there were two extraordinary ones.

Angel had PA of 155. And her finishing was 20. A hundred goals a season? No wonder!

"What is it?" said Ruth.

Oh. Problem. How did I explain my reaction? I hadn't even seen her kick a ball yet. The first thing that came to mind was to make a joke of it. Pretend like she was *so* beautiful I had lost my mind. That was patently dumb, but what else could I do?

The solution I chose was to flee the scene.

I jogged to Jackie and asked to borrow his whistle. He had the Dani whistle, and gave it to me.

"New plan," I said, calling out to the group. "Finishing drills."

"Fucking hell, Max," he said, pointing to his meticulously placed cones. "We need to get this right for the Alty game. We were sloppy against Litherland."

"We won well enough. Ah, yeah, fine," I said. We needed to get promoted. "Fine, fine. You do that. Angel, Robyn, with me."

I walked towards the goal to my right, realised I wouldn't need the whistle, and threw it back. Robyn grabbed a few balls and Angel looked from the group of women to me.

As she came closer, her appearance crystallised. She was tall and moved with the graceful power of a tennis champion. She was gorgeous in a kind of innocent-yet-bratty way, and I felt uncomfortably aware of why her looks would trigger some men to go tonto.

"Will you take some shots, please?"

She looked back at the main group, then hit me full beam with a pair of vivid blue eyes. "Don't you want me to warm up with the others first?"

I found myself frowning. I'd been *this* close to doing as she wanted. I had the strangest feeling I'd just passed some sort of test. "No."

Robyn rolled a ball towards her.

I took a couple of steps back and watched as Angel played a simple side-footed pass back into the goalie's arms. Her striking movement was very fluid. I felt I could already mentally sketch out how she'd make various kicks. There was an elegance and economy of effort that was incredibly suitable for a striker. Her height was the icing on the goalscoring cake. Her jumping was low, but her heading was fine. I imagined it could be trained to be a threat from crosses.

She hit a couple more side-footers, and then hit one with her instep, medium strength. She wasn't going to overextend until she'd warmed up, which was absolutely correct.

"Come here, please. Robyn come out about five yards. Angel, low square pass to here." I tapped a spot as though flattening a mole hill. She played the pass I wanted, parallel with the goal line, and I did the spinning, dipping chip I'd done against my former club. Robyn watched helplessly as it sailed over her head and into the goal behind. "Can you do that?"

"Yes," said Angel.

I waved my finger in a circle to say we should switch places, and then I hit the appropriate pass to her. She met it sweetly and did a decent approximation of what I'd done. "Needs more spin," I said.

"No, it doesn't," she said. "That was perfect."

"Robyn, you can join the others. Thanks."

"Yes, Max."

I pushed at my eyebrows. This Angel situation was way out of control already. She had the potential to be one of the best strikers in the country, and easily the most marketable. She could make *millions* from her sporting career, and her agent could cash in, too. That could be me, via Ruth. Millions of pounds. Her own perfume, her own makeup line. Documentaries, reality shows, announcing her next club live on Instagram to an audience of fifty million. There were less talented women who'd turned minor fame into a billion-dollar industry.

But Bonnie didn't want that for her sister. And I didn't want another striker with low teamwork. "What do you want?"

"What?"

"You're a decent striker. Your sister wants to keep you out of the limelight. What do *you* want?"

"I want to go join the session. And by the way, I'm an *amazing* striker. I'm the best you've ever seen."

I smiled. "I've seen a mirror, mate. I'm the best player there has ever been in every position there has ever been. I choose not to play striker because it's boring. There's no challenge. All right. Finish the session if you want and I'll talk to Bonnie about other clubs you might want to join. I've got mates at Tranmere."

Her bravado turned to dust. "What? You've seen enough? After three shots?"

"I've *heard* enough."

Her eyes darted left and right as she replayed our conversation. "But . . . you like cocky players. You like Henri Lyons."

"Confidence is good. Intelligence is better. When I tell Henri his shot wasn't good enough, he's intelligent enough to know I'm probably right. He'd think, like you, that his shot had been perfect. But he'd ask how it could be better. Because he has a brain."

That hit the spot. "I have a brain."

I extended my arms and turned ninety degrees in either direction. "When it comes to football, this is my city. Football will be played here the way I want it to be played."

She tried to turn me to ash with her laser vision, but she hadn't unlocked that perk yet. After smouldering for a bit, her jaw moved left and right. "What was wrong with the shot?"

I moved to the edge of the penalty box and got her to do the same. I pointed at the goal. "Block this. When I say go, go." I did a couple of kick-ups. "Go."

My volley was flat and straight, and she intercepted and blocked it easily.

"Again," I said. She came back to her starting position, and this time, I put lots of spin on my kick-ups, as though I was spinning a basketball on my fingers. "Go," I said, and she hared back towards the goal, but as she stuck her leg out to block the ball, my shot spat up like a leg cutter in cricket, up and over her knee.

"Again," I said. She came back slower this time, staring unhappily as I spun the ball. "Go," I commanded, and she started to run. But she stopped when she saw I'd kicked the ball much too far to the right—a full yard wide of the post.

Of course, it spun back *inside* the post, crossed the goal line, and almost seemed like it would keep going round in a spiral. I probably could have done more to keep the smugness off my face.

I waited, hands behind my back, to see how she'd react.

Her expression was unreadable, and she was almost inaudible when she spoke next. "I can do that."

Bad answer. "I know you can. That's not the problem. The problem is the hunger for improvement. The problem is you remind me of another player. Good striker. Didn't listen to the coaches. Didn't listen to me. Thought he knew better. Thought he was already good enough. Didn't want to add strings to his bow. Thought he was so good a rubbish shot from him was better than an open goal from a teammate. He was an absolute *idiot*. It took me a year to get through to him, and I don't have a year to spend on any one person. It's no good having all the talent in the world if you're too stubborn to let us coach you and if you think you've already got all the skills." I paused and thought about Tyson. "We coach *teams* here. Most games we need you to play the percentages. Some games we won't get *any* shots, and we'll need you to suffer and sacrifice. You need to be willing to learn to pass, learn to press, learn to shuffle and slide, learn to leave your ego in the dressing room."

"Like you."

I nodded. "Yeah. Like me." I looked up at the floodlights. "The games I'm most proud of aren't the ones I scored no-look backheel nutmegs, or outrageous free kicks, or direct from a corner, or dribbled the length of the pitch to score, or—"

"All right," she said, annoyed, and after a tiny glare, we both smiled and looked away.

"The games I'm most proud of are the ones where I suffered. It's absolutely mad when I think about it, but that's how it is. Kidderminster. I did everything I could. I was so frustrated I had nothing else to give I was almost in tears. Kettering. Two–nil down with nine men but they had to peel me off the pitch. Salford. Forty-five minutes, most of which was spent being absolutely rubbish and feeling like a piece of shit but at the end of the match I knew I'd done all I could to help the team get over the line. Bonnie's one of my favourite players because she plays like that *every match*. I'm really not interested in selfish players. If I ever think you're putting yourself before the team, you're out. I don't care if you score five goals against us every time you play for your new club. Long term, teams win."

"I'm a team player."

"Team players don't score a hundred goals in a season. That's a shot every time you got the ball. How many assists did you get that year?"

She shrugged. "Loads."

"I bet it was three. A hundred goals, three assists." I shook my head, smiling slightly, then got serious. Bonnie wanted us to not use her in promotions, to not put her on posters. We'd have sponsors offering double the money if they could make Angel the face of their campaigns. We'd get hundreds of calls a day from media pricks. I pinched my nose. It sounded like a fucking nightmare. I'd need to hire someone to take all those calls. I'd have to get extra security. "You know what? Enough talk. Let's see if you can hack it in my world."

"What does that mean?"

I nodded in the direction of Jackie and we walked to him. "Jackie. You doing a little match later?"

"Quick one, yeah. Ten minutes."

"Make it twenty. I want to see how Angel does with one slight restriction."

Jackie half-closed his eyes. "Restriction?" He looked at the girl he knew was a striker, and in a moment of remarkable perception guessed what I was planning. "No, Max. Don't. We haven't even seen her play!" But his pleas fell on stony ground. I didn't so much as twitch.

"What?" said Angel.

Jackie put his hands on his hips and looked up at the few stars that were visible. "You can play. But you can't shoot."

iv.

On the fourth day of Christmas, the cosmos gave to me . . . a chat with the constabulary.

Friday, December 8.

For once at training, there was absolutely no friction between my two assistant managers, and that was because the Brig spent almost thirty minutes on his phone. Finally, he murmured something to Sandra, and she blew her whistle.

"Max, the Brig wants you."

I left the session, not quite willingly, since dicking about with footballs all morning was better than most jobs, but not very reluctantly either, since I knew I wasn't improving. "'Sup, dude?"

"Would you please take a shower and get dressed? I need to take you . . . somewhere." His tone was sombre but not urgent, so I strolled, deep in thought, to the showers. Inside, I considered Sandra's first full week of training. It was hard to tell with such a small sample size, but we'd had a full week, no Tuesday-night match, and it had gone well. The canary in the coal mine, I had decided, was Ryan Jack. He was a super talented guy who would respond to good coaching. It was hard with him because he was so very old at thirty-five, and at some point I knew his CA would fall off a cliff. But for now, him dropping below CA 60 was a disaster, keeping him at that level was fine, 61 was good, and 62 would be amazing. That's what I told myself, anyway.

After a week of being top dog, Sandra had added a point to his CA, taking him back up to 61.

And the guys had been quietly impressed with her sessions. I didn't get the sense of delirious happiness like when Jackie had been the manager, but a general feeling of, yeah, that was really good.

I zipped my hoodie up, grabbed my kit bag, and followed the Brig to his car. Not long after, we pulled up in the car park of the local police station, and he handed me a note to give to the officer on duty. The note said *MAX BEST,* which was really fucking weird.

"I can't go in with you, sir."

"What's going on?"

"It's better if I don't say anything."

"Am I going to be arrested?"

"No. If I had received information *that* was about to happen, we'd be on a speedboat right now, heading out to the Isle of Man where we'd take a helicopter to Dublin. Quick trip down to Cork, onto a cargo ship where we'd pose as deckhands, a role where I would excel and you would flounder, for several weeks until we landed in the new world. At which point I'd hand you your new passport and spend three weeks drilling your new identity into you."

"Cliff Daps?"

"It would be a name I thought you could remember, sir."

I looked down at the paper he'd given me. This was absolutely mental. I walked away from the car, up some steps, pressed a buzzer, looked into a camera, approached the desk, and handed the dude a piece of paper with my name on it.

He nodded and turned away, picking up his landline. Thirty seconds later, a woman I'd met precisely once emerged through a door.

It was the partner of DI Barton, the stupid fuck who had tried to frame Mr. Yalley instead of going after my actual murderer. This woman was his girlfriend and according to Old Nick, she was just as culpable as Barton. I'm sorry to say that as soon as I saw her, my face went hard and I very nearly stepped out. And I'm even more sorry to say that the only reason I stayed was that the Brig had spent three thousand of my pounds already, and I was on the hook for an unspecified future amount. There were nights where I woke up, heart pounding, wondering how I would find fifteen to twenty thousand grand in a hurry.

"Mr. Best," she said, not attempting to smile. "Would you come this way, please?"

She led the way to a small interrogation room. Next to her sat a beefy boy who at first I assumed was there to protect her from me, but later I realised was her new partner.

She told me her name, but I wasn't listening for the first minute or so. I was trying to control my fear and fury at being put in this tiny room with this woman I despised. It was only when the beefy boy offered to get me a tea and left the room that I started to relax.

"What was your name?" I said.

"Rowan."

"DCI. Rowan."

"Just detective inspector. But, fingers crossed, I'll get a promotion soon."

"Yay," I said, with minus a hundred percent enthusiasm.

The tea arrived, and Rowan explained what the eff was happening.

"Mr. Best, this is a courtesy call, so to speak, to inform you of developments relating to your case."

"My murder?"

"We class it as attempted murder, since it didn't technically succeed. I am happy to inform you that this morning, we made an arrest."

"Oh."

She waited for me to say something, but the word *arrest* had fried my brain. I suppose I'd completely abandoned all hope of justice ever being done. "We just wanted to let you know before we informed the media."

"Where's DI Candyflip?"

"He's no longer on the case. I'm the senior officer now."

I closed my eyes. There was very little going on upstairs, just when I needed it. "So . . . you're in charge, now it's all solved. Sorry, what?"

She glanced at her beefy boy. "New information came to light."

I tapped the desk, an unconscious expression of my bewilderment. "So, where was he?"

"Who?" Rowan seemed confused.

"Welly. Welly. My hooligan murderer. The world's biggest twat. Welly."

She stared at the one-way slash two-way mirror that made up one half of one wall. Who was behind there? Something told me it was the Brig. "It wasn't Welly."

That woke me all the way up. She'd made a fucking horrendous mistake. "Of course it was. He threatened me, he was at the match, he's a violent prick. What's happening?"

"Mr. Best, please. It wasn't him." She cleared her throat. "Er . . . you reported that your car keys were missing, right? And you correctly surmised that whoever attacked you took those keys and held onto them. Something like a trophy. I'm not a psychologist, but I think they were taken in a panic, an option for an escape vehicle, perhaps. Later, they turned into a trophy—he buried them in his garden like treasure—but as we closed in on him, they became a noose around his neck. This individual dug up his entire garden looking for them. It was pure chance we found them after a tip-off. He must have shovelled the keys into a pile of earth as he was digging, not noticed, and reburied them, again without noticing. One in a million, but panic will do that to a person."

I leaned forward, neck long. "What are you saying? What are you talking about? It's all gibberish. Go to the start. Who are you talking about?"

She inhaled. "Mr. Sullivan. Father of Chris Sullivan. Football name Sully. You cut him from the youth team."

"No. It was Welly."

"Then why were your car keys buried in Mr. Sullivan's back garden?"

I couldn't get my head around any of it. "What?"

She sighed. "We just wanted to let you know that we got him. We got him, Mr. Best. It took some time, and I would privately admit we made some mistakes, but we got him."

"You got . . . Sully's dad?" I'd convinced myself it was Welly. Welly made sense. Just the name Welly was enough to convince me. "But, er . . . how?"

"I reinterviewed Mr. Yalley and your physio. They had been interviewed before, of course, but I had a new angle: Sullivan. The assailant had known you would be in the Blues Bar, because you told everyone, and everyone saw Mr. Sullivan there. So why was he seen by your physio coming *towards* the Blues Bar, outside in the pouring rain with no umbrella, when just moments before he had been indoors?"

"But he was with Sully. His son."

"He sent him to get some cash from the cash machine on the far side of the stadium. I'm sorry, Mr. Best, but it was definitely him."

"Oh," I said again. It was such a mindfuck. But the confusion didn't last all that long. I'd check all this with the Brig, of course, but it was certain that my assistant had been the real driving force behind this investigation. There was something very strange about Rowan's tale of the keys. Maybe the Brig would explain it, maybe he wouldn't. "Huh," I said. Sullivan. What had he said to me? That I wouldn't survive the season, something like that. That *prick*! He'd get what was coming to him. I tried to get my face as neutral as possible. As robotic a face as I could achieve. I imagined I ran a social media company and didn't actually experience human emotions. "Where is he now?"

Rowan, despite being an absolute idiot and probably a racist, had enough emotional intelligence to see that I was seething. She backed away a half an inch. "He's in custody. You don't need to worry about him."

"Worry," I said, trying to smile. "I just want to talk to him. Ask him why he did it."

"That won't be possible."

"Quick chat," I said, trying to be flirty. It died a death.

"That won't be possible."

In seconds, I was on my feet, smashing my chair into the floor. It didn't break. I'm not sure it even dented. "I'll kill him! I'll fucking murder the twat!" I kicked the chair away, noting in the non-insane part of my brain that the beefy boy was, while scared, standing in front of Rowan, protecting her from me. I allowed myself one last surge of anger, then I showed him my palms and backed into the far corner. It wasn't far enough to really make a difference. "I'm sorry. I'm calm." I took a breath, and Rowan pushed the guy's arm down. That was the moment I stopped despising her. I formed my hand into a fist and lightly punched the wall a few times. "He ruined his son. I tried to undo it, but what chance did I have?" I grimaced, thinking of Sully playing safe passes so his dad wouldn't shout at him. "Did he hit his kid?" Past tense. He would never do it again.

"I can't answer that."

"How long will he get?"

The beefy boy answered. "The problem, Max, is that he didn't use a gun or a knife and has no priors. The weapon he used was lying around. So it's hard to say it was premeditated. There was no financial gain, racial or religious motive, and your full recovery counts against us in terms of sentencing."

"Say a number."

"It's almost a wild guess at this point, but I'd say seven years."

"Seven years?" I cried.

"Seven to fifteen. If he shows remorse . . ."

Seven years and I'd need eyes in the back of my head again. I'd live in fear again. Dark mode was looking more attractive by the second. I bit my thumb. "What if . . . what if I forgive him? Forgive him in court? When could he get out?"

The police looked at each other. "Why would you do that?"

They were onto me. Better to keep my mouth shut. "No reason. I wouldn't. Course I wouldn't."

The Brig was by the car. He put his fingers to his lips, drove to a wood, and we walked a hundred paces from the car. Then he told me a few things.

The clue had indeed been in Dean's email draft from after the attack. Sullivan jogging towards the scene of the crime, but from totally the wrong direction. Dean recognised him from times he'd been the physio on duty at youth team matches, but hadn't known Sullivan had been in the Blues Bar mere minutes earlier.

And then the smoking gun: my car keys. The Brig had snuck in when Sullivan was away. Used a metal detector. Dug the keys up. Then a lot of surveillance by the Brig and his old army buddies, trying to catch Sullivan going to places I frequented. But he kept his nose clean. So the Brig let it be known—he wouldn't say how—that the police were closing in on Sullivan. This was true, thanks to the Brig. He'd made a deal with the Chief: Barton had to go, Rowan would take over, the Brig would hand them the culprit on a plate. Case closed, and Max Best would say nice things about them.

That pissed me off, but I understood it. Honey to catch the fly or whatever.

So then, what must have been a hilarious scene for those watching on various hidden cameras, Sullivan digging up every inch of his garden for three days. Then him watching in horror as a police technician found the keys in thirty seconds, exactly where the Brig had replanted them.

I could see it vividly. The good-looking murderer in his puffy jacket, being turned around while handcuffs were put on. His wife and son looking out of the kitchen window, bewildered. *"You have the right to remain silent." "What's happening?" "Your dad tried to kill Max Best."*

A car came past and we watched it. It struck me then how quiet the wood was. Where was all the life? The noise?

"So that's it," I said, and we stood there for ages. I should have seen some beetles. Some spiders. Surely? "I don't feel good."

"No."

"What about his kid?"

"I don't think that's something for you to worry about, sir."

I picked up a club-like branch that had fallen off a tree in a recent storm. You could use it for sport—hit a stone with it and you've invented golf. Cover it with dog wee, call it "The Patriarchy" and you've invented modern art. Or you could swing it at someone's head so that they wouldn't be alive anymore.

I gulped, tears in my eyes.

"What are you doing?" said a man who called himself John Smith.

"Little insects love logs and stuff," I said, as I went away from the road to find a suitable spot. I placed the branch down under a shrub, then grabbed some twigs and made a sort of tent of twigs. A twig-wam. "Little shelter for them. First it's shelter, then it's food. Then it's a coffin. Circle of life." I watched for a minute, waiting for the first little beetle to scurry into his new home. Nothing came.

"Perhaps you might want to tell your friends the good news, sir."

"Good news?" At first I literally couldn't think what he was talking about. As I wiped away the tears, I understood. But no. "A man tried to kill me for absolutely no reason, and now he won't see his son for seven years or more. The son's going to blame *me*. And at some point, the dad'll be back on the streets. What's good about that?"

The Brig pulled a face. Twisted his mouth in a rare show of uncertainty. "I know, sir. I know. But while your feelings may be complicated . . . Emma's will be quite simple. In fact . . ." He checked his watch and thought.

"What?"

"We could drive up and tell her in person. And then you'll see what it means to the people who care about you."

"What does it mean?"

"Finality. Think of it as an early Christmas present."

I'd had enough of this wood and started making my way back to the car. "That makes you Santa Claus, I guess."

His upper lip quivered. "Call me jolly old Nick." I stopped dead and must have looked at him with something like horror, because he explained himself. "Like the song."

"Song?"

"Jolly Old Saint Nick," he said. "It's a Christmas classic. Saint Nicholas performed miracles." His philtrum twitched again. "Like me."

8

THE TWELVE DAYS OF KIDSMAS, PART 2

v.

On the fifth day of Christmas, the cosmos gave to me . . . FIVE YELLOW CARDS.

Saturday, December 9. FA Trophy third round: Chester versus Swindon Supermarine.

Swindon Supermarine. Amazing name, amazing logo. The badge looked like a World War II fighter plane with a letter *S* snaked round it. They played in the Southern League Premier South, yet another competition I'd never heard of. How many leagues did we have in this country? There were more leagues than disgraced former Prime Ministers, and more teams than disgraced former cabinet members, and that was saying something.

As it happened, Swindon were second bottom of their distant, little-known league, and I knew before even seeing them warm up that they would need a Christmas miracle to beat us. I very nearly put Sandra in charge of the game, but it was too soon to be handing out presents.

I was in a bleak mood. There had been something comforting about the thought that it had been Welly who tried to kill me. He was a nobody, a hoodlum, a hooligan. He lived a life of violence and couldn't conceive of anything else. Sullivan was a normal, middle-class dude. A dad. A dad dude. He wore smart clothes and had a good haircut. If people like him were going around murdering wonderful people like me, then how could we even survive as a society?

The Brig had been right about Emma, though. Yesterday, when we'd driven to Newcastle and gathered the Weavers around their kitchen counter to tell them the police had arrested my killer, Emma had been ecstatic. Shocked, yes, but so utterly happy to get closure on a horrible part of her life that I had to pretend to be equally happy. Maybe that had been the Brig's plan. To stop me scrabbling around in the mud looking for dung beetles.

Her dad had listened in silence, then left the area without a word. He came back a minute later and showed me a bottle of wine. "Château Lafite," he said. "1983. Was a gift for winning a big case. Chap said to save it for a special occasion."

"We could have it with Christmas dinner," I said, before pretending to get shy. "If I'm invited, of course. I don't plan to play in the Boxing Day match. I can have a few sips."

"Perfect," said Sebastian, pulling the bottle away.

The Brig made the tiniest little noise. I glanced at him. "Actually, let's have it now. Truth be told, it was John who solved the case. He deserves a taste. Only a taste, though, since he's driving."

"We've got a spare room for the hero of the hour," said Rachel. "Why don't you stay, John? Tell us all about it."

"Oh, yes please," said Emma.

The Brig seemed stuck. He wanted to accept the offer, but didn't think it was his place or had a date back in Chester or whatever. I helped him out by opening the fridge and making a show of thinking about dinner. "Great, sorted. Start with the celebration wine, then onto the Aldi plonk until John gets delightfully sozzled. I'll make us some frozen pizzas." I slapped my hands together, job done.

Rachel pushed me away from her fridge. "Tempting, Max, but I think I can rustle up something a little more serious."

Sebastian had uncorked his antique wine and was gathering big glasses from a high shelf. As he was ready to pour, he said, "So, John. Tell us the story."

The Brig hesitated. "I really can't."

"Oh, you bloody can," said Sebastian, pulling the bottle away just as the first drip was about to fall.

I intervened. "You'll get the outline, not the sketch, and no follow-up questions." Sebastian nodded. "You can tell them what will be said in court, right?"

"I . . . yes." John seemed satisfied with that compromise. Those details would soon be a matter of public record.

"Sebastian and Rachel are masters of discretion."

"What about me?" said Emma.

"Sebastian and Rachel are masters of discretion."

Emma folded her arms. "You cheeky sod!" But she had to laugh.

That had been an evening of celebration, of free-flowing wine, and, once we got past the stuff the Brig couldn't really talk about, an evening of free-flowing conversation.

But now I was in the Deva stadium, my first time since learning the identity of whodunnit. Sullivan. Godactualdammit. And I could feel the wine in my legs. I tried to focus on the good things. Our cup runs. Our improving team. My growth in skills. And my Emma.

Emma was here, in Chester, up in the VIP box, smiling easily, talking to Crackers and Sumo and the new board. She wanted to spend some time with me, but she was also hoping to get a glimpse of Angel, our agency's new client. She wanted to see the fantastical creature Ruth and I had described. For some reason, she had been expecting Gemma to be in Chester, but it hadn't happened. I left her with MD and went to do football manager things.

In the manager's room, I couldn't concentrate. Kept getting flashbacks to the police room, to being told who had tried to kill me. I told Sandra what I expected from Supermarine—4-4-2, wholehearted but limited—and invited her to propose one of our seven formations and pick a team to fit. I pitched it as a sort of fun test of how well she'd absorbed my principles, but let's be honest, there was no mystery to what I did. She pitched a 4-2-4 with attacking roles for Trick, Pascal, and D-Day, and a rest for all our important players. She suggested I might want to play right back, since I'd made Andrew Harrison do it.

"If you play there, you'll learn how hard it is and you'll think twice about dropping guys into that position."

I shrugged. "Fine. I can play right back."

She frowned. "I was joking."

"No, let's do that. We can rest Carl. I feel like kicking someone, anyway."

She laughed, but she stopped when she saw my face. "Max, Magnus can play right back."

But I'd already started filling in the team sheet.

From Cheshire Live

Chester 5 Swindon Supermarine 0: Back to His Best?

Max Best led Chester to a thumping win over Swindon Supermarine in the FA Trophy today, playing in an unfamiliar right back role. From there, wearing the captain's armband, he shut down Swindon's dangerous left winger, linked beautifully with Pascal Bochum, and sent in a series of inch-perfect crosses which Henri Lyons and Tony Hetherington feasted upon. Best scored a hat trick of assists, and his first stray pass came in the seventieth minute when he was obviously bored to death. After that mistake, he switched from a contained, masterful examination of the narrow confines of his role, to spraying increasingly dramatic passes all around the pitch.

These passes drew gasps of admiration from the small crowd, but also drew the ire of Chester's new assistant manager, Sandra Lane, who subbed Best off and gave him a dressing down, much to the amusement of the rest of the Chester squad.

At the final whistle, I raced to be first to the shower, leaving Sandra to do all the boring stuff. I got dressed and went up to find Emma to see if she wanted to go out for dinner or visit Henri's House of Hams or go to the Christmas market in Chester, or what.

She wanted none of those things—at least, not yet.

"You've got a special guest," she said, and I felt someone come up behind me.

"If it's the Ghost of Christmas Past, tell him to fuck off. I signed up to his newsletter and the unsubscribe button is fake."

"Max," said an unfamiliar voice. It was possible I'd never heard it before in my life, which was bonkers.

I turned and saw Chris Beaumont, often known as Goliath. He was a gigantic man, six foot five, four foot wide. His goalscoring record wasn't impressive; he averaged less than one goal every four games, but I'd been pursuing him relentlessly for weeks, making increasingly demented offers to his club, Banbury. I'd finally hit on a deal that they couldn't refuse.

"Chris! Why are you here? You shouldn't be here. Do Banbury know?"

He smiled. "They know. It's all right. This is Rob. My agent. And my mate."

I shook hands with the guy. I'd seen him in the last twenty minutes when I was on the touchline. The Parasight perk had kicked in and was telling me that a handful of agents were visiting our matches. This Rob guy represented talent worth £300,000. I was guessing that meant six or seven decent clients. He was probably scraping a living. He seemed cool, though. We'd had a couple of quick chats on the phone, mostly him checking if I was serious about this move or not. "Your girlfriend has been making us feel at home," said Rob. "She's a much better salesman than you."

I squeezed Emma sideways. "No doubt. But you didn't say why you were here. I mean . . . you're not scouting Swindon Supermarine, are you?"

Chris laughed. "I've been getting loads of messages about how you're the best penalty taker in non-league. I wanted to see the competition."

I explained it to Emma. "Chris is a bit of a penalty specialist."

Rob said, "That left winger of theirs is highly rated. Banbury were looking at him to get crosses in for Chris. But you made mincemeat out of him."

"Oh, I wouldn't say that," I lied, smugly. "Oh, hey! How did Kidderminster get on?" They had already been knocked out of the FA Trophy and had played their scheduled league match.

"They won," said Emma.

"Oh. There goes Christmas number one."

"MD was keeping an eye on it. He said Christian Fierce got his fifth yellow, so he'll miss their game against your former team. And one of their strikers hobbled off."

"Oh, no." I smiled.

"You were hoping to be top of the table for Christmas?" said Rob, looking at his phone. "They're six ahead now, and there's two matches before the twenty-fifth. You *could* . . ." He trailed off. He didn't believe what he was about to say.

"It was a long shot but it would have been nice for my holiday. We told you about that, right, Chris?"

He nodded. "Manager taking a two-week break in the middle of the season. Anyone else, I'd think it was batty. But you deserve it. I just . . . The timing? With the transfer window?"

I shrugged. I wasn't sure where he'd got two weeks from. Not from me, that's for sure. "The transfer window is irrelevant, really. I'm not selling anyone, and I plan to have all my business done by nine a.m. on January first. For once, I'm being ultra, ultra professional about it. No one can be mad at me." The thought struck me as ludicrous. "They will, though."

He sipped his drink. "You asked why I was here. I just wanted to talk to you. See the place and talk to you. It's all loopy. You're basically talking about making me the most expensive player in non-league, *pro rata*. I . . . I'd like to know why."

I hadn't expected him to bust out the Latin. He sounded like he had gone to a good school. How had he ended up playing football instead of rugby?

I pushed my bottom lip out. "To me, you guarantee promotion. Over your career, you've scored one goal every four games. Here, you'll score two a game. If teams sit back, we'll smash them. If they come at us, we'll smash them. I just want to smash everyone and get out. And if I make you a cult hero and double your wages for the rest of your life, that's fine by me, too."

"I know you don't want to talk tactics too much before we've signed," said Rob, "but we can't quite understand how you're going to do it. It's something of a stumbling block."

"For one thing," I said, with a light laugh, "Henri Lyons, the best striker for miles around, is going to use his substantial gifts in service of you. It's like you start your first day in an Amazon warehouse and Jeff Bezos is bringing you coffee and every fifteen minutes he gives you a little shoulder rub. It's like your first day working for Microsoft and Bill Gates meets you at reception, shows you around, and sets up your computer for you."

Emma boggled. "Does Henri know about this?"

"Yes. And he'll make my life miserable. He'll whine and sulk. But he'll do it."

"Why?"

"Because there's one thing he values almost more than anything else. Purity. What I'm proposing will be truth and beauty writ large. Very large," I added, giving Chris a playful slap on the nearest (colossal) arm.

"Max," said Rob, smiling, "you're trying to persuade *her*."

"Yes."

"You should be trying to convince *us*."

"Ha! I don't think so. You know it's right. You're excited, and you're right to be. But you think this would be a fun little adventure, a chance to make a bit of extra cash and have an amazing story to tell. This isn't what you think it is."

"No?" said Chris.

I stopped smiling and felt my eyes start to blaze. "No. It's much, much more than that. People will remember the next six months of your career for as long as they live." I had got myself worked up and I had to shake the excess excitement off. "Whoo! I feel evangelical. Do you mind if I say something a bit unpleasant to Emma?"

Curiosity. Anxiety. "No."

"Bebs, Chris here is often held up as some kind of avatar of all that's shit about non-league." I put my hand on his shoulder and looked right at him. "But if he lets me, I'm going to turn him into the apotheosis of all that is good and holy about English football. Low blocks are an abomination, and Chris Beaumont will be my paladin, bathed in cleansing light, slicing through the palisades. Together, we will purify the National League North." The air was crackling with mad energy, as billions of competing universes were born and spun off with that precise moment as the start of their timeline. In half, my high priest of football schtick made Chris sign for Chester; in the other half, it repelled him.

In *this* universe, Emma said, "That's nice. Oh, that reminds me. MD was worried about you fighting with Sandra."

"What?" I said, bringing my hand back down to my side. "What?"

Rob helped me understand. "Your assistant subbed you off. That situation is unusual, to say the least."

"Ah, no. She was right. I lost concentration."

Chris leaned forward from the neck up. "You hit a fucking *spectacular* sixty-yard diagonal onto the number seven's toes and that really pissed her off. Your number came up on the board and she gave you an earful."

"Pointless show-off Hollywood pass. She knows I hate that crap. I'm not allowed to do it just because I'm the boss. And the row was entertainment. It was . . . what's the thing in wrestling where they pretend to be mad?"

"Kayfabe," said Emma, which freaked me out.

"Right. It was that. The more she stands up to me, the more the players will respect her."

"Did *she* think it was fake?" said Emma.

"No, she was really mad at me," I said, delighted. "Said I'd promised to play good football and I had to set an example."

"But who's in charge?" said Chris.

"Me. But I've worked really hard to get a top football brain in. I'm on the pitch, exhausted, struggling to do two jobs at once. She's clear-headed, she has an overview of the match and the wider sitch. I'm not stupid. I'll listen to what she says. And her subbing me off is like in *Star Trek* when the doctors relieve the captain when they start firing proton torpedoes against the Kardashians. I want pushback. I want the best outcome."

Chris looked at his agent, had a rapid nonverbal conversation, then turned back to me. "What will you do if I don't agree to come?"

"Ooh," I said, as though the thought hadn't ever occurred to me. "Then we do it the hard way."

"So I'm the easy way."

"Yep. The easy way and the fun way."

Emma poked me in the ribs. "What about drama? What about telling a story?"

I playfully tried to grab her fingers so she couldn't poke me again. "There will be plenty of that." I jerked my head towards the pitch. "Just not out there."

"I'm cup tied in the FA Trophy," said Chris, meaning he wouldn't be able to play for us in that competition.

"Oh? So the other teams will have a chance." I grinned at him until he smiled back.

He turned to Rob and shook his head. "The guy's potty."

"I'll tell you what the opposite of potty is. Which team in England goes up against low blocks the most?"

"Man City."

"Right. Most teams we play now low block us. And I've just hired a coach from Man City." I tapped my temple. "On my holiday, I'll be working on my free kicks and corners. We've got a coach who's perfect for the challenges we're going to face. We've got ten players ready to work their butts off so that you can hog all the glory." I got smug. I had outdone myself. "Have you got any medals?" I *had* been studying his career but as often happened immediately after a match, I didn't have all my faculties available.

"Won the National League before, and League Two."

"Fuck," I said. "That's good. Well, you know what it feels like. I'm offering you that feeling again. Er . . . there's only one thing you might not like."

"What's that?"

"Round here, *I* take the penalties."

vi.

On the sixth day of Christmas, the cosmos gave to me . . . the tiniest winning spree.

Sunday, December 10.

I was trying to have a lazy morning in bed with Emma when there was a knock on the front door. That was very strange, since my post got delivered to the club, and almost no one knew I lived in that barn. One of the few people who did, the Brig, would invariably text me before coming.

It turned out to be Ruth, in a slight panic.

"Max, it's the Yorks. Can you help?"

"Sure. What do you need?"

"Put your hoodie on." A few seconds later, Emma and I were following Ruth along the dirt path behind her property, and she explained. "There's an old couple who live here. The Yorks. Every morning, they open the bathroom blinds, there, and every evening they close them. It's a signal. That's how I know they're all right."

"Huh," I said. Ahead was a cute-ish cottage. The blinds were still closed. It woke me up pretty fast. Action stations. "You don't have a key or anything?"

"No. But they've left that window open. See? Maybe you could . . . ?"

I jogged ahead, partly to get to the scene faster, partly to warm up. If I did have to climb up there, it would be pretty tough going. By the time the ladies caught up, I had a plan. "If I move the wheelie bin over, climb on that, onto that windowsill, if I can get from there up onto that little roof, sideways there, might have a chance."

"Oh, I don't know," said Ruth, looking at my plan. "It's awfully risky."

"You get started," said Emma. "I'll push the window wider from the inside." She had tried the back door and it had swung open.

"Oh, thank God," said Ruth, racing inside, calling, "Hello?"

Emma and I hung around in the garden. Neither of us wanted to see a dead body, if that's what the deal was. But it turned out that Mrs. York had a bad cold and Mr. York had gone to the "big shop" that was open on Sundays to get some Lemsip or chicken soup or whatever, and had forgotten to do the blinds. So it was all good, big relief all round, and Mrs. York was ecstatically happy that Ruth had checked on her.

So nothing much had happened, but the old adrenaline had been pumping for a quick minute, and lazing in bed didn't seem like the plan for the day anymore. I went through a mental list of my options. "Ladies, can I interest you in a quick pop to Liverpool? I'll check in on the under-twelves at their futsal tournament, and then we can find a nice place to eat or a Christmas market or whatever."

"Absolutely," said Emma. "But first, what's futsal?"

Futsal is indoor football with a small, heavy ball. The nature of the ball promotes technique, passing, and skill, instead of traditional English virtues like kicking it long to a big man (Goliath), getting stuck in with tackles (Sam Topps), or complaining that a referee made a mistake so the entire match should be replayed and replayed until the team that feels they have a right to win, win (Liverpool Football Club).

When we got there, I felt something in the atmosphere. Something off. I frowned as we sat down at the back of the stand that looked down on three small pitches. What was it that I'd detected? I mean, the obvious thing was that the sports hall was packed with parents of footballers who wouldn't make it as professionals. Fifty or sixty of the same sort of person who had crashed a metal bar into my skull.

I shuddered, but it wasn't *that*.

Over there were the hosts, wearing a certain shade of red. Liverpool FC. They ran this December tournament, calling it Yule Never Walk Alone. Urgh. Emma had complained about my anti-Liverpool rants, so I'd tried to stop making fake vomit noises when that football club got mentioned. But I was pleased to note they all seemed vaguely depressed.

Next to them were a bunch of people in blue: Everton. Again, not many happy faces there. Then bunches of coaches and parents from smaller clubs and local teams, with a normal mix of excited, happy, and unhappy parents and children.

And over to the right, wearing gorgeous blue and white kits, a bunch of familiar faces lying around playing card games. Unlike most of the teams, there was no separation between parents and children. It seemed that Future's grandmother was on a team with Mark Nelson, while Future himself was paired with Tadpole, and Simon Black was in deep discussion with Stephen Watson's dad about what card to play next.

"Our lot look very relaxed," said Ruth.

"They do, don't they? Something's weird. I want to find out the standings without disturbing them. Can you see any organiser types?"

"There," said Emma, pointing to a table laden with documents being guarded by a middle-aged woman and a gangly teenager. "Want me to go and find out?"

"No, you're too sexy. You'll cause a scene and our lot will notice. Ruth, you go."

"Hey! I'm sexier than you. I cause more scenes than you two combined."

"I'm a superstar footballer," I whined. "Everyone knows what I look like."

"Here," said Emma, fishing her West Didsbury bobble hat from her handbag.

I pulled it as far down as I could manage, and in that disguise, went the long way round to talk to the organisers. I returned the same way.

"Well?" said Ruth. "No one even glanced at you, by the way."

"Turns out we are slapping."

"What?" laughed Emma.

"We slapped Liverpool. We slapped Everton. They're playing each other next and the winner of that will be in the other semifinal. So we've knocked one of the favourites out, have an easy game in the semi, and will play the final against a team we already beat."

"That's amazing," said Emma.

I scratched my head. It *was* amazing. How was that happening? "Can we postpone the Christmas market?"

"Course," said Emma. "We can't leave. You're about to get your first trophy. Or cup. Or vase."

"Oh!" I said, as ten tiny little kids from Liverpool and Everton took to the pitch. Five-a-side, red against blue, a real classic. And yet . . . "We've got the best team here," I said, astonished. At this age, most players still had CA 1, perhaps 2, and a powerful boy was more impressive than a skilful technician. But based on PA, we were by far the most talented team. Nine of our twelve would make it as professionals, and the other three would walk into the West Didsbury team.

"You already said that," said Ruth.

"No, I said we beat them. But look! They're not all that good. Liverpool have one good forward. Couple of decent midfielders. Everton have a good goalie and a good midfielder. That's it. The rest are fool's gold."

"What have *we* got?"

I looked around. "We're fucking stacked. We've got the best player in the tournament. Stephen Watson. Big Sam is the second-best goalie. Tadpole is the best, actually, but he's only ten. I hope he got some minutes. But Big Sam's second best of the starters. Mark Nelson might be the best defender, except if you count Future, who's been training with the fourteens and was even with the sixteens for a while. And the organiser told me Simon Black is top scorer by far. He's a menace at this type of football. He's too fast and sharp to stop." I laughed. I'd been getting annoyed at Playdar for underdelivering, but this was very much a team that Playdar built.

I watched as Spectrum, relaxed and happy, adjusted his glasses and looked down at a clipboard he was holding. Then he looked up at the time and across at the Liverpool versus Everton match. Then he spasmed, reached for his mobile, and when he finished typing, my phone buzzed.

Spectrum: Just FYI, I think we have a good shot at winning YNWA with the under-12s. It's in Liverpool. If you're not doing anything and you can get here soonish, you'll catch the final.

Me: Wouldn't you prefer to do it without me breathing down your neck?

Spectrum: No! But I don't think it matters. The kids are relaxed. I'm rotating the players as fast as I can with no drop in quality. The other teams either don't rotate or have bad subs.

If I took over for the final, I could use the Fantasy Football perks to give us a massive boost: Triple Captain, Bench Boost, and a Free Hit. It seemed like a guarantee of success. But what would that prove? Nothing. Spectrum deserved a chance.

Me: Sounds like you've got it under control. I'm about to do a 120% Hollow Knight speedrun so I won't be able to make it. Enjoy yourself!

He sent me a thumbs-up emoji and wandered over to watch the rest of Liverpool versus Everton. Liverpool won, and then it was time for our semifinal against Bootle.

The ref blew the whistle, and Bootle attacked.

Try to imagine three cute little corgis racing each other to the other side of the pitch, enthusiastic, yapping (in Scouse accents), arms flailing, their tiny knees pumping while Emma went "aww" because they were so tiny and so cute.

Then imagine a level-9,000 defensive midfielder approach a kid who was about to shoot, lazily dab the ball away, jog onto it, and pass it accurately forward, where little Simon Black accelerated to a hundred miles an hour and rolled the ball into the bottom left.

Seven seconds, one goal.

"I don't think it'll matter if you go down," said Ruth.

"I just want to enjoy it," I said. "Even if there's a slight chance I'd ruin the vibe or distract them, I'd rather not."

"Oh, look at that one!" said Emma. "What is he? Ten?"

"That's Benjy. He's seven."

"Holy shit. Can I keep him, Max? Can I? Oh, can I just pet him though?"

I smiled. He *was* cute. "Benjy. Seven. Attacking midfielder, can play left or right. He'll slap this tournament in a couple of years. Yule Never Walk Alone. Please. You'll never win again, more like. They should rename this, er . . . Merry Christmax. Oh, that's terrible. Merry Kidsmax."

"Give it up."

"I'm going on a coffee run," said Ruth.

Also going on a run: Theo White, a ten-year-old right midfielder with PA 55. There were so many kids running around I couldn't remember where I'd found him, but there he was, dribbling past two Bootle kids and pulling the ball back for Simon. He thought about passing wide to Das Tournament hero Adam, but scored a goal instead.

Spectrum subbed him off and put Benjy on for a couple of minutes. In that time, Bootle had more attacks, but one of Stephen Watson, Future, or Mark Nelson blocked or intercepted. It was all incredibly controlled. Spectrum was giving everyone minutes and the kids were reshaping how they played based on who was on the pitch. I'd taught them some of that when I was training with them, but almost all of this was Spectrum and the other coaches who had chipped in.

With Simon back on, we scored two more goals and then Tadpole came on to see the match out. Ten years old, the best goalkeeper in our system with PA 130, and he was getting minutes in a semifinal.

I got emotional and tried to hide it from Emma. Don't ask me why.

Ruth returned and handed out coffees in branded paper cups. "There's a Costa. Bonus. Coffee's not bad there. So we won?"

"Yeah," said Emma. "Max had a little inside cry, but I pretended not to notice."

Ruth smiled and leaned over to rub my arm. "They're all talking about Chester in there. This came out of nowhere, it seems. Liverpool have won this four years out of the last five. One of their coaches was raving about Stephen Walton."

"Watson."

"Said he's unbelievable. The woman doing the drinks said, 'We should sign him then,' and he said, 'Yeah. *And the striker, too.*'"

I nodded. It wouldn't be long before Stephen's talent was attracting scouts from every major team. How on Earth were we supposed to keep him for the next two years, let alone the next ten? "Ruth, you should butter up his dad. Let him know about the agency and all that."

"I've met him, remember? We've had this conversation before."

"Stephen needs these experiences to improve, but these experiences put him on display. We need to keep the dad happy and believing we're the best place for him."

"Are we?"

I scoffed. "We're already the best under-twelve futsal team in the world."

"How much of an exaggeration is that?"

"Big one. It's my *favourite* under-twelve futsal team in the world. That's no exaggeration."

"Anyone else we should get?"

"Tadpole."

"Who else?"

"That's it. Stephen's the big fish, though. He'll make the club and the agency a lot of money." I imagined getting a call that Stephen had left to join Liverpool and we'd get no fee. My blood pressure rose. Emma sensed it and pushed herself into me. What more could I do to keep young players at the club? Keep giving them chances in the first team, obviously. Keep improving the coaches and facilities. Keep winning tournaments.

Keep winning? We hadn't won this one yet.

"Oh, no," said Emma.

"What?" I said, head jerking left and right while I looked for danger.

"That little baby's dressed up like a frog. Oh my God. I want to pinch his cheeks and say ribbit. Am I allowed, Max?"

"You're a strong independent woman. But if you're going there, ask which kid on that team is theirs. They've got a good right back I wouldn't mind signing. Also, it's an owl, not a frog."

Emma bounced away and Ruth gave me a certain smile before returning to her coffee and phone.

Ribbit. The word reminded me of something. Something about football . . . Ah! On my first trip to FC United, they'd had a player with the nickname Ribbit. He was incredibly talented. Why hadn't I thought of him since?

Because, I realised, he wasn't in my database.

Me: Dude. What happened to Ribbit?

Ziggy: Oh! You mean Frogger. Haven't heard that name for ages. He met a Turkish woman and they moved to Marmaris. He runs a bar.

Me: Oh, shame.

Ziggy: No, I think he's happy now. If we win the league, we're going there for a piss up.

Me: Better stop throwing away two-goal leads, then.

Ziggy: I'll pass your advice onto our goalies. Hey, where's my boot deal?

Me: All sorted. Go to nike dot co dot uk, put whatever you want in your cart and use offer code MERRY CHRISTMAX for ten percent off.

Ziggy: Mate.

"Ruth, did you get anywhere with a boot deal for Bark?"

She closed her eyes, recalling some unpleasant memory. "They didn't laugh at me, exactly, but they suggested I might want to, let's say, come back later."

"I think you'll find it easier with Angel."

She scoffed. "You think?"

Emma came back, cheeks flushed with pleasure. She told me which kid the couple with the baby were watching. He wasn't of interest. "I heard you mention Angel. I realised, you know, that you've talked about her looks and her story and all that, but you didn't say much about her as a player."

"I can help with that," said Ruth, to my surprise. "When Max saw her, he became fully erect."

"Mate," I said.

"I mean that he stood up."

I shook my head. "Can you *not*? She's not even sixteen."

Ruth was unrepentant. "It was quite strange, Max. Even for you. What had you seen?"

This was my fault. I'd been getting sloppy about responding to players as soon as I saw their profiles. I'd started out bad at that and had trained myself to be better, but now I was so comfortable in my position I was falling into old habits. I'd done it not twenty minutes ago when Liverpool and Everton had taken to the pitch. "She's tall and she has a quality of movement that's hard to put into words. It just looked right. It suddenly clicked that Bonnie hadn't been exaggerating. So I went over, and yeah, that's a goalscorer all right."

"But you told her not to shoot."

"She's no good to us in her current form. She needs to become a more well-rounded player. She'll have to work really hard on her passing, technique, and her defensive work a bit, too. You saw how she struggled in that match."

"Bonnie was stressed to bits, but you seemed happy."

"Angel tried, she was shit, and now she knows we all know the things she can't do. Jackie stopped the match a couple of times to explain things to her and she was paying attention. As long as she's hungry to learn, everything will be all right."

On the pitches, the tournament organisers were moving goals around and generally reshaping the space. The final would be played on centre court, so to speak, giving everyone interested the chance to see.

"So you've signed Venus," said Ruth. "I'm almost more interested in Mars." She saw I wasn't following her. "Chris Beaumont."

"Ah."

"MD came to ask me if your gamble failed, whether the club could use the money I'd invested in the women's team to shore things up."

"What did you say?"

"I said no. Even though the real answer is yes, of course. But it's no until the very last second, Max. Until we're actually falling off the edge of the cliff."

"We're nowhere near that."

"I know. But it's MD's job to worry. The numbers involved must be frightening. How much are we buying him for?"

"Oh, we're not. Banbury can't sell him. Their whole team is built around him. No, we're loaning him."

"Loaning him? Then we're only paying his wages."

"That's often the case, but you can also pay a fee to loan a player. On *top* of his wages. It happens a lot at elite clubs. They can't just give away assets for a year. Yeah, I suppose it's rare down at our level. Unheard of, maybe, I don't know. I just want the player."

"So what's the loan fee?"

"Forty thousand pounds."

Ruth stared at me. "That's more than we paid to buy, outright, Ryan Jack, who has played in the Premier League."

"Yes."

"Forty thousand? To use him for six months?"

"Yes."

Emma went, "Oh!" She nodded. "That's what he meant about being the most expensive player *pro rata*. He'd be eighty thousand for a year, and that's more than that guy Jonathan Hurts. Are you sure about this, bebs? It sounds a bit crazy." The numbers were worse than she thought; Hurts had a three-year contract, if reports were to be believed. I'd know for sure when I started buying the Contracts perks, but you could argue his transfer fee was £23,000 a year.

"Crazy like a frog. All right, it's nearly time. God, this is exciting! My heart's going. The Liverpool kids look really intense. Ours are still chill AF. Holy smokes!"

Yule Never Walk Alone. The final. Hosts Liverpool with their fast boys, their strong boys, their tall boys. Mixed morale, mixed talent. A throng of coaches. The visitors and underdogs (question mark) Chester. Often known as tiny Chester. Minnows Chester. High morale, high talent. One coach. Spectrum, pushing his glasses up, enjoying himself. The wizard's apprentice.

Ruth and Emma were into the first half like no other football match I could remember. Maybe Emma was this animated when I played, but I would never see it. Now she kicked every ball, yelled, yelped, whelped, whined, whinged, moaned, groaned, and shrieked. Ruth was less vocal, but the way she shifted in her seat told a tale.

It was a journey.

We started with a seventy percent sort of team: Big Sam in goal, Future and Stephen Watson as defenders, Adam as the midfield, and Simon Black as the striker. Liverpool had their strongest lineup.

It was pretty end-to-end stuff, but we scored first. Simon—who else?—latching onto a nice pass. Spectrum rang the changes, bringing our relative strength down to sixty percent. Liverpool had shots that Big Sam saved, and John, another veteran of Das Tournament, scored on the counter.

Two—nil, and another flurry of changes. Off went Stephen Watson, on came Simon Black. Liverpool huffed and puffed, but we scored a third. The Reds finally clawed one back, but we were back to Black—Simon made it 4–1.

That's when Spectrum lost his mind.

Still smiling, chatting to his substitutes, and generally looking like a good-hearted Fagin, he weakened us to fifty percent, then allowed Tadpole to go in goal for the last two minutes of the half.

Liverpool couldn't believe their luck, and they struck twice.

Four—three at halftime, but the momentum was with the Premier League team. Ruth and Emma spent the halftime break chatting away at a mile a minute, excited, desperate, stressed.

Me? I needed to see one more thing before making up my mind. But I couldn't help but feel that . . .

Over on the far side of the pitch, the Liverpool head coach was pumping his players up. They would come out fighting, they would come out swinging, and if they got the next goal, there would be absolute carnage. The crowd felt it, too. There was plenty of support for ten-to-one outsiders Liverpool, but enough of the smaller teams had stayed behind to watch this most unexpected of finals, and they were almost all cheering for a Chester win.

So what would Spectrum do?

He had two valid choices. One, start weak and let his team get stronger through the half, ending with a thrilling last two minutes, a finale for the ages. Two, put his strongest team on the pitch, crush the Liverpool insurgency and demoralise their players. Honestly, either way sounded fun, but one was obviously much more likely to end with Stephen Watson lifting the first trophy of my management career, and the first of Spectrum's, too. The only option I wouldn't accept would be a halfway house. A compromise. As long as Spectrum chose a lane, I'd support him.

The Liverpool kids were in a huddle, and as the ref blew the whistle, they roared and clapped their hands and looked aggressive and ready to charge.

Onto the other side of the pitch sauntered Big Sam, Stephen Watson, Future, Mark Nelson, and Simon Black. One hundred percent strength. I flew to my feet and punched the air.

Spectrum's head snapped over and he saw me. I clenched my fist, grinning like a madman. He grinned back and whipped out his phone.

Spectrum: I take it you approve.

Me: Crush them like ants. Then release our ants. I saw Benjy had played. Has Biggins?

Biggins was an eight-year-old centre back with PA 35.

Spectrum: I'll give you two guesses.

He smiled in my general direction and slipped his phone back into his pocket.

Three minutes later, I almost felt sorry for Liverpool. Their best players had played most of every match, while ours had been given plenty of rest. Our reserves were ready to come in and play, even our backup goalie. And as their legs faded, so did their morale. Every Stephen Watson interception, every Mark Nelson block, every Simon Black goal stripped away some of their spirit, and I'm very, very sorry to say some of the Liverpool kids spent most of the second half in tears.

A four-goal lead turned into a five-goal lead, and for the last five minutes of the final, Spectrum took the piss by rotating the team, bringing on increasingly tiny players, until we finished with Tadpole in goal, Benjy, Biggins, Theo White, and Adrian Tomkins, aged ten, seven, eight, ten, and eleven respectively.

Liverpool scored the last goal, but somehow that made things even sweeter.

The three of us rushed down to join the celebrations, with me focusing on the players and Ruth and Emma wading into the parents, our sudden appearance flicking the switch from smiling pleasure to dancing joy.

Stephen Watson flushed as he held the trophy aloft—it was a cup with big handles; Emma approved—and flushed again as he was named Player of the Tournament and got a medal and a little man-kicking-a-football trophy. On the pitch, he was cool as a cucumber and played simply but with cheeky, extrovert flourishes. Off the pitch, he was quite shy.

Simon Black got a trophy, too, for being top scorer. His closest rival was six goals short. I noticed the coaches from the Premier League teams eyeing him greedily. Simon played like the reincarnation of Liverpool legend Michael Owen. Oi! Eyes off my players! But then again . . . he only had PA 77. By the time he was ready for the first team, the first team would be way ahead of him. He'd keep improving for a long time yet, though, and just as the hype was building, I could sell him as the new Michael Owen and rip off some club I didn't like.

The idea of rug pulling Liverpool made me even chirpier, even more willing to pose for selfie after selfie, made me make outrageous promises to the parents like "your child will be the first footballer on the moon" and whatnot.

Then I went too far, trying to get everyone to come to Nando's. Ruth shut it down right quick, saying Nando's with ten hyperactive kids was not her idea of a good time, and anyway, she had been doing what I wanted. We ended up at a nice local restaurant. Me, Ruth, Emma, Stephen Watson and his dad, and Spectrum.

After we got settled at our table, with Stephen's trophies displacing the salt and pepper, and after we had ordered, I rested my elbows on the table, rested my chin on the backs of my hands, looked at Spectrum, and sighed, "I've never met a genius before. How do you do it?"

He laughed, and he told us about the parts of the tournament we'd missed. He was just getting to the final, which Ruth, Emma, and Mr. Watson had a thousand questions about, when I was filled with a warm glow. Like, a full-body toasty feeling, hands in front of the fire after coming in from the snow, feet warmed up by the big Christmas socks, head snugly wrapped in a West Didsbury and Chorlton bobble hat.

In my mind, I stretched my arms wide and screamed, "I'm the king of the world!"

And as I returned to reality, listening to Spectrum explain how he thought of a football match as a chapter in a story, and a season as a book, I felt like another chunk of coal had been added to the fireplace.

But then . . . something strange.

I'd been so busy watching the kids and thinking about their parents while admiring the new, confident Spectrum that it hadn't quite clicked. But now that my mind was fully at rest, I was ninety-nine percent sure of it. His tactics attribute had been 15. It had always been 15.

But today it was 16.

He wasn't just improving. He was *improving*.

vii.

On the seventh day of Christmas, the cosmos gave to me . . . some transfer chicanery.

Wednesday, December 13.

MD and I were driving away from Sutton United, which as you know is down in London. My second trip to the capital in as many days. On the maps app, I marvelled at the famous names that were nearby: Sutton United were in the middle of Epsom Downs, Wimbledon, and Selhurst Park. There were times when I found the idea of London big and exciting, and others when I thought it was all a bit much.

"That went well," said MD.

"Yep," I said, beaming. "You were amazing for a guy who doesn't want this to happen."

"I do want it to happen," he sighed, as he eased around a corner right into yet another traffic light. Boo, London, boo! "It's just a *lot* of finance. You're committing us to a lot of spend."

"You seem relaxed about it."

"This comes out of the BoshCard money. The only risk is if Agatha pulls out of the deal before then. Which is vanishingly unlikely. I suppose . . ." He sighed. "I suppose I wish I knew more about the player. Or saw anything in him. I suppose it's not just you, for once. The scouts like him, too. Is it left, somewhere? What does it say?"

I concentrated on the app for a few minutes, giving MD directions to a bar. I texted the Brig and he was outside when we got there. He shook hands with a few guys who had the same sort of posture as him. He got in the back. MD pulled away and I heard the Brig struggling to click his seatbelt into place. I turned, amused, and gave him a thumbs up when he finally succeeded.

"I am pleased to inform you," he intoned, with much solemnity, "that I am delightfully shozzled."

"What were you on?" said MD.

"Four Horshemen," slurred the Brig.

"Not familiar. What's in that?"

"Jim, Jack, Johnnie, and Jameshon," came the surreal reply, and I was all set to laugh but MD instantly comprehended.

"Sounds good. Have to try that. Max, put some smooth jazz on so John and his four mates can have a little shnooze."

While I waited for my bodyguard to sober up, I thought about my scouting trips to see Sutton. They were rock bottom of League Two and while they were still fighting on the pitch, in the boardroom they were resigned to their fate. When I offered to take a player off their hands, they were interested. They'd get a fee and save on wages for a guy who was, for them, a mostly unused sub.

Eddie Moore had been recommended by a scout I'd befriended. His tip had cost me £100 in cash, and I'd sent Fleur, our scout, to check him out. She'd sent a glowing report, and so I'd been to see Sutton play at Tranmere—convenient—and at Wrexham—tickets thanks to Eve (who, by the way, sat next to me and flirtily complained I hadn't tried to make *her* my assistant manager; I somehow forgot to mention this episode to Emma).

Eddie had been on the bench in both matches, but he'd come on for twenty minutes in Wales. Of course, I didn't need to see him play to get his profile, but I had to persuade MD to let me spend even more of the club's money and all the effort was part of that. I'd worn MD down pretty quickly. After Benny's goal, I could have asked him to rebuild the stadium and he'd have said yes. But he was a legitimately good transfer target.

EDDIE MOORE		
Born 15.9.01	(Age 22)	English
Acceleration 13		
	Handling 1	Stamina 9
	Heading 8	Strength 7
		Tackling 10
	Jumping 6	Teamwork 14
Bravery 11		Technique 12
	Pace 13	preferred foot L
	Passing 11	
Dribbling 9	Positioning 10	
Finishing 4		
CA 41	PA 75	
Defender (Left)		

The scouts had painted me a picture of a player who was underrated by most managers because he wasn't physically dominant, didn't win headers, all that crap. But they'd spotted that Eddie had the core of a Max Best player, and the numbers suggested they were right. He had some speed, positioning, was good on the ball, and he had that sweet, sweet teamwork.

The Brig stirred. He'd driven us to London and then gone on the piss with his old army mates. It seemed a crime to make him leave so early, but it was a long drive home. "Did we win?"

"Yes," I said.

"Gleaming. *What* did we win?"

"Eddie Moore will join us on loan for the rest of the season."

"On loan? You hate loans."

"If you'll give me more than six microseconds to put one word after the previous word . . . He'll come on loan . . . with an obligation to buy."

"Gosh," said the Brig. Then after a while. "What does that mean?"

"It means to the outside world, he's on loan. But actually, we've bought him. But we pay next summer."

"My mother never used to let us buy on the never-never. She said never to the never-never." The Brig giggled.

"MD isn't a big fan of it, either. But it's only twenty-five thousand."

"That sounds both cheap and expensive. Erm . . . perhaps we could get a coffee somewhere. And a tartlet?" he added hopefully.

The word tartlet started me thinking, but I never completed the thought. MD was giving his opinion. "It's a lot of money for a reserve left back at a team that will fall into the National League. It's a lot of money for a player all my contacts say is nothing special."

"Why do you want him, sir?"

I turned to him. "We need a left back for when Trick leaves. MD is friends with the Sutton lot and they're going to say that Eddie is a right winger."

"Oh, this again." He blew some unwanted air out. "How about that coffee?"

Ten minutes later, we were in a motorway services drinking their appalling coffee. I went through the plan again. "Right. January first in the morning, we sign Goliath on loan. He's really on loan."

"And he's going to win us the league even though he's not that good and has almost no upside."

"Exactly. A minute later, we sign Eddie on loan. We say he's a right winger and Sutton do the same on their side. He's only coming in on loan, we say, to cover me for my holiday."

"And people will believe he's a right winger?"

"Who's going to check? Why wouldn't he be? We don't mention the obligation to buy. It's just a loan. At this point, we start briefing that we're way over budget and all the money from the cup run has been wiped out. Something like that. Any time from there, Trick can leave and it will come as a hammer blow. Rymarquis might leave it till late in the window to give me another deadline day headache, but Trick will push for it to be done early, and my holiday will help."

"He could ruin your holiday by stealing Trick. But Trick's under contract. He can't just vanish."

"His contract, my enemies have learned, includes a release clause if he can get higher wages elsewhere. He negotiated it last summer."

"That was clever of him."

"Get some more coffee in you! He did no such thing. It's just an excuse so he can leave for free. So, right, Trick's gone, got his pay raise and all that. We've spent all our money, Rymarquis and his mates are laughing their heads off. Soon as Trick's safe, Sutton can mention the obligation to buy, like if they need to placate their fans or whatever. And Sandra can start using Eddie Moore as a left back."

"What if Trick stays?"

I shrugged. "Then we have two left backs and can use Magnus as cover for Carl at right back. But we'll have massively upgraded and Eddie will slap next season, too, and after that, he'll be our backup left back in League Two."

MD smiled. "What about in League One? The Championship?"

He was joking; I wasn't. "You'll have to write more cheques when we get there. Bigger ones. Number goes up."

The Brig stirred his coffee. "So this year's TV money is going on Chris Beaumont. The prize money is going into equipment for the lads. Next year's sponsorship money is already being spent. Don't you think you should reconsider how much you'd accept for Raffi?"

"No. He's an England international."

MD hadn't drunk any alcohol, but the thought of me presenting him with bigger and bigger demands had sobered him all the way up. He tried to see the bright side of this year's spending. "At least we'll have done all our transfer business on day one of the window. Except for signing off on Trick leaving, and Max doesn't need to be around for that."

"Mmm," I said. "We'll get a right winger, too."

"What?" said MD.

"I didn't want to scare you. Don't worry, he'll be free. He's the kid Tranmere signed from my former club and they'll cover his wages if we give him some first-team experience." Barkley. A PA–130 right-sided attacking midfielder. His CA was still in the 20s but he'd be able to cover a few minutes and he could hit a good cross. "He can come for a month or two if we need him. That's all agreed. Basically, if we get any kind of serious injury, we press the Bark button. He's very raw, but the price is right and he could be useful if we're up against a low block. I wouldn't put him in against York City or anything, but he's talented. And he knows the level so it's not like signing some kind of prima donna."

There was a silence. "Max," said the Brig. He looked around, laughing in disbelief before fixing me with those ladykiller eyes. "Can I just check, please? Just because I've been drinking." He looked up, theatrically, then down again. "You, who are so very opposed to loan signings, intend to make three loan signings this January?"

My eyes were shining and my smile was devastating. I know because a bored-to-death cleaner who was walking past got a full blast and was suddenly having the best day of her life. "Guys. This is the part where you say how much fun it is working with me."

The older men looked at each other. "More coffee?" said MD.

"Yes, please. Irish, if you can arrange that."

viii.

On the eighth day of Christmas, the cosmos gave to me . . . a chance to close the gap to three.

Saturday, December 16. Match 20 of 46: Chester versus Boston United.

Before kick-off, Henri asked for a word. He wanted to check I had plans for Christmas dinner, otherwise he'd invite me to his place. He said he wanted to ask me "while we were still on speaking terms," which was odd, but I found out what he meant at the men's first team Christmas party six days later.

"I've accepted an invitation to Weaver Manors," I said.

He feigned surprise. "I thought you weren't keen on her father."

"While I think it's *perfectly* reasonable for me to demand that he stops supporting the team he's loved since he was able to walk just as they're about to start winning everything, I have decided to try to overlook this one, huge, unforgivable character flaw in the interests of spending more time with his daughter."

The features of his face spread apart as he admired me. "You're simply wonderful, did you know?"

I grinned. "I recently learned he has an amazing wine cellar, and I'm not going to be playing from Christmas to New Year, so . . ."

Henri experienced a pang of regret. "Andrew will be there, in my place. If I'd known there would be wine . . ." The buzzer sounded, so I didn't have time to investigate what he meant. "Let me shoot you to the top of the league, my friend. A win today will give you something to celebrate. He might upgrade from Italian wine . . ."

"To Spanish?"

He pulled a face. "You are supposed to motivate me, *gaffer.*"

I hugged his shoulders. "If you're struggling to motivate yourself for matches, you can always fall back on your writing career."

This harmless half-joke hit like a cloud of pesticide. Henri looked . . . guilty?

I'd decided to go for a 4-1-4-1 with Raffi Brown not in the match day squad. His big match would be on Tuesday and I didn't want him getting injured. He was both pleased and annoyed. More annoyed, I think, but I didn't care. We'd bought something like seventy tickets and his England debut was going to be our unofficial Christmas night out. The official one would be on the 22nd and I had no idea what to expect from it.

The match kicked off and I spent ten minutes patrolling the halfway line as Boston fell into a low block. Eleven men behind the ball, trying to deny us space, trying to stop us from getting into good crossing positions while also flooding the box with tall boys so if we did cross, they'd probably deal with it.

Grim.

And what made it worse was how much fun our last meeting had been. If you remember, a guy had called *talkSPORT* to rave about it. With good reason. It had ended 6–0 and there had been red cards, fights, the debut of my 2-6-2 formation, *my* league debut for Chester, me putting my knee on the ball inches away from the Boston manager, Sam going off injured and hobbling back on. Just a wild ride.

From that to *this.*

I'd put Trick in the lineup to help with the pretence that he would be hard to replace, and to be fair, while his CA was low, he was far better than Magnus in a game like this. He dragged our average CA down to 50.3, but Sandra's coaching was very much working. She'd squeezed an extra point out of Henri. He was on CA 63 now, and that felt like a huge achievement. Pushing back against the tide of shit facilities and shit opponents. Yes, Sandra mate!

Aff, Trick, and Ryan combined on the left to create a half-chance. Trick's cross wasn't terrible, but Henri couldn't get to it.

At the back, Carl Carlile had finally caught up with Glenn Ryder—both were CA 54—and Steve Alton was starting to leave poor Gerald May in the dust. Youngster was closing in on gold, Pascal had turned silver, and Andrew Harrison was about to hit whatever the shittest metal is. Tin? Anyway, after six months of regular training, he was CA 19. Which . . . felt slow, but I'd plucked him from a beach and turned his life upside down. I was more than willing to be patient with him, but he was making me wonder about how many CA-1 players I would sign in the future. We could end up training them for two years before they were useful.

D-Day dribbled past one player and rolled a simple pass forward for Carl to chase. He smashed the ball across goal, but there was only Henri in the area, surrounded by seven defenders. Raffi was useful in those situations—he often surged into the penalty box, adding another body to our attacks. Ryan and Sam didn't have that desire or the knack of finding themselves in the right place. No wonder Raffi was being courted by so many clubs.

I glanced up at the main stand and saw more scouts and agents than usual. Putting the hours in before the January transfer window. Made sense. A lot of moves to be made. A lot of money to be made.

Boston weren't currently a threat, so I moved forward ten yards, leaving Glenn and Steve on the halfway line and everyone else in an attacking position. Except Ben, of course. He'd moved to CA 45, which was good, but again, it felt slow. Maybe I'd have to upgrade our goalkeeping coach, or find Angles a talented young assistant or something. It couldn't be that I focused all my attention on the outfield players. The goalies needed to improve at the same rates.

I got the ball, shaped to pass left, did the cut-back move Cody Chambers had taught me, and sprayed the ball wide to D-Day. He now had a little more space, and he used the time to concentrate. He whipped in a cross perfect for Henri. Almost perfect. Henri needed to add power to his header but couldn't quite generate enough. The ball looped up harmlessly into the hands of the goalie.

Sandra was waving at me. *Get back! Get back!*

I shook my head and pointed to the spot where I was. *I'll play farther forward than you're comfortable with, thanks.*

She nodded.

Boston booted the ball away, not even bothering to pretend to start an attack.

The crowd groaned.

Attendances were slowly rising, which is what you'd expect when a team is playing well and winning most of their matches, but I'd been disappointed in the numbers. I wanted more. MD said word had got round that teams were coming to Chester to defend and as a result, the matches weren't that interesting for casual fans. It was one of the reasons he had allowed me to go nuts on the Goliath fee. We could make some of that forty grand back by selling more match day tickets.

We got a free kick and Ryan Jack went to take it. I was still pretty down on myself when it came to set pieces, penalties excepted.

I stayed on the halfway line while Glenn and Steve went up. Almost everyone was in the penalty area now. I walked forward ten yards, then another five. Sandra was going tonto, but I wanted to invite Boston to launch a counter. If they did, we'd have much more space to work in. I looked at her and took one step back. She threw her hands up, exasperated.

Ryan's free kick was fired in, and Ryder got his head to it. It went just over the bar.

I shook my head. Quarter chances. Half chances. We'd wear Boston down, make them run and concentrate for eighty minutes and hope to get space in the final ten minutes.

A Boston guy was on the floor, pretending to be injured. Trying to run the clock down. Sandra was waving at me, so I jogged over.

"What? I know what I'm doing."

She was annoyed. "I've been trying to call you."

I gestured vaguely towards my ears. "I don't hear much when the match starts. Tune it all out so I can focus."

"Weird. Forget DM for now. Try being a right winger."

"Hmm? What about D-Day?"

"He'll be right mid. We'll overload them on the right. You, Donny, and Carl all on that side of the pitch. See what mischief you can get up to."

I laughed. "Hang on. I thought you were trying to stop me going all-out."

"No, Max."

"You want . . . more mischief?" It was hard to believe. "No one's ever asked me to go *more* crazy."

"Putting the league's best right winger at right wing isn't crazy."

I closed my eyes in an attempt to contain my frustration, not at her, but at the truth. I was no longer Max Best: Mystery Winger. But there was no point having a tactical brain on the touchline if I wasn't going to listen to her.

I wandered back to the DM slot, let play stabilise again, and drifted over to be close to D-Day. I played six-, seven-, eight-bounce passes with him, trying to annoy a Boston player into leaving the low block. It worked. He came at me, lunged, and I dabbed the ball back to Carl. I sprinted and looked over my shoulder to see where the ball was. I had wanted it played slightly to my left, but he'd shanked it right. Mate.

I scrambled across, annoyed that a promising move had lost momentum. But then I thought, why not cross with my left foot? I looked up and saw Henri was surrounded. We needed Raffi. We needed bodies in the box, or we needed every pass in one move to be sharp and accurate.

With a push of the ball towards our own goal, I retreated, watching as Boston's players fell into shape, some slower than others. I passed to Donny and jogged to the other side of the pitch. Sandra's general concept was good—it was what we'd done against Kidderminster in the late stages. Why not start early?

At halftime, I had three or four minutes of quiet massage. My fitness had been improving steadily until I'd hit the plateau, and in a game like this where I wasn't storming up and down the length of the pitch doing long sprints, I felt I could just about last the ninety.

When I got down, thanking Dean, I went to Sandra and was about to tell her the plan for the second half when I remembered she knew the game, too. "Thoughts?"

"We might win like this, but we need bodies in the box," she said. "Four-three-three."

"Width is more important than numbers." From wide we could do a lot more damage than if we tried to attack centrally.

"Right. I forgot you do that narrow four-three-three. I'll never understand it. Four-two-four, then," she said.

"Better. But the fullbacks might end up not doing anything." We hadn't practised the Art of Slapping from a 4-2-4. It would probably work in the end, but one fullback would typically be out of the game, doing nothing. "Three-five-two," I said. "I'll be the third centre back but I'll go roaming. Could be a two-five-three with me wide left."

"Left?"

"Link with Aff. Really hammer that side."

She calculated. "So Trick and Steve come off. Tony as second striker. Who goes into midfield?"

"What do you think?"

"Pascal?"

"Bingo."

"What if we score and they come at us?"

I smiled. "Then we'll have a lot of fun, won't we?"

It was hard to explain, but just having Pascal on the pitch gave me an injection of energy. There were certain players I had a good on-pitch connection with. Guys who understood what I was trying to achieve and would help me do it. Henri, Raffi, and Pascal topped the list. I found myself wanting to drift infield to combine with Pascal, and darting forward to be a third striker. Most of the time, though, I stuck to the plan of overloading the left. Now we had two to aim for, with Pascal under instructions to arrive late in the box, if he could, and cause a nuisance.

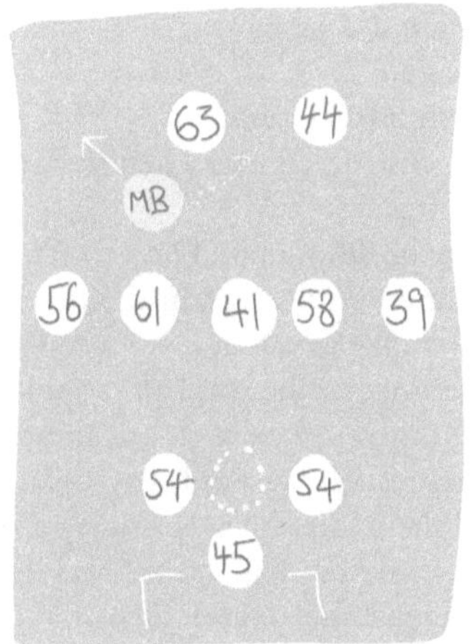

MAX BEST'S TACTICAL INDISCIPLINE
16 DEC '23   BOSTON (H)

As we tried this concept, it became clear that while Raffi Brown's late drives in the danger area were a genuine nuisance, Pascal was something else entirely. He was more like a pet who had decided to wander between your legs while you were checking your phone for the latest score from Darlington versus Kidderminster. Chaos, but not the sort we wanted. We'd have to work on that. Something for some private sessions, perhaps.

By the way, I really wished I had the Live Scores and Live Tables perks. They weren't worth the cost, not when I had so much else to buy, but on days like these it'd be so much fun, or so very stressful, to see what was happening in the other games and how that affected the standings.

While I'd lost concentration, Aff had surged forward with no support. With a slight panic, I hared towards Henri, feeling the effort drain my battery.

Aff fired the ball high, but now I was the third player in the box. The ball went all the way to the right, where D–Day collected it, took a touch, and looked up. He had three of us to aim for and I quite fancied scoring another towering header. So I nearly erupted when he played a weak, lame pass side-ways. What the fuck?

My skin went bonkers: goosebumps, tingles, hairs on end, the works. He'd laid the ball to Pascal.

I zipped sideways, paused, then darted towards the young German. He fired the ball at me, low and hard, and I deflected it with the side of the back of my heel into Henri's path. He lashed it past the goalie.

One–nil, relief, and the crowd finally had something to cheer.

I celebrated with the lads, then peeled myself away and jogged to Sandra. "What's the score?"

"Still nil–nil, but Kiddies got a man sent off and their other centre back has done his hamstring!"

Wow. They'd lost both centre backs in consecutive games. "That's what you get when you don't rotate. Fuck."

"What?" She'd seen that I was disappointed.

I shrugged. "Just thought it'd be harder."

"To what? Win the league?"

"Yeah," I said, with a hint of sadness.

"Go back to DM," she instructed me. Then she added, "Please."

"What about entertaining our fans?"

"Sorry, Max, but we're professionals. They won't thank you if we all have fun and come out with a draw. You've given them a moment of magic, but if Kiddies slip up and we don't take advantage, it's a bad day. Now do your job."

I walked away, a bit downcast. She was right, but if I had another 30 points of CA I could really go gung-ho. Really smash these teams up. But I didn't. And that's why I was going on holiday. And why I was signing Goliath.

Sandra was smart and she hadn't been sprinting around. She was thinking clearly. Not only that, if I made her feel valued and listened to her, she might stay at the club longer. Maybe she would turn down the first offer she got because she was having so much fun.

And most of all, the more often I deferred to Sandra, the more my players would respect her. Henri pitched his ideas, as did Pascal, and sometimes I took small ideas of theirs. But when it came to influencing my decisions, Sandra was many levels above those guys, and she'd had the balls to sub me off when she didn't like what she was seeing. Yep. It would be good if I played up that side of things.

The commentary alerted me that Boston would come at us more. In the tactics screens, I saw that they'd abandoned the low block and would try their normal 4-4-2 defensive style. Direct balls to the strikers, load the box at free kicks and corners.

"Glenn, Carl, you awake?"

"Yes, boss."

"What I want for Christmas is a clean sheet."

Glenn frowned. "Boston are there for the taking, boss."

"Sandra says shut it down."

Glenn's face lit up. "She does?"

"Finally," said Carl. "A boss who understands football. Merry Christmas to one and all!"

The three of us dominated their strikers, our midfield dominated theirs, and we had chances to get the second goal. It didn't come, but there were no scares. No surprises. One–nil, three points. Not quite the football of my dreams, but the home fans went away happy enough.

When I got to the touchline, Sandra told me the news. Kidderminster had lost. That put my former team back into title contention, but that wasn't the headline. The headline was that we were only three points away from being top of the pops.

	TEAM	P	W	D	L	F	A	GD	PTS
1	Kidderminster	22	14	7	1	39	14	25	49
2	Chester	20	15	1	4	53	20	33	46
3	Darlington	21	12	7	2	32	19	13	43
4	York	23	11	9	3	38	25	13	42

There was one more match to play before Christmas day. We were away to Bradford (Park Avenue), the worst team in the league. Kidderminster were away to South Shields—a tricky match at the best of times, but they'd lost both their starting centre backs and one of their talented strikers.

If we won and Kiddies lost, we'd be the Christmas number one.

It wouldn't happen. No chance. It wasn't even worth thinking about.

But it's all I did think about, and later I realised the wins and the transfers and the wine had pushed away all thoughts of Sullivan and his metal pipe. My mind's eye was firmly fixed on one thing: the remarkable Christmas gift I hoped to wrap up for the people of Chester.

9

THE TWELVE DAYS OF SILKMAS, PART 3

ix.

On the ninth day of Christmas, the cosmos gave to me . . . a match to boil my wee.

Tuesday, December 19.

England's left-sided centre back had time and space. He took a couple of strides forward, calculated, gambled on a couple more. Still no Welsh player bothered with him. One more stride? Why the devil not?

Now a Welsh dude, bedecked in all red with flashes of white—very Santa Claus—sprinted at the ball. Behind him, his teammates were spread out, ready to press, ready to compete. The England guy passed into the feet of a midfielder, who was immediately swarmed. He fell over, somehow, the ball bobbled around, and Wales tried to launch a fast break. It *broke* all right, broke down at the first vaguely complicated pass. Instead of using the chance to counter Wales's counter, the England guys passed back to the defenders, allowed Wales to reset, and the whole farce started again.

So went most of the first half. Long periods of tedium—the Welsh goalkeeper took one full minute for every goal kick—interspersed with tiny moments of frantic activity that ended with no progress on either side.

"Argh!" I yelled, and got to my feet. "Glenn, am I allowed to boo England?"

"Depends if you think they're Marxists," he said, in reference to a *Daily Mail*–led media campaign that had tried to recast England's bland, inoffensive first team as some kind of raging socialists. That particular culture war had flared up, died away, and now the gammons were on to something else.

Our big evening out was not going well. Seventy-four people from Chester had boarded three specially commissioned buses. Men's and women's first-team players plus WAGs and BAHs (boyfriends and husbands), our coaches, Inga, Joe, MD, and so on. MD had decided to let the club pay for the transport. That was a good gesture and pretty cheap as Christmas gifts went.

We'd arrived early enough to see Raffi warming up, wearing his England kit, laughing and joking and looking around Altrincham's stadium with disbelief writ large on his face. Shona, Raffi's wife, and Moss, his dad, were near me, and we yelled out at him. "Raffi! Give us a wave! Raffi Raffi give us a wave!" More of the Chester mob joined in until Raffi shyly gestured in our direction. Our cheer was one of the biggest of the night.

But then, as our carnival was getting going, the teams had been announced.

England were 4-4-2 with lots of players from the National League. I knew about a third of them from my scouting. They had CAs ranging from 50 to 80, but most were around 70. Chester's average, remember, was just over 50. We'd be in the same division as these guys next year. Seven or eight months from now, in fact. Mildly worrying.

If we could finish this season with an average CA of 55, we'd still lose a bunch of games at the start of next season. But as we kicked on to 60, we'd be competitive. At 65, we'd start winning. Could we scrap hard enough at the start so that a late run would put us in the playoffs? What a lame ambition; the playoffs were *such* a lottery.

I shook my head. Those were problems for future Max.

Back to England C. Four-four-two, lots of physical boys, hard runners, hard tacklers. Not a lot in the way of technique. And no Raffi in the starting eleven. I suppose that didn't come as a surprise. He was CA 52 and playing in the division below everyone else. He scored goals from midfield, though. There was no split between football hipsters, dinosaurs, and floating megabrains—goals from midfield were priceless.

But when the subs were read out and Raffi wasn't among them, there was serious deflation. That's when everything else started to grate.

The rain. The abysmal football. The queues for the burgers. The burgers.

"Max," said Shona. "Sit down. Tell me all about it."

"About what?"

"About what's boiling your wee."

"The pitch is a bog. The rain feels vindictive. There's loads of scouts here and that Welsh goalie is doing everything he can to waste time in the match. Imagine that. You've got the chance to show what you can do in front of scouts from England, where all the money is, and your goalie is trying to bore them all into leaving early. I'd go and punch him in the mouth, if it was me. But their manager must have asked him to do it."

"There's scouts?"

"And agents." I pointed to a section of the main stand where there was, no exaggeration, over a hundred and fifty scouts, and at least twenty agents. "Your mate Bradley Rymarquis is here."

"He's not my mate, Max. I wrote to him once."

"And the football. Christ. No ambition, no flair, no style. This is the worst game I can remember seeing. It's Sunday League quality." I ruffled my hair. "Raffi would change the dynamic. He can take a pass from a defender, hold it, and retain it in midfield. None of these pricks can do that. That one thing would unlock Wales."

"Do you think they came to see Raffi?" said Moss, who I thought hadn't been listening.

"Probably more interested in the Welsh lads. In theory, all the best Welsh players who aren't playing for big teams are here. They have some handy players, by the way. Give them a proper manager, for example *me*, and they'd do well. But urgh! Raffi's one of the most talented guys here. It just didn't occur to me that he wouldn't play. They've seen him in training. He can do everything these pricks can do, and more." I shook my head, genuinely getting angry. "This England C manager was in charge of like twenty League Two games, won three. He's rubbish. And he's got himself made boss of England C and that's his little fiefdom. It's typical of the sport and the country. We don't want anyone good in charge. He gets points for taking a look at Raffi, but loses them all by not even having him on the bench." Also, it was embarrassing to me, personally. We'd come all this way and it had been a bust. If I'd come alone, I'd have been annoyed. If I'd brought Sandra, I'd have been apologetic. But I'd brought every-fucking-one. It was flat-out catastrophic.

"I hear you've been stopping Raffi from leaving," said Moss.

"Don't," whispered Shona, though I wasn't sure who it was aimed at.

"He'll leave when it's the right time for him. This summer, I reckon. Move him up to League Two, see how long it takes him to get up to speed. Another three-year contract there, people starting to look at him near the end of the second year. He'll be 25 when he gets to a Championship club. A year to break into the first eleven. Five good years running their midfield. Couple of cup runs, couple of shots at making the Prem." I nodded. Every time I said it out loud, it sounded better and better. "Thirty grand a week minimum. That's one point five million a year, Shona."

"He'll get there even if you let him leave this January," whined the doddering old Ian Evans–loving fool.

"Nope. If he signs for a club that's too far ahead of his, let's say *current ability*, he'll never play. If he never plays, he'll never improve. He'll never get to those levels."

"You just want him in your midfield, scoring goals, winning you games."

"Yeah? Except I just said I'd let him leave in the summer. I just said he could skip the National League level and go straight to League Two. It's not about me. It's about him and his career and providing for his family. Five million pounds over three years. That's the goal." Half a mill of that going into my pockets; damn right I intended to do it the right way and not try for a shortcut.

Shona squeezed my arm and shook her head. I calmed down, and she released me. "Do you have a club in mind? In League Two."

"Not right now. I've got friends at Tranmere and I'm going to meet the guy who owns Grimsby. The Chester fans wouldn't be too pleased if I sold Raffi to Wrexham, but they don't get a vote. Wrexham have got the money; that's for sure. I had thought about Stockport County but they've won like fourteen games in a row. They're going to win the league. I'll be doing a lot of League Two scouting soon. I'll meet some of the head honchos along the way."

"At least find a club in London," whined my tenth-least favourite person in this stadium. "Where it's warm."

I brought up my shitty mental map of the country. "Crawley Town are somewhere south. They've got a good manager. Timo Jentzsch. I don't know much about him, but they bought him from Benfica to be their player-manager. He only played a few games, so it was like they were buying a manager which is an unusual way to go about it. He kept them in the league and now they're in playoff contention. I want to learn more about him because that club had been chaotic before he took over. It's owned by Bitcoin guys. I suppose if Bitcoin goes up, they'd have the money to buy Raffi. AFC Wimbledon is south, but I don't know if they've got money for transfers. Forest Green might be down there, somewhere. They're that vegan club. They're struggling in the league, though."

"Raffi can eat vegetables so long as his dad can be warm in the stadium," said Moss.

"I'm going to mingle," I said, and wandered along the rows of seats looking for someone less annoying to talk to. "Donny, go get me a Four Horsemen."

He blinked, showing that he knew what it was. How did everyone know these random things? "We've got Bradford on Saturday."

"I don't want a drink. I want to sit in your spot. Go and talk to Shona for a bit."

"Oh! Right."

He scarpered and I sat next to Trick Williams. One thing that could cheer me up: confirmation that he'd be leaving soon. "Trick dude."

"Gaffer."

I did a theatrical look around to see if we might be overheard—our section was rammed. "Any news?"

"Yeah. It's on. Eastleigh."

What a buzz! How did I keep so outwardly calm? "That's Southampton, right?"

"Right."

"Fuck. Lot of travel."

"It's all right. I like the banter on the team bus. The logo's a spitfire. Looks just like Swindon Supermarine we just played. National League, too. So I'll be able to prove you wrong about hacking it."

I smiled. "Good money?"

"Pretty good, yeah. Brad fucking hates you, mate." He laughed.

"Top. Top top top. So . . . probably won't play you the next few games, just in case?"

His head dropped. "I want to play."

"And get injured and in six months you've got no money coming in? Come on. Think."

He exhaled. "Yeah."

"When's it going to happen?"

"Third of Jan, they reckon. Just as you're settling into your holiday. Really trying to twist the knife."

"Cool. That's good. Yeah, that'll do."

"Where are you going, anyway? You haven't told us."

"Not too far. You won't want a postcard. All right. Looks like a win-win."

"Will I get a league winner's medal?"

"Yep. If you can't get up here for the final day, we'll find a fake Trick to dance around the pitch and all that."

I got up and thought of giving him a friendly pat on the shoulder, but I didn't, just in case Rymarquis saw it. I looked around and went to sit near Magnus, kicking Livia out of her seat. "Dude. You happy with us?"

"Yes."

"Want a new contract?"

"Maybe. What are the options?"

"You're not doing much coaching. I reckon we formalise you as player-physio. I'd like to tie you down to a long contract, but you don't seem the type."

"I'd prefer to be flexible. I have dreams that extend beyond football."

"Just another year, then, with a pay raise that kicks in if we get promoted."

"I will meditate on it."

"Great. Choose someone for me to talk to next."

"Don't you want to watch the match?"

"No. It's aggravating."

"Andrew Harrison."

That got my pulse racing. While the squad's overall morale was very high, individual players seemed to become happier or sadder on a gentle curve. Henri, to nobody's surprise, was one of the moodier characters. He often had two-point swings in his morale. Youngster and Pascal, despite being teenagers, were two of the most stable.

Recently, Trick's morale had spiked up and down like a seismograph. I guessed the ups were him looking forward to his new club, his new contract, and a general feeling of being valued, while the downs were him thinking about missing his friends, being apprehensive about playing in a higher league, and so on.

Only one player's morale had been trending downwards with no prospect of a rebound.

"What makes you say Andrew?"

Magnus frowned and leaned closer. "He can't ground himself."

"But he touches grass."

Magnus broke into a big smile. He enjoyed it when I teased him about his beliefs because, since being cursed, I'd been pretty open to believing all kinds of mad bullshit. One day, when I didn't have seventy careers to look after, I'd try some Reiki or one of those things where you talk to candles.

"His radiance is diminished."

"You say that like it's a bad thing." Another big smile. "But it's interesting you'd choose him. You're very perceptive." I went over and made Michael and Noah leave the area. "Andrew, bro."

"What's he done now?"

"Who?"

"Noah."

"I don't know." We both frowned. "Has he been making a nuisance of himself? Well, it hasn't reached my ears, which means the coaches can handle it, which means it isn't worth mentioning. No, I wanted to talk about you. You all right?"

When we were talking about Noah, he was mega interested, mega present. Now I wanted to talk about him, he shrank. Eye contact stopped. "I'm fine."

I folded my hands in my lap and waited, eyes half-closed, not amused. I had just enough of my vision on the pitch to keep collecting XP, not that there was much of that. The curse was treating this like watching a National League match, which made sense given that was the level of the players. The Welsh league was considered a much lower standard, but the curse generally gave XP based on the higher level of the two teams.

Andrew closed his eyes, counted to some inordinately high number, and when he opened them found I was still there. "It's Gemma."

I leaned away from him. "Hhhhh what?"

He crunched his shoulders into his neck, defensive, asking me to keep the volume down. Maybe because Henri was nearby and he knew about their fling. "You set it up!"

"Me?"

He rubbed the skin around his upper eyelid. He couldn't get *too* mad at me because I was his boss and he was mortally afraid of the Brig. "Anyway. I was thinking of . . . you know."

"Asking her to marry you."

"Of ending it."

"Right. She's not your type. You prefer uggos."

He quashed some burst of anger. "Do I have to talk to you about this?"

"No," I said, standing up. But I sat right down again. "Actually, yes. There's some Christmas dinner bullshit tangled up in this. You've been invited to the Weavers', right?"

He nodded. "Emma said you'd behave in front of one of your players."

I laughed, but he wasn't joking. She'd really said it! "Right. Relationship advice. I can do that. What's the problem?"

He spread his elbows so he could pull at his hair. "There's no problem. She's just . . . It's me."

"Oh, fuck that," I said, annoyed. "Spit it out, Jesus Christ."

He counted to a billion again, in which time Wales's keeper took one goal kick. "She's trying to change me and stuff."

"Yeah? She trying to make you give it your all in training? Well, it isn't working, is it?"

Another annoyed look. I was slapping this conversation. Ten-out-of-ten material here. He swallowed, opened his mouth, thought better of it, dipped his head, sighed, and looked at me. "She wants me to dress good and stuff. Always wants to go shopping and that."

Waves of cosmic information flooded into me from all angles. This was something I could understand; I'd been in his shoes! "Okay. Gemma's a hot brunette who likes to dress nice. She wants to go to nice restaurants and bars and show off her body and her hair and, yeah, her man. Have you been doing that?"

"Not much, no. You don't pay me enough." I went to his player profile and opened the Contracts tab. It showed me what I already knew: weekly wage, salary length, future increases, release clauses, and so on. Adding this screen had cost me a 1,000 XP but only showed me data from my own players. Excitingly, though, my purchase had led to Contracts 2 becoming available. And, miracle of miracles, it offered exactly what I wanted—it would show me the contracts of players *from other clubs*. It was a hefty 5,000 XP, but that was cheap. I'd have paid four times as much. This knowledge would supercharge me. The price had made me recalibrate *when* I'd buy it, though. Maybe I would unlock an attribute first so that I kept the feeling of forward momentum.

I touched his coat and flicked at his fringe. "You're not blowing all your dosh on *drips* and Christ knows you're not spending it on *trims*. So what are you doing that you don't like doing?"

He inhaled. "It's not about what we do. It's about what she *wants* to do. I live in a glorified hostel. I'm poor and I've got my brothers to take care of. That's my priority and always will be. I can't spend hundreds of pounds on meals and shoes and aftershaves."

"Emma wants me to dress nice and she likes being taken to fancy restaurants and having nice holidays. You might have noticed that I dress like a tramp most of the time. And that's fine with her because she knows I'm busy and don't care much about that kind of thing, but every now and then I wear a suit or do something fancy and she enjoys it, and I enjoy it, too, truth be told. Wouldn't want to do it every day, but she's my special little pumpkin and I like making her happy. And do you know why I don't mind a bit of hoodie-related banter? Because we talked about it. Right at the beginning, I told her how I felt about clothes and style and fashion. Easy. Now Gemma is a bit more into that stuff than Ems, but she's smart, she's a lawyer, she has a career. She isn't some pointless WAG who's obsessed with looks and only looks. If she's dating you, it's because she likes you as you are. And sure, she can imagine a future where you look and smell amazing all the time. She's not wrong to imagine you better. That's what I'm doing. Because as a player, right now, you look and smell like dogshit. You're ranked last for improvement across every team, every age group. Michael's fine, Noah's fine. Your family is in a good place; you've done your job. Now it's time to get selfish. Get your head on your career. Talk to the hottest woman you'll ever date. It'll be fine. And on Christmas Day, you'll smile and be charming and laugh at my jokes." I nodded and got to my feet. "Max Best has spoken. Boom. Smashed it. Next."

I wandered around, looking for my next opportunity to spread seasonal goodwill. I didn't think anything of it at the time, but Henri was nearby and had heard my final words. He scribbled into a notebook, looking slightly demented.

The match finished 1–0 with England scoring after a Welsh defender made a mistake. But my restless mood had made me bounce around the travelling contingent, forcing people to move around and sit next to different people, and that proved to be a big hit. Every time there was a change in the seating arrangements, there was a little bump in energy, and by the time we set off home, everyone was having a good time.

Not what I'd wanted, then, but by the time we got onto the buses, my wee was a healthy, normal temperature.

x.

On the tenth day of Christmas, the cosmos gave to me . . . the fruit of a writer's psyche.

Friday, December 22.

I'd never been to a football club's Christmas party. Last year I'd got myself uninvited to my former club's do when I said I wanted to leave to become Chester's director of football.

My guess was that there would be rivers of booze, dozens of scantily clad party babes, pumping music, and a final drunken message from the manager reminding the lads not to overdo it since they had a match at three o'clock the next day. And hey, maybe that's how it went down at other clubs, but for some reason, Henri Lyons had been placed in charge of our event.

It was scheduled to start at 5 p.m. Henri wanted it later but I had a date with destiny at Tranmere that evening and even starting at 5 was pushing it. By the appointed hour it was basically pitch-black, and if anyone wasn't feeling especially Christmassy all they had to do was stand outside for a couple of minutes and they'd get a jolly red nose and, depending on how thick their undies were, a couple of snowballs.

At one minute to five, we parked and the Brig pushed me into a secondary school's assembly room. There were paintings on the walls, a raised platform at the front, and lots of fancy details in the wood that made me think we were in Tyson's expensive private school. I had been deep in thought on the drive, not paying much attention to where we were going.

It looked like I was the last to arrive and that was very much intentional. The men's and women's first teams were there, all mixed up, but no partners. This was strictly internal. With all the backroom staff, we were getting up to fifty people in the group. There was one empty chair near the front, but while everyone else was on the school's shitty hard-backed wooden numbers, I had a red armchair covered with an embroidered dresser scarf.

I flopped into it and Kisi Yalley appeared to my side, handing me a flute of champagne.

"I can't drink that. We've got Bradford tomorrow afternoon."

"It's alcohol-free," she said. "All the drinks are, except for Vimsy's. Henri says he's to be our sin-drinker. I don't like the phrase, but Vimsy is happy about it."

"What's— Oi!" I looked down at my feet where Charlotte was trying to push a red ottoman under my feet. "Oh!" I looked to my left where the nearest players were shaking their heads and laughing. Did they think I'd insisted on VIP treatment or did they know this was Henri's idea?

I didn't have time to think. A red curtain fell, hiding the stage from us. Lots of stomping happened behind it, and in the main hall, the lights dimmed. Then spotlights shone on the red curtain, sweeping diagonally around like air defence lights from World War II.

A voice boomed out from speakers built into either side of the stage.

"China. The year 3000. An AI entity known as Cow Cow has allowed small quantities of silksteel to be sold to the west, specifically France."

What? A single, nervous laugh popped out of me.

"President Napoleon the Professional is obsessed with silksteel and is determined to discover the secret of its manufacture."

A young face popped out from the gap in the middle of the curtains. FA Cup hero Benny! "It's spiders," he said. "Spoiler alert." He vanished.

The narrator continued. "Napoleon sends his top agent and cousin, Ohnree-Leon to steal the secret of silk from the Chinese." Dramatic pause. "This is that story."

Benny's hands emerged from the same place his head had been, but now he was holding a wide sign that read, *APPLAUSE.*

So we applauded.

To my left, Trick and D-Day were cackling, which made me get hot. There were loads of other players, and then to the side, an annoying light. I leaned up and felt pretty sure the light was next to Dani. Huh. I supposed if she couldn't hear what was going on, it was all right if she was on her phone. We couldn't ask her to wait outside or whatever. This was Henri's version of including her.

The curtains slid apart and now I saw the stage.

On the right was a big sign, about two metres wide, that said *SILK!* There was smaller writing underneath but it wasn't well illuminated. I think it said, *by Henri Lyons* or similar.

Right at the back of the stage, in the middle, was a projection of an image. It was the Deva stadium, but with some photoshopped cyberpunk elements such as a hovercar going past. I nodded—this was much cheaper than having to make real sets and you could get really creative. Shame for professional set makers, but that's progress.

Entering stage left were Tyson, Captain, and Bomber from the under-six-teens. The defenders were wearing yellow plastic coats and sunglasses—to show it was the future, I guess—while Tyson was in red.

"What's happening, Glenn Junior Junior Junior etc?" said Tyson.

Captain straightened. "Not sure, journeyman striker Tony Hetherington."

Now might be a good place to mention that from this point, unless specifically mentioned, at least one person in the audience laughed at every single line in the . . . the . . . the *play?* This time it was Tony laughing hardest, along with those sat near him.

Captain, apparently playing the role of a descendent of first-team captain Glenn Ryder, continued. "All I know is that the hero of the age, he who glitters in the dark, he who knows fourteen ways to look at a blackbird, Henri Lyons pronounced in the French way, repeat for the avoidance of doubt, Henri Lyons, asked us to meet him here."

Fifteen-year-old right midfielder Sevenoaks, also in a yellow coat, fake jogged onto the stage. He looked a lot more nervous than the others and his delivery was stilted. "I just got the message. Am I in time?"

"Yes, Donny D-Day Dorigo." The two pricks near me cheered to see that one of them was part of the story. See? Representation matters. "We're just waiting for Henri to come."

"I wonder who will be playing that role?" said Sevenoaks.

"What?" said Tyson, hands on hips. "Don't get meta! And don't break the fourth wall, either." He turned and wagged his finger at us, the audience. "That goes for you, too!"

"What's all this, then?" said Dan Badford, the −1 PA midfielder I'd discovered at Das Tournament. Unlike the other cast members, he wasn't dressed in any sort of futuristic style. In fact, he was wearing the clothes of a Victorian street urchin, except he had a long, twirly villain's moustache which he caressed sensually whenever he said anything funny, which was often. He had a minor part, but he really stole the show.

"Oh, bother," said Tyson. "It's that bloody Trick Williams again." Trick's nonstop giggling ceased, his eyes went wide with amazement, and then he laughed twice as hard. "You get out of here, Trick Williams! You know what will happen if Max Best sees you."

Dan Badford twisted his moustache. "Best? Huh! He'll get sacked any day now. I'm just bidin' me time."

"It's been almost a thousand years!" complained Tyson. "As established, it's the year 3000! Give it up!"

"Mwaaaaaaah," said Dan, an extraordinary noise that conveyed that while he knew Tyson was right, he wasn't going to change. He slunk away behind the *SILK!* sign.

Angelic music flooded the hall, which after a half second delay, led to more laughter. We all knew where this was going: the arrival of the great man himself. Which kid from the under-sixteens would be playing him? Benny, maybe. Lucas Friend? It would have to be the most handsome kid, and that would probably have been Tyson. Would Tyson play two roles? He was absolutely killing it as Tony, so why not?

Henri Lyons himself strode onto the stage—more laughs at his arrogance—in a silver macintosh. He was also wearing a shiny silver and gold glove on his left hand. "You have answered my call!" he said, hamming it up big time. We in the audience were having a blast, but no one was enjoying this more than Henri. "The weather is foul, my friends, and the tidings are grim. But here you are, steadfast and true. I award you five relationship points." He tapped on the back of his glove like there was a computer in it. One by one, the young cast members reacted as though receiving a power-up.

"How may I assist you?" said Tyson.

Dan Badford came out again and a snide look came on his face. "What would *you* know about assists? Bwaah." He left the stage again.

Henri stepped to the edge of the stage and swept his gloveless hand in a wide arc. "I have been given a mission. A dangerous and difficult one. If I go alone, I will surely die." He dipped his head, but lifted it again. "I need a team! A merry band of brothers, a unit, a squad. Each with complementary and overlapping gifts. A getaway driver, a hacker, and someone who doesn't know about life in the year 3000 to act as an audience surrogate."

"Okay," said Captain. "I'm in, right, but we'd better hurry up and get on with it."

Henri frowned. "Why the rush?"

"You know why! Because if Max hears about this, he'll want to take over like he always does!"

"Not this time. This time I will stand up for myself. This time I am the one with the skills, the knowledge, and the passion for the project. Yes, this time, I will be in charge."

The curtain closed. A few people clapped but were stifled by the narrator's voice.

"One minute later."

The curtain opened again, and now there was Benny, wearing a cheap black hoodie, looking at some plans on a table, with the young actors to his left and Henri sulking behind him to the right.

"So what we'll do, right," said Benny, "is we'll take the screamjet to Beijing, which as you know is sponsored by a beer company and is now called Gan Beijing."

Two people rushed out of the wings. One was Kisi, wearing a black macintosh and a white priest's collar. She also had a halo of tinsel that hovered an inch above her head somehow. The other was Charlotte, wearing a yellow mac. They got close to Benny.

Kisi said, "Very good joke, Mr. Best."

Charlotte said, "*Sehr lustig!*"

Benny clicked his fingers and the scene behind him changed. Now it looked like one of those old buildings in China, but again with the same flying hovercar in exactly the same part of the screen. I hoped it would be there on every image and wondered how many in the audience would notice. "I've analysed the sitch and I can say with a billion percent confidence that the secret of silk is definitely here, inside the Forbidden Palace, and it's definitely not a trap."

Dan Badford, playing Trick Williams you remember, came back to his little part of the stage and leered. "Did someone say Palace? Talk about a tough away trip! Why's it forbidden, anyway? It's health and safety gone mad!"

Benny clenched his fists. "Get lost, Trick!"

Dan slunk away again.

Kisi said, "Well done, Mr. Best!"

Charlotte said, "*Gut gemacht, mein Lieber!*"

Henri coughed. "Max, I think we should focus our efforts on the city of Luoyang. It's on the historical Silk Road, there's an enormous factory there that came online a week before silksteel became available for purchase, and a new quarter called Silk Factory Number One is guarded day and night by killer robot dogs, swarms of drones, and old men who sit around drinking tea playing mahjong."

Benny sighed. "Mate. It's not there. It's in the Forbidden City. It's obvs."

Kisi and Charlotte intoned: "Max Best has spoken."

Benny continued. "Now, look, don't stress. I've got a plan. What's the last thing they'd expect?"

Henri looked up at the stage lights. "I do not know. Perhaps we go there pretending to film a movie, but in fact it's a masterfully plotted, meticulously prepared heist."

"My plan's way better than that. Ready? It's four-four-two."

"Pardon me?"

"They'll never expect four-four-two! Knock it long to a big man! No one's used four-four-two for eight hundred years; they'll never see it coming. Yep, that's the ticket. It's absolutely foolproof and nothing can go wrong."

"Max Best has spoken."

The curtain closed, and this time stayed closed for longer. A hubbub of chat exploded in the cheap seats, interspersed with big belly laughs as people remembered lines.

The curtain opened, the picture had changed to a throne room or some such, and Benny was rubbing his hands, delighted. "We're in! I knew it'd work! Now to find the secret of silk production. Um . . . Henri, try that box."

"You want me to open this box? Box number one?"

"Yes."

"What about . . . box number two?"

Music from a gameshow played, causing Trick and D-Day to go all the way back into hysterics. "Open both boxes, you twat!"

Henri opened the first one and the background image changed to be a portcullis. "It's a trap!"

Benny pointed. "What are those mysterious lights that are coming closer? The lights! They're coming closer! Everyone in the audience can use their imaginations to— Argh! The lights got me!"

The curtain closed again, and quickly reopened. The sign that said *SILK!* had gone, freeing up more space on the now totally bare stage.

"Where are we?" said Tyson.

Benny snapped his fingers. "Got it! It's an escape room. What you do, right, yeah, got it. Let me try first. Okay so you pour the five litres into the three-litre jug. Then you've got two litres left. Pour that into the four-litre jug and pour *that* into the three. *Voilá.* You've got minus two. Wait. Where are the jugs?"

"Max 77," said Henri. "It's not an escape room. We've been portal fantasised."

"What does that mean?"

"It means we've been sucked into a time loop and the only way out is to revisit scenes from our past and learn things from them."

"I was just about to say that," said Benny.

"Well done, Mr. Best," said Kisi.

"So kluggy kluggy," cooed Charlotte, and the laugh from Pascal in the audience sounded like it was genuinely painful.

"Everyone get ready," said Henri. "The first scene is about to start!"

Benny nodded. "Top. Through here is it?"

Henri reached out to stop him. "No, Max! That's the time paradox room! We can't go in there until we've educated the audience about the specific rules of this specific time loop story! Max, noooooo!"

The curtain closed.

Somewhere behind me, Pippa leaned over to Sam and said, "This is the best play I've ever seen." And it was hard to disagree.

The curtain opened, and now Sevenoaks was on the right, wearing Chester kit, his foot on a ball. The background picture showed a penalty kick situation from the point of view of the penalty taker.

"I know this scene!" said Henri. "It's where D–Day took a penalty, made a mess of it, and the original Max Best kicked him in the balls."

"What do you mean, the original Max Best?" said Benny. "I'm the original Max Best."

"No, you're his seventy-seventh clone. Hence the name, Max 77. It works. Shush."

"So what do we have to do?" said Tyson.

"Well," said Henri, rubbing the back of his neck. "I think we should stop Max kicking Donny in the balls."

"But that will change history and Max Prime wouldn't have taken over as Chester manager," said Captain.

"That's true," said Henri. "So we should let him kick Donny in the balls."

"Hang on," said Tyson. "But then . . . if he kicks Donny in the sack . . . Donny's great great etc grandson, Donny, who is clearly visible behind us now—" Laughter at Henri's solution to the two Donnies challenge. "—won't be born. He'll vanish and then we'll be down a teammate."

"Wait," said Benny. "If past me kicked past Donny in the two-pack, how come Donny had kids and grandkids and all that?"

"It's a paradox," said Henri. "And we have to solve it to get to the next scene. Tricky. Very tricky."

They all leaned their foreheads into their fists in an exaggerated show of thinking. Just as the energy in the audience was dipping, the picture behind the actors changed to one of Benny kicking Sevenoaks in his special area. Benny was giving a double thumbs-up to the camera, while Seven was doubled up in fake pain.

When it was quiet enough to hear the actors, they continued.

Tyson said, "I've got it! We let the kick happen, but we save the swimmers." He nearly corpsed delivering that line.

Henri, also fighting a battle to keep a straight face, said, "How? A codpiece? Max will know. His foot is so sensitive it enjoys French poetry."

"Paper!" said Tyson. "Find some paper."

"Here," said Captain.

"What is it?" said Henri. "It can't be a vital document, or we'll change history."

"Er . . ." said Captain, reading the two pages he'd picked up. "Looks like proposed contract extensions for Gerald May and Joe Anka."

"Perfect," said Henri. "No one will ever notice those are missing."

The audience, collectively, winced. The play had been taking jabs at people, but that was below the belt. This was a proper roast, now, and no one was safe. Incredibly, everyone fucking loved it.

Captain tore the pages up and crushed them into balls, which Seven shoved down his shorts. Benny kicked Seven in his newly protected groin area, turning to do a thumbs-up, just like in the image. Then Benny took a few steps to the side and rejoined the others.

"It worked!" said Henri. "We're going to the next scene!"

Curtains down, hubbub, and we were back.

Tyson was where Seven had been, spotlit. He'd taken his coat off to reveal that he was wearing a simple red football shirt, but incredibly, he was now sporting a ballerina's skirt. He was rolling a football around under his foot.

"What's this?" said Captain.

"I know!" said Henri. "My great etc grandfather was there that day. This is when Max Prime discovered Dani."

"Oh!" said Benny. "But Dani wasn't playing football that day, was she?"

"No," said Henri. Benny went over to get the ball from Tyson, and it was clear that Tyson did not know what was happening.

"Hey, er, that's not . . ."

"No improv!" snapped Henri. "So, Max 77. Scan your genetically hard-coded memory banks. What do you remember from this day?"

"It's coming back to me. Dani was . . . I think she was miming."

"Miming?" said Henri.

"You know, like pretending she was stuck in a glass box."

"Stuck in a glass box?" said Henri, doing a fucking unbelievable piece of mime work. For a second, I really thought he'd slid a piece of glass onto the stage that we hadn't noticed. "That's right, Dani was miming like she was stuck in a glass box. She was miming . . ." he repeated, nodding while Tyson shook his head vigorously, "that she was stuck in a box."

"Come on, T," shouted someone in the audience.

Tyson sagged, held his hands out, and felt for the glass in front of him. He was a rubbish mime, which made it funnier.

"And then what did she do?" said Henri. None of the actors spoke. Instead, he held up a big sign. It said, *AUDIENCE PARTICIPATION.*

"Dance the robot!" called someone.

"That's right!" said Benny. "He danced the robot."

"She," said Henri, with a twinkle.

Tyson grimaced, but felt he had no choice. He made little jerky movements, rotating his arms in increments of ninety degrees. It wasn't bad. He got some applause.

"I think there was one more thing, though," said Henri, cruelly. Tyson was really shaking his head now. Henri said, "Walking like a certain animal, wasn't it?"

"Chicken!"

"Giraffe!"

"Mollusc!"

"T-Rex!"

"That was it," cried Benny. "T-Rex. She was walking around like a T-Rex and that's how Max Prime knew she'd be good."

Tyson glared at his mate. *I'll get you later.* But with the cheers and jeers from the first teamers ringing in his ears, he shortened his arms and plonk plonk plonked across the stage, finally looking back the way he'd gone and letting out a big roar. He got half a standing ovation.

"So what do we have to change in this scene?" said Benny.

"Er, nothing. Just don't fall and get knocked out."

"What?"

Someone threw a foam brick onto the stage. I think it was supposed to hit Benny on the head, but it didn't even get close. My young striker collapsed, clutching his ear. "Argh," he said, proving that we didn't teach our young players to simulate injury.

"Oh, no," said Henri. "The mission! We'll be stuck here forever. Unless . . . is there a doctor in the house?"

"You could try Dean," said Tyson.

"Dean?" said Henri. He took a few almost drunken steps around the stage—bewildered didn't even start to describe how I felt—before kneeling and pulling up the hatch of a trap door.

Chas Fungrieve, a lanky striker who went to this school, popped his head up. "Go away."

There was fucking pandemonium—some of the biggest laughs yet. My head was reeling. How did Henri know about the "Notes from Underground" thing?

"Dean! We need a doctor."

"You just want my magic spray."

"It's the year 3000. Doctors are basically magic spray operators."

"Where's the patient?" Henri pulled Benny close to the hatch and Chas sprayed him with hairspray. "Can I go now?"

"Yes, thanks. You've saved the day again. What are you doing, anyway?"

Chas got shifty. "Nothing." He lifted a pointed tinfoil hat onto his head and regressed into the depths.

That was the last we saw of Chas. All those rehearsals, all the stress and worry, and the payoff was the top of his head being visible for twenty seconds. *That's* dedication.

"Okay," said Henri. "I think we can handwave scenes three, four, and five. Onto six!"

The curtain closed, some furniture got scraped around, and it opened again.

In the "look at me" slot on the right was Tyson again. Still wearing the tutu, but now in a long, dark, flowing wig. He was gyrating gently from side to side while turning his hands over and over.

"Ah!" said Benny. "This is the day I met Livia."

Biiiig laughs when people realised Tyson was cosplaying our gorgeous physio. I craned my neck to see if I could see her. I saw a ponytail shaking wildly and guessed she thought it was funny.

Henri pointed. "I need to marry her. That's what this scene is about."

"I don't think it is," said Benny, who suddenly had a copy of the script in his hands. He was flicking through it. "No, there's nothing about that."

"I have written a song," said Henri, and he wandered to the back and picked up an acoustic guitar. He pranced around the stage, making it clear he was about to serenade Tyson. Tyson was even more embarrassed than in the previous scene.

"Oi oi oi!" said Dan Badford, rushing onto the stage. "Yellow card! Stop the match! You can't do this. She's in a relationship!"

"No, Trick," said Henri. "On this day, she was single. She's fair game!"

"You have defeated me with logic and historical correctness," said Dan. "Give her your best shot." He moonwalked stage right. I saw him fumble with his hair as he went.

We all fell quiet. I had a ghastly sinking feeling. Henri was going to profess his love for Livia and we were going to have fucking mega drama for Christmas. I felt my breaths coming in irregular jolts. What was I supposed to do? Let it happen?

He strummed his guitar in a way that suggested he knew how to play. To the left of him, as we in the audience saw it, the rest of the team put arms around each other and swayed gently. And when Henri sang, so did they all.

He started with a single *hummmmm*.

There was a burst of laughter from the far side of the hall and Henri smiled. He made Benny hold his guitar while he went to his collection of big signs. He held one up that read, *DANI STOP READING AHEAD.*

So he'd given her the script so she could follow! I wondered how much of the seemingly improvised bits were actually on the page. Most of it, I reckoned. He took his guitar, settled, hummed once more.

And then, the song:

"Fair of face and flowing locks,

We agree Liv-i-a rocks,

How did Jackie bag that fox?

We all have much *bigger*—"

"No! No! No!" Dan Badford burst back onto the stage, but this time he was in one of those bald caps, hurriedly pulled on, and a garish 80s shell suit. "That's a no from me, dog. Shut dat down. Shut dat down."

"What?" said Henri. "You weren't even dating her then, Jackie."

"Nah nah nah. Replay the scene. Replay the scene till I like it." He pulled a card out of his pocket. It said *REPLAY.* "I'm playing my Liverpool card. Replay it. Curtain. Curtain!"

When the stage came into view next, Henri was at the front with Tyson dressed in his future gear again. Back to being Tony Hetherington, then.

"And so," intoned Henri. "We have collected all six crystals from all six zones."

"Sorry, what?" said Tyson. "We don't have any crystals. You never said anything about crystals."

"We have to collect six crystals to end the time loop. I said it eight or nine times. I'm basically a professional writer. I wouldn't have forgotten that."

The kids looked around. "Here's one," said Bomber, and I think that's all he said in the entire production. He looked very nervous but game to contribute.

"Where are the others, though?" said Henri.

At once, everyone on the stage looked up.

"Magnus?" said Benny. Silence. "Magnus, have you been eating our crystals?"

"No." The voice echoed cosmically from all around us. Everyone in the audience looked left, right, down, up. Henri must have hidden speakers all around the room for this one bit.

"Did you eat the crystals, bro?"

"No," came the voice again, but it was followed by a deafening burp. It was so disgusting that there was a silence of about three seconds before the laughter started again.

"Mate," said Benny. "Right, we do the time loop again, gather the crystals, and that's the end of the play, right?"

"Great summary, Mr. Best."

"*Danke für den Überblick.*"

"Yes," said Henri. "All we need is some physical energy to recharge the portal so we can go through."

He smiled at Tyson, who sagged again, knowing some prank was about to happen. "No, Henri. The portal's right there. Fully charged."

"It *looks* fully charged but it needs someone to do ten push-ups to make it totally safe."

"We could all do one push-up each," suggested Tyson.

"I've heard you brag about how good your push-up technique is," said Henri. "I'd feel safer going through the portal if *you* did them."

"Come on, Tyson!" shouted a male voice.

"Show us what you got!" shouted a female voice.

Again, the teenager felt he had no option. He got down and did a quick ten push-ups to massive acclaim and some wolf whistles.

"Wonderful," said Henri, pretending to examine the portal. "Oh, perhaps it's not quite . . ." He glanced at Tyson, who huffed, annoyed. Henri smiled. "Yes, it's very stable now. We must travel through the portal and live our lives in the year 2023. At all costs, we must not meet our past selves. Youngster, avoid evangelical churches and food banks. Pascal, avoid libraries and walking tours. Glenn, stay away from hair salons offering ten-pound trims. Tony, stay away from the poorly lit car park on Tarvin Road on Wednesday nights after ten."

"What about me?" said Benny.

"You're staying here, Max. I can't deal with two of you."

"But there will be two of *you*," cried Benny.

"And that is my Christmas gift to the world!" said Henri, stepping back and holding his arms out to indicate that his doppelgänger would be walking on stage. What sorcery was this? My chest tightened; I couldn't breathe. Henri got cheeky. "Aha! But if only for just a few seconds, I allowed you to dream. And . . . curtain!"

The curtain closed and immediately reopened with the entire cast in a line. The narrator said their real names and who they had played, and one by one they took a bow.

But there was one final gag.

When the voice was telling us that Benny had played Max 77, it hesitated. "You said he was the seventy-seventh clone. But that would make him Max 78?"

"No," said Henri. "He's the seventy-seventh clone of Max."

"The first clone is called what?"

"Max 2."

"Right. It goes Max Prime, Max 2, Max 3, and so on. So this is Max 78."

Henri stewed, realising he'd made a mistake. "I don't take notes!" he yelled, then stormed off.

The lights came up, doors opened, and people wheeled in trolleys of snacks and alcohol-free drinks. A special trolley was for Vimsy and Vimsy alone. Cheerful Christmas music came on, suddenly everyone was wearing party hats, and the Brig was grabbing my elbow and shepherding me towards the exit.

With my head still spinning from what I'd just seen, the Brig pushed me to his car and whizzed me up to Tranmere.

They were playing a relegation six-pointer against Grimsby Town. Grimsby is on the east coast, one of those places that sounds like it's in Yorkshire but isn't. In 2016, it was voted Worst Place to Live in England. The football team featured in the sensational final episode of season one of *Welcome to Wrexham*.

We arrived late, missing kickoff by five minutes. Mateo's version of the Brig, John Driver (not his real name, that's just what I started calling him in my head), met us in the car park and whizzed us through the badged doors until we burst into the director's box like a pair of Christmas fireworks.

"Whoo," I said. The thirty seconds we'd had to wait outside had turned the tips of my fingers into little ice domes.

"Max Best!" said Mateo, rising to shake my hand. You know I don't like handshake culture, but I gripped his hands, held them in place. He looked startled but then understood. "How about a hot drink?"

"Yes, please."

"Alcohol?"

"No, thanks. Game tomorrow." I glanced around and recognised Chris Hale, the lad from Grimsby turned multi-millionaire who had bought his childhood team. I was about to introduce myself, but Mateo intervened. I realised he was blocking my view of the pitch.

"Wait, Max, wait. Have you heard the lineups? The tactics?"

"No," I said. "We rushed here from the Christmas party. Henri Lyons wrote a fucking . . . thing. The rules kept changing with every scene. My head's jelly. Where were the spiders?"

"Good, good. Fresh eyes, then. Take a look and tell us what you see." He stood aside.

I frowned at Chris Hale and his much younger lady friend. They were wearing sceptical looks, and it dawned on me that Mateo had been raving about this floating megabrain he'd found and they rightly didn't believe him. I had no interest in amusing them. I turned back to Mateo. "You want me to do my tricks? Like a performing monkey?"

He grinned. "Come on, Max. It's Christmas! Give us one little treat. You never know, if you impress Chris, he might buy some of your cast-off players."

John Driver handed me a cup of hot chocolate. I took a sip—delicious—and some of my crankiness evaporated. And maybe Grimsby would be an option for Raffi Brown one day. I decided to impress them while being a bit more careful than usual to "see" what the curse told me in an instant. "Tranmere are four-three-three," I said, taking another sip. I paused, pretending to be scanning the pitch, before rattling off the lineup. I thought about going next level by saying something like, "If those are the starters, I'd expect to find X, Y, and Z on the bench." But I resisted the temptation and moved on to the away team. "Grimsby. Four-two-three-one. Ha, my assistant would love that. Shame you've not got the players to do it."

"What do you mean?" This was the first thing Chris had said to me directly. It wouldn't be the last.

I answered by naming the Grimsby starting eleven. "The back four and goalie," I added, "are fine for the level. There's something weird there I can't put my finger on, but in theory it's all fine. Then you've got two defensive midfielders. One's good but his legs have gone, and in this system you're asking him to do a lot of running. The other is that Simon Green. He's dogshit. But anyway, he can't play DM. If he's your best midfielder, holy shit. But at least give him a chance. CM or go home. Then it's three attacking midfielders, and you need good technique and passing for that. I rate you one out of three. And your striker? Wow. You paid a lot of money for him, didn't you? Bad news. He blows. He blows hard." I laughed. "I'm Max Best," I said, stepping forward to shake the guy's hand.

"Chris Hale. This is Candy."

"Hi, Candy," I said. Look how polite I can be!

"I read your manager notes," she said, gloomily. Perhaps it was supposed to be sultry? Whatever she was doing wasn't working on me in the slightest. "You're unprofessional."

"Understood," I said, turning away. "I'll make a big effort to correct my behaviour." I sipped the hot choc.

"Is there any hope for us?" said Chris, vaguely amused by my analysis.

I shrugged. "Don't really care either way. I've pair bonded with Tranmere. I'm Tranmere for life. If you go down, that's Tranmere safe."

Mateo smiled. "That's nice, Max, but Chris is a friend. There aren't many good guys in football, but he's one of them."

"'Kay," I said. "Sack the manager. Get someone else in."

"You, for example?"

"You can't afford me."

"You might be surprised."

I turned to look at him again. It struck me that he was a strange friend for Mateo, and the owner profile provided by the curse showed they were quite different sorts of people. Chris was a much better businessman; he would make the club generate more money. Mateo had a far, far higher interference score, meaning he'd get involved in football matters much more than Chris, who would leave things to the professionals. Chris also had more patience, resources, and ambition.

Chris was resources 14 (compared to Mateo's 4). He wasn't just rich, then, he was filthy rich. He didn't look it; he had the air of an architect. Sort of a flat, mechanical intellect hidden behind short, white hair and round, dark-rimmed glasses. He was wearing a plain jacket, nothing fancy, and normal dad jeans. His, er . . . companion was in a more wealth-appropriate little black number, ready to hit the trendiest hotspot in Soho. I wondered what Andrew Harrison would have made of her.

Mateo spoke. "Chris was like you, working a dead-end job, but he took over the company and turned it into a behemoth."

"Architects," I said, pointing at him.

"Business-to-business services," he said.

"Oh." On the pitch, not much was happening. Both teams were near the bottom of the table and they were playing safety-first garbage. One of the Tranmere defenders panicked and hit the ball as far as he could down the line. "Fuck me," I said. Then I remembered where I was. "Sorry."

"What should he have done?" said Mateo.

I sighed and put the cup down on one of the little tables; my hands were warm now. "It's not his fault. Both teams are playing through the middle, and they're so scared of losing, they're reluctant to commit their fullbacks forward. He doesn't have loads of options."

"If they lose, they'll get shouted at," said Candy.

"It's three points for a win," I said.

"Zero for a loss," she said.

With superhuman effort, I kept my gob shut, but that had the effect of filling the room with awkwardness. Unlike with Henri's special brand of cringe, there wasn't a joke lined up to relax everyone. Mateo tried to restart the chat. "Chris built his company on Max Best principles."

That caught my interest. "What does that mean?"

"How would we describe it, Chris? Inclusivity, diversity, taking care of your staff? People first, profit second?"

Chris took his jacket off, showing that he was wearing a plain blue shirt underneath. The only hint he was rich was that he'd released one more button than most British people would be comfortable with. "Max, when I was young, I read a book called *Liar's Poker*. Do you know it?"

"No."

"It's about sociopaths making money on Wall Street. One of the companies with the biggest arseholes had a guy working in the mail room. Just a nobody who went round handing out letters to the staff."

"On a sort of trolley thing? I've seen it in movies."

"Could be. I don't know. The book didn't mention if it was a trolley or a basket." He paused, and I realised he'd made what he thought was a joke. The surprise in my face was enough for him. "This kid's married and his wife gets sick. She's in hospital and they can't pay the bills. The kid's only been at that company a few weeks but it's his wife so his embarrassment isn't relevant. He bites down his shame and goes to ask a partner for a loan so she can get the treatment she needs. The partner listens, says not to worry about it. The bills get paid. No one ever asks for the money back. They said they'd take care of it, and they did. Done. No questions asked."

"Huh," I said. I wondered if I'd do the same with a Chester employee. Maybe when we had Wall Street bank money.

"That kid ends up becoming a trader. Becomes head trader of mortgage securities. He and his team create a new financial instrument, and people can't get enough of it. For a few years, that one desk with a handful of traders makes more money than the rest of Wall Street combined."

"The rest of Wall Street combined?" I repeated, because it sounded nuts.

"Yes. They invested ten thousand dollars and retained an employee who made them hundreds of millions. I read that story and I thought, that's the kind of place I want to work. When I became a manager, that's how I treated my staff. None of them created a financial instrument that would one day crash the world economy, thank God, but the better I treated them, the harder they worked. The longer, and better, too. The company became innovative, dynamic, and a great place to be."

"They won awards, Max," said Mateo. He seemed to love telling and hearing this story. He was rich because his family owned land. Sure, he invested the profits wisely (except for buying a football club), but he clearly looked up to this man who'd created his own fortune. "And made money. Lots of it. Whatever your price is, he can afford it."

"Nope," I said. "Clubs should be owned by their fans. I'll only work for a fan-owned club."

"Our fans own twenty percent," said Chris. "Is that enough for me to get an interview?"

Again, I realised late that he was joking. He was actually funny, this guy! I cracked a smile. "You know what? Yeah. Can't be *too* picky, can I? Grimsby, eh? What have you got there for tourists?"

"Do you like fishing and learning about fishing?" said Mateo.

Chris stuck his tongue in his cheek and shook his head. "It's a lot more scenic than Birkenhead, Max. And it's a lot closer to your girlfriend."

That made me sit up straight. He'd been scouting me!

Mateo scoffed. "It's not! It's the same distance, you idiot."

"It's half an hour closer. Max, it's a wonderful part of the country, believe me."

"Top. One more reason to look forward to next season."

"What do you mean?"

"I mean we're going up, you're going down, and we'll meet in the middle." I smiled. "Unless you sack your manager. He's rubbish." The guy had low scores in coaching, tactics, man management, and judging players. His only strength was massive determination, which was pointless if he had no actual tools to work with.

"He's respected. Has impeccable references, did a great job at his last two clubs. Signing him was a coup." Chris was mad at me—he'd chosen the manager himself. Done the interviews, taken soundings, believed he'd chosen well.

I didn't feel the need to bicker about it. "Okay," I said, raising my hands in surrender. "What do I know? But everything you said is about his reputation and the PR you got. What about on the pitch? That kid on the bench, Tom Hickman. Very, very talented young centre back." Tom was nineteen, CA 50, PA 120. "Is he improving? How fast? He should be pushing for a starting spot by the end of the season. What about tactics? Is there any flexibility? Do his substitutions turn defeats into draws? Not from what I've seen. When he comes to you in January and gives you a list of five players he wants to sign, do you track the ones you don't buy as well as the ones you do? Because you'll quickly find he's no better at spotting talent than anyone else in the stadium."

"Oh, and James O'Rourke is better, I suppose?"

The truth was James was even worse than Grimsby's clown, but I wasn't going to say that out loud. Ever. "James has one thing no other manager in the football league has."

"What's that?" said Candy, eyeing me with less distaste now.

"A guardian angel," I said, spreading my wings. "Something tells me Tranmere are going to get at least ten points in January. And James is going to survive the season and all will be right with the world. What do you think, Mateo?"

"That's one way it could go," he said carefully.

"Nope. That's the only way it can go. That's how it *will* go." My lips quivered as I thought back to Henri's play. "Max Best has spoken."

xi.
On the eleventh day of Christmas, the cosmos gave to me . . . CA fifty and three.

Saturday, December 23. Match 21 of 46: Bradford (Park Avenue) versus Chester.

I'd decided to assume a low block was coming and go all-out attack from the start. Just wanted to get to the stadium, crush it, and get home. Thinking about this match exhausted me, but when we pulled into the stadium's car park, seeing stewards smiling and wearing Santa hats, seeing dads bringing their kids to the match, I felt alive again.

I'd decreed that Trick wasn't available for the next three games—if he didn't leave on January 3, we might use him again—but the squad was looking good. Morale was high despite, or because of, Henri's bonkers stage show. Tyson had travelled with the firsts as though he might be named as a sub, and if we'd have seven slots, he would have been. His selfless performance in *SILK!* had endeared him to all the first teamers—he felt like one of the gang now. Apparently, such Christmas plays were pretty common in football clubs; it was a rare chance for players to have a dig at their manager, and everyone was meant to take the barbs with good grace. Henri had even apologised to Sandra for not slagging her off, but he said he'd written most of it before she'd arrived.

So far this season, we'd been crazy lucky in terms of avoiding long-term injuries and that had allowed the group to keep training hard. We'd had a few good pops in the past week. Raffi led the way with a two-point gain after training with his fellow England internationals.

Urgh. That match. He hadn't gone on the pitch, so they hadn't presented him with the customary cap. I hoped he'd get one someday, otherwise that travesty would linger.

He'd marched forward to CA 54, though, and suddenly he was looking like one of the very best midfielders in the division. Carl was now our best defender, and Andrew Harrison must have spoken to Gemma, because his morale had gone up and he'd trained like a lunatic. He'd finally cracked CA 20, and Sandra agreed we should increase his minutes on the pitch so he could kick on to the next level.

Bradford were the worst team in the league with an average CA of 36. It hadn't been long ago that *we'd* been putting teams out with CA 40. Our progress had felt glacially slow at times, but here we were, cock of the walk.

In goal I gave Robbo a Christmas match—he was delighted—and at the back started with Carl, Glenn, and Magnus. We'd play a solid defence for ten minutes in case Bradford had ideas of attacking us. Keep it tight first ten!

Ryan, Sam, and Raffi were the three central midfielders. Aff on the left, obviously, with me theoretically lining up as the right mid. In fact, once the game had settled, Magnus would go right mid and I'd do whatever I wanted.

Then Henri and Tony as strikers. Average CA a monumental 53.5. Hoo-rah!

Run up the score in the first half, then give some minutes to Pascal, Youngster, and Andrew Harrison.

Bradford scrapped, worked hard, dug in, and made life as hard as they could. Aff got into his stride pretty fast, easing to an 8 out of 10 rating. Raffi kept surging into the penalty area causing havoc. Our only weak spot was the right, where Magnus wasn't the ideal candidate for whipping in crosses or going on mazy dribbles. So I spent most of the half on that side of the pitch, dragging two defenders to cover me, opening space for everyone else.

After getting no shots on target for the first twenty minutes, we got a move to click, then another, another, another. It was 4–0 at halftime, with two goals for Henri and two for Raffi.

At halftime, I asked Sandra for her thoughts.

"This one's in the bag. We've got Warrington in three days. Local derby. Our fans will be well up for that. We should take you off, and two others. Henri and Raffi, maybe. Wrap you up in cotton wool."

I leaned closer and whispered, "I'm not playing in that one." I moved away and I saw her making calculations. She understood me well: I intended to let her manage that game solo. The tops of her cheeks suddenly flushed with excitement and apprehension. She'd be the first woman to manage a match in England's top six divisions, even sooner than she had expected. Home to Warrington was a potential banana skin—the best team against one of the worst. It could go very, very wrong for her. Whatever happened, she'd get her name in the history books. "If, say, you were picking an eleven against Warrington . . . which three would be the first names on your team sheet?"

"Max Best," she said, with a hint of a plea.

"No."

Her eyes widened, but after a few seconds, she nodded. Of course she couldn't be the manager if I was playing. At least not until she'd got a few wins under her belt. But more likely, I'd take over even if I didn't mean to, just like in Henri's play. She took a breath. "Glenn. No, Aff."

"You can have both." She surprised me by hesitating even further. I made the obvious suggestion. "Henri?"

"Or Raffi."

"Huh," I said. So that's where her mind was. I had the CA ratings to fall back on, but a floating megabrain had Raffi and Henri pretty close in terms of value to the team.

"Well, Henri, yeah. Got to be."

I waited. "Raffi versus Glenn?"

"Need that leadership."

I agreed. "Okay, work out three subs for the guys you want to take off today. I can play left mid if you need."

She scoffed. "Oh, can you?" Almost instantly, she closed her eyes. "Of course you can." She moved some magnets around. "Steve, Donny, Pascal. You slide into DM. Make it boring." It was her turn to whisper. "Just so you know, Kidderminster are losing. We're top on goal difference."

Oh! Amazing. I hadn't made a big deal of that since I knew Kidderminster would pull something out of the bag and we would only waste our mental energy and be disappointed.

Still, we were top of the league in the "as it stands" tables. Better than a kick in the teeth. I went back out with a spring in my step.

For the second half, I made the game boring, just as Sandra had requested. Every time I blasted the ball far and away, I looked over for a score update and it came back in the form of a thumbs-up.

Our fans knew the score from the Kidderminster game and were chanting, "We! Are! Top of the league! Said we are top of the league!"

I took my intensity down so that I could hear them, and they kept at it. When the final whistle went (4–0, no injuries, no red cards) I jogged over. "Kiddies?"

"Last-minute equaliser."

"Argh!" I laughed. "Why did I let myself dream?"

Sandra smiled. "One point behind, two games in hand. It's like you said. Why is this so easy?" She showed me the league table on her phone.

	TEAM	P	W	D	L	F	A	GD	PTS
1	Kidderminster	23	14	8	1	40	15	25	50
2	Chester	21	16	1	4	57	20	37	49
3	Darlington	22	13	7	2	35	20	15	46
4	York	24	11	10	3	40	27	13	43

"You know what this means, don't you?"

"No."

"Whoever's in charge of the next two games is going to get six points. And that person will very probably take Chester to the top of the league."

"Don't."

"And become a hero, forever."

"Stop."

"Her name an instant legend."

"Go to the fans."

I smirked and spun around, walking away as commanded. But then I stopped, turned, and caught her all excited, like a kid who'd discovered that the massive box under their family's Christmas tree had *her* name on it.

xii.

On the twelfth day of Christmas, the cosmos gave to me . . . a nice day to go and ski.

Christmas Eve. Went to the care home and spent an hour with my mum and Anna while the Brig took Solly for a walk. The guy came back looking all sheepish. Turned out he'd got two phone numbers on his walk. Shocking behaviour. When we got back to Chester, I gave him his Christmas present.

"What's this?"

I'd given him a little envelope. "Open it, open it."

He did, and slid out a card. "Bring Your Nephew to Work card. Oh! You remembered. That's . . . But what is it?"

"He likes football, you said. You'll bring him to watch training in the morning. Then you can fuck off to Chester Zoo or something, then at five he can train with the under-twelves."

"He's thirteen."

"Oh! Cancel the whole day, then! There's no solution! No way round this impasse!"

He smiled. "Perhaps he could train with the fourteens."

"Think he'd like that?"

"Oh, very much, sir. Very, very much."

"And then the VIP box for whatever match is going on that night. Champagne, truffles, er . . . all washed down with Four Horseman. Something like that. And I'll score a hat trick for him."

"I'm moved, sir. Moved."

I offered him a hand. "Thanks for everything."

Christmas dinner. A smashing success. I was charming, Andrew formed an unlikely alliance with Sebastian. The elder Triplet shamed himself and his ancestors by raving about how much he enjoyed the way Newcastle United were playing this season. How well the players were coached, how much they'd improved. Sebastian *preened*.

When it came time to drink the fancy wine, I said something along the lines of "fill 'er up, Jack." You know, classy.

"Can *you* drink, Andy?" said Sebastian, dangling the bottle in a tempting way. He knew Chester had an important match the following day.

"He won't be playing," I said sternly. "He is to be sent for immediate reeducation."

"Max!" complained Emma.

I grinned. "Warrington are almost as bad as Bradford. He might get twenty minutes if he stays sober. But, er . . ." I stole a look at Gemma. She was dressed very slightly more casually than normal, and Andrew was a bit smarter, in turn. They'd worked it out. "Wine's bad, but pre-match copulation is worse. If Andy wants to do one, he might as well do the other, too. We play Warrington again on the first of Jan."

Gemma stared at Andrew, who turned a similar colour to the wine. Emma glared at me. Sebastian and Rachel glanced at each other. I *think* they were amused. I couldn't let Henri have all the Christmas fun, could I?

"Maybe half a glass?" said Andrew.

"I think you can manage more than *half*," said Gemma, and for two minutes, that was the funniest thing any of us had ever heard.

Tuesday, December 26. Match 22 of 46: Chester versus Warrington Town.

I borrowed some gear from Sebastian and took the train back to Manchester, and then across to Chester, getting some very funny looks as I went. Emma came with me, turning a very shitty journey—Christ, our trains are bad—into a fun sesh. We did crosswords together and I let her show me some TikToks.

MD picked us up at the station and drove me to BoshCard HQ.

"I heard the Christmas play was quite something," he said. "Sorry I missed it."

"When we first met, you said Henri was a nutjob. Later you took it back. Turns out, you were right all along."

He grinned before his smile faded. "Your holiday is going to cause all kinds of problems."

"Don't give a shit."

"I know," he said. "But . . . would you please pop in . . . before? So I can ask you questions. Check things."

I tilted my head. "New Year's Eve work for you?"

"Yeah, sure," he said distantly.

"Are they inside?"

He snapped out of his brief funk. "Yes. All ready."

"'Kay. I'll be in soon."

MD went ahead while Emma helped me get into her dad's ski gear. The helmet was a bit tight, but I didn't need to strap it closed for a quick visual gag. I walked into the meeting room and coughed. Twenty players plus staff sat up straight or pushed themselves off the walls they'd been leaning on.

"Lads," I said, coughing a few more times. "I'm sick. I'm dead sick."

Lots of head shaking and smiling. They'd known something like this was coming.

"Are you looking for the best white powder?" said Dean, which I didn't totally understand, but Henri and Pascal laughed, as did a few others.

"Ker," I said, fake coughing. "I think I'll leave Sandra in charge for today. All good?"

"What's the formation?" said Sam. "Who's playing?"

In my normal voice, I said, "How should I know? Sandra's in charge. Ask her. I'm fucking sick, remember." I switched to a sickly hunch, picked my skis back up, and flicked my goggles down. I clomped out—ski boots were heavy!—and Sandra walked to the front.

As I left, she was opening her notebook and wheeling the flipchart forward. "Well, this is unexpected, but I made some notes I was going to discuss with Max. I suppose they'll work for you, too." She looked up in surprise. "You still here, Best?"

"No, Miss," I said, and with one last fake cough, left her to it.

I left the ski stuff in my office and locked the door behind me. It'd be safe there for a few days. I sighed. Carrying that stuff around had been a drag. Unburdened, I felt lighter. Freer.

"What now?" said Emma.

"Huh. Don't know. What are you in the mood for?"

She thought about it. "Go somewhere?"

"Grimsby," I suggested.

"No. And don't suggest Tranmere, either."

New Year's Eve.

I went to BoshCard HQ to meet MD, reassure him one last time, and sign some papers. My office was the same but different. "What's all this? Where's the ski stuff?"

"The Brig took it back to Newcastle. Said it was a good scam for getting top plonk."

"Did he say good *scam*?"

"He did."

That was one of my phrases. I wasn't sure I liked him taking my material. They'd replaced my crappy chess set with a nice, hand-carved one, and given me some comfy armchairs, too. On the top of my bookcase, I had a fancy coffee machine. Maybe that was a gift from BoshCard so I'd stop bothering their employees. Then I noticed the walls. "Oh!" I pottered over to where someone had hung up a framed England shirt. It said *Brown 8* on the back, and it had been signed by the man himself. "Will you look at that? That almost makes it all worthwhile. God, that looks great."

"You've done well, Max. I'm . . . beyond pleased. I don't have the words."

"Relax, Mike. There's loads more to come. Hey! Little stealth gift. Look it!"

"I know. We gave one to Sandra, too."

It was a newspaper headline and subheading that had been carefully cut out and set into a frame. "'Memory Lane'," I read. "'Chester boss becomes first woman to win professional men's match as Seals slay Yellows'." I closed my eyes and when I opened them, it was still there. It had really happened.

"Max . . ."

I turned round and smiled at the man whose life I sometimes made miserable. This little holiday of mine would cause him a lot of grief, but he'd suck it up because he loved his football club. I felt a surge of affection for him. "Mike."

"You're . . . you're coming back, right?"

I puffed my cheeks out as though it was a long shot. "Next year, maybe."

His eyes widened with panic, but then he remembered the date. "Fucking hell, Max."

xiii.
On the thirteenth day of the twelve days of Silkmas, the cosmos gave to me . . .
a flash forward to January.

January 1, 2024.

I was in the shower area. I'd just gone to check if someone had left a window open in there—the whole space was bloody freezing. Two players entered the dressing room and seeing no one was around, immediately fell into gossip. From the voices alone, I wasn't sure who they were.

"Did you see who we've signed?"

"Yeah. It's fucking mental. I never would have thought that *he'd* come here."

"Only on loan, but I hear he's on big dosh."

"He doesn't fit the team. What's the point of him?"

"The boss likes him. That's all that matters round here."

"Might win us a few points, though? Wouldn't say no to that."

"He can take the penalties, I suppose."

They dropped their bags and walked out, laughing.

I walked back to my kit bag and pulled out the football boots my mother had bought me as a present. Something told me they were going to see a lot more action in 2024 than in the previous year. A lot more goals and assists. And maybe, I thought, as I fiddled with the laces and checked the studs . . . maybe I'd find time for the occasional no-look backheel nutmeg, too.

10

HE'S DONE WHAT?!

Life glossary: *Busman's holiday. The kind of holiday where you do things you do in your day job. For example, a bus driver from Chester whose idea of a break is driving around the Wirral.*

Monday, January 1, 2024.

I woke up, slightly confused, as per usual, and grabbed my phone. 7 a.m. and my pristine inbox had been defiled by hundreds of emails and texts. Some from people wishing me a happy new year, some from agents offering me players, plus about fifty from ghoulish online retailers trying to "build a relationship" with me.

We had a match at 3 p.m., so I had to—

No, hang on.

I was on holiday.

After some contented stretches and an extremely decadent yawn, I texted Ruth to ask if I could gatecrash her breakfast. She replied almost instantly with a selfie in which she was rubbing heads with a horse called Tempest. A few seconds later, she sent a text.

Ruth: You're only just getting up? The early bird gets the worm.

Me: But the second mouse gets the cheese.

Ruth: There's remnants in the fridge. Help yourself.

Me: Thanks.

But I lay there, wondering. Maybe there was a better option: breakfast in another part of the world entirely.

There was no rush, so I took my time going from room to room in the barn, making sure there was no food lying around to attract rats, no windows slightly ajar, nothing in the fridge that would sprout mould, and so on. I had already packed a couple of bags, and I chucked those, plus my footy gear, onto the passenger seat of my Subaru (for some reason there were two mattresses squashed into the back) and drove off.

Forty minutes later, I was in the training complex, pottering around, getting my bearings. The dressing room was crazy cold, so I popped into the shower area to see if someone had left a window open since Christmas. They hadn't, but I overheard a couple of players chatting about me. When they were gone, I checked I had cash in case something I ordered cost money, then wondered how long to wait until I followed the pair into the canteen. Five minutes? Nah, I had a better idea. It'd be fun to let them know that I'd heard them.

First, though, I checked the Transfers screen. There were a lot that had already gone through. Two stood out.

Mon 1st Jan - Chris Beaumont - Banbury - Chester - loan

Mon 1st Jan - Eddie Moore - Sutton United - Chester - loan

Here we go! I love it when a plan comes together! Yes, mate!

Hmm. Thinking about it, there might be some mild interest in another item, though if you ask me, it barely warrants a mention.

Mon 1st Jan - Max Best - Chester - Tranmere Rovers - loan

The canteen was warm and smelled of chicken and rice. Two employees in smart aprons and hats were there nice and early, one going round wiping tables and checking there was enough salt, pepper, and ketchup in the appropriate containers while bantering with some early birds. Another was at the food counter serving two players—surely the two who had been talking about me.

The first was James Gladfelter, the cheeky chappie left back who had flirted hard with Emma while I was learning to walk again in Tenerife. She liked the flirting—he was good-looking and funny (her words, not mine)—and while it was annoying, he never overstepped. In the meantime, I'd learned that no one called him James. Everyone called him Jack the Lad.

The second was Reece Cox, a young midfielder who had been out on loan at Dunfermline but hadn't played much so had been recalled. There was a reason he hadn't played much: He was garbage. For League Two, I mean. With PA 45, he'd do all right for most National League North teams.

I made a beeline right to them. "Jack the Lad! And you must be Reece. Very, very pleased to see you again, Jack, and very pleased to meet you, Reece. And you lads must be *delighted* that I'm here. You're made up, aren't you?"

"Er . . . yeah," said Jack. "Is your bird with you?"

"My bird? No, she dumped me after Tenerife. Said she had her heart set on another."

He looked ecstatic until he realised I was taking the piss. But there was a reason everyone liked him—he took the joke with good grace and turned up the charm. "But *you're* here, at least. Reece, this guy's a tactics nut. The lads were raving about him in Tenerife and Henri was telling us mad stories. You gonna help the gaffer, then? What's the deal?"

"Nothing like that. Just gonna train. Have a break from working so hard, being on call, all that."

"You'll play, though?"

I smiled. "I don't pick the teams, mate."

Reece was looking from me to his phone. He had WhatsApp open. Guess I was the hot topic of discussion. "But you're the manager of Chester."

"I don't pick the teams *here*."

"No, I know. I mean. How can you play for us if you're the manager of . . . Chester?"

"Reece. Eat your breakfast before it gets cold. And don't worry about it. It's all perfectly simple." They took their trays to a table while I walked along to the end of the counter and looked at the scran that was available. It was all in metal rectangles. "It's just like being back in school," I said.

"Aye, it is, right," smiled back the kitchen worker. "You're the new guy?"

"I'm the new guy," I said, staring at the options. There was bacon, scrambled egg, beans, sausages, and fried brown. Not hash browns. Just brown. The colour brown, fried. "Can I have smashed avocado on toast?"

"You can have mushrooms on toast and I can flatten it with a spatula."

"Tempting. Can I have a little bit of everything that isn't brown, please?"

The guy lifted things onto my plate. He hesitated over the bacon. "Is this brown?"

"Give me two slices and I'll subject it to a barrage of tests. Is the scrambled egg made from egg?"

He knew exactly what I was worried about. I wasn't the first to hear reports that so-called scrambled eggs were made from a gross powder. "It is, yeah, don't worry. It's all fresh here, not like that hotel crap." He hoisted a big blob of it and my mouth started to water. It looked soft and fluffy and moist and when he slapped it onto the plate, I felt a full-body shiver of something like ecstasy. "If you don't mind me asking, is this all a publicity stunt or what is it? No one can get their heads around it."

"Is me eating breakfast a publicity stunt? I think you've got me confused with . . ." I hesitated, trying to think of someone for whom eating breakfast would be a media circus. "Er . . . let's have this conversation again tomorrow and hopefully I'll have thought of a way to finish that sentence. Thanks!"

"Oh, here he is! It's really true! Max Best in the house!" Lee Contreras, a full-of-himself midfielder who ran pretty abysmal YouTube and TikTok channels, was clambering over tables and benches, pointing his phone at me. His mad toddler energy nearly killed my holiday vibe. Behind him, about eight other players had come in at the same time and were amused by his antics. Most of the first-team squad were around, so this would be a good time to set some boundaries.

I set my plate down and wrapped my arm around Lee's shoulder, smiling as he turned the camera to selfie mode. I leaned my head against his as I said, "Hey, Lee?"

"Yeah? Whoa, man! I can't believe this! What a story!"

"Lee, you remember you guys were nice to me in Tenerife and all that?"

"Yeah, that's right! You were there! Tenerife was wicked, yo! If you're new to the channel, check out the videos I made. They're bangin'!"

"So I like you and, as a mate, I'd suggest you press that big red button there, delete the file, and never do this again. And I'll say nothing about it to the people who are going to decide on your next contract. If you want some fun content for your channels, you come and ask me, but not this morning, because my mind's completely set on the Notts County game, isn't it? Same as yours."

The threat to his contract cooled his fires. They all knew I hung out with Mateo and had killed at least one incoming transfer. "Notts County, right," he said, as he went through various calculations.

"You'll be up against that Irish lad in midfield. Have you noticed the way he tends to take loose touches as he accelerates?"

"He . . . what? No."

I smiled. "No problem! There's still, like, *ages* before the game. You can use your top tech skills to find the clips I watched. Of *your* opponent."

He realised this footage was not good for his brand and finally hit red. "Er . . . But where are *you* going to play?"

"It doesn't matter," I said sweetly. "Because I know the strengths and weaknesses of every Notts player, and I can play anywhere. If I decide to play as the middle of the central three, you'll be the first to know." That was me gently threatening to take his spot in the team while hinting that I had powers beyond a normal player. "Hey, do you think we should call them Notters or Nottsos?"

"What?"

"Never mind. We're going to have a lovely time this month, Lee. It'll be just like Tenerife, but we'll be having our parties on the pitch. Getting points, getting out of trouble, and getting our careers moving in the right direction. You with me?" I'd frazzled the guy's brain. "You can say 'Yes, Max.' It works in most situations."

"Sorry, hang on. Are you our new manager?"

I gave him my best Cheshire Cat grin. "We've *got* a manager. And it will stay like that . . . if we win." I picked my plate up and came as close as I've ever done to whistling a jaunty tune.

Hmm. Where to sit? I wanted to chat, but I didn't want to chat about *me*. I sat next to Jack the Lad and got him started on his favourite topic. "So how's *your* season been so far?"

After brek, I drove to my home for the next four weeks. It was a stupendously ugly block of flats in an area called Wallasey. It was unfurnished, had no wifi, and did I mention it was ugly?

But I was on the top floor and the view was top drawer. Unspoiled grass-lands leading to a sandy beach, then the endless, choppy blues of the River Mersey and the Irish Sea. I planned to get all maritime with my free time.

I hauled the two mattresses from my car into the lift. They were the ones from my old "office" at the Deva stadium; I hadn't used them recently. They'd do. I looked around my new base. I'd need a little lamp so I could read in bed. And some more books, maybe. The ones I had didn't quite hit the spot. Ever since I'd seen *SILK!*, I'd found that most content didn't quite captivate me.

A little shopping would give me something to do in the next few days. A mission. Instead of scouting for fullbacks, I'd go scouting for books. Instead of buying big lumps, I'd buy little lamps.

But first, I had to earn my pay.

At 11, I drove back to the Solar Campus and joined the rest of the lads in milling around. Despite my little warning shot at Lee, I was once more the centre of attention, which you *know* I hate. I chatted fairly happily but when people asked me about Chester, I got confused and said, "What's that?" and if they insisted that I was the Chester manager, I looked down at my new training top and tried to read the letters on the badge, upside down. "Says here . . . F . . . R . . . T . . . G. Fried rice to go?" After five minutes, they'd basically given up trying to understand why I was there and were asking each other about what they did for New Year's Eve.

I mostly hung out with Junior, who I'd rescued from the northeast by recommending him to Mateo. Junior had improved up to CA 60, which was obviously great, but he was still short of the level needed to succeed here. My scouting had suggested that 75 was the minimum. When he hit his PA of 80, he'd be a regular goalscorer in League Two and would have a decent career. Until then, he'd struggle to get minutes. I was looking forward to training with him, anyway—he had good movement and was fast. We worked well together.

We boarded the team bus, drove the ten minutes or so to Prenton Park, and after some of the guys stopped to sign autographs for some of the early birds, we made our way into the players' lounge. This was a comfortable space with PlayStations, comfy chairs, table football, ping pong, and a darts board. The guys chilled for twenty minutes, and then it was through a corridor with murals of past players and their achievements, into an events room to listen to James O'Rourke give his pre-match instructions.

It was great to see him and shake his hand again, but holy shit his talk was remedial. He said it would be our 4-3-3 against their 3-4-3 (wrong!) and droned about passion, desire, duels, spaces, making things difficult for the opposition. I nearly laughed when he talked about giving the fans something to cheer about in a withdrawn, apologetic tone.

We were playing Notts County, who were third in the league. They had scored twice as many goals as Tranmere, but had conceded the same amount. One small, gobby part of my brain was begging me to scream "Attack the bastards!" but the rest of me was saying "Chill, fam, we on vacay."

And anyway, Tranmere weren't exactly a free-scoring team. Notts already had three players who had at least ten league goals to their name. Tranmere's top scorer, a Nigerian powerhouse with the single name Samuel, had five. After twenty games that . . . that was diabolical.

"So we'll keep it tight," James said, bringing his talk to a close. He was normally a funny guy, charming and lively, but I'd noticed that football pitches diminished him. Here, again, he was a shadow of himself. I reckoned he was always like this in his pre-match talks, but now the pressure had been dialled up a few more notches. Fans were calling for his head and his owner had taken a very, very public step towards replacing him. "Try and make it hard for them. If we're still in it near the end, we can have a wee go, but obviously they're a top, top team so we'll have to be on our toes for ninety-eight minutes and maybe if we make things hard for them, we can nick a draw and that'll be a good point against these lot."

Wrong! Wrong! Wrong!

He should have been saying, "Lads, let's go slap. Lads, they can score a few but so can we their defence is shit let's get ready to rumblllllllle!"

I kept my face blank as I checked what the players near me were thinking. Amazingly, they were paying attention. A few were nodding. It was a good group. They liked James and wanted to do well for him. No problems with the attitude. The biggest troublemaker, from what I'd seen, was Jack the Lad, and while he was pretty slappable, even he was more the lovable rogue type than the malicious dressing room virus type.

James hesitated. I think he was battling to control his tone, trying to make what he said next sound like what he'd said before. "And we've got Max with us for January. He'll be on the bench today. It's a shame we're playing on January first so there's no time to integrate him into our system, but that's football. Every other match this month is on Saturday, so plenty of weekday training sessions for him to get up to speed."

"Er . . . question about that," said Jack the Lad.

"Not now, son. That's it. Warm up."

We got changed in the dressing room—twice as big as Chester's (life goals), but covered in cheesy motivational messages (why? vom)—and went onto the pitch to get the old juices pumping. I didn't need a warm-up for that; the stadium itself was enough. It was filling slowly, a few flags waving in the simply ginormous Kop, a bumper crowd expected since everyone had the day off and there was nothing better to do. The music was too loud, drowning the fans if they wanted to sing, but it all helped add to the sense of expectation. Gave the occasion a sense of weight. Was this bigger than the first-round FA Cup match against Salford? Maybe. I got a few butterflies in the stomach. Wow! Hadn't expected that.

When my name was called out as one of the subs, there was a big buzz around the place. *So it was true. But . . . but how does that work, exactly? How can a manager loan himself out? Is this a prank or what?*

We started by jogging around and doing some stretches. Coach Colin led this phase. He kept yelling about "mobility" and "activation." We did ten full minutes of hip stretches. "Hips don't lie!" he yelled. Then we worked with resistance bands—for example, with them tied around our ankles, pushing the legs out to the side or cowboy strutting with them. Lateral movements, hips, glutes, A-skips, aaand relax. Some players took this chance to blast themselves with massage guns, but I didn't have one, so I took another look around the stadium—wow!—and wanted to go round talking to all the inexplicably busy workers to see what they were doing.

I remembered I was on holiday. That shit could wait. I went back to the lounge to see what games they had on the PlayStation.

I'd just picked one when a bunch of lads burst in. They saw me and hesitated. I was that manager-in-waiting guy. How should they act around me?

I smiled to show I was pleased to see them. "Hey, who knows how to play *Mortal Kombat*? Lee?"

"Not really, Max."

"Perfect. Me neither. Come over here and let's punch each other in the face for ten minutes."

"Yes, Max," he said, all friends again.

Either he lied about not knowing how to play or I was as bad at beat-em-ups as I was at chess. Everyone in the chill room stopped what they were doing at the exact same moment, responding to the same inaudible cue. Time to get back to the dressing room for the final pep talks, where a seemingly calm James O'Rourke gave us the usual speech about winning duels, keeping it tight, and sticking together. I wondered what Sandra would have been telling the lads at that exact moment? Probably something like, anyone kicking a high, aimless ball towards Chris Beaumont is going to wake up unemFUCKINGployed!

"Something funny, Max?"

"What?"

James was eyeing me. Having another *manager* as a player must have been a bit of a mindfuck. I hoped he wouldn't try to establish dominance over me or some crap. We hadn't been able to get together and talk about this new phase of his life. I'd offered but he had said he was busy. "You were smiling."

I blinked and realised everyone was looking at me. I got to my feet and beamed. "Just happy to be here, boss! Excited to play alongside such legendary players as . . ." I stuck my finger out and swept it slowly around the benches. I completed my sweep and put my finger away. "Well, I'm happy to be here."

"Cheeky bastard," laughed Colin, and I got middle fingers from some of the guys.

The bell rang and there was lots of incoherent shouting. Our captain, a centre back, of course, clapped his hands and led the lads out.

All very familiar, all very soothing.

"Max," said James. "Quick word?" We glared at a physio until she left, and then it was just James and I. "I've put you on the bench for obvious reasons, but realistically I can't actually use you today."

Ah. So he was going to be difficult. "Huh," I said. He'd been told by on high to select me, so I *had* to be on the subs bench, but after the game he would go to Mateo with some bullshit about why he didn't feel it was the right match for me. He thought this was the best route to self-preservation. He thought I was after his job.

"You've come from a low level, you haven't trained with us, Notts are one of the best teams in the league, it just doesn't make sense. Let's see how you get on in training and we'll see about giving you minutes against Barrow."

"Yeah," I said, amiably. "That's one option. Another option is you give me twenty minutes today so that I can do a full half next week and start the three games after that."

"Max," he whined.

"James. Do you remember Tenerife?"

"Yes."

I smiled. "So do I." One of the moronic messages on the wall was *The body achieves what the mind believes.* If I took over here, my first task would be to paint over all that guff. "James, you're not thinking straight. You think I'm here for nefarious purposes. I'm not! I've come for the exact reasons I told you. A break from the grind, get my levels up, and get paid silly money for five matches. Then I'm fucking off back whence I came. But even if you think I'm here to steal your job, what better way to stop that happening than to throw me on for twenty minutes against a strong team? We both know I'll play shit, we both know we'll lose today. It's not going to be a very effective whatsit, is it? Audition. But twenty minutes today will do me the world of good. I can feel it." I bounced on my heels. Very springy! Body was feeling limber. "Right, let's get out there and get at 'em. What was it, four-four-two and hit the channels?"

"It's four-three-three. As you know." He wanted to say something else, but I had the ear of the owner and if there's one thing he knew better than me, it was not pissing off rich men and decision-makers.

As luck would have it, the big man himself appeared. Mateo put his head round the door and came in. "Knock knock! My two favourite football managers! Good to see you getting on well."

James opened his mouth, but I got there first. It was slightly cruel, in a way, but I had to save him from himself. "We were just talking about Notts," I said. "They play three-four-two-one so James was thinking there would be space in the fullback areas I might be able to exploit. He promised to put me on for the last twenty and see what havoc I could wreak. Oh, and he was saying that Notts have a habit of getting ahead in matches, thinking they've done enough to win, and switching off." Boom! Look who'd done his research. "He's expecting a tough game but if things land right, we might have an exciting finish. Oh, and he promised to let me take the penalties because he's studied my technique and proclaimed it to be flawless."

Poor James had listened to all this with his mouth agape. He closed it now, frowned, and was again *this close* to sabotaging his future.

This time, Mateo was the one who saved him. "Splendid!" He slapped James on the back. "Rachel said you'd be moody about Max coming, but I said, no chance. He'll see Max as a resource. Someone to bounce ideas off. Yes, it's great you're getting on. Makes me optimistic about the future!" He rubbed his hands together. "Bloody cold in here. I'm going to my box. Talk to you later!"

He left. James looked pretty furious. As far as he was concerned, I'd just confirmed that I wanted his job. But what could he do?

He could get out of my way while I saved his skin.

That's what he could do.

Prenton Park is huge. Way bigger than the Deva. This place could hold 16,500 people! The Kop and the main stand were so big, so chunky, so perfectly what a football stadium should look like, that when the match kicked off, I got dead excited about taking to the pitch.

Of course, there was zero chance of that happening in the first half, so I stretched my legs out and switched off my brain.

Junior was next to me. I asked for his impressions of the players, and he gave me a running commentary, or a walking commentary in the case of Samuel, the striker, who lumbered around doing almost nothing. He had good scores for pace and acceleration, even for dribbling, but he just didn't want to break into a sprint. Junior liked him and refused to confirm what I was seeing. His 4 out of 10 was a stark contrast to his opposite number Bailiff, who was fast, furious, and clinical.

After twenty minutes, in which time Notts battered us and quietened the crowd by scoring the opening goal, Junior finally cracked. He leaned over and whispered, "What the fuck are you doing here, man?"

I grinned as though I would launch into a hilarious cock-and-bull story but decided to tell him the entire truth. "Being murdered set me back to level one as a player and I've been grinding to get back to where I was. I believe I'm blocked in my recovery by an almost arbitrary game mechanic taken from an ancient version of what is now called *Soccer Supremo*. That mechanic caps how much I can improve based on the division I play in, but I've found a loophole. By coming to a League Two team, I'll benefit from their coaching and infrastructure ratings, and any game time I get will be a huge bonus. I reckon I can move from CA sixty to somewhere in the region of one hundred. Not only will that give me the boost I need to make a difference in matches when I go back to Chester, the time away also affords me something of a much-needed break from the strains and stresses of running a football club. Last but not least, I'm very slightly exploiting my relationship with Tranmere's owner, who I suspect wishes to sack James this month and offer me the job while I'm *in situ*. Although it was my idea to come here, he's so keen on me taking over that he's paying me five *thousand* pounds a week, which is big money for me and will get the Brig off my case. What Mateo doesn't realise is that if my CA increases as fast as I suspect it will, and if I ignore James's shitty tactics and do what's best for the team, we will win at least three of the five matches. Nine points will really shoot Tranmere up the table, and I'll achieve my secondary goal of repaying James for his kindness."

"Max?"

"What?"

"You're just, like, smiling."

"Didn't I say all that out loud?"

He tsked. "No."

"Oh. Weird. Okay, short version, I need a break from managing and here I can work on my fitness, push myself to become a better player, and get some sea air."

"But what about your team?"

It was my turn to tut. "I've sorted it. It's all done. They can do without me against fucking Warrington. Fucking Rushall Olympic. Jesus. It's four weeks."

"I'm sure you already know but it's kicking off. Chester fans are going ballistic."

"Oh, no," I whimpered, putting the back of my hand to my forehead. "My team is top of the league playing the best football for miles, Tranmere included, by the way," I added in my normal voice, pointing to the feeble display from the team in white. I returned to a sarcastic whine. "We're on track to win the league by fifteen or twenty points and I'm still not happy. Waaah."

Junior shook his head. "You're absolutely mental, you know that? There isn't a single person who would do this, this, this madness, and act like everyone *else* was crazy."

"You know what the real shame about all this is?"

Junior narrowed his eyes, suspicious. He suspected I wasn't going to address the conversation with sincerity. "No. What?"

"It's not a good progression fantasy."

"Why do I bother?"

"See, we've got five games in January. This one, Notts County. They're third. They're really good, though not quite as good as James thinks. Saturday is away to Barrow and they're sixth. Next is MK Dons, eleventh, then Swindon, sixteenth. Last game is Doncaster, eighteenth. So the games get easier."

"Ah. I can see how that would ruin it for you."

It was something of a miracle that we were only losing 1–0 at halftime, but then again, the team's morale was only a bit lower than County's and the players were willing to suffer and sacrifice for the collective. All except Samuel, who was less use than a statue. His attributes were good and he had very high PA: 128. But he looked unmotivated.

When I finally sauntered into the dressing room—I'd paused every three yards to take in more of the sights and sounds—James was in discussions with Coach Colin. I eased past them to the tactics board and slid two of County's three "strikers" back to the positions they were *actually* playing: CAM.

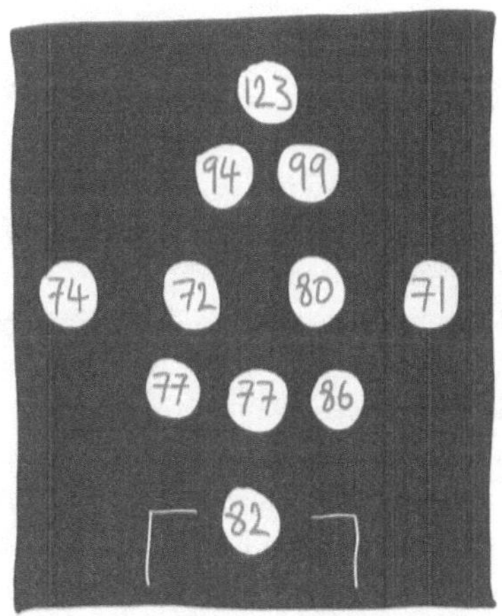

The two CAMs were set to make forward runs, and perhaps that was making James think they were playing as strikers. They weren't, though. They were starting from deeper and neither the midfielders nor the defenders were taking responsibility for picking them up. Me moving the magnets was a big signal to James. A reminder that I'd told him this before the game had started. He absolutely *had* to change something, or Notts County would score at will and literally the only thing that would save him was that Notts had that habit of taking the lead and mentally switching off.

James and Colin looked at the board. Colin nodded, he knew I was right, but James didn't want to talk about it. As far as he was concerned, Notts had three strikers, or he didn't think the exact positioning mattered.

That's what was great about the whole holiday thing. It wasn't my circus and I wasn't the ringmaster. If the circus wasn't selling enough tickets, if the jugglers were sloppy, if the lions were timid, what did I care? I had a beard of bees, and unlike the gymnasts and tightrope walkers, I'd always land on my feet.

As I lazily followed everyone down the stairs that led to the tunnel, I paused to read the Latin text written in huge letters: *Ubi Fides ibi Lux et Robur.* It was the same text that crossed the club badge.

My Latin is pretty exceptional, as you know, but that one had me stumped even though I'd looked it up in the past.

"Junior, what's this motto mean? Everybody believes in lights and robots?"

"Where there is faith there is light and strength."

"That's too complicated. Too long. It should be short and snappy. *Chat shit get banged. Who dares wins. Eat my goal.*" I went through the words again. "Why does a football team need light?"

"I kiss the badge, Max. I don't read it."

After sixty minutes, Notts finally got the second goal they deserved. Their players, who I will call Notters, visibly relaxed, while the grumbling from the home fans doubled in intensity.

After sixty-five, Notts began making substitutions that weakened the team. This took their average CA down from around 85 towards 80. Ours was a smidge over 70, which was higher than Sutton United's, but might have been the second lowest in the division. Mateo said he planned to bring a hotshot player in during the January window. I shook my head—it had just clicked that he meant *me*. Well, he'd need more. This team needed an injection of quality.

And a bit of something else, too. What *was* it this team lacked? Pace? They had a couple of quick lads. Leadership? Experience? I couldn't put my finger on it. Jack the Lad was playing all right. Lee was battling. Only Samuel was truly absent.

Seventy minutes. No sign of a substitution. More signs of the fans turning against their manager. "You're shit, O'Rourke!" cried someone who must have been sitting near Mateo. But generally, the home fans were trying to be positive. Trying to find something to cheer.

There were massive gaps all around the stadium, blocks of empty seats, but there were pockets of singers. "TRFC! Ooh!" was one chant. Four out of ten. "Superwhite army!" was another. An old chant that was perhaps somewhat unfortunate in the modern world. It came from the 60s, when a manager had decided that since Liverpool played in red and Everton in blue, there was a gap in the Merseyside market for a team that played in white. The Superwhites were born. Yeah, anyway. Not a song *I'd* be singing.

At seventy-two minutes, James turned and mumbled that I might want to warm up.

"No need, boss," I said, whipping my tracksuit off. "I'm ready to go."

I went right to the touchline, pulling my feet up behind me, jogging on the spot, all the stuff substitutes did.

The kit was all white with blue details. The sponsor was a company Mateo owned. My number, 77, was on the front of my shorts as well as on my back, below the word *BEST.*

The fourth official, the guy who helps the referee by keeping control of the managers, complained that he hadn't been told what the change was going to be. "I'm going on for number ten, Samuel," I said.

"No!" said James, almost in a panic. He chose a different striker—the guy playing farthest to the right, the only one who'd been playing okay. Fine. As long as I got my twenty minutes, I didn't give a shit. This match was basically over, anyway. It was pretty much a consequence-free environment.

So then there was a free kick and the ref held up the game so that I could make my League Two debut. I high-tenned the unlucky striker and strolled onto the pitch, waving at the fans in all corners of the stadium. The home fans were applauding me politely, and the away lot were jeering.

Notts had a free kick deep in their half, and my sixth sense kicked in. I jogged towards the DM slot, and just as I arrived, so did the ball. One of County's tricky CAMs dropped to get it, turned, and accelerated to the left, from which position he'd chip the ball into the penalty area. I knew because I'd seen him doing it since kickoff, and no one had thought to stop him.

He was pretty surprised, then, to find that the ball had long gone. I'd picked his pocket so cleanly he didn't notice until it was too late. I popped the ball forward to Lee and darted left. Lee exchanged passes with a fellow CM, brought the third CM into the move, and by then I'd made up the ground to the left mid slot. Lee fizzed the ball out to me, but my first touch was unusually poor—all I could do was a protective move I'd seen Jackie teach the women. I put my body between the ball and the nearest Notter, sorted my feet out, and was about to play a short pass back to Jack the Lad when I realised he was nowhere to be found.

A Notter slid in and knocked the ball out for a throw-in.

Yeah, this league was fast! But it wasn't like when I'd played against professionals for the first time. That day I'd had a minor meltdown, believing I was dogshit and would never be a player. Now, I was pretty sure I had once been CA 150+ and was certain I could get back to that level.

Losing the ball here hadn't been my fault. Why hadn't Jack come to help? I checked his individual instructions: He was allowed to make forward runs. He simply *hadn't.* Weird.

I pottered around while play went on around me. Sometimes I'd accidentally be in a good position for a pass and I'd one-touch it, keeping it moving. After a few minutes, I was starting to feel frisky. My match rating was a solid 7 and Notts were an attack-minded team, which meant they left spaces all over the pitch. Space I was happy to invade. Check *this* out, Pascal!

If we wanted to get back into this game, I mused, the priority had to be not to concede another goal, so I found myself dropping into the DM slot more and more. I fucking crushed it. Either I straight-up won the ball before one of the twin CAMs could get it, or I put enough pressure on them that they lost it, or if the CAM *did* get there ahead of me, I positioned myself between him and his mate, using the cover shadow concept I'd learned from Salford City. If the CAMs couldn't combine, they couldn't do shit.

As my confidence grew, I spun these turnovers into breaks. Proper, direct, fast breaks, limited only by how accurately I could pass and how fast I could get to County's offside line.

A dangerous ball is hit long.

Best rises to head it away.

Contreras controls and plays a neat one-two with Dodd.

He combines well with Best.

Best shapes to pass to Samuel, but pushes the ball past the defender.

The crowd are getting to their feet for a rare Tranmere attack.

Best is on the left with only one defender ahead of him.

He plays it square, looking for the return pass.

Samuel gathers, uses Best as a decoy, turns onto his right and . . .

His shot dribbles harmlessly wide.

Best looks distinctly unimpressed—he would have been clean through.

I was on one knee, rubbing the bridge of my nose. This twat Samuel was ruining my holiday.

Perhaps like many other people, you have been in a house or a car when it has been raining outside. And you've watched, fascinated, as a certain raindrop has hit the glass, dribbled, stopped, dribbled some more. Perhaps you willed it to stay motionless, to defy gravity. Perhaps you cheered when it reached the edge. But if someone takes a shot with all the power and purpose of a slothful raindrop, you do not cheer. Unless, maybe, you support Notts County, in which case you might sarcastically jeer the fact your opponents finally had a shot against you.

I got up and tried to relax my jaw.

Tyson. This is what it was like playing on the same team as Tyson. This is why I'd kicked Tyson out of the youth system.

Because it fucking *sucked*.

Why would James keep this guy on the pitch? It was like we were playing with ten men. We weren't all that far away from getting a result; one piece of quality would get us back in the match. At 2–1, we would activate the crowd. The last few minutes could be epic.

James was perhaps trying to balance various factors. Long term versus short term, different factions and cliques within the dressing room, players returning from injury, workload, contract discussions, and so on. None of that mattered to *me*. While I was on the pitch, my job was to get points on the board.

I walked across the grass while the match was going on. No one was in our DM slot so there was once again a massive chasm between our defence and midfield that Notts were more than happy to exploit.

"Max, what? Are you injured? Get back out there."

"Take Samuel off. Put Junior on."

"What?" James wasn't angry—he couldn't believe he'd heard what he thought he'd heard.

"We could get something out of this," I said, as I pottered away.

Seventy-seven minutes gone. When I died, there would be an emotional applause in the seventy-seventh minute. That'd be nice. All heartwarming and stuff.

I didn't feel motivated to chase the ball around or help the defence out. There was no possible world in which Max Best on holiday should care more about winning this match than the manager whose full-time job it was to care. CAM felt good. I hovered there for a while, walking up and down in step with the rest of the players. Notts kept the ball for a while, and I concentrated on them.

They had lower CA than Salford City but were far ahead of them in the league. A lot of that was because they had a superstar striker and two clever players feeding him. But a couple of years from now, a much-improved Youngster in the DM slot would shut down half their attacks. A midfield partnership of Raffi and Andrew Harrison would dominate the centre. Pascal would be so dangerous on one of the wings that Notts would almost certainly change formation, especially if I was running riot on the other side. Nah, they'd have to switch to 5-4-1 or something equally cautious or we'd absolutely smash them.

Jones, our captain, put in a thundering tackle that got the crowd roaring. The ball spun out to the right back, who passed it to Lee. I waited as long as poss (not very long) before pointing to one side of a midfielder. Lee understood my intention and rolled the ball to that position. I got there, took a touch, and dabbed the ball forward to the feet of Samuel. I ran back the way I'd come, already plotting what I'd do when the ball was laid off. I glanced left, but Jack the Lad was still stuck at left back. Why hadn't he raced forward when the transition had started?

But it wouldn't have made the slightest bit of difference.

Samuel, who was enormous and had strength 18, grappled a strength-15 defender. The pair battled for half a second before Samuel gave up. Notts countered our counter—naughty—and we were lucky to see a shot rocket over the crossbar. The Notts forwards were laughing and joking, having a blast.

I walked over to the left mid position to be as far away from James as possible. The guy was pissing me off. Pissing the Tranmere fans off, too, by the sound of it.

When there was a little break, I tested myself with some stretches. Body? It all felt good. Mind? I was clear-headed.

The speed of the game was impressive. I'd had a bad touch and struggled in a couple of moments, but it wasn't way above my level. The match against Salford must have really helped me. Next Saturday, now, that'd be interesting. How much CA could I add in a week? Five points? Why not? So what could I do now, in the last ten minutes of this match, to make sure I got the most CA growth?

First-team minutes? Check.

Good coaches and facilities? Check.

The only other factor I thought I'd detected was that maybe, maybe, players improved more when their match ratings were higher. It made sense—playing a guy out of position would lead to him getting bad ratings and then why should he improve? But a striker played in the right position could still improve even if his form was bad. However, he would improve faster if he was playing well and scoring goals. That was obvious.

So, fine. I decided to see if I couldn't bump my match rating up.

I was currently on 7 and the curse liked it when I combined with other players to progress the ball. Samuel was a big stumbling block. (Good nickname for him, there. Write that down.) I decided to wander back to the DM position, where at least I could play some passes to Lee and the other midfielders.

Something unusual happened then. I lost a header.

Hunt plays a quick, low pass to Hemmings.

He turns inside and passes to Murphy.

His first touch is poor, but he recovers. He chips it forward.

Best is in the way—but he loses out.

Reynolds nods it into the path of Bailiff.

He's crowded out but finds Edwards.

He cocks his leg to shoot . . .

But Best is there!

Fantastic block. He had to time that just right.

Corner to Notts County.

As I got to my feet, our goalie and Gareth, the captain, came to give me high fives and congratulatory slaps. They were still fighting. They still had pride.

Samuel, the world's most expensive totem pole, was placed on hundreds of logs and rolled back into our penalty area. Future generations would ask: But with their primitive technology, how did they do it?

He was one of a mass of bodies in the middle of the goal. I knew that Notts liked to play corners short before whipping in a cross, so I scanned the area and decided to place myself where I thought the ball was most likely to go: past the mob of players in the six-yard box, all the way over on the edge of the area.

Sure enough, Notts played a short pass, then another, and the ball was returned to the original corner-taker. He took a swing at the ball and lots of players—and the goalie—jumped to try to make contact. Someone did, but it was a glancing blow from the top of their head. He couldn't have passed it to me more accurately if he'd tried.

I touched the ball forward and ran as hard as I could.

One defender realised the danger and ran towards me (dumb) but I cut inside and outside in two fluid moves, leaving him on his arse. Another five yards forward and it was me against the world (what's new?): their two smallest players who'd been left as defenders, plus five or six guys who were screaming back to help.

I didn't have many options, so I ran. The constellation of defenders was forcing me a little farther right with every stride, and I was starting to get boxed in. Even though I was rampaging into their half, none of the defenders were as stupid as the first one, and they all kept on their feet. I needed to do something. Needed an option. But as I scanned and scanned, I found no teammate had come to support me. They'd hung me out to dry.

Enraged, I lashed the ball out of play for a throw-in, right in front of the main stand. Right in front of Mateo.

I was a player-manager playing for another manager. You didn't see that very often. Nor was it a common sight to see a guy on a break angrily smashing the ball into the advertising hoardings.

I was really treating this Tranmere lot to some of my best material.

One of the Notts guys tapped me on the back. *He* understood what had just happened. "Played, mate."

The main stand had a lot of families, executives, and corporate types. The curse showed me there were more than a few scouts and agents around. But there were still enough normal fans for it to get fierce at times, and they did so now. Bald, pasty heads, bellies groaning under the strain of their own magnificence, these men were the pride of England, three lines on their foreheads, flecks of spittle exploding from their mouths as they screamed bloody murder. I stood facing them, hands on hips, as they vented their spleens. I couldn't tell if they were raging at me, at the rest of the team, at James, or at Mateo.

And I didn't care. I was on holiday.

Some red and green lights to my right made me turn. Tranmere were making a substitution. I was one hundred percent sure James would sub me off. Subbing off a substitute could be explosive enough to bring this manager-on-loan nonsense to a quick end. A footnote in history. A joke at a handful of parties in the Wirral, Chester, and Darlington. And you know what? Good. I'd go and have a proper holiday. A big one with Emma, not just a few nights in Airbnbs between Christmas and New Year. Not one where I'd have to spend my precious time and energy making a shit manager look good.

The red number was 10.

Samuel.

The green was 25.

Junior.

I shouldn't have done it, but I slapped my hands together and went, "Come on!" In an instant, I was in full prowl mode. Pacing around, barking at the midfielders. There were at least ten minutes left, maybe eleven or twelve. We couldn't go too crazy, or we'd get done on a counter.

Samuel, the twat, took his sweet time getting off the pitch. We're losing, you idiot! That's *our* time you're wasting! But then Junior sprinted on and my neck tingled.

I dropped to DM and watched as Notts took the throw-in and passed the ball around. Junior and the other forward pressed. Notts went into midfield, trying to use their width to draw us out of our shape. But eventually they did what they always did: played through the centre. Something clicked, some pattern recognition. I'd seen this particular sequence before, in the videos of Notts. They'd pass there, there, *there*, and then boom, Bailiff would be one-on-one with the goalie. It was almost too late to stop it, but I put my head down and raced back to my own goal. I zipped past a startled Gareth Jones and arrived at the penalty spot at the same time as County's deadly striker. I shoulder-barged him and took the ball in a tight circle to my right. I passed left, to Jack the Lad.

Running forward, I overtook him and he was more than happy to play it into my path. I slowed just a fraction, marvelling at how much space I had, how many options I had. No low blocks here. This was chaos. Notts didn't know what to do about a player who popped up in every single position, but they knew I was a threat now, and three of their players came at me. I took another stride, feigned as though I'd knock the ball down the line and chase it, but instead thrashed a low diagonal pass through no fewer than five opponents, right onto the toes of Junior at the edge of the centre circle. He and his striker partner combined while I made my way—suffering now—up the pitch.

Junior held off a defender, touched the ball back in my direction, spun and sprinted. I played a first-time chip with the outside of my foot, the ball curving beautifully onto his favoured right foot.

A golden chance!

The angle was fairly tight, the goalie was storming out to narrow it even further, and two defenders were about to slide in. But Junior was favourite. He looked up, looked down, steadied himself . . . and passed sideways.

I appeared between two startled midfielders and side-footed the ball into the net.

Two—one, and at last something for the home fans to cheer.

My first thought was to glare at the bench looking at the options. Did we have a different left back? One who might get forward? League Two allowed seven subs and this season you could use five. Tranmere used to have that amazing left back that Blackburn had poached. Imagine him, here, playing with me, with all that space in front of him.

"Yeah!" cried Gareth.

"Whoo!" yelled someone.

"Yes, Max!" screamed Lee.

They'd encircled me, were pushing me, jostling me. I laughed—I wasn't the manager, and I didn't need to think about the subs. I was on holiday. "Come on," I cried, pulling them to the Kop so we could pump our fists and show our biceps and all that shit fans loved. When we'd done that and I had some space, I stood there, smirking, full of myself, cocky Manc twat, and they loved it.

But Notts were dangerous, so I dropped to DM for a couple of minutes. That extra-long sprint I'd been on had taken it out of me, so I needed to catch my breath. A Notts midfielder was on the ball and about to fire a low pass to a CAM, but he saw me moving that way and hesitated. Pleasing. While he was dawdling, Lee barged him off the ball and we were away. The move came to nothing, but our fans were up for it now, and in the away end, there were lots of guys in black and white bobble hats biting their nails.

As I noted that our average ratings were flying up and Notts's were in decline, as I looked around at the fans and the pristine pitch with its wide-open expanses, inviting me to visit, I felt myself smiling.

This. *This* was a holiday.

My legs started pumping and I crashed—fairly, said the referee—into a midfielder and nabbed the ball from him. The counter-punch was on me almost before I could blink, but for once the bounce went our way and Lee came up with the ball, like a prize truffle pig. I raced towards Junior but suddenly felt claustrophobic. I hated this narrow 4-3-3 shit. If the fullbacks didn't get forward, everything was compressed into a fraction of the pitch. So I veered to the right, to the empty spot I'd told Mateo I would attack.

The midfield bounced the ball around a few times, then the most technical one swept the ball in my direction. The pass was shit—too high, too slow, too much spin—giving a centre back time to shuffle across and make life hard for me. His plan was to stand me up and—

I was already past him. Instead of cushioning the ball and thinking of what to do, I'd done what I'd told Dani, Maddy, and Sevenoaks to do. Aggressive, decisive, forward-thinking play.

I sprinted—legs burning now—the main stand were rising to their feet in waves, heads turning to follow—"Go on, son!"—quick glance, two-on-two in the middle—darted towards goal, nightmare to defend against—so fast! Goalie forced to come—feint, push to the byline—open goal!—but a Notter was sliding in. Had to put my foot on the ball, wait—cut it back for the second striker. Open goal for the lad!

But the ball didn't go in. The roar from the Kop was one of outrage. Baying for blood, a spine-chilling, guttural noise that resolved itself into the chant, "Off! Off! Off!"

What had happened? I went to the commentary and discovered the last defender had decided to foul our guy, to wrestle him to the ground. It meant a red card and a penalty—the ref made no mistake—but if we missed the pen, his manager would be ecstatic with the decision.

While the mess got resolved, I checked the tactics screens. My match rating was 9, but there was something more important than that: I hadn't been set to take the penalties. Fucking James, man. What the shit.

The Notters finally started to leave the penalty area. The home fans were making a helluva noise. Gareth Jones, a centre back, was holding the ball. That was odd—one of the midfielders was supposed to take the pen.

"Best," he called, and as I looked up, he threw the ball. I caught it and tried to be calm. Tried to be professional and serious.

Not very hard, though. I placed the ball down on the penalty spot and punched the air like I'd already scored. I turned away from the Kop, and the goalie, and double-thumbed my name and number. And while the ref did his final referee things, I laughed as I did kick-ups and a little bit of tekkers.

Peep!

The ref gestured that it was time.

I looked up into the Kop, where the most manic Tranmere fans were. I picked one out and gave him or her a Maxy fingerguns, a wink, and a cheeky smile.

I laughed to myself again. This was so much fun, holy shit, why hadn't I done this earlier? Then I started my routine.

Forward an inch, feint left, forward two inches, feint right, inch, eyes left, big step, eyes right. Normally when I took penalties, I wasn't laughing the whole time, but apart from that it was the technique I'd come to rely on.

The goalie, his own technique disrupted by my slowness, finally hurled himself to my left, so I rolled the ball centre right.

One day, I'd miss a penalty.

One day, I'd look a right twat.

Today, though? Nah.

The roar hit me like a sonic weapon. It was overwhelming, literally stunning. Our fans celebrated the goal with the force of 6,000 alphorns. Christ, though, what a feeling. I'd never experienced anything like it. Retired players talked about the hit of adrenaline, of dopamine, of *something*, they got from scoring goals. It's like a drug, they say. It's addictive. You miss it.

I know that for the first time in my short career, I celebrated wildly, nothing held back, whipping up the Kop. Later, I saw footage of me running into a mass of Birkonians slash Squirrels, quickly swallowed whole with a wedge of teammates coming in behind as if to rescue me. Later, I was told I'd got a yellow card for inciting the crowd or jumping into the stands or some garbage. That was funny—if I got five yellows, I'd be suspended for one match. Would that suspension be kept on my record for years and years until I played League Two again?

The fans had whipped me up into a frenzy, but by the time I crossed the halfway line, I was ice cold again.

We were slapping and Notts were down to ten men. The three points were there for the taking. I checked the clock: We'd gone over the ninety minutes. Notts took their star striker off and put on another centre back. Hello, low block, my old friend!

For two minutes, I stood on the left wing, being fed the ball, which I whipped into the box as best I could. Right-footed inswingers, mostly. Crosses, free kicks, corners. Just because I'd played twenty minutes in League Two didn't mean I was suddenly great at them again. But I was able to put the balls into the box more or less where the strikers wanted them. Notts County clung on, though, until the final whistle, like the good team they were.

An unlikely draw, a useful point, a bit of drama, and a couple of goals for yours truly. I've had worse days off.

In the dressing room I lay down to get a massage, and no one questioned why I was first in the queue. Someone asked if I wanted to talk to the media. I was in my usual post-match haze, completely drained. I'm pretty sure I said no, and they said I had to because I was Man of the Match. I'm ninety percent sure I told them Lee was *my* Man of the Match and they should interview *him*.

Junior came to admire me, and I asked where I could get dinner at this time on this day in this part of the world. He tsked and said we always ate together after games, so that was a bonus.

I went through the motions of showering and exchanging hand slaps with everyone, getting more and more sullen until I got some carbs in me. That cheered me up, and I even joined in with some of the banter.

The only fly in the massage oil, and I suppose it was a big fly, was when Barkley shuffled towards me during dinner and asked if he could have a word, but more on that later.

Tuesday, January 2.

Light flooded the flat, turning it into a warm, welcoming space, rays reflecting from every surface, rebounding like benevolent, healing lasers. However, *that* flat was located in Sydney, Australia. *I* was staying in the Wirral, a peninsula that used to be in Cheshire, I'd learned, but had been given a big-money transfer to Merseyside in the 70s. Inexplicably, people from the Wirral were *not* known as Squirrels. It's right there, guys!

In my flat in the Wirral, close to New Brighton Beach and The Promenade, the sun didn't flood in. It didn't wake me up. It didn't do shit.

I woke up naturally, and early, after a fitful, restless sleep caused by too much smugness in the bloodstream. Playing—and scoring—in front of 7,000 fans was not comparable to playing in front of 2,000. I closed my eyes and relived the moment when I'd scored the penno. What a rush . . .

A book would help calm me down, but I didn't have a lamp, and the big light was harsh. So I got up, grabbed my kit bag, and drove to the campus, where I read a few pages of *Going Infinite*, a book by the same guy who'd written *Moneyball* and *Liar's Poker*.

Then we met for a video debrief on yesterday's match. James, who was now treating me with even *more* suspicion, gave an overview of his thoughts. Then Colin went through ten key moments, pointing out things that the team had done well or badly. It was fine—way better than what Chester did on video, which was nothing—but in my opinion only scratched the surface of the problems and completely missed the two things I thought were most troubling. He didn't mention Jack the Lad failing to go forward—they must have noticed!—and there was almost no mention of Samuel.

I spent much of the time rubbing my temples silently going *holiday holiday holiday* like a mantra.

After that, we had breakfast together, did a light session on the all-weather pitch, and that was it. My whole workday! I was free to go round the second-hand shops in my new home looking for lamps and fast-paced action thrillers.

There was just one thing I had to do first.

Tue 2nd Jan - Calabash Barkley - Tranmere Rovers - Chester - loan

I swaggered into the hospital, smiling and happy, still bathed in the light of my own radiance. I knew the room number and found it soon enough.

In a bed, his leg splinted up, trying to look cheerful even though I knew his morale was rock bottom, was Joe Anka.

He saw me and tried to sit up straight. He winced.

"Joe," I said, clapping hands with him like one of the cool kids.

"Max, holy shit. Why are you here?"

"Can't have you in hozzie alone, feeling sorry for yourself while I'm having a whale of a time. Can I?"

He looked around. "I'm not alone. My whole family's here."

"Yeah, well, I've come to save you from them. Blink twice if you want me to kick them out."

He smiled, but winced again. He introduced me to his mum, one of his aunts, a cousin, and two nephews.

"Top," I said. "I promise to remember everyone's names. Now, tell me what happened."

He balled his hands and pushed them into his forehead. "It's a blur. I was going for the ball. Fifty-fifty, but I came off worse. They said there was nothing in it. Nothing malicious, you know. The guy's been texting me."

"Clean break?"

"Yeah."

"Six weeks out?"

"At least."

"I still have to pay you though, right?"

Joe's mum tutted, but he smiled. "He's joking, mum. He's winding you up."

"Not now, Max. My baby's got a broken leg!"

"That's payback for all the hearts he's broken. You got an assist, I heard."

Joe smiled and I had to stop myself going into his player profile every five seconds to see what his mood was. I'm pretty sure it briefly went up three or four points. "You'd have loved it. We had a free kick over on the right. I sent it into the mixer. Chris headed it in. It was like . . . Hey, that was easy! It's like you planned. Like you said it'd be. Warrington didn't know what to do. The low block was just inviting us to hit crosses to Chris. It was over by halftime."

"How's Sandra?"

He nodded. "She's very professional. Lots of detail. She's really crossing every T, if you know what I mean."

Of course she was. Otherwise, if it went wrong, she'd get savaged. "Well, we're top of the league now." I checked the time. "Right. You're going to be all morose and shit and I can't stand it. So I was thinking when you're out of here you could do the music in our home games for a while."

His face lit up. "Really?"

"Yeah. I'm thinking themes. Sixties night. Mostly hits, stuff the olds know. Know what I mean? But you can sneak in a couple of lesser-known bangers. Seventies, eighties. Get people into the idea that DJ Joe Anka is at the wheel. Then! Then we hit them with the really good stuff."

"The noughties?"

"Er . . . what's that? Backstreet Boys and Shakira?" I pulled a face. "It's your gig . . . I was thinking . . . guess the theme."

"Guess the theme?"

"Yeah. You play songs an hour before kickoff. There's a theme that connects them all. First person to text the right answer wins a prize. So, like it'd be Abba, then Bananarama, then the Cranberries. ABC. Or they're all songs from movies. They're all one-hit wonders. They're all bands with a replacement singer. The songs were all banned by radio stations in a moral panic."

"Oh, Jojo, you'd be so good at that!"

"Great, that's settled, then. If you get bored, there's millions of things you can do to help the team and the club. Watch scouting videos. Q and As with fans. Write letters to old timers who renew their season ticket for the twenty-fifth year. We send you three goals from the youth players and you choose your favourite. All kinds of stuff." I got up to leave. I would have stayed longer if he'd been alone, but he had all his peeps there.

"Max, wait," he said. "What about you? What's going on? It's all kicking off round here."

"I'll tell you what's going on." I pointed at one of the kids. I do remember his name, I'm withholding it here because of his privacy. "Guess my lung capacity. Go on, guess."

"Whaaat?" said the kid.

"That's right. Four point two litres. Four point *two*. Can you believe it? I've only been there a day. It's the sea air, Joe! It's full of healing salt."

"That water is rancid. You've not been swimming in it, have you?"

"No."

"Don't swim in that water, boss."

"Oh." That was ominous. "Okay, anyway, number goes up, finally. It's happening. And while I'm there, I'm going to have a pop at Dixie Dean's records."

"Dixie Dean?" he laughed. "MD said you'd be gone for a month. You can't score all Dixie Dean's goals in a month."

"Ah!" I said, holding up a finger. "What if I play for Tranmere every January? If I do that for ten years, I'll have played ten months. That's like a season. He scored, like, twenty-seven goals for Tranmere in one season. That's not loads. I can do that, even if it takes me ten years to do it. Then I'll play one month a season for Everton and shoot for the big one."

Joe mashed fists into his head again. "I know you're joking but even to *have* the idea, even to think of it. You and Henri, you're not normal."

"Who's Dixie Dean?" said the kid, less shy now that I'd addressed him.

"When he was twenty-one, he scored sixty goals in one season. Last year, everyone thought Haaland might catch him, but he ended with thirty-six goals in the Premier League. So the best striker today having an unreal season can score thirty-six. Dixie Dean scored sixty. I can see your mind is blown."

"And you're going to score sixty goals, too?"

"Nah, that sounds like a lot of work. I don't feel like working hard. I'm on holiday!"

"But Max," said Joe, who looked like he needed a bit of peace and quiet. "Why don't you aim for the Chester records? Score more than Smasho. Dick Yates. Stuart Rimmer."

I sighed. "Joe, be serious. I'm a big League Two star now. I can't even remember the name of the division you play in. Okay? Now, if you don't mind, I'm going back to my glamorous League Two lifestyle."

"All right, boss," he said. "What's first on the list? Mani-pedi at an exclusive salon?"

"Close. I'm going to a charity shop to buy a second-hand lamp and some paperbacks with short chapters."

"But Max, Max, sorry. I just . . . I've seen you. You don't do what you're told. How does it even work with another manager picking the team and everyone knows you're better than him and all that?"

I shook my head. "Joe, it's really easy. Smooth sailing all the way." I became introspective. "I can be very obedient, you know. Very disciplined. And what I think I'm going to learn from this experience is that sometimes, sometimes I *don't* know best."

He eyed me, waiting for the tell-tale signs that I was joking, but my eyes didn't crease, my lips didn't twitch. I gave him a final handshake and went down to my car. As I started the engine, I checked Joe's morale. It had gone from abysmal to poor—a two-point jump. Yes! Some world-class football management right there.

I'd earned a treat, so I brought up "Holiday Road" by Lindsey Buckingham and blasted it through my car stereo.

I drove down the street with the most charity shops and parked. When I walked back along it, I saw a shop with a dark brown aesthetic that I hadn't noticed before. An ancient and faded sign proclaimed it was called Needful Things.

When I opened the door, a bell rang and it reminded me of an old bicycle. I was immediately struck by how awesome every item was.

Here was an old Panini sticker of Rudi Völler sporting the quintessential German football look: porn star moustache and permed mullet.

There was a lampshade with the repeating motif of a goose biting the tail feathers of the goose in front of it. A hand-written label attached by a frayed piece of string said, *LIGHT NO WORK*.

I picked up a hardback copy of *What Newcastle United Fans Know about Football*, and found that almost every page was blank. *Amazing* gift right here. I flicked through again and the "by the same author" page showed the publishers had printed similar books for the top twenty teams in the UK. Good gag but the existence of the other books ruined the joke for me.

I bent to admire a medal in a glass case that was inscribed with the words, *For Outstanding Achievement in the Field of Excellence.* Next to it was J.M. Barrie's actual hook hand.

While I was scratching my head at a pile of human bones labelled *Piltdown Man*, the shop owner came in and stood behind his counter. He'd been reading the newspaper, it seemed, and he placed it down on the counter. I was drawn to the headline: *He's Done WHAT?!*

My gaze moved up to the masthead. It wasn't one of the newspapers you'd get in this part of the world; it was from Chester. I finally looked at the shopkeeper, but I knew who it was.

Old Nick bared his teeth. "Max. How pleasant to see you. Why don't you and I have a little chat? Hmm?"

11

DIXIE DEAN

Dixie Dean (1907–1980) was an English footballer who played as a centre forward. He is regarded as one of the greatest of all time.

The shop was from a bygone age. An age of muddy pitches, heavy leather balls, brutal tackles, and no substitutes. Still, an age where a PA–190 striker competed against PA–180 defenders every week. Could he survive? Could he thrive? Could he live up to his talent despite all that bedevilled and beset him?

While the shop's fixtures and fittings seemed authentic, down to the till that looked like a typewriter and twee decorative plates sitting proud on shelves, it wasn't quite right: There was no dust, no old carpet smell, no creaking floorboards. Not quite convincing when you knew where to look, or sniff, or step. It was no more convincing, really, than the static projections from Henri's production of *SILK!*

Nick, though, was twice as real, twice as vivid, twice as furious as when I'd last met him. Then, I'd been in a hospital bed, more helpless than a newborn, and he'd been pretending to be a doctor. Now, though, I was the all-time goals-per-minute king of Tranmere Actual Rovers and his mood swings didn't interest me much. "How much is the lamp?"

"What?"

"How much for the lamp and do you take Scottish money?"

Nick massaged the knuckles of his left hand. He looked up at some point on the ceiling. "I gave you a gift, Max."

"Oh! *You* were my Secret Santa! I'll use that voucher to buy one of those big candles. You know the *big* ones?"

Rage poured off him in bone-shaking ebbs and flows. Jaw set, teeth grinding, eyes blazing, he turned his head like an animatronic executioner towards the fake till in his fake shop. A very real Post-it note had been stuck there. Before he plucked it away I saw the text: *NO KILL GOLDEN GOOSE.* I relaxed, *almost* completely. He could rage and shout and give me the hairdryer, but he wouldn't hurt me.

He became quite still, only moving his lips a quarter inch, whispering in a way that some may have found blood-curdling. "Do you know the story of the goose who laid golden eggs? His owners *ate* him. The story is meant to teach long-term thinking, but never before has such a tale involved a goose who *chose* to stop laying eggs. A goose who left the farm where he *belonged* for a languid cruise around Guadeloupe and Grenada where he *didn't*. That animal would lose his *protections*." He smacked his lips as though he was imagining eating me. It's possible I was reading too much into the gesture, but he had the teeth for it. "You have made my life very difficult."

"I do that, yeah," I said, examining one of those wire rotating postcard racks. Nick's pop-up shop stocked postcards from all kinds of random places, but the newest ones were from the Middle East. Made sense based on the little I knew of his movements. The most aesthetically pleasing ones were from Asia, though, so I rotated the rack to that section.

Nick growled, "You've guessed, it's clear, that when you gain what you call experience points, I also benefit."

"Yup. Hey, what's Singapore like? I heard the Prime Minister shaves your head if you're caught chewing gum."

"So imagine my surprise when I discovered that instead of earning the predicted amount from *managing* Chester versus Waddington Town, you were *playing* for a completely! Different! Team!"

He was worried about 60 experience points? What? So he was angry because he didn't understand his own curse. And now I had to explain it to him? Abysmal. "Yeah, the difference in XP was pretty small, actually, because I only played twenty minutes and the base XP was the same. No biggie. I mean, if I'd played twenty minutes for Chester, you'd have got the exact same amount. What's the problem? Oh! You've been to Jeddah. I hear the cheese is good there. Nick. Right? Do you get it? Jeddah? Cheese?"

Nick pulled his hand behind him, arced it round in an unnaturally perfect circle, and slammed his fist into the counter, which cracked into a spiderweb. I couldn't help but imagine what he could do to my precious, precious skull, but I quickly mastered the fear. He couldn't do *anything* to me. Not really. I was his golden goose and all that. He didn't even realise how golden I was. I was Dixie Dean reborn.

He looked left again and a new Post-it had appeared in the exact place the previous one had been. It said, *REMEMBER HE DO OPPOSITE.* Nick inhaled so massively he grew two inches, then he fixed his steely eyes upon me. "I'll try to be patient. I would appreciate your assistance."

"Boom," I said, slapping the counter, giving him my full attention. "You only had to ask."

Again the stillness, but now with a hint of a twitchy eye. "Max. I like when you earn experience points. I do. It's good for you. It's good for me. It's good for my colleagues!" He added the last part almost manically. His words hinted at why he'd chosen me for this curse, or why it was working so well. We had a lot in common. For a start, we were both selfish team players. But although I was sure he was some sort of eternal being, a demon, a hell-spawn, he was also doing a really fucking good impression of someone who hadn't slept for days and was stressed off his tits. "We like when you use your gift as your gift was intended. We don't like publicity that attracts attention to the fact that you're abusing the system." He tapped the newspaper. "And we really, really, like stability. Guaranteed income, you might say. When you announce a hypothetical plan to go to Exeter to watch a cup match and at the last minute you decide it's too cold and you'd rather stay home watching *Sunderland 'til I Die* for the thirtieth time, we take it on the chin! We accept it with good humour, even if we've already spent the money, so to speak."

"*Sunderland 'til I Die* is top," I informed him. "The first five watches are tragedy. The next ten are comedy. Eventually you realise: This is horror."

He bared his teeth, snatched and crumpled the latest Post-it note: *HE HATES WHEN YOU NAG ABOUT WIBWOB.* Clearly the writers of the notes were only guessing what we were talking about. Or they could hear but knew I was watching and wanted to nag me by not nagging me. The little shits! Nick was still blabbing on. "But when you are scheduled to manage a double-header against Wallington, we really expect you to be in harness for those. We can estimate how much you will abuse the system in those matches. My colleagues are really quite good at it. *He won't play against Tamworth—he's saving himself.* Accurate. *When he comes on against Darlington, he'll stay on the pitch.* Accurate. *He won't play against Wallington—he thinks they are beneath him.* All too accurate! Not only do you not play, though, you don't even manage! You give the honour to your subordinate! So you may experience yet more indolence!"

Okay, so he had the power to create pop-up shops and grant wishes and smash things, but no one was allowed to talk to me like that. "What is your problem? Who are you shouting at? Calm the fuck down. I'm not one of your imps. Jesus Christ, get a grip."

Nick took my suggestion far too literally—he gripped the edges of the counter, head bowed, desperate. Without looking up, he asked, "Do you know what a derivative is?"

"Yes! It's *this shop.* It's derivative of a Stephen King story. If I were him I'd sue you for plagiarism."

"Plagiarism? Where do you think he *got* the idea?" He briefly blazed at me, but his attacks were futile now. When I went on the front foot, he backed away, like all bullies. He was hanging his head in defeat again and talked to the epicentre of the spiderweb he'd created. "A derivative is a financial contract that can develop when economies are stable. Stable, do you hear? If person N has an extremely stable income stream, he can use derivatives to do all sorts of wonderful things including leveraging, hedging, and speculating. Person N might be literally superhuman in the assessment of risk, and person N might be able to turn stable income into riches beyond the dreams of avarice."

I scratched my neck, pretending to be lost. "Hedgehogs?"

"Person N," continued Nick, his voice dripping with venom, "might back the wrong horse. He might back a horse expected to run at three p.m. in Wallington, only to find that selfsame horse wearing flip-flops, sauntering around Merseyside, feathering his own nest!"

"Am I a goose or a horse? Make up your mind." I tried to process what the guy was saying. I wasn't in the mood for Nick. I wanted to think about scoring goals in front of massive crowds, soaking up the acclaim and adulation. For the first time, I'd had a taste of what it was truly like to be a PA–200 player, and I wanted more. Not only that; someone I'd met recently had planted the idea in my tiny mind that I might take a shot at Dixie Dean's goals record. And why not? The curse had given me the skills and I was adept at using them. With a big effort, I brought myself back into the room. "You want to know where I'm going to be so you can spend money you haven't earned yet. How is that my problem? I didn't sign up for any of this shit. You're lucky I'm still motivated to do it." I matched his glare for a few seconds, then relaxed. This was a chance for me to learn some things. "What if I'm sick? Are you going to throw a tantrum every time I catch the flu?"

"Being poorly is a good excuse. Taking a good month off to abuse the system is a poor one."

Ah. I understood things a little better now. He was relying on my XP income and he thought I had just cut off his supply. I grabbed the newspaper with the provocative headline and pulled it closer. Then I looked for a pen and found one right there next to the till for impulse buyers. "Ha! Look at this. This pen has a picture along the side. It's a naked woman but you turn it upside down . . . ha! She gets dressed." I smiled at Nick. He had heat coming off him like the boiler of a steam train. I laughed. "Mate, relax. Watch this."

I wrote some numbers down in the margin of the paper. Despite himself, he was interested. "What are you doing?"

"You've been leveraging my XP to buy helicopters and shit. You need to live within your means. Drag yourself up by your bootstraps. First thing we need to do is make you a budget."

He turned and smashed four shelves of decorative plates in one fell swoop. "Insolent child!"

The noise of the plates disintegrating was upsetting. It sounded like a whole body of bones being broken, but after a slight pause to remind myself that the plates were almost certainly not real, I kept on with my maths. I soon had to consult my phone. The intensity and duration of my work brought Nick from rage 10 to rage 3. "What is it?"

I cricked my neck. "If you're counting on my XP to buy helicopters, then fuck you. I don't give a shit. All right? But don't call me indolent. This month is going to be mega. Probably the number-one month for XP ever. Dixie Dean has the record for the most league goals in a season, and I'm about to smash the record for the most XP in a month. See here? Each one of these numbers is a football match taking place in January. There isn't a lot of footy this week. There's West Ham tonight but I couldn't get a ticket. So the first game is this Friday. Queen's Park versus Dunfermline in the Scottish Championship. I'm not sure but I reckon that'll be four XP per minute. So let's say three hundred and sixty." I tapped the number I'd written. "Plus up to thirty new players in my database, and coaches and physios and I might meet a super scout I can poach. Saturday I'll play the second half for Tranmere, I hope, so it's a hundred and eighty for the first forty-five mins, forty-five for the second. Let's put two twenty-five. And, of course, the money I get for playing will pay for the Brig. Who you foisted on me, so once again what looks like chaos is me cleaning up your mess."

"I didn't—"

"Sunday there are some FA Cup third-round games, or I could do Notts Forest Ladies against WBA in the third tier. I haven't decided where I want to go yet—that's the beauty of being on holiday—but let's pencil in four hundred and fifty for that match. Tuesday the ninth I was thinking of Wealdstone v Aldershot. It's a long drive but it's much more tolerable when you know you won't have a full inbox to work through the next day. No chance I'd be going to that one in a normal month. What I'm saying is I'll be in Glasgow one night, London the next. Watching three or four matches a week in addition to training and playing and everything else. What did you say? Indolent? This is legendary grinding, you prick! This is *unreal* levels of dedication."

I wrote 270, followed by a couple of 630s, more 270s and 360s and mumbled names like Everton, Burnley, and Man City Women. When there was a choice, I was limiting my travel to the north of England, as usual, but on some days there was only one place to go, and that place was never local. Nick watched and listened. Out of the corner of my eye, I thought I saw him licking his lips—this time because I was laying golden eggs—but when I glanced up he was regarding me with a look of bored civility. "Is that the end of the list?"

"Nope. These are just the pro matches. There are untapped five-a-sides all over Merseyside, and I might be able to get to some Sunday League matches. I'm going to sneak into the training sessions of pro and semipro teams. There's so much talent on Merseyside. I love making fun of them but they're brilliant at football and they don't need to be asked twice to go visit sick kids in hospital. Yeah, it's going to be just like the old days. Me, on my own, running around earning experience points, finding players, turning your bicycles into helicopters. I don't want to ruin the holiday vibe by setting an arbitrary target, but I'm thinking I could get ten thousand XP this month. That and twenty untapped talents, two hundred coaches and scouts, two thousand new players in the database. And you know my favourite thing?"

"I do *not* know your favourite thing."

"The twenty-eighth of January, the last day of my loan, is Liverpool Women against Arsenal. Big game! Seven XP per minute! And you know where Liverpool Women play their games? Prenton Park. Same as me! I'll get in for free. Which makes me think this whole thing was planned. Not by you, because you're utterly fucking clueless, but by a higher power."

Nick seemed dizzy. He very much had the demeanour of a man whose prospects had gone from extreme poverty and a short life of long beatings to one of incredible wealth. "You've been telling everyone this is a holiday."

"Yes, you fucking cretin. So they'll leave me alone. If I said they could call me if they had questions, I would never get anything done. This way, this *genius* way, I get hundreds of things. One, I get to increase my playing level. I was motivated to do that, but after scoring in that big stadium, even more so. I'm addicted already, holy shit. I recently realised I'm quite vain. Isn't that strange? I want ten goals in these five games. A hundred years from now, people will look at my Wikipedia page going, what the hell was *that*?! Two, I get paid. Humans need money, right? You know that by now. Three, I make sure Chester will get to a higher level because if I can get my skills up, winning football matches will be easier than skimming stones. Four, I get the XP to buy an attribute and the Contracts perk. Contracts, mate. That's going to be such a power-up! Five, I get new players and maybe some new staff. Six, I get a break from being responsible for everything. I get to switch my phone off if I want. Everybody wins, mate. Including you. Oh, and seven, I get to play for the same team as my boy Dixie Dean, whose record I'm plotting to smash. It's all gravy. So why don't you get out of my face?"

Nick stared at nothing for a long time. Finally, he nodded. "Ten thousand experience points? My colleagues made a mistake, Max, in doubting you."

"Don't blame the imps! Look, leave me out of all your stuff. Okay? I'm unpredictable. That's not a bug, that's a feature. Deal with it. Don't gamble on me doing things the normal way, and don't do this again." I swirled my finger around, indicating the shop.

Nick didn't seem to be listening. He picked up the newspaper and ripped off the part with my numbers. He screwed them up into a ball which caught fire and turned to ash in an instant. "Good. I understand it better now. Leaving the farm to lay more eggs. Very creative. You value creativity, and it has served you well so far. But you must be careful; creativity is inherently risky." He took out his pocket watch and fussed with the crown. He was trying to put some thought into words I would understand. "When one steals a famous painting, one does not display it in one's drawing room. That would be foolhardy, would it not?" He tapped the headline. "You have stolen *La Giaconda*, displayed it, and invited the local constable to come and admire it."

I tutted. "What are you talking about?"

"I refer to your ambition to beat a longstanding record. To bask in unearned acclaim. Try to imagine—this will be hard for you—a universe with rules. One rule is that I'm allowed to give you a gift and you're allowed to use it. Nothing you do as a manager will raise so much as an eyebrow. When you play, imagine a policeman is watching, wondering how such a treasure came to be in this place."

"Are you saying I need to stop playing?"

A Post-it appeared, and I thought I caught some imp-sized fingers vanishing into nothingness. It was the same one as before: *REMEMBER HE DO OPPOSITE.*

Nick pushed his hands back through his hair. "You should stop, yes. That's the truth of it. But I know you won't. So work with me. Let us get creative." He looked at the watch again, shook his head, and put it away. He paused for a long time. "I have it. There are rules. There is a person who enforces the rules. The person is impartial, incorruptible, and entirely without humour. The person is, in fact, a referee."

I nodded. It hadn't occurred to me until then, but when he said it, some out-of-focus thoughts became foregrounded. "Right . . . because this is all a game to you lot. So there are rules. So there's a referee. Okay, I'll buy that. It's another demon, obviously. A referee for demons. The Refereemon."

Nick gave me a withering look that was far more effective than most of his outbursts of temper. "That is not even close to its name. As I said, you are allowed to use your gift. Have at it! But you would be wise not to attract the attention of . . . what's a more suitable translation? *The Sentinel.* It seems logical to me that you can play for Chester. The level is not so high—yes?—and you are young and not stupid and you train with your players. Why should you not reach their standard? And slowly, slowly, as your team improves, so do you. Yes, why not? Who could argue with that? Many years from now, you are offered a role in a Premier League team and you perhaps have one final season as a player in your legs. You score a few of your unearned goals and dance around the sides of the field like a dressage horse. Tolerable. Enjoy it. Then you cease to be a player and enjoy many long and happy years as a famous manager. Risk free."

"So there's no time limit on the curse?"

He ignored me. "Let me take the other extreme. Next year, you get bored with the challenge of managing Chester and find yourself playing for . . . What is the best team?"

"The *best* best? Luton Town, maybe."

"You play for Luton Town in the World Cup final and you score six goals. Your name is engraved into metal, there are parades in your honour, books and songs are written about you. That, anything like that, would be . . . inadvisable. The Sentinel would be sure to notice. That would be bad, for *both* of us."

I grunted and rolled my neck around. Nick still didn't know about football, and he didn't know that I already had two chants. But he knew the rules of his own games. That said, I didn't want any restrictions placed on me. I wanted my name in lights and there had to be a way to get it. "Right. Here's the thing. So far, I haven't done anything noteworthy. Yesterday I scored a tap-in and a penalty. Easy. I did some good things and some bad things. No expert who watched that match would think I was better than Henri or Ryan Jack. In a month I'll be the exact standard of a Chester player who has had a few weeks of better training. It's a totally believable story. Now, Chester's good and all, but I'm smashing it there and there's still only two thousand coming to the games. I'm wondering if I might not skip a few divisions, learn my trade in the Championship for a couple of years, then mess up the Prem. Dixie Dean, right, his family was from Chester, he played for Tranmere, he had his skull smashed in, two years later he set a record people say will never be broken. I'm way along that path! It can't be coincidence. I'm his regen. Don't particularly feel like going to Everton, truth be told, but a club with a smart owner. Brighton. Yeah. I could do for Brighton what Dixie Dean did for Everton. People will talk about me for as long as the game is played."

Nick stared into space. "I'm not getting through to you, but I can't tell you the consequences. It's one of the rules. What are my options? Regulation. Intervention in your economy. A forcible realigning of your incentives. Every minute spent playing loses experience points, and when you hit zero you begin to destroy your purchases. Harsh but clear. Threats. You don't respond well to threats, but I think a small threat is in order. You see, you are not the only one with a Retire option. I can end our arrangement, too. Will I suffer? Of course. But there could come a point where the result of this—"he tapped the newspaper for the millionth time—"is banishment from this realm for a thousand years." He shook his head. "From what I've seen, next time round, there will not be helicopters. I would very much like to stay while the going is very, very good. Do you understand?"

"If I attract too much publicity, you'll pull the plug. Sorry, but that's out of my hands. People think I'm weird. They love talking about me."

"As a manager it's fine! Let them talk! As the third or fourth best player on your team? Perhaps! Use your brain! My preferred option, Max, in almost all things, is self-regulation." He turned around, and as he did so he trod on some broken ceramic. He kicked out at the debris, and I swear time slowed and my eyebrows were singed with the heat of some unseen flame. Nick flicked part of the counter up and walked through. I realised the counter had been keeping me brave, and now that there was nothing between me and him, I was literally frozen with fear. He paced around me in an endless, irritating loop. "You are restless because you are overpowered for your level. There is little challenge for you until you reach the next step. I understand that much." He paused, whispering into my ear from behind. "I can help you. A few off-the-cuff remarks here, planting a few ideas there, and hahu! The challenge is back. The struggle returns and you are kept busy." He was off again.

"Ah, veto. No, thanks. I'm doing just fine without your help."

"Too late. The wheels are in motion. Don't worry, there's no charge."

"Fuck me."

And then that particular moment had passed and Nick was leaning against a display of jars and containers. He gently rubbed his bottom lip, a gesture intended to be casual. "It was interesting what you said about earning ten thousand experience points this month." Casual casual casual. "That would be quite a feast. You mentioned there is a high-level match tonight. Surely attending that would be a considerable help?"

"West Ham are at home to Brighton. Six hundred and thirty XP, plus injury time."

"Fascinating. Injury time, you say? That's when the injuries happen? No matter. If you are willing to travel to Ham, I am willing to use my contacts to ensure your admittance."

"Oh!" I exclaimed, faux-surprised. "You're willing to help me and you have no skin in the game?"

"Let's just say it would go a long way to repairing the damage you have caused."

I ignored his jibe; I wanted to go to that match. "If you want me to drive to fucking London I'll have to leave right now and I'll get back home at four a.m. or some shit. So there are conditions."

"Oh?"

"I'm only here in this shop because I want a lamp. So I want a lamp. It doesn't have to be amazing, but it has to work. I want to read books in bed. Right? And I want some books. Page turners. Something like *The Da Vinci Code*. Holiday stuff. Because, Nick old bean, this is my holiday. My holiday on my terms. All right? Ticket, lamp, book. What do you say?"

He took out his ancient pocket watch and fussed with it. "The ticket will be waiting for you. As will a lamp and a book."

"Great," I said. "Bye." I strode to the door and rested my palm on the handle. "One last thing. Did you ever do a deal with Dixie Dean?"

His eyes darted around as he went through his personal memory banks. "Dixie . . . Dean. You mentioned him, but the name does not, shall we say, ring a bell."

"Fuck me," I mumbled. "You're telling me he did that for real?"

"What?"

"Nothing. If I drive to London and there's no ticket, I'm hitting Retire. Just so you know. Say hi to the imps for me."

In the 1933 FA Cup Final, Dixie Dean became the first-ever footballer to wear the number 9 shirt. (The match was the first where players wore numbers to help spectators identify them. Everton wore numbers 1 to 11; a small team from Manchester wore numbers 12 to 22.)

West Ham versus Brighton was a fascinating clash of styles, with one team playing hard-boiled, stripped-down football not a million miles away from what Ian Evans would do with a £500,000,000 squad, and the other trying to evolve the sport in real time.

West Ham's number 9 was Michail Antonio, a player who had started his career in non-league. He'd started as a winger, like me, but now was a hard-working striker. He scored a first-half header and ran around the huge stadium while fans screamed with delight. I was pretty jealous.

The match was also a chance to see Brighton's double-dribbler, Mitoma, cause havoc on the left wing. He was fantastic, but his final decisions weren't always the best. He could take a difficult pass, dribble past two players at high speed, and then give the ball straight to the opposing goalkeeper. He was better than me at everything except decision-making.

While I watched and my XP counter ticked higher, I thought about my meeting with Nick. He'd confirmed that he relied on me getting XP and had finally said out loud that he didn't want me to play football at a professional level. He didn't want me to catch the eye of the Refereemon, but as long as I avoided *that* I could do whatever I wanted. Self-regulation, he'd said. That was clever. Make me set my own goals and limits and if I messed up, I'd only have myself to blame. Something to try on my players!

West Ham were soaking up pressure and then hitting long balls for Antonio to chase. He had started at a tiny club and bounced around the lower leagues for a while, gaining experience. It took him seven years to get from non-league to Premier League. If I did the same, who could argue? Luton Town had brought players all the way from non-league to the Prem. It *did* happen. It just had to happen slowly. Well, fine—until recently, that had been the plan, anyway.

I was twenty-three. If we got one promotion per year, I'd get to the top flight aged twenty-eight. One year to inject some CA into me, then aged twenty-nine, I could have a bash at Dixie Dean's record. Injuries permitting, I'd probably get three or four years at the top level as a player. That was enough, right?

Another way to think about it was that I could improve as fast as I wanted as long as I did it in private. Playing for Tranmere in January had seemed like a fun template, one I could repeat with a League One team next year and the Championship the year after. That plan was out. That plan, I hadn't realised, was me walking into the crosshairs. What about that idea I'd had once where I paid a club to let me train with them? If I paid Birmingham City £20,000 to let me spend next January cosplaying as one of their players, would they? Maybe if I included it as part of the deal when I sold them a player. I could get my levels up without making myself more visible.

Ah, but what was the point? If I couldn't get on the pitch to use those skills, why bother?

Mitoma took the ball on the left and tried to thread a pass through the eye of a needle to a teammate. It was ambitious; if it had come off, his teammate would have had an easy chance to score. It didn't come off, and West Ham were back in possession. Mitoma's match rating dropped one point. The curse did not approve.

The move gave me an idea. I could be a CA-200 player as long as I didn't *look* like a CA-200 player. Coming on for the last ten minutes to turn a defeat into a draw? Yes, as long as I stank the place up in the next match. I could play like dogshit in matches we were winning easily. Passes could bounce off me, I could miss headers, hit free kicks into row Z. Then against good teams I'd put on a show, though not too much, and make sure we smashed the league. "He plays better against better teams," people would say. That was a thing in sports. That happened.

Creative, he'd called me.

This was very creative thinking, since I was nowhere near CA 200.

I wanted to do something extraordinary as a player. Scoring two goals a game wouldn't go unnoticed no matter how many passes I mishandled.

Mitoma got the ball again, waited for the defender to commit himself, burst past, and was fouled. A pretty wild tackle. Orange-card level—it needed more punishment than yellow but maybe wasn't quite a red.

As the Japanese winger rolled around in agony, I remembered why I hadn't ever wanted to play every league game. Things were different, now, though. Now I wanted another rush of the goal drug.

If only the Refereemon had a yellow and red card system. I could go crazy as a player until I got the yellow card, then stop. But I felt certain the dude only dealt in red.

All right. Frustrating, but the upshot was that I wouldn't be signing for world champions Luton Town anytime soon. I would keep my head down. Keep out of the papers. Self-regulate like a champ. If I stayed with Chester, I'd find ways to increase my CA and be ready for when we got to the Premier League. Maybe five years from now I could ask Nick if he thought it was safe for me to take a tilt at Dean's record. Or, even better, I'd ask one of the imps. They were more likely to give me an honest answer.

Pockets full of experience points, head swirling with desires and fears, I drove way, way, way back up north. I parked and went up the lift to find a little present outside my door. A plain, silver lamp and a book.

Something like *The Da Vinci Code*, I'd said. Nick had picked up another book in the series by the same author. This one was called *Angels and Demons*.

I shook my head as I flicked through it. Not a very creative choice, but the chapters were lovely and short.

Dean's family on both sides hailed from Chester.

Wednesday, January 3.

I wasn't at my freshest for training, but I did the work. It was a tough day, physically, but even though I was struggling and failing to match what the other players were doing, I couldn't help but keep a manager's eye on proceedings. There were a few lads, I started to realise, who were coasting. Doing the bare minimum. The list, you'll be shocked to hear, included Jack the Lad and Samuel.

After lunch, I went back onto the pitches to take free kicks. Beckhams and Cannonballs spluttered off my feet. No risk of the Refereemon mistaking me for a talented footballer today.

As I showered, I thought about Chester. I was trying to keep out of the squad screens—a digital detox of sorts—but it would have been unprofessional not to keep an eye on the latest transfers. A lot was going on!

3rd Jan - Trick Williams - Chester - Eastleigh - free

3rd Jan - Vivek Purwaha - Chester - West Didsbury - loan

3rd Jan - Michael Harrison - Chester - West Didsbury - loan

3rd Jan - Calabash Barkley - Tranmere Rovers - Chester - loan

The squad was pretty full now. Twenty-four slots filled, including Michael, who would be back in a month unless he wanted to stay longer. With Trick safely gone (hurrrrr!) Sandra would be able to use Eddie Moore at left back. Bark was cover for Joe Anka, and Sandra knew we'd promised him minutes. Today, Tyson's name was included in the squad list, meaning he'd trained with the first team. Yesterday, it had been Benny and Lucas Friend. The youth system was well and truly linked to the first team.

With the new signings, we were £900 a week over budget, but MD understood we needed bodies and said he would make it work. The truth was, we'd been under budget for most of the season.

The women's squad had a few minor injuries and was looking threadbare, especially in defence. I needed to send Jackie some reinforcements, ASAP.

He left school at fourteen and worked for Wirral Railway. He was a late starter; his father had done the same aged eleven.

While I watched the horror unfold in front of me, I tried to remember the last time I'd watched a five-a-side match simply for XP. Before I became director of football at Chester, surely? Before the World Cup.

Well, I was back! There was no danger of me finding a useful player; I'd stumbled across an over-forty-fives league playing in a flat-roofed *soccer dome*. One team was a bunch of rail workers playing under the banner Railway FC. They were playing a team of bus drivers called Park the Bus FC and the score was currently 8–8 with two minutes to go.

I'd like to say all the stray passes and mistakes were because of the pressure of the situation—next goal wins—but it was no different to what I'd seen in the previous fifty-eight minutes. Neither team found a winner, face was saved, hands were shaken. Players would go home and tell their wives and kids how many goals they had scored. Perhaps they would write them down in a book. A record of their achievements. Something for people to remember them by. Every goal a slice of glory; the numbers on the page humming for all eternity.

The next lot came on: Queen's Park Vets against Park Road Vets. Once I'd added them to my database, I went round to check the other pitches were empty, then hit Playdar. I probably wouldn't find a good player, but it would lead me to another park, pitch, field, or gym where football was played.

Dean took a night job so that he could concentrate on his first love, football.

Me: Sending you a DM to take a look at. She'll come to training when she can, but she works nights so it's hard. Sorry about the accent.

Jackie: What's her name?

Me: You know the rules. Can't ask me questions. I'm on holiday.

Jackie: I need to know her name.

Me: Fine. I think she said Diane but it's hard to be sure. Her English isn't very good.

Jackie: Where's she from?

Me: Merseyside.

Boom! He walked right into that one. Diana was a twenty-two-year-old DM. CA 1, PA 60. Jackie didn't often play with a DM but now he had the option. The hit of dopamine when I found a low-CA, high-PA player was really something. Nothing like scoring in front of 7,000 maniacs, but it was in that direction.

While playing for Tranmere reserves, Dean was fouled and lost a testicle. To help with the pain, a teammate rubbed the area. Dean is said to have shouted "Don't rub 'em, count 'em!"

Thursday, January 4.

Nick's warning had been working its way through my tracts and pipes and a nugget of wisdom was excreted soon after I woke up. My epiphany was thus:

If this January was the last chance for me to improve my CA to a higher level than the average of the team I was managing, then I needed to be extremely careful about how I spent my improvement points.

For example, did I really need stamina? Emma might have spent *all* my points there if she had a vote, but I tended to play less than half a match, and from the DM slot I could manage my fitness quite well. So there was maybe no point going flat out on all the running drills Tranmere did.

Did I need more strength? It was useful in situations where I had to grapple an opponent, hold the ball up, or release myself from someone's clutches. A few more points would be okay, but I didn't need to be an ogre.

Dribbling, pace, and finishing? Sure, if the plan was to be a mystery winger again. A more feasible plan was to stick to being a DM, where my anticipation and the curse would do a lot of my work for me. But I could be a DM who took amazing free kicks and penalties. With Chris Beaumont in the team, I wouldn't need to shoot all the time. Turning goals into assists would keep me away from the notice of the Refereemon.

I'd need to score *some* goals, though. I had a taste for it now, big time. Everton's new stadium was being built not all that far from my temporary home, and seeing that several times a day really got my juices flowing. If I was going to stay at Chester, we needed to expand the stadium and, more importantly, fill it. My goals needed to be met by deafening roars. They needed to produce that buzz. That hit. More, please!

When I got to training, I took my intensity down to about eighty percent of the day before. They say if you aren't a hundred percent committed you're more likely to get injured, but I wasn't so sure about that. It sounded like an excuse for idiots to throw themselves into reckless challenges. After the usual drills, we played a fairly serious full-sized match with the first team playing 4-3-3 and the rest of us matching the 3-5-2 we expected from Barrow. That meant I played right mid, so I was up against Jack the Lad. At one point, I had the ball on the right and I was strolling around, being all dickish and annoying. I bent to put my knee on the ball and the sky went *CRACK!* I looked up, expecting to see a thousand-foot-tall demon with twin Uzis, but it was just a plane that had gone supersonic.

Jack had taken my pause as a chance to get me, but I recovered just in time and passed the ball left. I sprinted forward into the slot Jack had vacated, and sure enough the ball was played there. I accelerated as the goalie rushed out to intercept. If I got there first, I could boop the ball over the keeper, but he would wipe me out and I wasn't much interested in that.

So I swayed, pretended to do the boop, but ran around the keeper without touching the ball. I didn't expect anything other than the goalie to collect it, or kick it clear, or something of the sort. But my move bamboozled him, and I found the ball rolling clear. I passed it into the unguarded net.

When I looked back, chuckling, I saw that the goalie and Jack had crashed into each other and somehow they were both prone, holding their groins, lightly moaning. What you do in this situation is, you wait to check how serious things are, then you make jokes.

I knew right away both players were fine—certainly no attributes had turned red—so I skipped the first part. "Don't rub 'em, count 'em. How many have you got, goalie?"

"Three," he gasped. He untensed his body a fraction. "Got one of his."

"It's meatballs for lunch, isn't it?" I wondered, as the physio arrived. I looked around at the half-dozen players who'd come over to check on the sitch. "Seriously, though. We should start calling Jack's girls to let them know he's gonna be out of order for a while. Anyone free this afternoon?"

"Best," he groaned.

"What?"

"Shut the fuck up or I'll steal your girl."

"Yeah, I'm not worried about that. I've put her somewhere you'll never get to her."

"Where?"

"The other team's half."

Sharp inhalation of breath from the nearby players, followed by Reece Cox hiding behind Mark Dodd so he could laugh. Carlos, the team's exotic Spanish DM (who was returning from injury), shook his head. "Juu are savage, Max. Remind me not to cross you."

"Don't worry about crossing me. Worry about our only left-sided player crossing the halfway line."

"Fuck off," said Jack.

"I've been waiting for the right time to get that off my chest," I confessed. "I feel good now. Better out than in, as they say."

We had lunch—Jack sat away from me—and I asked Trev Northcross, the reserve goalie who Emma liked, if he'd let me work on set pieces with him. He was up for it. I did twenty minutes of corners, ten minutes of direct free kicks, and ten of swinging crosses for him to catch—that was good practice for him, too.

In the shower, the monthly perk arrived.

January Special Offer

New perk available: Masterpiece Theatre

Cost: 1,000 XP (If your total experience point income in January exceeds 10,000. If you fail to reach that target, the perk will be added to the shop as a permanent option priced at 4,000 XP.)

Effects: Allows for more precise deployment of players at set pieces.

I mean, wow. I'd wanted some kind of perk like this almost since I'd realised I could control football teams, but the fact Nick had taken my suggestion I could grab 10,000 XP and turned it into an actual goal was almost as annoying as the whole Sentinel thing. (I'd finally given up on the name I'd invented. Sentinel was better and more threatening.)

Fine-tuning where players would go would be fantastic. Even from the limited description, I was already fizzing with ideas. What about putting Goliath at the near post and everyone else at the far post? How would you defend that? Most teams tried to get two or three players near him. That would leave us with a three-man advantage on the other side. Fuck, what if I could get Goliath *and* Christian Fierce?

"Max?"

"Yep?"

It was Trev, the goalie I'd been training with. "Are you laughing because you're thinking about Jack?"

"No." I turned my shower off.

"Aren't you worried he'll give you a hard time?"

"No. I'm worried I won't be here long enough to annoy him into changing. Do you know what's up with him?"

"I didn't know anything was off. I thought he was playing well."

"He's *defending* well. Can we do this same time tomorrow?"

"Yes! It was great. Most players get worse as they get tired. You get better!"

"Top top top."

I dried off. After I got dressed, I sat and stared at nothing while I thought about the next perks. The curse was presenting my XP stash slightly differently.

XP balance: 3,659

January income: 973/10,000

Masterpiece Theatre was desirable but not urgent, and I'd only be able to buy it when I'd reached 10,000 XP, or on February 1 for an inflated price. Basically I needed to have 1,000 XP in my balance at the end of the month. Easy.

So the next ones on my list started with Attributes 5, which was 1,900 XP. That was top of the list mostly because it had been so long since I'd unlocked any attributes.

Then there was Contracts 2 for 5,000 XP. That was expensive enough that I could justify using one of my discount vouchers. The five percent one would take 250 XP off the bill. Being so close to the perk was absolutely mouthwatering. It would show me how much money players at other clubs were on, their contract expiries, release clauses, and so on. That info was much more important than unlocking a single attribute, but I was in a holiday mood, and when you're on holiday you chuck your money around recklessly.

The third thing on my shopping list was Wibwob. Base price 10,000, but I'd use the ten percent voucher on that one. At the start of February, I might have something like 5,000 or 6,000 XP, meaning I'd be in range of Wibwob at the start of March, or by mid-April.

Yeah. By the end of this season, unless I got turned into a bug by a cosmic referee, I would be a very powerful football manager.

For now, though, I bought Attributes 5 and watched as the crappy animation happened. I'd forgotten about that! I saw a generic player profile with almost as many empty cells as full ones. The first empty one turned yellow then returned to being blank, and the next changed giving the illusion of movement, highlighting only the empty cells, about fifteen of them, and the coloured one went round faster and faster, slower and slower, making it look something like a roulette wheel.

Finally, it landed on . . .

Creativity.

Fuck me. Did Old Nick have his hands on the scales there?

What did creativity mean in terms of a football match? The ability to do something unexpected? A reverse pass? A no-look backheel nutmeg? It had to be something like that.

I quickly took a look around the men's and women's squads, and there were no great surprises. D-Day's creativity was high and Glenn Ryder's was low. The women had a set of creative midfielders: Kisi, Dani, Maddy, and Charlotte. That made sense.

Well, I was pretty pleased with it, and I would enjoy working out exactly what difference it made to players and how they played.

In the shop, Attributes 6 appeared, retailing at 2,050 XP.

He is best known for his exploits during the 1927–28 season, which saw him score a record sixty league goals. In total, he scored eighty-four goals that season. He also scored eighteen goals in sixteen appearances for England, which, as you know, is more than one per game.

Friday, January 5.

Me: I DON'T KNOW HOW TO SAY THIS BUT I HAVE MET SOMEONE ELSE

Emma: One day you're going to go too far with this sort of thing. Who is she?

Me: Goalkeeper! There are two of those goalkeeper school things here. One's down the road from the stadium. I called the guy and said have you got a tall, lithe woman who can handle balls.

Emma: Why do I feel these messages are going to be in a court case one day?

Me: I've just seen her in action. She's perfeck.

Emma: One for the agency?

Me: Not quite that good, no.

Emma: Shame. What is XG?

Me: xG. Expected goals. It's how many goals you should score. A penalty kick has xG of 0.76, so you should score 76 goals for every 100 shots.

Emma: Okay. My friends who are boys who like football WhatsApp group said you were in a podcast. I'll send you the link.

Excerpt from *Pyramid Schemers*, the original and best podcast dedicated to the other seventy-two teams in the Football League.

Rocky: So that's my pick for over two point five goals. Mike, what have you got next?

Mike: It's my pick for long shot. The listeners really liked it last week when we picked bets with looong odds, so I'm doing that again. Going extra long.

Rocky: Spicy. But not longer than Juan Rosario to score against the tightest defence in the Championship? What was it, ten to one?

Mike: That nearly paid off! He hit the crossbar. This one's even longer odds. It's in League Two, for Tranmere.

Rocky: Hang on. You're not advocating for our listeners to bet on Tranmere Rovers . . . to score?

Mike: Unorthodox content, I know, but hear me out. For once, I think the market has made a mistake. After his two-goal haul last week, the bookies slashed his odds, but in my opinion, nowhere near enough. Max Best to score any time is twenty to one.

Rocky: Twenty to one is the longest pick in this show's award-winning history. You're suggesting that lightning will strike twice. That's what this pick is. Who are they playing?

Mike: Barrow.

Rocky: Barrow! With one of the meanest defences in League Two! Best won't start the match. He's a defensive midfielder. Yes, he takes penalties but twenty to one is the stingiest price in the history of sports betting.

Mike: Hear me out.

Rocky: Go on.

Mike: He plays DM for Chester.

Rocky: Maybe for some listeners this is a good time to mention that this player is, in fact, the manager of Chester Football Club. If you think it's bizarre that we're talking about him playing for Tranmere in League Two, there are many who would agree with you. Please continue.

Mike: He plays DM because he's doing a job for his team. When they're behind he gets forward and he's a different beast. For Tranmere, he's playing as one of the front three. He dropped deep against Notts County because they have such dangerous players, but Barrow don't have the same threat. I think he'll play in forward positions, and I think that'll mean he gets chances, and if he gets chances, he'll score. He's extremely clinical. I think when he's played enough games in higher divisions, we'll see that he's an xG machine. We'll never see odds like this again. That's why he's my [gunshot sound effect] long shot pick of the week.

Rocky: Okay. [coughs] Maybe this is a good time to remind listeners to gamble responsibly. Never bet more than you can afford to lose. Visit be gamble aware dot co dot uk to learn more.

This was fascinating. First, the existence of a podcast specifically designed for EFL teams—those NOT in the top twenty. Second, the way the hosts were named after boxers. Third, their analysis was really good! Fourth, neither were fans of Chester, or Tranmere, or me, so if one was saying I was good and one was saying I was shit, that would help with the old Sentinel business. I could use these guys as canaries in the soul mine: If both were raving about me, I might need to consider dialling down my performances.

Me: That podcast was interesting. Tell your mates I'm not an xG machine and they shouldn't bet on me. Tell them I have no intention of scoring against Barrow and the match will be of absolutely no interest to anyone. Tell them Dixie Dean's record is safe.

Emma: They're laughing at you.

Me: Is that right?

Emma: Said the closest you'll ever get to him is his statue.

Me: Send them some middle finger emojis then leave the group.

Emma: Okay, done.

Emma: [eye-rolling gif]

A statue of Dean was unveiled outside Everton's stadium in May 2001.

Saturday, January 6.

James O'Rourke hadn't spoken to me much during training, and that was fine with me. What I needed most in the world was someone with whom I could discuss my problem of how to do whatever I wanted with no interference and no penalties if I went too far. Yeah, James was the last person I wanted to talk to. In some ways, he was like a feeble version of the Sentinel. James couldn't chop my head off and send it to a different ring of hell to my body. All he could do to hurt me was not let me go on the pitch.

Huh. That wasn't so feeble, was it? Right now, that was the main thing I wanted.

Fortunately, I was friends with James's own Sentinel, Mateo, and if I didn't get on the pitch today there would be hell to pay.

I was feeling pretty glum, slumped on the team bus with my earbuds in to make sure no one talked to me. What was I going to do? We needed to get points to save the club from relegation. Given the chance, I'd have to score a goal. Maybe two. Would the Sentinel give a shit about a match in League Two? Did it even know what Cumbria was? It would be a bad day if I scored a hat trick but Nick hit Retire.

Tricky. Messy. Annoying.

The bus passed Everton's new docklands stadium, looking gorgeous, and made a right turn. That seemed to surprise everyone, so much so that I felt it even without hearing what they were saying.

A few minutes later, the bus stopped outside Everton's current home, Goodison Park. Huh? We were playing two hours away, in Cumbria.

"Here you go, Max," said James, with a little smile.

I frowned and got up. "Have you sold me to Everton?"

He laughed. I hadn't seen him in this good a mood the whole time I'd been at Tranmere. "You asked if we could stop off at the statue, remember? Said it'd only add five minutes to the journey. Said it might inspire you."

"Right," I said. It was all coming back to me. "But you said no."

"I said I'd think about it."

"But you meant no."

His smile faded, but came back. "But then I really did think about it, and what's the harm? He played for Tranmere, after all. I like that you care about the history. Go on, fill your boots."

The doors opened and I found myself walking towards the larger-than-life statue of Dixie Dean, a player so good that Stanley Matthews and Tom Finney were in awe of him. The rest of the squad disembarked behind me, confused but interested.

Lee Contreras asked if he was allowed to record in the area. "What?" Oh. For his YouTube. "Better idea. Let's do that interview you wanted. Tell me when you're ready."

He couldn't believe his luck. "We're on."

I stared into the lens. It didn't come naturally to me, but I'd found that if I didn't think about how I looked, I tended to look fine. "All right, Contrarians?" Lee blinked as I said the name of his tens of hard-core fans. I think it blew his mind that I'd watched any of his stuff. "Max Best here with all the Tranmere players. We're off to smash Barrow and I said, 'Hey, let's pop by the Dixie Dean statue on the way there.' Bit of a pilgrimage sort of thing. Lee, you been here before?"

"No, Max," he said, keeping the camera on me.

"So here's the man himself," I said, looking up. "Stocky, wannee? Powerful. Sort of a South American look to him. Down here, Lee." Lee dipped his phone. "People leave flowers and that. Everton aren't even playing today. And come over here." I'd read about this on Wikipedia or somewhere. "This metalwork here, see? The little circles there? There are sixty. This guy scored sixty goals in thirty-nine games. A year or two before, he had a crash and smashed up his skull. Remind you of anyone?" I rubbed the back of my head.

"You gonna score sixty goals, Max?"

"I was thinking about it," I said, talking to myself, now, pottering around, looking at the big man from all angles. "You can't be a fan of English football and not come across the name Dixie Dean. None of us have ever seen him play and there's no good footage. But we're still talking about him a hundred years later, and we'll still be talking about him a hundred years from now." I reached up to touch the nearest knee. "He had a crash and shattered his knee-caps. Metal plate in his head. Imagine how many goals he'd have scored if he was totally healthy. It boggles the mind. Guys like this built the sport. You're on big money now, Lee, because this guy made everyone in the Wirral want to watch football."

"We're standing on the shoulders of giants," said James O'Rourke, who had come to listen.

"That's it! Yeah. You know how good players from the past were because of how people talked about them. Bill Shankly said Dixie Dean was on par with Beethoven and Rembrandt." I blew air out of my cheeks. "Don't you want people to talk about you like that? What would you give?"

There was a brief silence, broken when Junior bent down to check out the flowers. "Hey! There's a Tranmere scarf." He picked it up and threw it around Dixie Dean's neck.

"Team photo!" barked James. He looked more like a manager now. More in control. I slipped away. "Best! Where are you going?"

"I'm not in the team," I said.

"Yes, you fucking are. Get over here."

I stood next to him at the back row, while the front row knelt. I had a feeling this would blow up on Tranmere's social media accounts. When James announced it was time to go, most players were keen to get out of the cold and onto the warm bus. I was the last, along with Lee. He pointed the camera at me again, and I put my hand in front of it. He didn't argue, but he glanced up at the dominant player of his age. "You can't score sixty goals in one season. It's impossible."

"No," I agreed, but not for the reason he had given. Apart from the fact that the Sentinel would make me live inside out for a thousand years as a warmup to the real torture, it suddenly seemed disrespectful to think of myself in the same breath as Dixie Dean. He had earned everything he achieved. Earned through blood, sweat, and tears, not by exploiting a loophole. "I can imagine having a season where I score twenty in ten starts. You know, just for shits and giggles."

"Sure, Max."

I took one last look at the Tranmere scarf. Someone had put that there today. I looked around, my neck suddenly tingling. Was there a PA200 ten-year-old in the area just waiting to be found? Heading 20, strength 20, finishing 20? "And you know what? If I can't be Dixie Dean . . . I can find the next one."

12

THE REGULATION WILL BE TELEVISED

We arrived at Barrow's weird stadium and I spent much of my time before kickoff in a weird mood. I wanted to play, but I wasn't allowed to play too well. I wanted to help James O'Rourke, but James O'Rourke didn't seem too interested in helping himself.

He had named his usual 4-3-3 and the only change from the Notts game was to bring Carlos back into the midfield. Carlos was a silky-smooth playmaker, so I had no problems with it in principle. Personally, I wouldn't have thrown a player returning from injury straight back into the starting eleven, but that was me. No, my main problem was that Samuel was in the team. Samuel the 4–out-of-10 striker. Sam the Sloth. Fireman Sam—if you want someone to extinguish your own attacks, give him the ball. When James announced the enormous lump was keeping his place, I actually gasped, and the players and physios near me turned to stare.

Such decisions weren't spur-of-the-moment impulses. You had to discuss it with your assistant and sit and write out your team sheet and hand it to the referee. That meant it was the product of *some* amount of thought. In the marketplace of ideas inside James's head, he'd sold Junior and bought Samuel. He might as well have handed the referee a piece of paper that said, *I'm going to be fired today, lol.*

I got changed and warmed up without enthusiasm, even when I noticed that Barrow's badge featured a bee and an arrow (B, arrow) and that one of the stands was named after a former manager called Brian Arrowsmith (B. Arrow). There were two main things dampening my mood.

First, there was EFL branding all over the stadium. It must have been the same at Prenton Park, but I hadn't noticed because I hadn't had the Sentinel swinging the Sword of Damocles in my general direction. The EFL had signed a TV deal which meant all its matches (Championship, League One, League Two) were filmed and if not shown live, at least cut up into YouTube clips and TV highlights packages. If I, for example, scored eight goals from the halfway line, a couple of fucking people might fucking notice. I had to think that all publicity was bad publicity.

Second, James was a wonderful person but the curse rated him as dogshit in all aspects of football management. Unless something drastically changed, and I'd only ever seen minimal changes in staff profiles, he didn't have much of a future in the role. The best thing to do would be to go down the Kidderminster route. *Their* manager had a tactics wizard who he trusted, and he had an assistant manager who was good at scouting. James could be the guy in the middle of some talented specialists. But if I was Mateo, I'd want someone like *me* surrounded by the same specialists.

The game got underway.

The Barrow manager was a real hothead. He barked nonstop, which was extremely aggravating when I was trying to have deep thoughts. His numbers weren't amazing, but he was better than James in every department. Louder, too.

I sighed and pulled my hoodie tighter around my head. Most teams had rules about all their players wearing the same kit, and those rules were ruthlessly enforced by the captain. If you see a football team at an airport going to a big match, they'll be wearing club suits and club ties. It shows that everyone's equal, no one's bigger than the club. Tranmere's subs were wearing a black and green bench coat, but I didn't like it and didn't want to wear it, so I didn't. Fortunately, no one was too interested in telling me how to dress. Maybe they'd heard what I'd done in Darlington. At last, something positive from the scurrilous article!

I watched James for a minute. Like most managers, he pointed a lot and shouted. Micromanaging where players should pass and what they should do with their bodies. "Left! Left! Eyes open! Turn! Tracking back! Tracking back! And again!"

Just a stream of pointless instructions the players couldn't possibly take on board. Wasted energy. Being seen to be doing something because he felt the TV cameras on his neck, because Mateo was taking some practice swings with the Sword of Jamocles, because it was all James had ever known in football.

James, man. Saving him would require me to play my absolute best, but that would risk the ire of Nick and the Sentinel. Would I really risk everything to save *James O'Rourke*? He had a weak squad and no clue what to do with it, meaning even if I helped him out, he would be back in this position soon enough. Maybe it was kinder to let him fail so he could get on with the rest of his life. Dixie Dean bought himself a pub and ran it for almost twenty years. James O'Rourke was a good name for a pub landlord.

The first half was agony. Since my murder, I'd been super careful with my head, but I spent at least half the time banging my skull on the back of the dugout. *Dum, dum, dum.* It might have killed a few brain cells, but it relieved the frustration wonderfully.

Barrow were playing three at the back, and we had three strikers, so you might have thought, wow, we'll create lots of chances here. Nope. For a start, Barrow swarmed the midfield, giving Lee, Carlos, and Doddsy no time and space. Fine, right? Because the defenders could lift long balls to Samuel, who was bigger and stronger than the defenders he was up against. He would cause mayhem and the other two forwards would slap. Nope! Samuel quickly settled into a 4-out-of-10 match rating. Yeah but Max, the fullbacks will get forward and do damage. Soz, weren't you listening? Jack the Lad never attacked! He was like a yapping dog securely attached to his kennel, except his owner had removed the lead and the idiot pup hadn't realised.

No, forget all thoughts of parity, of an equal contest; the first twenty minutes was all Barrow. Then they scored and things changed. They became even more dominant. In the final five minutes before halftime there was yet another twist—a twist of the knife. Barrow scored again and had a feeding frenzy around Tranmere's penalty area as they battled for another, their players laughing and joking, their fans munching on pies and teasing us in weird north-of-north accents.

The buzz from our comeback against Notts, the goodwill we got by visiting the Dixie Dean statue—James had set fire to it then poured petrol all over himself and his career. His team had two giant holes that he made no attempt to plug, he never changed his plans, and despite using an attacking formation, his team was defensive as fuck. If he ever got a manager's job again, it would be a miracle.

Junior tried to talk to me, as did Coach Colin and the physios. I grumped them away, and with a minute to go in the half, stood up and looked around. I spotted the little cluster of guys with owner profiles. Mateo was there, of course, looking grim. As soon as an hour from now, he would offer me the position as Tranmere Rovers manager.

My legs felt heavy. The spring in my step had gone and I had no appetite for schemes and plots and secretly saving people. I didn't know what to do, didn't know how to navigate these side quests in the optimal way. In front of me were many literal lines and one metaphorical one. Did I really want to wrest control of a match at halftime? The last time had come back to bite me in the arse.

But this whole Tranmere thing was only partly about me. I'd told MD some of the truth, and I'd told Old Nick some of the truth, but I hadn't told anyone *all* of the truth. And I never would. My motivations were all built on the same foundation: Emma.

Emma hugging James because I'd smiled. Emma hugging James because I'd laughed. Emma hugging me because I'd smiled and laughed.

My heart turned into a fucking flamethrower. I was going to do battle for this football manager, big time. Yes, mate! I love the smell of three points in the morning!

Decision made, I burned with the fury of a thousand suns.

And then I relented and changed my mission statement.

James would get my help, but only if he wanted it. Really wanted it.

I checked where the TV cameras were and cross-referenced them with what I remembered from clips of Barrow. The main camera was up in the middle, somewhere . . . There! Found it. Okay, so if I stood with my back to it, about *there* . . .

I crossed the Rubicon, going into Barrow's technical area. Their sandy-haired manager was your typical proper football man: beyond gobby, screaming gibberish at his players and spitting venom at the referee virtually nonstop. He was certainly making the most of his limited gifts and had turned Barrow into a team with a shot of making the playoffs. "What?" he yelled, turning his face to me, and the camera. If he did anything dumb, it'd be caught. If *I* did something dumb, there'd always be some doubt about exactly what.

"Can I use your room for two minutes?"

"What you fucking say?" His bench had cleared, and they were all up in my business, ready to throw stings and arrows at me.

"Your manager's office. Can I use that for a private chat?"

"Can you fuck! Get lost!"

I didn't get lost. I stared at him until Junior pulled me away.

"What's going on?" said the referee. He'd rushed over to stop tempers from boiling over. Fat chance with the Barrow boys—they were born simmering.

"There was a boy in my school with the same name as him," I said. "I was only asking if he was that kid, and he went bonkers."

"You're twenty years younger than him, Best, and you're not allowed in his technical area. You know that. I should give you a yellow card."

"Oh, ref," I said. "You've got that little room. Can I use it for two minutes? I need to make a private phone call."

He tried to process what I was saying, but couldn't. "What? Jus— I'm running a match!" He jogged off.

James finally responded to my antics. "What are you doing?" he growled. He growled like someone who had never met Ian Evans doing an impression of Ian Evans. It didn't move my needle in the slightest.

"We need to have a private talk."

He tried to sneer, but again, rubbish. "Oh, do we?"

"Yes. As soon as that whistle goes."

"You're not in charge around here."

I showed him my phone with its countless unread emails and texts. "I just got a text from Mateo asking me to come up to his box right away." I let the threat hang in the air. The implication was that James would be sacked at halftime. It had been known to happen. It could be interesting to categorise the levels of humiliation: sacked the day after a match versus sacked at full time versus sacked at halftime. I suppose the worst would be *sacked in the warm-up*. I pressed home my advantage. "I can talk to *him*, or I can talk to *you*."

The ref blew the whistle and while James was reeling, I took his arm and led him under the main stand. We went past all the rooms and stopped by some double doors. People kept coming and going, but it was as private as we were going to get.

I grabbed his shoulder. "We don't have much time. Listen up. Are you here?"

He looked at my left hand, the one I cradled my phone in. "What did he say? Am I out?"

I took my hand off his shoulder so I could make tiny but powerful gestures. "We met in Tenerife. You remember, right? Some weirdo kid turned up, said he was manager of Chester. The only reason to believe him was his *unfathomably attractive* girlfriend. Emma. You remember Emma, right?" I showed him my home screen.

"Emma. Yeah. Emma."

He was a mess. His head was everywhere all at once. "In hozzie, I was all crazy. Got to get fit for the holiday. Got to get on that plane. You'd have been proud of me, mate. Fucking grafted. I had that goal, and I put the work in like a pro. I was wobbly on my legs, but I made it. So then what? I didn't have a plan for *the holiday itself*. It was just *be there*. But I was so full of anger and frustration—James, focus—so angry all the time, so lost. And I didn't have anything to *do*, so I took it out on the only person who was there, the last person I wanted to snap at."

"Emma."

"Right. I'm not saying I was a monster or anything, but it was frustrating that I'd take out my mess on her. Do you know what I mean? It was getting to be a vicious cycle. I'd think about the attack, what the police did, what Jackie did, all sorts of stuff. It'd bubble up and Emma would say something and I'd just . . . vent. It was really aggravating me that I couldn't stop myself from doing it. But then I did it again, but more." I shook my head. "Horrible. Dispiriting. And then we bumped into you lot, and that was it. You gave me what I needed: a bit of purpose. Some physios and coaches and the pool and the dinners where you sat outside in the dark for me."

He was present now. Listening to me for the first time since I'd arrived at Tranmere. "I preferred it to being inside with those rowdy idiots."

"The thing is, I owe you. I've tried to tell you a hundred times I'm not here to take your job. I've paid Mateo back."

"The tribunal."

"Yeah. And Junior and Bark. The worst thing that can possibly happen is he sacks you and offers me the job. How do I turn it down and stay friends with him? I've imagined the scene a hundred times and it doesn't end well. We've got to avoid it. I've paid him back and I'm trying to pay you back. But I've got to ask, do you want to keep this job?"

"Course I do. I'm a fighter. I won't quit."

Typical macho gibberish with no substance behind it. But it'd do. "Okay. The tactics aren't negative, but the messaging is. You can't fix that in five minutes. Fight by sending your allies in. I'll fly in like, er . . . Lord Flashheart. Let me fix it."

"What?"

"Let me fix it. Barrow? They're shit. Let me do a Max Best special. Insanely positive. They've never seen anything like what I've got in mind. We'll get back in this game, get a draw, get a point, maybe go for all three. I can't do this one on my own, though. This isn't a superhero story. Flashheart needed Blackadder. I need your team."

"Sounds like you want to be the manager of Tranmere Rovers."

I tutted and looked up at the ceiling. This guy. I brought my phone out of my pocket like the genie's lamp it was. "If I wanted that, you'd have been sacked already." I slipped it away, then mashed my fists into my face. "God, this is frustrating. You need to stop being so negative. Stop thinking the worst. Go back to the sun and the sea and all those big plans you had for the season. Let's get the fuck on with it or go our separate ways. You're in a death spiral and you can't think straight. You need someone on the outside to get you back on course. Come on, there's no time. I have to do the tactics. Let me help you! For me, and for Emma. For Emma, James!"

He thought for a while. "What's the plan? Tell me and I'll tell them."

"No time. Trust me. We go back, clear everyone out, and I'll tell them."

"What?"

"Get everyone out who isn't playing. We're subbing Carlos and Samuel off, by the way."

"I don't follow."

"There will be twelve people in that room, including you and me. If any of this leaks, we'll soon find out who did it. Neither of us wants an audience for this." The fewer people who saw me do a halftime mutiny the better. Lesson learned.

"But—"

I shook my head and turned him around. "You've got twenty seconds to save your career. No joke. Come on, now." With a gentle push from me, he started moving his legs. I wasn't sure what the odds were. Eighty–twenty in my favour, I supposed. The home fans had been singing "you're getting sacked in the morning." James knew he was on the brink.

He went into the dressing room and the hubbub died down. I stayed outside in the corridor, my back to the wall. If he didn't go for it, I wouldn't play. I'd claim my calf was feeling tight or whatever. If he wasn't willing to grab the rope I'd thrown him, he couldn't blame me when he fell down the well. There were long-term reasons not to play, too. These end-of-an-era matches tended to linger in the memory. The Tranmere fans would remember the team who got James O'Rourke sacked. Being involved in the worst Tranmere performance in living memory would not do much for my brand. Or my ego. Also, if I didn't play, I couldn't catch the eye of a demon.

"Okay, fellas. That was not acceptable." James coughed, then grunted. I felt him looking around, still coming to a decision. "Couple of changes at halftime. Carlos, you're off. Samuel, you too. I'm going to ask everyone who isn't playing the second half to leave the dressing room." Weird silence. "Come on, now. Everyone out."

The physios left first, then some coaches, then the other players. Junior went past—I hadn't told James who was coming on—and I reached out to grab him. When the last guys were out, I pushed Junior back in, and closed the door behind me.

Coach Colin hadn't left. He was leaning against the wall, arms folded. He was a good coach and I liked him, but if James was fired, he'd probably take over as caretaker manager. He had an incentive to do James dirty. He wouldn't, but why risk it? And if I needed to hunt down a traitor, why make the Brig's investigation harder?

I went to him and mumbled that he needed to leave, too. He reacted badly. Fuck him. If Tranmere were relegated, dozens of people would lose their jobs. His feelings didn't matter.

"Everyone over here," I said, quietly, when it was just the eleven players and James. I pulled the tactics board away from the wall, to establish dominance over it more than anything else.

"The fuck is going on?" demanded Jack the Lad.

"Shut it," I suggested. "I've been out in the corridor telling James an idea that could get us back into this. Right? My teams use three-five-two a lot, so I know how to play against it. Here's the plan. We're going to play four-four-two low block."

"What?" said Gareth Jones, the captain.

"What?" said James. "What happened to being too negative?"

"Genius, isn't it? To attack, you must first go ultra, ultra-defensive. Sun Tsu. Back four as normal. Jack'll be happy—he gets an excuse not to run forward."

"What is your problem?"

"Dizzy, you're left mid. Dodds, you're right. Shuffle, slide, look after your spacing. Here's the twist: Junior's going to play wide left. I'm going to play wide right. The goal of everyone on this team is to defend for your lives and get the ball to me as fast as poss."

"To you?" said Jack. "What a surprise."

"It's a head scratcher, isn't it? Get the ball to your best player? Hmm. Tommy Tactics rides again. Goalie? Punt the ball at me, low and hard." Punting in this context meant kicking it long. "I might be hiding near one of these guys, but hit this space. Fast, mate. No dicking around. Get the ball, punt it. I can cope with some spin and some height but too much and you'll give them the chance to get back into shape. Defenders? Block, punt. Midfielders, block, punt. If you can get the ball just over the halfway line when they're even slightly out of shape, we're going to slap."

"What do I do?" said Junior.

I laughed. "You score the goals. What do you fucking think? When I'm running onto that ball, you're drifting left, away from danger. When you think I'm about to hit it, you fucking go at goal. Straight for goal from whatever angle you're at. Be calm. If you can first-time the finish, top. If you need to take a touch, great. But that's it. No turning back to pass to runners. There won't be any. Now," I said, touching the tactics board. "This will fuck with their heads. They've never seen anything like this. They'll respond. Probably drop their wide mids back and play five-three-two. Or they might switch completely. We'll have to see. At that point—I'll tell you when—we go right back into four-three-three and it's your usual playbook again, but this time it'll work. Dizzy and Junior up top, with me as the third striker."

"Third striker?" scoffed Jack. "Don't you mean playing anywhere you want?"

"That's right, Jack! But not left mid. You'll notice I leave that space open for you to run into." He thought about stepping to me, which made me laugh. "You useless prat." Was I trying to rile him up so that he'd want to prove me wrong? Nah. Just liked calling people names. The bell rang. "That's it. Oh!" I snapped my fingers. "I'm thinking about winding their manager up. I probably won't—I'm on holiday—but I might. If it happens, let it happen. You don't need to get involved. Jack, that goes double for you. Don't want a tough guy like you wading in."

Junior raced onto the pitch, leapt to practise a header, and pumped his knees up to hip level like pistons. I walked behind him, fretting. Losing wasn't the issue;

if this plan blew up, James could tell Mateo he'd tried things my way and it had failed miserably. That would be fine with me. James would know I'd tried to help him, and Mateo would think twice about offering me the job.

No, the problem was Old Nick. This plan made me the creator and all our attacks would flow through me. Even the tactics screen had me listed as the playmaker. We needed at least two goals. Two assists . . . against Barrow . . . in League Two . . . in front of just 3,000 people . . . surely *that* was allowed?

Barrow kicked off, having made no changes at halftime, and began pushing up the pitch as our guys fell into a shuffle and slide. Junior hung out on the extreme left of the pitch and I did the same on the other side with no one anywhere near me.

Barrow pressed forward, passing left and right, probing, looking for openings. They were winning 2–0 and were in no hurry. They kept the three centre backs on the halfway line, but one by one their midfielders moved farther and farther forward.

A cross was sent in, and Barrow had plenty of numbers in the box to attack it. The mass of defenders did enough to make the header difficult and the goalie ran out to pluck the ball from the air. In the same movement, he drop-kicked the ball in my direction. I strolled towards it. The important thing here was *not* to do anything flashy or eye-catching. I did *not* want to end up on some tekkers highlights reel or whatever. I played for Chester and had to act like it.

He'd kicked it sort of sideways, and it was spinning and dipping pretty wickedly, to my right, perilously close to the right touchline. If I didn't control it first time, it'd go out and the move would have ended before it had begun.

I controlled the ball, still strolling forward, on the inside of my foot. It blooped up in a way that demanded a volley. Nick might have raged at me, but anyone who has ever played football will understand it. I *had* to volley it. Free will does not exist when the ball pops up just right!

Up it went, about chest high, and I watched with mild interest as it began its descent before thrashing it, much as our goalie had done, diagonally to the left.

Junior had sprinted as soon as I'd controlled the ball and now it was arcing into his path. His eyes widened and his first touch was poor—it squirted almost perfectly square. But he was fast enough to recover, and as the defenders hared backwards, the keeper made the moronic choice to come out. Junior didn't have time to think, so he struck the ball low to the keeper's left.

Two–one, and Junior ran over to the crazily designed away end, full of Tranmere fans.

I didn't want to be in the celebration highlights, so I walked the opposite way, going past the Barrow dugout. I winked. "Next time, let me use your room."

That annoyed him and he danced around, puffing himself up, generally behaving like he was playing a party game where he had to act as two different animals simultaneously and we had to guess which ones he was doing.

He was a dick but he was no mug; he ordered the left mid to drop deep to cover me, so as Barrow pushed forward again, this time with more urgency, I walked across the pitch and told Junior to swap sides. This time, Barrow's spell of possession was more prolonged and more intense, but we held firm. Still, it was a good while before anyone could get the ball to me.

It was Jack the Lad who did it. He won possession, played the ball back to the goalie, who had no choice but to play it straight back. Jack feinted, cut inside onto his right foot, and chipped it out in my direction. I'd have liked some more pace on the ball but that was okay.

I accelerated. Ooh, that wind resistance was coming back! I checked where Junior was and found him making a perfect run. I hit a left-footed curler that went behind two of the centre backs and held up with the spin. The goalie came out a few steps, remembered how he'd made it easy for Junior before, and retreated. Junior latched onto the pass and his first touch was heavy. The keeper *did* go running then, throwing himself at the ball sideways to cover most of the angles, but Junior scooped the ball up about two feet, over the keeper's body. It plopped onto the goal line and rolled a couple more times before coming to a gentle rest. Junior followed it and absolutely smashed it into the back of the net. Just to be sure.

Now the home fans, not a noisy bunch at the best of times, were even more quiet and the Tranmere lot were going tonto. We'd come back from two goals down—again!

Jack ran past me on his way to join the celebrations.

"Well, well, well," I said. "Look who can play."

While the guys wrapped up their party, I kept an eye on the Barrow tactics and the commentary. Sure enough, they made a change. They took off a striker, put on a specialist left back, and changed to 4-5-1. Holy shit! It almost looked like he was clinging on for the point, and he'd dropped his average CA in the process.

I walked to Barrow's half of the centre circle so that they couldn't restart the match and called our guys in for a quick tactics update. "It's James o'clock!" I said. "Got it?"

"Yes, Max," called Lee. I liked this side of him. With a clear plan and a vision and some hope of it working, he was serious and disciplined. I could imagine him maturing into a Sam Topps type. Sam with much higher technical qualities. Hmm. I liked the sound of that, but not as much as Lee liked the sound of his own voice. It'd be interesting to know when his contract ran out, just in case.

We lined up and Barrow stormed forward, stung by our recent double whammy. But we weren't in the low block now, so they overcommitted.

Dodd slid into a tackle, Lee poked it wide, and Jack the Lad ran out to collect. He had twenty yards of space in front of him, but he turned and played a sideways pass. I put my hands on my head. What the fuck? A golden chance tossed away.

Barrow realised things had changed and spent a minute reassessing. I was happy for the time out, too. I bent and placed one knee on the turf. We were back to James's tactics. My legs felt fresh and springy. As things stood, a few football hipsters would drool over my passes, but Junior would get all the headlines. If we could get him a third goal, he would be all of the story. Especially if the third assist came from somewhere else.

Or maybe . . . maybe 2–2 was enough. Another point against a top-six team, James's job safe for a week, and the next three games were against increasingly easy teams. Maybe it'd be more . . . more *Emma* if I sort of . . . asked him for his opinion instead of giving it to him.

I walked over to the dugouts and asked James what he wanted. "Go for the win or keep what you have?"

He looked ten years younger. "You joking? This is a great point. This is an amazing point!"

"All right."

I dropped to DM and we shut up shop. When Barrow got too excited, I dribbled through their lines and sent Dizzy away. The manager got the message and his team didn't commit too many bodies forward after that.

Finally, with one last look up at the TV cameras, I decided not to try to get the manager sent off. Helping James was a risk I thought was worth taking. Acting the maggot to stir up trouble was self-indulgent.

Still, the fact that I couldn't be myself was pretty depressing. There was a good thirty seconds near the end where I couldn't get my legs moving. Then I thought, hang on . . . *Chester will be here in a couple of years. This manager might still be in charge then, and in that game I'll be free to go full Max.*

That cheered me up. I sprinted left to help my best buddy Jack the Lad defend an overload, and patrolled the width of the pitch being a proper team player slash untethered puppy until the full-time whistle blew. Two–all, job done, end of the Barrow story, back to Merseyside for chicken and chips.

Yeah. As if it was going to be that simple.

Barrow had the strangest away end I'd ever seen; all the seats were squashed into one section and then there was a huge Perspex screen and then just loads of dead space. While the real Tranmere players went over to the away end to applaud the fans, I zoomed straight into the dressing room to avoid attention and to get a massage.

The physios were out collecting their gear and chatting to their fellows from Barrow, so I had to wait. I sat on a treatment table, kicking my legs. A fairly cute woman knocked and let herself in. "Are you decent?" she said, pretending to shield her eyes with a clipboard. I wasn't that familiar with the Cumbrian accent—it was a bonkers mix of Yorkshire, Welsh, and just, like, Scandinavian.

I wasn't sure who she was, so I bit back some very flirty responses and went with something pretty mild. "I could be."

"Saw you come in. I'm Emma." Two Emmas in the world. Who would have thought it? "I'm the media manager here at Barrow."

What did media managers do? Liaise between the journalists and the playing staff? There was one at Tranmere always trying to get me to do interviews. I'd have to talk to him to find out what exactly the position entailed. "We'll need one of you when we get to League Two."

"You're *in* League Two," she said, before slapping herself on the forehead. "You mean Chester. So you're going back? Yeah, you will need someone. You're not making the most out of this story and your socials are pretty bleak."

She was about to continue, but I interrupted like a true gentleman. "Emma, help me out. Barrow were a non-league club recently, and now you've moved up and you're doing well. You could go to League One! But I was looking all over the maps for your training ground and I couldn't find anything. Where is it? Do you train in the stadium or what?"

"No, we train in Manchester."

"Wait, hang on. *Manchester* Manchester? *Best chips in the land* Manchester? That's two hours away. Barrow AFC, from Cumbria, train in Manchester? You're messing with my tiny mind."

She shrugged. "That's where we train. FC Manchester United," she said. She meant FC United of Manchester. Ziggy's team. So a tier-seven team had tier-three or -four facilities. That couldn't be right. I needed to investigate that. Also, training two hours away? That was absurd, but if it worked it opened up half the country as locations for our new training centre. Land too expensive in Chester? Buy some in Barnsley! She didn't realise the enormity of what she had said, because she ploughed on all chipper and bubbly. "So's now anyways, there's lots of journos want to have a chinwag with yer."

"No, thanks."

"Sorry, I wasn't clear. There's, like, a *record* number of journos here to talk to you. They're spilling out into reception."

"Why?"

"Oh, I don't know. Something about you've put a woman in charge and done a runner? Something about the first manager to loan himself to another club? Could maybe be connected to the absolute *storm* you've whipped up."

"Got to be honest, Ems, none of that is cutting through into my day-to-day. I'm pretty focused on my reading. I'm nearly done with the Dan Brown collection. Do you know a good book with short chapters?"

"A good book with short chapters? The Bible. So who do you want to talk to first? There's the BBC, Sky, *The Sun*, *The Athletic* . . ."

"No, thanks."

She winced. I'd just made her life very, very difficult. "There's one. Nice girl, lovely girl, very pretty."

"Nah."

Emma pulled out her secret weapon. "She says you'll do it because you owe her fifty pounds."

I smiled. "Tell her she's used that one. No, Ems, I'm not talking to any media today. I have a hot young guy who does that for me. His name's Lee; I'll send him out when he gets here. He was my Man of the Match."

"We say Player of the Match, now."

"See? Lee knows all the media things. He's perfeck. I'm one of those dinosaurs. I only talk about conspiracy theories. I've gone full gammon."

Emma looked dubiously down at a clipboard and swallowed. How was she supposed to explain my refusal? "Right. Well, there's one other thing. I was told you're big into the disabled football and all that and there's a couple of not-able-bodied TV reporters and they've specifically asked if they can speak to you. They're big fans of Max, they said. I did sort of make a promise to them. I didn't realise you wouldn't—"

Our players came in, chipper and loud. They were happy with the point, same as their manager, and were high on the adulation they had just got from the travelling fans. "Lee. Get over here."

"Yes, Max."

"You're doing my media stuff again. Get Junior and go together. Don't mention me."

"Don't mention you?"

"If they ask about me, talk about Doddsy. If they ask about me again, talk about how well we defended. You get the idea. I don't exist. Don't mention me! Emma, can you separate those two journos? So I can talk to them but the fifty-quid woman can't see me? If you can do that, I'll do it."

"Yeah, I can, aye." She wanted to ask why, but didn't. She led me, Junior, and Lee along some corridors. "You wait here, Max." Lee and Junior followed her to the main media area, and half a minute later she was back, holding the door open while a short guy pushed a dude in a wheelchair through. As Emma left, her voice floated backwards. "I'll leave yers to it."

"Thanks, bebs." When she was gone, I counted to three and slapped my hips. "What the fuck?"

The two disabled TV reporters were, in fact, two of the imps. The one pushing the wheelchair was the tactics imp. He was wearing a crisp white shirt, open to the third button, under a smart jacket. He was wearing all-white trainers. His overall look reminded me of something I couldn't quite put my finger on. The one in the wheelchair was the one I'd caught playing Snake on an old Nokia. He was wearing a cheap black hoodie. He was holding, I'm very sorry to report, one of those big, fuzzy microphones with a box around it, where the box displays the logo of the media company the microphone holder works for. The branding said *IMP TV.*

Tactics Imp looked depressed, and Snake Imp wasn't much happier. "What's up with you two? Oh, shit. Is it the Sentinel? Did I piss him off?"

"No," said Tactics Imp, not looking at me.

"Can you guys give me a warning if I'm getting into the danger zone?"

"No," he said again, but when I didn't show any sign of saying anything else, he added a single word. "Soz."

"I don't," I started, but then wondered if there was any point. These guys thought they had carte blanche to interfere in my bizniz. "I don't want to be meeting demons and imps every ten minutes. We can't do this. And not in public." Tactics Imp's surly teenager vibe was getting to me. "What's *his* problem?"

Snake Imp pulled the microphone back to his own mouth, and I realised he'd been pointing it at me, like a real interviewer. "Sulking." He pushed it back.

I scrunched my face up as I peered into the fluorescent lights above us. With a big sigh, I looked down at the imp who had tried to help by directing me to buy the Wibwob perk. As ever, after my initial anger I felt vaguely sorry for the wretched creatures. "What's the problem, dude?"

"Don't understand," he mumbled.

"What don't you understand?" I said, with more patience than I knew I had.

"Low block four-four-two against three-five-two. Why did it work?"

"If I tell you, will you tie Nick's shoelaces together so when he tries to walk he falls flat on his face?"

He kinda grinned. "Can't."

Snake Imp went, "Hurr!"

"Give me your stupid notebook." He did, along with a pen. I squatted to use Snake Imp's lap as a writing desk, using crosses to represent the enemy and circles for me and my team. "Look, it's dead simple. Barrow are doing three-five-two. We're four-four-two low block but the front two are way wide."

"Two midfielders are forwards!" he whined.

"It's fine for twenty minutes. Low block's not about what they do on the ball. You know that phrase, right? On the ball is when the ball is at their feet. No, defending is about what they do *off* the ball. All professional players have done a four-four-two low block at some point in their lives. You just need discipline and to be willing to suffer for the team. It's not a problem."

"Oh."

"So we've got eight defenders and a goalie. Barrow aren't going to score with just the two strikers. Bit by bit, they push midfielders forward. It's typical to get wide players involved so they can send crosses in. So the left mid and right mid go forward and when they smash a cross too hard it might go all the way across to the other one and they can keep putting pressure on. One of the three central midfielders gets involved, too. If they're desperate, they'll send another, and move a centre back to DM, and so on and so on."

"But he was winning."

I shrugged. "He? The other manager? It's a league. Goal difference matters, he's at home, and we're rolling over to die. Why shouldn't he tickle our belly?"

"Hurr!" laughed Snake Imp.

"So what happens when I get the ball? This is me on the right."

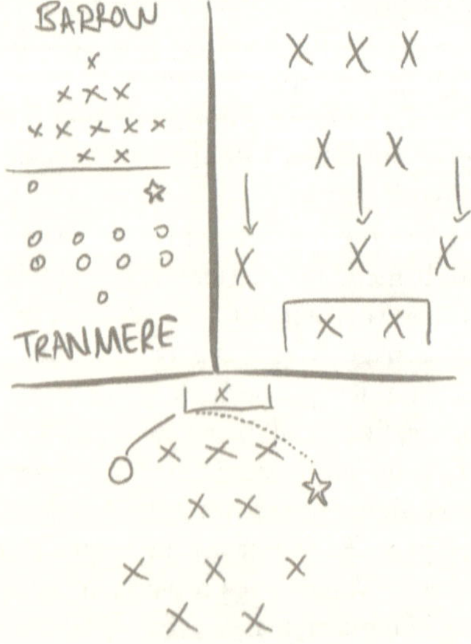

"The star."

"Is it? No, it's just a wonky circle."

"Junior's on one side, and he's going to make a run here, behind the defenders. I pass to him, boom, easy. Shot on goal. I thought it might take a few goes to work because his control isn't the best, but he's fast and the defenders were surprised. We got lucky, but the overall principle isn't hard. What I love is that the two central midfielders aren't attacking or defending. It's like I took them off the board. And there are three centre backs but only one is involved—the one nearest me. If I was too slow, he might have blocked the pass or tackled me. Which is why I did it fast. And these other two are pretty useless if the pass is good and Junior's touch is decent. And look how much space I'm in! They can't even kick me."

"Why no Chester do this?"

"Most teams don't attack us. And everyone in the National League North knows what I can do. They'd get sacked if they gave me all this space in the fullback areas. Also, I don't really have a Junior comp. Pascal would be closest, I reckon. I suppose it would work with him, but I haven't been able to get these passes going since my murder. Not ones this complicated. I feel like I'm passing twenty again."

"Creativity twenty," said Tactics Imp. His mood had flipped completely.

"Oh, am I?" I said.

He got shifty. Turned away, side-eyed me, and in an arch tone said, "Maybe?"

I scoffed. He'd just confirmed it. "So do you get it? The low block was to draw them onto us. Make all these gaps here. They're attacking with five against nine, we're attacking with two against three, but to me it's almost like two against one. It could blow up and we could lose five–nil but all you can do is try to move the percentages in your favour, and in this model, our chances are going to be way better. *Way* better."

"Max wins," he said, taking the notebook from me and staring at the sketches with great reverence.

I stood up. "Next time bring coloured pens." I suddenly wondered what was going on. They hadn't come for a tactics lesson. "Is that it?"

"Eh?" said Tactics Imp, barely listening.

Snake Imp smacked his colleague with the microphone. "Mission!"

"Don't want to."

"Get on with it. Fookinell."

Tactics Imp gave the other one a dig on the arm. "Gobbymanctwat. You do it."

Were they . . . swearing? In a Manchester accent? Were they listening in on my every conversation? No, they would have heard me explain the tactics to the team. "Oi, Tommy Tactics. Tell me."

He scratched the back of his neck and looked away. "It wasn't us."

"What wasn't you?"

"It wasn't us. Mission complete. We go now."

"No no no. Hold it right there. It wasn't you. Okay, something bad has happened. Nick thinks I'll throw a tantrum about it." Tactics Imp was nodding. Suddenly, I felt sick. "Is it my mum?"

Tactics Imp pulled a face. "Max mum *old* sick. Not us! Not us!"

"All right, don't have a fit." It wasn't mum, then. "You can't tell me. I'm going to find out, am I? Fine. It wasn't you. Why should I believe that?"

Snake Imp wedged the microphone between his leg and the side of the wheelchair. The interview was over. He whipped out what looked like a vintage Nintendo Gameboy. "Not us."

I wasn't going to get anything else out of them. "Last question. If you're Imp TV, where are your cameras?"

Gameboy Imp rolled his eyes as his mate swung him round the way they'd come. He gave me a look of pity as he said, "Imp TV not real. Duh."

Back in the dressing room I found I'd lost my place in the massage queue, so I decided to skip it. I didn't like being the last one that everyone was waiting for, so I got showered and dressed. I sat on my part of the bench, wondering what could have happened to make Nick worry about me lashing out. Who should I call? I had no clue.

I got my phone and checked the Chester result: a 4–0 smashing of Rushall Olympic with a hat trick from Goliath. I went to the *Manchester Evening News* website, then *Cheshire Live*. Nothing jumped out in the way of bad news that might affect *me*.

Mateo came into the dressing room. Owners weren't really supposed to do that. There was a growing trend of it happening, especially with American business boys who thought it was normal, but most European footballers hated it. They needed a place to vent and rage and complain. A safe space, you might say.

"Max. Can we talk?" I should have realised he was there to deliver the bad news, but I panicked, thinking he was there to offer me the Tranmere job. Surely James had done enough to buy himself one more match? The blood drained from my face. The imps! They had somehow reported my tactical ideas to Mateo, confirming that it had all been me! It didn't matter if the Tranmere players never told anyone what happened at halftime if I fucking blabbed not two minutes after the final whistle!

"Yep. Is it something you can't say here?"

Everyone in the dressing room had got quieter and a few inches closer. Mateo pressed his lips flat. "Up to you."

"Hit me," I said.

He took a breath. "Your player, Ryan Jack. He's done his knee. They think it's bad. He's had gas and oxygen. Stretchered off. They're thinking ACL."

I whipped my phone out. The score was now 5–0. The match was ongoing! There had been a huge delay, obviously. I opened the curse screens but they would show the Tranmere match overview until I left Barrow's stadium, if the past was anything to go by.

I put my phone away and tried to process the news. "Cruciate ligament! He's thirty-five. Is that him fucked?"

One of the physios nodded, but another shook his head.

Mateo looked at his watch. "We were going to have dinner with the Barrow directors, but I'll drive you back if you want."

I bit my nails for a while. "He'll have loads of people with him now. Tomorrow his family will pile on. I'll go see him on Monday after training."

"You can skip training, Max," said James.

I rubbed my head. "I can't skip training," I muttered. "I'm on holiday."

Monday, January 8.

On Friday, I'd gone up to Glasgow to watch Queen's Park against Dunfermline in Scotland's second tier. The curse rated that as worth 4 XP per minute, suggesting the Scottish Premier was a 5-per-minute league. Saturday was the Barrow match, and Sunday I decided to watch Notts Forest Women in the third tier. With a bit of Sunday League and some five-a-side minutes thrown in, I had blasted past one-fifth of my monthly target.

XP balance: 2,812

January income: 2,150/10,000

I trained cautiously and skipped the extra free kick practice. If Ryan's injury was as bad as the curse feared, I might need to play as a central midfielder. What would that mean? It'd still be disproportionately valuable to be able to turn free kicks into a deadly weapon, but a case could be made that the team would equally benefit from me adding a few more points in jumping, heading, and tackling. Some stamina, too, since I'd have to throw myself into lots of matches in a short space of time towards the end of the season.

The plan was to spend some time with Jack, then go and have a chat with Sandra.

When I went into the hospital room, Sandra was there. Convenient! Also present: Physio Dean and Jackie Reaper.

I went to the patient and tenderly placed his hand in mine. "Ryan. Don't try to open your eyes. It's me, Max Best."

"Me eyes are wide open, bosh."

"Don't go into the light. I've ordered you a cheeky charcoal chicken and chips."

The pain and gloom lifted from his features. The word charcoal followed by the word chicken did something to an Englishman's brain. Created a need that had never been present before. "Charcoal chicken? What's that?"

"Jackie will explain it to you later." I let go of his hand and checked his morale. It had gone up since I'd entered the room. "How you doing?"

"Not too well, bosh, to be fair."

"Yeah. What was it like?"

"Just went to do a turn. Normal. Thing you'd do a thousand times a week. Heard a pop. Felt like I'd been shot."

The Injury perk had finally proven its worth. On the day itself, when I could finally get into the Chester squad screen to check Ryan's profile, it simply said *suspected knee injury*. When I woke up the next day, it said *cruciate ligament injury—12 months*. I had to go through the motions, though. "Dean, what do you think? Partial tear, maybe?"

"We might not know till we go in. Could be good news. Absolutely could be. But for your planning, er . . . Max and Sandra, I'd expect a long layoff."

"I'm finished," said Ryan, wringing his hands. "I know I am. That's me done."

"Come on, Ryan," said Jackie. "Don't be like that."

"For once, Jackie's right. You'll be miserable for a while then we'll find you a sexy nurse to take care of you. You'll fall in love with each other and eventually, she'll ask you out."

"Fucking hell," mumbled Jackie.

I pretended I hadn't heard my subordinate. "I've not been idle, Ryan mate, since I got the news. Based on my research and following a template I found in *Cosmopolitan* magazine, I've got a questionnaire for you that will really kickstart the healing process."

"Er, Max," said Dean, but I knew I was on solid ground.

"Dean, I got a B in biology. We didn't do knees but we did whatsit. Water going round in a circle. You know, clouds." I settled onto the chair and coughed. "Okay, question one: You have messed up your knee. Do you A, resent watching your teammates play? B, blame yourself for not listening to your body? C, find hope in the ponytail-and-baseball-cap combo of a ravishing medical professional?"

Dean got up and pulled me away from Ryan. "Okay, Max, thank you very much. I'll take over the rehab, I think. You go back to your holiday."

"What the shit is this?" I said, pointing to a newspaper on Ryan's side table. It was the same rag with the *He's Done WHAT?!* headline. But today's edition said, *CALAMITY LANE*. "What's that? Is that a pun?"

No one wanted to explain it. Jackie bit the bullet. "It's from Calamity Jane. Someone from the Wild West. Don't know the story."

"Calamity Lane. Are they . . . are they fucking blaming Sandra for this? And Joe Anka? It was fucking random." I was seething. Boiling to the point my vision turned into a snowstorm.

"Not now, Max," said Sandra. "Today's about Ryan. We're happy to see you. That's good. We're positive. And you're a bit of an inspiration, aren't you?"

She'd reached through the wild, birth-of-the-universe static and switched me to a better channel. My eyes went back to normal. "What?"

"You and your tekkers video. If anyone knows what it's like coming back from a bad injury, it's you. Tell Ryan what it's like."

I looked at my midfielder. "You've never had a bad injury before?"

"Oh, loads. This is the big one, though, isn't it?" He eyed Jackie and the hand wringing started again. He was more likely to end up like his mate than me, so he thought. Well, fuck that. I pulled Dean away and took the seat next to Ryan again.

"Mate, it's horrible. It's awful. It's weeks of suffering and loneliness. You want some human contact but when it comes it drives you mad. Everything's aggravating and the worst part is you don't know if you should bother doing the rehab because you don't know how broken you are." I took his hand again, but this time there was no irony in it. "That was me, though. Head injuries are wild. Your knee is fucked, mate, and you'll be out for a year. But it's mechanical and the surgeons fix more knees than I score no-look backheel nutmegs. You're not going to suffer and be lonely, not for very long, anyway. I'll keep you busy. I've got fucking *tasks* for you, mate. If you want to quit playing, that's all right, we'll look after you. But you shouldn't. You'll be out, then you'll be back. We're going to be in the National League. You'll come back in the side just as we're getting good. Making a drive for the playoffs or something. And you'll come back better. We'll have better players around you, better facilities, more physios. And then we'll get promoted to League Two and then we'll bin you off because you'll be like thirty-seven by then and I mean, come on."

He smiled at the last bit.

Dean sighed. "We need to work on your bedside manner, Max." I think that was a callback to something I'd said to him once.

"I'm actually smashing this," I told him. "Now, I'm all into personal choice these days. So Ryan, I can finish by giving you a tender kiss on the forehead, or I can start looking for hot single nurses in your area."

Sandra snorted. "It's my job to end this conversation, I reckon. Come on, Max. Let's go do some planning. Ryan, I'll be back in a bit. All right?"

The patient relaxed back onto his pillow. "All right, Miss."

Jackie and Dean laughed.

"What?" I said.

"D-Day is running a book on who'll be the first to say mum instead of Miss."

I smiled. In school, there was always one boy who did that. It normally took a few months into the new school year, if I remembered right. "Has anyone done it?"

"We think Youngster came close because he suddenly stopped mid-sentence and blushed."

"Huh." It wouldn't be Henri or Pascal, unless they had the exact same verbal setup in school, which I doubted. They probably addressed teachers by their full titles including qualifications. Nah, it would be someone British and someone young. "Get your money on Bark."

As I left I turned round and saw Jackie take my seat. He and Ryan had big smiles and were shaking their heads at my antics. A mad story to tell each other as they aged. *Remember when Max came to see you in hozzie?*

Sandra and I went to the hospital canteen and caught up. Our 4-4-1-Goliath was smashing through the low blocks. Henri had started out grumpy at all the attention Goliath was getting, but after Goliath's first goal he'd pointed at Henri, whose selfless running had created the chance, and bear hugged him. Goliath gave all the credit for his goals to whoever set them up, which was often Henri, and with such a reliable supply of attention and affection, Henri was in dreamland. The two were now thick as thieves, and their post-match interviews were one big love-in. Eddie Moore had been a bit shaky, feeling the pressure of coming into a successful team, but the lads were being patient with him. Bark was getting on better with Tyson and the other young players than with the older guys. He had minor imposter syndrome, Sandra thought, but he was obviously talented. She was on it, she promised me.

Yeah, things were great, except for the injuries. Two bad ones in two games.

"How do you feel about this Calamity Lane shit?"

She sipped her drink and leaned back. "I was told when I took this job that there was only one opinion that mattered. So the question isn't what does some clickbait-chasing hack think. It's what do *you* think?"

"I think you're crushing it. No notes. How are the rest of the media treating you?"

She thought about it. "Good. It's a good story. I think they'd have preferred if I lost my first, like, ten matches."

I tutted because she was right. "Fucking ghouls."

"MD wants us to do a documentary like Wrexham. Says we're doing mad stories all the time and we should monetise them."

"Tell him to boil his fucking head."

"Will do."

"Okay, let's talk central midfield. Looking a bit bare suddenly. Bit lacking in passing range and craft. Do I need to go to MD to beg for cash?"

She drummed the side of her paper cup. "We've got Sam and Raffi as first choice. We have a better left back now so we can play with two CMs for the rest of the season. No more three-five-two. We've had more bids for Raffi. Did you know?"

I smiled. "I did."

She leaned forward. "How much?"

"The last one was three hundred."

"Are you serious? That's . . . we should sell."

"Ooh," I said, wincing. "You just lost some crushing points. What's a level below crushing? You're no longer crushing the job. You're gripping it firmly."

"Why, though?"

"Because Chester's record sale was three hundred thousand. Ian Rush back in the old days. I want to beat that. And because Raffi's a fifteen-million-pound player," I said.

She paused. "You'll . . . take less than that, though?" She was wondering if I was as crazy as all the fans seemed to think.

I scoffed. "At four hundred I'll start to be tempted. Start, mind you. I really don't see the point of letting him go for less than eight. Okay, *realistically*, six hundred is a done deal. Between five and six is a grey area."

"What about four with a sell-on? Fifteen percent of his next fee."

"That sort of thing might come into play a few years down the line, but if I sell now I want the cash now. A mill in the hand is worth two mill in the bush."

She thought things through for a while, then decided Raffi's eventual fee wasn't relevant to the next few weeks of her life. "Sam, Raffi. We're sticking to four-four-two, right?"

"Unless you want to rest Chris. He doesn't seem the sort to need it, though. He never sprints, does he?"

"This weekend is Solihull in the FA Trophy. He can't play in that; he's cup-tied. Four-one-four-one?"

"Hmm." I looked around, checking we couldn't be overheard. "With Ryan, we'd have half a chance. Without Ryan . . . we're struggling. Solihull are going great guns in the National League and we've got three matches in seven days. The worst thing would be an injury to a key player in a losing cause. If you want to weaken the team, put Tony up front, that sort of thing . . . I'm okay with it. It's your call."

She inhaled and let it out over five long seconds. I'd given her permission to drop out of the FA Trophy in the fourth round, at the first sign of a stronger team. Permission to start conserving our dwindling resources. It wasn't like Max Best to be pragmatic. "If you were playing, would you weaken the team?"

"Depends. Our scout said they play three-five-two. I find I like playing against three-five-twos. A weak team with me and Pascal . . . maybe Bark and D-Day . . . We could get creative. On the other hand, that competition has served its purpose. What's that, three matches that got postponed? Top. But now we need to make sure we have bodies in the last months."

"Can Youngster play CM?"

"Yeah. Not as well as DM, but he'll have to learn. It'll be good for him, anyway. Teams won't always have DM slots for him."

"Sam, Raffi, Youngster, Magnus. Four for two slots. As you say, not much craft in that list. Then it's a bit desperate. Pascal, Donny, Bark. Not very natural. Oh, Andrew Harrison, but he's undercooked."

I nodded. "Push him harder. Make him do extra sessions."

"Not very Snowflake FC."

She took a sip as I said, "I'm not paying him to *suck*." It was pretty close to a spit take, which pleased me. "When I'm back, I can fill in at CM sometimes. I wanted to ask if you thought I should spend my extra coaching time getting my free kicks back up to scratch, or turn myself into a Ryan Jack comp."

"Free kicks."

"That simple?"

"That simple. You can already do most of what he was doing. You need some experience in there, but you can do it. And I've seen your old free kicks up close. Remember you gave Patricio a little slap? If we can get those back . . ."

I nodded and thought about if there was anything else that couldn't wait. I decided almost everything could be done by text. "Are you having fun?"

"Having the time of my life."

"Do you want me to come back?"

She sipped her drink and stared into it for quite a long time. Finally, she said, "Yeah." She grinned and looked down again. "Million percent."

That evening I went to south Wales to watch the FA Cup third round match between Swansea City and Leeds United. That was a mad, hectic match which earned me 6 XP per minute.

But on Tuesday I cancelled my plans and took Jackie and Raffi to meet Ziggy for a tour of FC United's training facilities. If they were good enough for Barrow, a club potentially heading to tier three, they'd be good enough for me. For a while.

I said something of the sort to Jackie. "Hold up. You want to rent this? Barrow get the pitch from nine to ten, we come ten to eleven. Is that your idea?"

I sighed. "Come on. I want to build something like this in Chester, or near it. Stop blabbing and show me the rest."

"That was it."

"Oh."

Broadhurst Park was a cosy 5,000-seater stadium. Jackie and Ziggy had shown me some of the facilities that were not immediately obvious from the outside, such as classrooms for the academy kids to study in, and a well-equipped kitchen.

Outside, across a road, were two grass pitches and an all-weather 3G one.

And that was it. I'd done some homework and found the entire thing had cost £6.3 million. But Ziggy had a useful data point: Half the funding had come from grants. There was loads of money sloshing around for well-designed sports programmes, he said, especially if the local community could use the facilities, too.

"Okay, but hang on," I said, turning this way and that. "This has one all-weather pitch. We've got two. We've got more pitches than FC United. Are our facilities better?"

"No," said Jackie. "This is better."

"Why?"

"This is football-only. Our men's team park next to someone from BoshCard."

"So?"

He shrugged. "It's amateur. Makes a difference to how you feel. Maybe it shouldn't, but it does. And we don't own anything. The women get kicked off the pitch by pensioners and walking football and an under-fourteens team who are the biggest bunch of gobshites in Cheshire."

"You're saying if we bought the credit card building, our players would improve faster?"

He frowned. "I don't think of it that way, but yes."

Raffi was listening quietly, as he always did. Now he spoke. "If you owned it, you'd change things. You'd put a massive Chester badge on the front and we'd drive there and be proud to go. You'd knock through the downstairs offices and make one big gym and a proper medical room." He tsked. "Even the handles on the doors. They're a pain when you've got your boots in one hand and a ball in the other. They're fiddly, them handles. You owned that building, you'd change that in no time."

"All right, so we buy some land, put up some pitches, some changing rooms. *There's* a million gone and we're no better off. I want facilities so good a League One team would call to ask if they could train there. What's next?"

"Kitchens," said Jackie, pointing to the stadium. "You get a nutritionist and your own chefs, the players eat better, train better, play better."

I nodded. "The shared meals at Tranmere are cool. I'm socialising with the team and saving money on food, too. Okay, that can be a priority, I think. Could we get a mobile kitchen for now? Someone in a caravan thing who comes to training and dishes out kebabs?" I thought of Emre, my old mate from Platt Fields. He could do it in the morning and drive back to Manchester for the evening rush. "Is that dumb? Your faces say yes. Okay, proper kitchen. I've seen home renovation shows. Kitchen's, what, twenty grand?" The others scoffed. "Call it forty. Fifty? And wages for two chefs and someone to tell us not to eat Mars bars."

Ziggy tutted. "They do tailored plans for every player and teach the kids about food. Don't be a dick."

What next? I scrunched my face up to help me think. "Gym. Swimming pool? Place to relax and hang out. How much is a bean bag? I don't need to fill the space yet, do I? I need to build a big room for all sorts of stuff. Or design it to be modular where we add one building for one function and then another when we have the money. Year one, gym. Year two, wellness area. Year three, infinity pool with views of Dubai."

Raffi spoke next, and everything he said increased the total cost by another few million. "Video feedback rooms, meeting rooms, space for the data analysts, space for the performance analysts and psychologists, brain training, ice baths, space for dads to chill while their kids are training, press conference room, somewhere for sponsors to come and do photoshoots and all that. Pascal told me about a German team that has this massive cube and you stand in the middle and it fires footballs at you and tells you where to kick it. Dead hard. You'd love it, Max. Oh, and some dartboards." He gave me his best lopsided grin when he saw my reaction to his shopping list. "My dad's been checking out what's on offer for when I move."

"Are you off?" said Ziggy.

"Max won't let me," joked Raffi. "And Ryan's out, so the team needs me. The summer, though."

"Where will you go?"

Raffi and I spoke at the same time. "Somewhere warm."

Jackie had thoughts. "Max, *you* don't need to do this. When it's time to do it, you hire people. Experts. They do all the grafting, find a site, sketch up proposals. You sit and listen and have a think. For you, the whole thing is a one-hour meeting, do you know what I mean?"

I was realising that the capital costs of what I wanted to achieve were mind-boggling. Raffi would buy me one all-weather pitch. Two if I sold him for what I wanted. Even turning a consistent profit in the transfer market, it'd take twenty years to upgrade everything to the standards I wanted. At *least* twenty. "When it's time to do this, it'll already be time to do the next thing. We need to get ahead of it."

"What do you mean?"

"Never mind. You're right. I should get a consultant or whatnot."

Jackie kicked a pebble. "The facilities are fine, Max. The men's team are pulling in two thousand a match. The fan base doesn't justify a big expansion."

That stung. He was right. But my hope was to do it without the fans. "If we increase the standards, I can make more money on transfers."

"If you want to raise the standards quickly, get the youth teams playing in harder tournaments. The Cheshire stuff is okay, but the twelves won that Liverpool tournament, didn't they? If they're ready to step up, put them in Merseyside and Greater Manchester leagues."

"Can I do that?"

"Course. It's easy. You need to show you're competitive enough, which winning tournaments will do. And then it needs to be organised. Can Inga take on more work? You might need a part-time youth coordinator. And it's more travel so it's more expensive. But if you want a quick upgrade, that's one."

I nodded and bit my nail. Lots of food for thought, but I'd seen what I needed to see. "Oh, look at the time," I said. "If we leave now, we could make the start of the West Didsbury and Chorlton match. Check on Vivek and Michael." Silence. "Not interested?"

Raffi snorted. "We knew you'd do this. My mates are already on their way there." I opened my mouth, but he knew what was coming. "Paying to get in, Max! Paying to get in." He laughed.

"They'd better," I growled, shaking my fist. "Good. We'll watch some proper football, then dinner's on me."

I fell into a groove that would serve me well for the rest of January. I'd train in the morning and either walk around Merseyside—the beaches were pretty good!—or look for Playdar opportunities. Then a pro match for the experience points in the evening, or five-a-sides, or a night off, reading.

James O'Rourke, now a lot more like the version I'd met in Tenerife, whistled to end Friday morning's training and called me over.

"Max, well done. You're improving at a rate of knots. The coaches are pretty astonished, I've got to say."

"Is Colin still mad at me?"

"Well . . . yeah. But he'll get over it when he realises you kept him in a job. No, he *will*. So tomorrow it's home to MK Dons, another three-five-two team. I want you on the pitch from the start."

I blinked. "I'm starting?"

"Yep."

"Samuel?"

He shook his head. "On the bench. You'll only fucking mither me if I make you play together."

"Any special tactical instructions for me?"

"If I gave you some, would you listen?"

I shrugged. "I'd *listen*."

"You cheeky sod!" He looked around at his domain. It was better than Chester's setup in lots of small, expensive ways. "Look, I think I should apologise. I haven't reacted very well to you coming here with your media circus but . . . that's in the past. I'm excited now. MK Dons are a nightmare. Very aggressive, very snide, there's always trouble. Having someone on the pitch who'll get them running back to *their* own goal, put pressure on *them*, get in *their* faces, yeah, I'm excited about it! Okay, but look. Everyone gets that you're in the group but not really in it, if you see what I mean. So we haven't been too bothered about you wearing your own gear around the place. But for tomorrow—just tomorrow—could you please wear the proper clobber?"

I pulled a face. "The black and green thing is vile. How about you just don't sub me off? Then I won't have to wear it."

"Come on, that won a competition, that did. It's quality." He smiled. "Let's ask Emma what she thinks of it. Is she coming to watch?"

"Emma? No." She'd had a bad experience at Tranmere last time she'd been there, but we hadn't told anyone. "She's swamped at work. Fine, I'll conform. For the team. But why tomorrow? What's the haps?"

He'd got what he wanted, and he was distracted now. He was looking at his phone. "Oh? Er . . . it's live."

"We're the live match?"

"Yeah, yeah. Early kickoff. Big media interest for this one. Loads of applications for accreditation. More than against Wrexham, even. You'll want to show your skills, yeah? Maybe blast one of those free kicks into the top corner. Our goalies are getting pretty sick of seeing it, eh? Yeah, unleashing prime Max Best against MK bastard Dons. I'll sleep well tonight." He went off laughing.

I rubbed my forehead. A must-win match that I was starting . . . live on TV . . . against a team of wind-up merchants . . . cameras everywhere . . . media circus . . . and worst of all, I had to dress like shit.

13

MAX BEST: A RETROSPECTIVE

Excerpts from Rovers Return, the third-most active Tranmere Rovers unofficial fan forum.

Max Best: A Retrospective Thread created by Fredly_Submarine, 2 Feb, 2024

Part 1.

The purpose of this thread is to document my memories of the short-lived Max Best era, to speculate on what it all meant, and to generate a discussion that will hopefully answer some outstanding questions. For those new to the forum, I am known to have solid contacts in the club's staff. I've also been trawling through other forums (the shame!), social media, and listening to every single Tranmere podcast from the past month. Putting all the pieces together has been both illuminating and confounding.

I shall begin by outlining certain indisputable facts.

1. On the first of January this year, Chester FC manager (and director of football!) Max Best was registered as a Tranmere Rovers player for a loan period of four weeks. There was no advanced warning this might happen.

2. Later that day, he was named as a substitute in the match against high-flying Notts County.

3. In twenty minutes, he scored two goals.

4. The entirety of Tranmere's fan base asked themselves: Who is this kid?

Certain conclusions were reached with impressive speed. Within days, we all knew that:

1. MB burst onto the scene as a right-winger playing for Darlington.

2. MB spoke of his ambitions of becoming a manager.

3. He joined Chester to fulfil those ambitions.

4. He won every match that he managed.

5. He was put in a coma by a deranged fan.

6. MB survived and while he had become a statistically unremarkable player, he continued to be an off-the-scales manager.

7. He took a very shit Chester team to the top of the league.

8. He found a woman to replace him and came to Tranmere. (I say "woman" not dismissively. She has a higher win percentage and more points per game than any of our last ten managers. I mention gender only because it links to the topic of the media, which I will get into.)

9. The top-of-the-league Chester fanbase debased themselves with a pathetic four-week-long temper tantrum that will forever taint that pathetic excuse for a football club.

Much of the speculation around point 8 centred around the idea that managing in the sixth tier had become too easy for him and he wanted a new challenge. Some of the discussion devolved into rants about snowflakery and MB being a social justice warrior. There are possible merits to that case, but I'm not interested in how he chose his successor, only why he came to Tranmere.

On the playing side, of particular note was Best's performance against Notts and even more so against Barrow that had many re-evaluating his statistics within the context of a long-term recovery from a very serious head injury. How could a player with three goals in eighteen tier-six matches score two in twenty minutes in his first EFL match and bag two assists in a half in his second? It was decided that Best's recovery was more or less complete, that the strain of managing had diminished him as a player, and that with better players around him he could express himself more on the pitch.

A big portion of the fanbase, notably every single intelligent poster on this forum, decided MB was the Second Coming and would awaken this sleeping giant. The hype reached amusing but captivating heights.

As we dug deeper, we discovered yet more delicious tidbits:

1. Best recommended Junior Howland and Calabash Barkley (a youth team prospect) to us.

2. He warned us off buying a much-regarded Scottish striker whose form has since turned to dust.

3. He sent his best mate Henri Lyons to train with us earlier this season, though it didn't lead to anything.

4. He helped the club in a transfer tribunal, increasing our fee by a "substantial" amount. (How exactly he did this remains a mystery, but Mateo is known to have gone into the tribunal carrying a cross and emerge walking on air.)

5. MB has regularly visited the training ground and watched matches with Mateo in the executive box. (There are many photos and in the first of such images, his girlfriend is with him. This is important in the context of Facegate, which I shall address later, naturally.)

6. There's an unsubstantiated rumour that Mateo provided the finance for MB to buy his local grassroots team (some hipster collective thing

in Manchester that I refuse to take the piss out of because they, correctly, hate the Tories).

In short, Best has been acting at least partially as our director of football, has been getting players into the club that he rates and would like to work with, is big mates with our owner, and unlike most people in the club is an actual subject matter expert. (For the hard of reading, I'm saying he understands football.)

Other important facts:

1. His girlfriend is just about the fittest woman I've ever seen (and I include Jet from *Gladiators*). As most of you already know, this is highly relevant to this discussion. I urge you to follow her on Instagram <here>. Thank me later. She also appears in the background of <this video> from the training camp in Tenerife and you can see Jack the Lad flirting with her to the right in <this TikTok>. Note Max Best watching them with a smile. Not angry, not plotting revenge. Most people think JTL's behaviour in the camp is connected to what followed on the pitch, but I do not.

2. MB is quite poor. Most of the sightings of him during the last month were in second-hand shops, pound shops, and cheap cafes. His car is a wreck, though I will refrain from stating the make and colour because of his issue with the deranged fan. Suffice to say, it is not an appropriate car for someone who can control a fifty-yard pass and send it accurately another forty yards without letting it touch grass.

The upshot of all this fact-finding and educated guessing was obvious: At some point, Mateo would sack James O'Rourke and install MB as our new player-manager. The only real mystery was why JOR would accept having his replacement join the squad and why he would select him for games. Most hot-blooded Rovers fans agreed it proved JOR is a cuck who enjoys being humiliated and the conversation turned to whether it was wrong to kink shame him, not whether the accusation was real. I took no part in such juvenile threads but enjoyed the memes <in this one> and did get a chuckle out of the infamous <soap opera script>.

All of this analysis was so compelling that we decided MB would soon be our new manager and it was impossible to imagine a different outcome.

I was, perhaps, one of the first to revisit the issue. I wrote match reviews of the Notts County game <here> and the Barrow game <here>, very much from the point of view of "Replacement Theory" (this name is a joke, don't inbox me, I've punched more fascists than you). After seeing how his goal celebrations changed (more on that below), I stopped writing and I haven't posted here since. Every day that JOR kept his job deepened my suspicion that we had got everything very, very wrong.

But how could that be? The facts only supported one conclusion.

Now it's time to pick up our facts and twist them into new shapes, because MB has gone back to Chester. Tonight is their Fans Forum, where he will face a roomful of manbabies (I heard they changed the venue because demand for seats was so high), and tomorrow he will be back in the hot seat for their match against Chip Shop FC (or similar. Who knows what the teams are called in that Mickey Mouse league?).

In short, he's gone, and the transfer window has closed, so if he's coming back, it ain't as a player.

This is what's breaking my brain . . .

If Max Best didn't come to Tranmere to become our new manager . . . what the hell just happened?

Part 2.

Why would a player-manager loan himself to another club? A rival club, in fact. Some theories:

1. He did it for the money.

2. He came to replace JOR but something happened on our side to prevent him.

3. He came to replace JOR but something happened on his side to prevent him.

4. Our existing squad warned Mateo not to hire him.

5. He failed a medical.

6. There's a legal reason he can't join an EFL team but he can work in non-league.

7. He lost a bet and the forfeit was to play for us.

I think I can disprove most of these in the form of mini match reviews.

But I do have one big question that I can't shake. I believe if we answer one question we'll be much closer to finding out his motivations. The question is this: Why didn't he speak to the media *once* in his time at the club?

That answer might also explain what he did in his last match, and for that reason I despair of ever learning the truth because the club and players, and my sources, have rallied around the lad. Facegate is especially frustrating because we all saw what he did, we know what he did, and we even know why he did it. Yet somehow that doesn't help us understand anything in the slightest.

vs Notts (home) and Barrow (away)

Two goals in the first, two assists in the second. Some shaky moments but overall Best showed great attacking qualities and he showed that he can defend, too. Interesting to note his interplay with Samuel (virtually non-existent) compared to his interplay with Junior (they know each other's games inside out). MB is a player-manager with favourites and is not shy of showing it. Already we can see he has problems with Samuel and Jack the Lad.

Goal celebrations: Note the difference. In game one, he runs into the Kop like he was born in Birkenhead and grew up with a John Aldridge poster on his wall. By game two, he's moving away from the celebrations. Something's happened in the meantime. Could be that someone at Chester has had a word with him, but why would Best give a flying fig? He holds all the cards if he wants to stay at that tinpot little outfit. So someone at *Tranmere* has told him not to get the crowd worked up? Makes no sense. There's footage of Mateo jumping around the executive seats when Best scored his penalty and there's one thing everyone agrees on when it comes to our owner: Mateo's a Tranmere fan through and through. There is zero chance *he* asked Best to stop celebrating. So why did Best stop celebrating our goals? Unknown.

Mediawatch: Best's signing took everyone by surprise and there was almost no media attention for the first match; lots of the reporters were at Chester watching the second match with a woman in charge. (The first was another unannounced MB surprise. Why not harness the media buzz?) Against Barrow there was a ton of press, but Best gave them the slip. Why? One thing's for sure: If it was all about the money he'd have taken the chance to raise his profile.

vs MK Dons (home)

This match disproves the "we saw something about him we didn't like" theory, in my opinion.

MK Dons had played 3-5-2 in eight of their last ten matches, and the other two were against small teams in cups.

JOR had played 4-3-3 in every match of his reign except for two. One, Notts, where Max Best had a free role and seemed to play DM most of the time. Two, Barrow, where for twenty minutes it looked like 4-4-2, which many fans have been crying out for given our squad. The team sheets, the TV formation graphic, the BBC report, everything had us as 4-3-3 against MK Dons with Best as one of the strikers.

They did line up like that in the moments just before kickoff, but as Dons got the ball, MB fell to his haunches and did nothing until the first throw-in. He had seen what it took the TV commentators another two minutes to realise: Dons were playing 5-3-2. They'd learned from Barrow that you don't leave huge gaps for Max Best to wander into! MB went to midfield, grabbed Carlos, and pushed him from CM back to DM. Carlos didn't want to go but Best yelled at him and manhandled him until he stayed put. They had another very visible on-pitch row when Best lined up next to him. Two DMs! We were playing 4-2-2-2, which I had never seen before but later all the hipsters said was the RB Leipzig model.

With Best shouting at Lee and Dodds to attack, it meant we were getting four players forward in central positions against three central defenders who were only sometimes supported by a fullback. Even from the stands it was clear to me that the Dons fullbacks weren't much in the match. They were defending against attacks that rarely came.

Next Best was in Bogle's face, telling him to join the attacks. I was on the far side of the pitch, but you could almost lip read what Best was saying—there's no-one here—all the action was central. Bogle got the message and started bombing up and down the right, but Best still wasn't happy. He pushed Bogle into a right wing back starting role.

So what was that? 3-3-2-2?

Notably, MB didn't do the same on the left. He didn't acknowledge Jack the Lad once in that first half, I don't think.

The overall feeling was confusion.

Our dugout was confused—Coach Colin was pacing up and down with his head in his hands, but JOR didn't change things back.

Our players were confused—the formation was a lopsided folly.

Our fans were confused—in the first half, the superstar player they'd come to see completed, what, ten passes? Won two headers?

MK Dons were confused—they were set up to defend against a player who barely went in their half while our workmanlike, unimaginative midfielders were suddenly popping up in their penalty area playing one-twos, doing stepovers and flicks.

I think even the referee was confused—he knew we were shit as well as anyone, and he knew MK Dons like to get stuck into a tackle. But he had the easiest first half of his life. No drama, no fuss, just whistling to signal our goals and to give an uncontroversial penalty, which Dizzy took.

Three–nil at halftime!

We went to relieve ourselves and get beers and the atmosphere was one of disbelief. Still some weren't optimistic. "You watch now," said my mate. "We'll concede early and fold like a cheap tent." I heard one fan tell the world, "Get that Best off. He's done now. Stealing a living." The people with *functioning* brains were smiling and happy. Three points would ease a lot of the tension around the place. Put a bit of distance between us and Forest Green, even put us above Col U and Grimsby until they played the 3 p.m. games.

What we now know is that there was yet another halftime bust-up in the dressing room. Unlike with what went down in Barrow, this one was witnessed by our moles and we have the gist of what was said.

Jack the Lad: What the fuck, Best? What is your problem?

MB: My problem is that I can't draw a perfect circle.

Jack: What?

MB: I try to draw circles but they come out as stars.

Jack: You know what I mean.

MB: If I knew what you meant, I'd know what you meant.

Jack: You're giving out instructions, running the match, bossing everyone around.

MB: Friendly suggestions as part of a collaborative process.

Jack: You've given orders to every fucker on that pitch except me.

MB: You want an order? Two chicken burgers, hold the cheesy chips.

Jack: What did you say?

MB: There's no point trying to involve you in the match, mate. You're useless. You're like a Subbuteo man who's been glued into place. If I was really giving the orders, you'd never get on the pitch. There's good young fullbacks in the reserves who want to contribute. You're a blockage. You're stuck in the pipes.

Jack: I'm fucking good at this game. I'm better than you!

MB: You're number one in the league for cash earned divided by yards run. James, MK are switching to 4-4-2 second half.

James O'Rourke: What? How do you know?

MB: I'll give you a billion pounds if I'm wrong.

Remember the theory that the players and coaches told Mateo they'd never play for Best? We know at that point he'd had run-ins with Coach Colin, Samuel, Jack the Lad, and Lee Contreras, which is impressive for two weeks' work.

So in the second half, what do we get? We switch to 4-4-2 as Best wanted. We know from our sources that Best was supposed to be playing left midfield—it was his idea. But then he played as a sort of left-sided DM, and every time he got the ball he passed to Jack the Lad.

I was on the wrong side of the stadium again, but my mate was close to it and described it to me. The passes got slightly farther and farther forward, forcing Jack to run higher and higher up the pitch. Whenever Jack turned back, safety first, Best threw a hissy fit. When Jack didn't make forward runs, Best collapsed to the pitch in disbelief.

It sounds childish now, but at the time everyone in that stand was sucked into the drama and turned on Jack pretty quick. "Get forward, you bastard!" "Jack, you useless twat, what are you doing?" Once they had noticed how he never went forward, it was all they could see. When Jack finally crossed the halfway line, Best ran around doing a goal celebration.

Bear in mind, there was a high-stakes match happening at the same time. MK Dons came out for the second half flying, and we were almost down to nine men while Best was doing his antics.

Dons got a goal, and then another. Three–two, they're on the march and we're in big trouble.

Best went to be CAM then. He got the ball, dribbled left, looked for support. Jack was nowhere, but Best passed to where he thought he should be. It rolled out of play for a throw-in and we were screaming our heads off. There was equal vitriol for Jack and Best, I think, but only one of the players was affected. Best was laughing at the abuse; Jack was close to tears. Best went over and we thought he was going to put an arm round him, tell him it's not that bad, something like that. But no. He waved his finger, gave him a tongue-lashing, and pointed to the subs bench. *If I were the manager you'd be off, son.*

MB made Lee go to left mid, and played central midfield himself. With a proper left side we looked more solid again and it looked like it was going to come down to who won the most duels. Best struggled in the middle, but when he lost the ball he sprinted back to help the defence, and when he did get a bit of space he slipped the ball to a striker nice and fast or waited for Bogle to get on the overlap.

The match was finely poised, really tense, when Bogle got fouled. We had a free kick over on the right of the box and Best wanted to take it. He hadn't been near MK's goal, so they didn't know what's coming. He smashed it between the defenders and the keeper, slap onto Gareth Jones's forehead, goal! Four–two and we've got some breathing space.

MK lost a bit of their fire and there was a chance the match would peter out, which I for one was okay with.

Best hadn't finished being a clown, though. He wandered around the pitch—never on the left—and every time he got the ball he pinged it at Jack the Lad. Running between the lines with options left and right? He turned and threaded the ball *back* through the retreating midfielders all the way to the left back. On the right wing with Bogle making an overlap? Sixty-yard diagonal back onto JTL's toes.

It was bloody infuriating and for the first time I had some sympathy for the Chester fans. If he's turning important matches into his own private pissing competitions, I get why some of them are upset. Rovers fans watching from home are fuming. *Best is diabolical. He's lazy. He's not up to the level. He should sort his passing stats out before he has a go at the other players.*

Now, about the squad going to Mateo to say "I won't play for this guy." You'd think so, and they'd be justified, but no. Bogle's pissed when Best doesn't play a return pass. Lee doesn't want to play left mid. Carlos doesn't like improvisational football. But they do what they're told, and do you know what football players like? They like winning. They'll play for Best because that means winning loads of football matches.

Ten of the players on the pitch would have no problem with Best as manager. Personally, I feel a lot of the "Bully Best" and "Jack the Sad" takes were overdone. Best *is* annoying, there's no getting away from it. But I've read an article describing how he fixed a young player in an unconventional way and I believe MB was working towards something in that match. I thought it at the time and I was proven right, though sadly we didn't get to see it on camera.

That was because once the three points were more or less safe, Best turned his attention to his most pressing need: to avoid talking to the media.

Near the end of the match, Best went up for a header. He didn't need to challenge for that ball—Dodds was there. Three players jumped, one fell to the pitch, clutching his head. Of course, with his recent head injury, the physios rushed on and there was a long, long delay as he got the oxygen mask and was stretchered off.

We were told that he was rushed to hospital. Nope. That was an outright lie from the club. He was rushed to his hotel room. He was rushed to a steakhouse. He was rushed to Manchester to watch his hipster team. My sources aren't sure *where* he went, but certainly not to hospital. We know this because he was spotted watching Everton versus Aston Villa the next day and he trained as normal two days later.

The whole thing was a ruse to get out of talking to the press!

vs Swindon Town (away)

We named an unchanged team against a side in good form. The graphics I saw before the match had Swindon set up in their usual 3-5-1-1, but the Swindon fans we talked to before the game said they'd made some changes "because of that lad." Their manager's idea was to have fast fullbacks playing as the wide centre backs, to match Best for pace. That was the plan.

We were supposedly doing 4-3-3 again, but none of us believed that would actually happen.

At the start of the match, Best did that thing where he watches what the other team are up to. He jogged around giving instructions to everyone, including Jack the Lad, and he trotted back up top. Third striker! We were actually doing 4-3-3!

Then we started pumping long balls at Best. He was up against a fast but short left back, and Best beat him to headers every single time. It was twenty minutes of old-fashioned carnage as Junior and Dizzy feasted on the second balls and peppered Swindon's goal with shots.

At 2–0, the fast left back got subbed off and they brought a big lad on. So what did Best do? He went out wide and used his pace to get to the byline. The centre back fouls him, yellow card. Best is hurt but walks up and down the front line looking for opportunities. Swindon are a good side so they adapt. They block the defensive holes and try to hit us on counters and nick something on a set piece.

Which they do and it's a tense last ten minutes, but even if they'd got an undeserved equaliser, that would have been a point against a top-half team.

Instead, we leave there with all three.

Again we had a lot of social media bleating about Best being lazy. A do-nothing with bad stats.

Apart from the shock and joy of watching a player turn his part of the pitch into a game of rock, paper, scissors against an opponent who only has rock and paper, what I took away from that match was how harmonious it was. We basically played James O'Rourke football but with an on-pitch general making rapid changes and the players accepting them. There was less shouting from Best, and a lot of in-game coaching.

Mediawatch: The paps were losing interest in following MB around, it seemed. He wasn't scoring dramatic penalties or doing volleyed assists, and he wasn't speaking to them, so what was the point of travelling? The only talking point was that his assistant manager had lost her first match and they wanted a reaction to that. Again, though, radio silence from him.

At this point, let me remind you of some theories about why Max Best came to Tranmere Rovers:

1.   He did it for the money.

The figure of £5,000 a week started doing the rounds as the terms of his loan— double the wage of any other player (as far as we know). Hard of thinking fans thought this was extortionate. Clearly, this is nice money for someone working in non-league football, but if he can get it at Tranmere he can get it elsewhere. He has shown no signs of picking his career moves purely based on money.

Note: He has a few clients from when he was a football agent and presumably that helps keep the wolf from his door.

2.   He came to replace JOR but something happened on our side to prevent him.

Mateo decided he didn't want rapid tactical changes and would prefer to watch us slog through the same steps and missteps week after week? I don't think so. MB is so fractious and unlikeable that Mateo couldn't imagine working with him? Please. We know Best turned up at our under-twelves training sessions, intervened in a girl's team match because he spotted an opposing player had concussion (later confirmed by medical staff) and was "caught" delivering cardboard boxes full of stuff to a local food bank. He might be manic depressive (Dixie Dean statue versus not celebrating goals) but the backroom staff liked him. They described him as "intense but funny."

3.   He came to replace JOR but something happened on his side to prevent him.

What could this have been? He was offered £5,000 a week for the first four weeks like a drug sample to get him hooked, but then the offer for the rest of his contract was much lower? Mateo doesn't strike me as that sort of huckster.

He was disappointed with our facilities and players? But he already knew them before he came. As mentioned, he was a regular visitor to these shores.

He didn't like living in the Wirral? Understandable! But he could live in leafy Cheshire and work here. Many do, and many have done.

4.   Our existing squad warned Mateo not to hire him.

MB's two-goal burst against Notts got the crowd going, but it was his assists against Barrow that got the players' attention, and when you listen to their post-match interviews from the other games, you'll realise how they look up to him as a player. With the younger players there's no little hero worship. Check out <this video> from Lee Contreras's YouTube where he's looking ahead to the Doncaster game watching clips of the midfielders he's likely to be up against. It's late at night and he's red-eyed and tired but he wants to find something he can contribute at the team meeting. He doesn't say it, but it's clear that he's desperate to impress MB.

5.   He failed a medical.

No. Unless Samuel did the tests while wearing a mask of someone else's face, *Mission: Impossible*-style.

6.   There's a legal reason he can't join an EFL team but he can work in non-league.

This makes little to no sense since he has recently played five matches *in* the EFL.

7.   He lost a bet and the forfeit was to play for us.

Many people found the <Dixie Dean statue visit> cheesy and twee but I found it quite moving. He appreciates the club and its history and if you watch the footage of him going on for his debut, he looks proud.

And so we come to the strangest and most controversial match yet.

vs Doncaster (home)

Donny had been playing 3-5-2 and if I were them, I wouldn't have known how to set up against us. They stuck with what they'd been doing, which seemed smart at the time.

We were unchanged again, but that only begins to tell the story. Some changes aren't shown on the team sheet. With a nod from Best, Carlos would drop back from CM to DM. With a scissors gesture, our strikers would go wide with Lee and Dodds rushing to fill the gaps.

And—wonder of wonders—the fullbacks had come alive. What had happened in the previous week? Not sure. For once, our moles were keeping mum but there was an insinuation that James O'Rourke finally stepped up and bashed some heads together.

Our third goal sums up the positive side of the Max Best experience.

A controlled passing move from the keeper to Bogle, across the defence, back across the midfield. Very patient. Doncaster got pulled around, then it was on. The ball was fizzed out to JTL. He took a touch past a midfielder, scampered away, hit it square to Best. He turned inside, faked a long pass wide, turned slightly away from goal. He pointed at someone, then no-look backheeled it diagonally forward towards the left touchline. JTL had continued his run, and he whipped it low into the area where Dizzy redirected it into the bottom left.

Glorious.

And now the negative side. First, while Jack the Lad is reminding us all of what he can do and adding to his transfer value, Samuel is nowhere to be seen. Our big summer signing looks like he's finished at the club already. Not exactly Best's fault we signed him, but he was utterly ruthless in excising him from the team and we have a big financial hole there now.

Second, the Facegate incident.

Facegate

Let's say MB is on £5K a week. He's got £20K in his pocket for playing five games—not bad—and he's helped the team get eleven points. After a rocky start with some players, there's buy-in to the way he wants to play. As a player, he gets into any team in League Two. As a manager, the same. So he's happy, right? All is well with the world. Yes?

No.

Let's do a moment-by-moment rundown.

1. With around seventy minutes gone, a Donny player finally gets a chance to land a reducer on Best and smashes into his shins.

2. The physio signals Best needs to be subbed off.

3. Best throws a tantrum. He's livid.

4. Best refuses to leave the pitch.

5. He hobbles around for a minute while Donny press their advantage.

6. The ball breaks for Best, who holds it up and spreads it to the other side of the pitch for JTL to run onto.

7. While we nearly score, Best talks to James O.

8. JOR prepares the sub, but appears to have agreed to give Best a few more minutes.

9. Best whispers something to Lee Contreras, who asks Best to repeat it.

10. In the next phase of play, Lee finds some space and plays a very careful ball *behind* Best, forcing him to turn onto his favoured right foot.

11. Best hammers the ball into the crowd.

12. The ball strikes someone in the press box flush in the face.

13. There is a moment of stunned, horrified what-the-fuckness.

14. Best points down the line and screams to demand a throw in. "Our ball!"

15. JOR subs Best off before the referee can yellow/red card him for . . . for what, exactly? Misconduct?

16. Best leaves the stadium early again.

17. This forum decides that Best will never be seen at Prenton Park again.

18. Best is spotted at Prenton Park the next day, watching Liverpool's women.

19. The identity of the person struck by the ball becomes public knowledge. He works for a media outlet and was present at MB's girlfriend's only visit to our stadium.

20. Tranmere TikTok is flooded with women saying the guy is a creep.

21. Jack the Lad posts on his socials defending Best for sticking up for his girlfriend.

22. That post is quickly deleted and JTL posts another one saying everyone's overreacting because it was an accident and that it was obvious Best was trying to play a long ball down the line and got it wrong.

23. The creep is banned from the stadium and a club statement uses phrases like "unwanted and inappropriate sexual advances will not be tolerated."

It's not hard to guess what happened. The creep had a run at Best's girl and Best has got very public revenge. Best will get a fine and a ban and he has also left himself liable to legal consequences.

Everyone has their own opinion about the incident. Mine is not relevant.

What fascinates me is that it does offer some potential clarity about the big question.

Why did Max Best come to Tranmere?

To smack a ball into a creep's face.

Case closed?

. . .

John King's_love_child
The title made me think he was dead.

. . .

Typo's_Intentional
I ain't reading all that.
I'm happy for u tho.
Or sorry that happened.

. . .

The_Bozster
Great thread, Fred. 11 points from January and JOR sure to be Manager of the Month. Jack the Lad been bullied into dominance. 20K to dodge the drop, drop the dough. Money well spent. Don't punch people but do punch a Nazi. Violence solves nothing, take your hands off my girl. Conflicted.

. . .

Challinors_Long_Throw
the guy's a lazy brat who thinks he will get away with smashing a ball into someone's face
and he will
there's no risk to his career. not in the slightest.

. . .

John King's_love_child
Could backfire, though. Can't imagine his girl's too happy about it. You can't even open a door for a lass these days without being cancelled. She's probably already broke up with him because he's a violent monster.

. . .

Geordie_Cruyff
He isn't a monster and she hasn't broken up with him. Max Best is a good man and I'd be happy for him to marry my daughter.

. . .

Morecambe_White
Oh thank fuck! I'm so happy someone did a proper post that got people thinking because I have a theory and now that there's context and people actually reading instead of just reacting, I feel like I won't get laughed at.
So hear me out, and don't jump down my throat right away.
This lad Max Best, he's proper autistic. I know you're thinking "oh mate come on it's 2024" but wait! I'm not saying it like a diss or a slur. I mean, like, medically. He must be.
We've all heard bits and pieces about summer training. And as Fred put in his links, you can fucking see him there in the background of videos. You can see Jack the Lad flirting with this unreal blonde and that's Max Best's girl! It's all there.
All you have to do is put two and two together and that's what I've done. Get this. Strap yourselves in, boys.
Max Best doesn't have loads of friends. He's a loner by nature. You can't see that on the pitch, but just trust me. Read and watch his interviews. He's a

loner, fact. So he gets his head cracked open and he's in hospital and all that. Shocking. They should hang the bastard who done it. He goes to Tenerife for some sun and some privacy. Hundred to one shot, bumps into our lads. James O and Mateo find out what's up and sort him out. Look, I don't rate James O as a manager and I think Mateo's made mistakes, but it brings tears to my eyes the way they looked after this kid. Dead serious, that's class, and that's what I want from my club.

So they let Best use the swimming pool, lend him a physio and a couple of coaches. What have we done? Like, three hours of work? I mean, seriously. And it's not work, is it, if you're in Tenerife and the sun's out and there's a fucking dreamy woman chatting to you the whole time. I mean, find a job you enjoy doing, know what I mean? But this Max Best kid, he's autistic AF. He doesn't think "oh that was nice bye." It festers. He's thinking, they helped me, how can I help them?

He goes . . . I know! I'll save them from relegation single-handed. It's about a thousand to one in terms of value but that's what I'm saying. Three hours from us is someone sitting by the pool so he doesn't drown. Three hours from him is eleven points and safety. Do you get me? His head's not right. He doesn't think like us. I'm not joking now. I happen to think he's a really good player, but his real skill is being a sort of footballing Mike Brearley. Older guys will get that reference. He played cricket for England. He wasn't that good but he was a genius captain and made the other players outperform.

Me? I'd have him back on a big contract. But he'll never come back here. He's balanced the ledger. We're over.

Edit: THIS EXPLAINS WHY HE DIDN'T DO ANY MEDIA. Think about it.

Last word: Kicking the ball at some lowlife? I mean, if it's proved to be on purpose he needs to be proper punished. Big fine, five-match ban, warning about his future conduct. It's going to weigh on him and there will be days that he regrets it. But fuck me, what a shot!

. . .

Honey_I_Shrunk_Pat_Nevin

Top work, Fred, you absolute madman. I thought your forensic analysis of <why Mellon should be sacked> was your masterpiece, but you've outdone yourself.

Only thing is, everyone's missing the point about Best and his missus and why not handle it in private? It's mad simple.

Best gets a fine and a suspension. Maybe there's a sponsor that thinks twice about working with him.

The sex pest loses his job, gets a lifetime ban, and now everyone in the world knows he's got wandering hands. His life is in tatters.

Next guy who's alone in a room with her is gonna think twice.

Fred, you've way overrated him as a player and my cat could manage in the National League North, but he's done well here. Good luck to him.

Liverpool, 11 a.m.

It had been almost a week since I'd launched a football into the face of the prick who had teamed up with his mate to harass Emma. When I left the pitch, I went straight to the dressing room for treatment on my shins. Mateo came to ask me what the fuck I'd done. I told him about what had happened when Ems had gone exploring the media operations and why she hadn't been back to the stadium since. He listened in silence and all he said was, "I wish you'd told me."

After he left, I grabbed my stuff and snuck out of the stadium. The fewer people I talked to, the better.

The pain in my shins was pretty bad and I regretted not taking a pack of painkillers home with me. But the worst thing was the awkward phone call I'd had with Emma.

There was a lot of stilted phrases and half-truths, but I couldn't be totally honest. The British press were notorious for hacking phones and listening to whatever private conversation they wanted. I assumed Beth and her ilk were listening to my every call, every FaceTime, and had access to all my texts and emails.

I'd stayed in my holiday rental for one more day, watched a women's match at a sparsely populated Prenton Park, then gathered my bits, posted the key at the estate agent's, and went back to Chester. Holiday over. One swollen bank account, one swollen shin, one demon gorging himself on all the XP I'd collected.

I used my rapidly healing leg as an excuse to lie low for the week. I trained in private and tried to get myself ready for the fans forum where, in theory, my recent escapades could see me kicked out of Chester Football Club. But I couldn't think beyond Emma and what I was going to say to her. And, more importantly, what she was going to say to me.

Friday morning finally arrived.

We hadn't seen each other for a while, but she had taken the day off to go sightseeing with me and for moral support during that night's Fans Forum. Of course, I was dreading that it wouldn't be long before she was back on the train, heading north. I met her at the station and my heart stopped as she looked at me and immediately looked away. So it was worse than I thought . . .

She lifted her eyes again and her face softened. "Oh, Max," she said.

"I know," I sighed.

"Come 'ere." She pulled me in for a hug. "Gemma's worried about you. She can't understand why you did it."

"Why I hit the guy? I promised I'd hit him the next time I saw him." I broke away. "Are we only going to talk about that?"

"No," she said. "But I want to talk about it once and I want the truth."

Fair enough.

I drove her across Liverpool and out towards the Irish Sea. We parked and went for a stroll, with me being a surprisingly enthusiastic tour guide. We were walking along a stretch of sandy beach across the water from New Brighton where my flat had been. "The beaches here are all right! You're not supposed to go in the actual *water*. One-third of people who go swimming around Britain's coast get sick. Did you know that? That's fine, isn't it? Absolutely *fine*. View's nice, though, and there's cool buildings and I sort of don't mind the Liverpool skyline."

"Did you miss Chester?"

"No. I enjoyed the break. Tonight will suck with them all yelling at me but I can make it through the rest of the season now. I feel pretty good." On top of everything else, I'd found half a dozen youth players and bought two new perks: one to let me move players around at set pieces and one that showed me how much players from other teams were earning. Much, much more about those later.

"My dad's been helping me follow the results. We reckon Tranmere are safe now. Twelve points from the danger zone. Is that right?"

"Not safe but pretty safe. And they're playing better. They should have enough about them to survive."

"And Chester? Did that go according to plan?"

"Yeah, pretty much. Sandra's league record is won four, drawn one, lost one. Got knocked out of the FA Trophy, made it to the semis in the Cheshire Cup. That's solid. B plus. And the transfer window is closed, the other teams didn't make any big moves, and we didn't lose Raffi."

"It was a bad result against York."

I laughed. "I'll be answering all these questions tonight. The league's sort of interesting now. York beating us brings them back into it. In theory." I showed her the league table.

	TEAM	P	W	D	L	F	A	GD	PTS
1	Chester	27	20	2	5	72	27	45	62
2	Kidderminster	28	17	8	3	50	20	30	59
3	Darlington	28	16	9	3	45	28	17	57
4	York	29	15	11	3	47	29	18	56

"Why only in theory?"

"The only advantage the other teams had was our fixture congestion at the end of the season, but we played all our fixtures in January and the others had at least one match postponed. So that advantage is pretty much gone. I'm relaxed about it."

"You don't seem relaxed."

I slowed. "I'll be relaxed when I make you smile."

"You make me smile when you're being you. The real you." I didn't know what to say to that. My high-minded liberal ideals hadn't stopped me sucker punching a dude. And while I deeply, deeply regretted it, I also didn't regret it and would do it again. The real me? What was that? Emma sensed my confusion and changed the subject. "What's in the backpack?"

I smiled, just a bit cheeky. "I'll show you in about sixty seconds."

We kept on across the sand. The cool sea air was giving her ruddy cheeks like the cutest ever gammon and her cute little nose was tinged with red.

"This is called *Another Place*," I said.

"What is? This beach?"

"This is called Crosby Beach. There's art here, and the art is called *Another Place*. It's by a dude called Antony Gormley."

It looked like a pretty empty expanse of sand with a few people dotted around. "Art on this beach? You pulling my leg?"

"No. You'll see. It's weird but great. You can ask that guy about it. He's here every day."

"Him? But how do you—? Hang on. Is that . . . wait . . . what *is* that?"

She picked up the pace, leaving me a few steps behind. I caught up as Emma leaned left and right. She was stood in front of a six-foot tall cast iron statue of a man looking out to sea. "But there's loads," she said, realising that every one of the people dotted around were all made of metal; we were the only actual humans there.

"There's a hundred," I said. "Some are half-buried and you only see them when the tide goes out. It's pretty amazing, really messes with your head. This is my fourth time here. There's something disturbing about it."

"It gives me the shivers. It's like there's an actual man inside, trapped. It's horrible. But it's peaceful, too."

"I think when your brain processes that it's really, really, really a sculpture, you start to like it. But that first shock is, er . . . shocking."

People had put hats and scarves on some of the statues, and we walked in silence to the next one. It was wearing a Liverpool scarf, which was really unfair on the poor dude, but Emma didn't seem to notice what she was touching. She pulled the scarf a little tighter so that the guy's neck wouldn't get a draught. "Is this what you feel like? A helpless statue looking for something you'll never find, far from your friends? Have you been lonely? Is that why you wanted me to see this?"

"Er . . . maybe. Lonely? In a way. But I was thinking less . . . poetically." I slung my backpack round and knelt to open it. I emerged with a football. "A lot of people are saying I was petulant and immature. I don't think I was but I'll take the punishment. I'll pay my fines."

"No, you won't."

"What?"

"Mateo's going to pay it, if there is one. He called me to apologise for what happened. He wishes you'd let him handle it. And so do I. Or you could have let John do it. Or if you really, really needed to punch a man in the face to defend my honour, you could have done it in private."

I shook my head. "No. It had to be public."

"Why?"

I squashed the ball between my palms and tried to bounce it like a goal-keeper. It flopped into the sand. As I cleaned it, I said, "It wasn't a punch in the face, it was a kiss."

"Max."

"There's a scene in the Bible where a mob has come to find Jesus. They don't know what he looks like; they didn't have Instagram back then. So they get Judas to point him out. He goes over to Jesus and gives him a kiss. That's how the mob knows. I've given my kiss, and now everyone knows. They know about him, and they know what'll happen if *they* try something." I looked up at the sky. A few seagulls were swirling looking for discarded chicken and chips. "I *look* petty and childish. Worth it, if you're that little bit safer. I'll get a ban. So what? I don't want to play if you're not there to watch me. Since he did what he did, you've been to a couple of Chester games but you didn't come to any Tranmere ones. I barely saw you in January." I looked at the smooth, clean ball. "So it had to be public. I want people to know that if they hurt you, I'll destroy them. It doesn't reflect well on me, I guess, but there's an easy solution: They can leave you alone. Then there's no issue."

Emma looked from the sea to the seagulls to the statues. A hundred cast iron replicas of an artist, some half-buried in the sand, some who got drowned twice a day. The installation made more sense than I did. "What's the ball for?"

"I . . ." I looked away instinctively and made a huge effort to look at her while I said something that was unquestionably childish and immature. "On the phone you said I could have hurt someone else by mistake."

"Yeah. You could."

Away and back again. "Pick a statue."

"That one."

"No, that's too far. Pick the one there." I pointed to a guy twenty yards away.

"That's not a choice."

"I'm kicking from sand. Do you know how hard that is? The degree of difficulty of this shot is insane. This is five times harder than hitting the press box from a nice flat strip of grass." I settled and looked from the ball to the target. I swung my foot—a travesty of a sentence which does nothing to convey the magnificent coordination of bone and brain—and with a dull thunk, the statue nodded the ball away. "Heading 20," I said. "Should sign him up."

Tiny creases appeared on her forehead. "You can make that shot a hundred out of a hundred?"

"I can make it one out of one. I'm just saying, there was no risk to anyone else. I promise."

She came close to me and put her hands on my sides. "I don't want people to think poorly of you and go on the radio and say you should be banned from football. I want people to see you the way I see you. Kind and generous and thoughtful."

"I don't care what they think. I only care what you think."

She leaned into me and rested her head on my chest. "You need people, Max. You need to talk to people. Next time you go to hit someone in my name, will you talk to me first?"

"You'll tell me not to."

"That's not . . ." She stepped away and I felt a massive, icy cold bubble form between us. "Do you still want to move in together?"

"Of course!"

She nodded a few times. The bubble wasn't icy, I realised. It was cool. "I have conditions."

"Right. Your own sink."

"I want you to talk to me. When it comes to something like this, I'd like to feel my opinions matter. Remember you said that to me once? It works both ways. If you want a me-and-you life, then we have me-and-you conversations. There's no 'you' in 'us'."

"Er . . ."

"You've got to include me, even—especially!—when you think I'll say no. I don't want a relationship where you're always *explaining* why you did something. I want a relationship where you involve me and value me and if you really," she said, holding her finger up to stop me interrupting, "if you really respect me like you say you do, why wouldn't you?"

"So if I offer you a forty-nine percent vote in our decision-making council you'll move in with me? That's the best deal in the history of trade."

"You work in Chester, and I work in Newcastle. We can't live together. Yet. But I'll talk to my dad about WFH one day a week. I'll go watch you kick a ball around and four days a week, I'll still be a hotshot paralegal with exceptional photocopying skills."

The wording confused me. "WFH?"

"Work from home. The cottage."

"What cottage?"

"Where you live."

"Oh, the barn."

"It's not a barn. Don't let Ruth hear you call it that."

"It's got wild animals living in it. It's a barn. Will your dad say yes?"

"He's . . . I had to tell him about what happened, and he was incensed. I mean about the guy, not you. Dad isn't seeing any moral grey areas. He joked that he was going on forums defending you."

"Forums?"

"You know, like Reddit. And the ones from before Reddit. What? What are you thinking?"

"I'm thinking it's not fair you have to come to me all the time. How about one weekend a month I put Sandra in charge and go to Newcastle to watch you read documents?"

"Deal. But Max. You . . . This is a me-and-you conversation, now. If you want me to move in, I'll need to bring clothes and furniture and things. I'll need to buy some stuff. It's not a huge, huge deal but I don't want that to be wasted time."

"Why would it be?"

"Are you going to stay at Chester? If not, I'll wait and move to where you *do* settle. That's fair, isn't it?"

"Huh." A thought shot past like a shooting star. Was my relationship with Emma similar to my relationship with Chester FC? Successful but always one mistake away from ending? Built on a foundation of sand? I tried to imagine talking to Chester the way Emma had spoken to me. "So . . . if I can look past their flaws and we can have a good talk . . . I'll agree to move in with my toothbrush, my knee-high boots, and my fluffy white jumper that makes me extra huggable. Okay . . . Okay. I'm going to tell them what I want from them and they're going to accept because they need me desperately."

She bit her luscious bottom lip. "Are you saying you're the Emma of that relationship?"

"Of course I'm the Emma of that relationship. I'm the Emma of *this* relationship."

That made her laugh—a proper, warm laugh that made me realise everything was going to be all right. "You're not the Emma of this relationship. But just so you know, I don't have any knee-high boots."

"Yeah, you do. I saw you in them."

"You didn't because I don't."

"Might have been a dream? You said Mateo's going to pay my fine?"

"Yeah."

While I was waiting for her at the train station, the £20,000 had landed in my bank account. It hadn't excited me at the time because I was busy catastrophising, but now it clicked. Yes, I needed to save some to pay the Brig, but for the first time ever, I felt I could splash some cash on my dream woman. I held my elbow out to her. "Then I'm rich. May I take you shopping?"

She took my arm and we started walking back to the car. "You hate shopping. It drains you. Don't you want to save your energy for the Fans Forum?"

I looked back at the ball I'd kicked. Some kid would take it home. "Didn't you notice? I've been training with a League Two team for a month. I've got almost seven litres of air in here." I thumped my chest. "And my stamina feels way better, too. It was weird, though. They didn't have any way to test it."

"Didn't they?" said Emma, her lips twisted. "While you're *behaving yourself* at the Fans Forum, I'll be thinking of some suitable tests. All right?"

Just then I didn't care about football or the future. I only wanted to be with Emma. "Why do you care if I behave myself? I could take over at Gateshead and we could live on the Tyne and you could walk to work."

We arrived at my shitty brown Subaru. "Because of Henri and Raffi and Youngster and Jackie and Dani and Ruth. Because I'm invested. And because you are, too. If you *tell* the fans how you feel, you might get what you want."

We kissed, then, and I felt so wonderful, so at peace, that I wondered if I could do things her way.

As I started the engine, I took one look back down the beach. The statues hadn't moved, but as always, they had moved me. "Art makes me retrospective," I said, as I navigated the car park.

"You mean introspective."

"That, too."

My mind was made up. I would go to the Fans Forum and patiently let the Chester fans vent their spleens and when they were done, I would talk about my lofty ambitions for the club, and we'd all get on the same page and begin to sketch out a road map that everyone could agree on. And if there was any unexpected drama, some sort of seismic shock, or a devastating bolt from the blue, it wouldn't be my fault.

14

THE SUPPORTERS TRUST

The Fans Forum had been moved from the Blues Bar with its 120 capacity to the weightier Crowne Plaza Hotel in the city centre. The conference room's primary colour was beige, offset by wood panelling and magnolia ceilings. The vibe was stuffy and businesslike, and the business of the day was shouting at Max Best. To that end, three hundred golden-legged, cream-coloured chairs had been laid out in rows. A flurry of late arrivals meant the hotel staff were rushing around adding more.

More than 300 Chester fans were sitting, most with their arms folded, glaring at me. Dotted around the crowd I saw plenty of faces I knew: Crackers (the blind architect) and Sumo (the Twitch streamer) from last year's board. Sean and Ollie, the xenophobic former board members who had tried to get me voted out at the last mid-season Fans Forum. On the front row there was Sandra and Ruth next to the Brig and Barnesy. The two army veterans looked relaxed and interested, but every now and then they'd scan the room and I realised they were both on the lookout for maniacs. Bulldog, Tyson, Benny, and Future's grandmother were part of a gaggle of parents from the youth teams.

Here and there were players from the first teams: Henri, Glenn, D-Day, Charlotte, Bonnie, and Angel. In a sort of halo around Angel the men weren't folding their arms and weren't glaring, but their wives and girlfriends were.

On the stage to my immediate left, without a microphone by request, was Emma. She claimed to be there offering moral support, but almost every time I opened my mouth to answer a question she coughed or poked me. What happened to self-regulation? She was the Sentinel made flesh!

Then it was me, and to my right, Jackie Reaper, to *his* right, Ryan Jack, followed by MD and Secretary Joe.

Starting in the middle but with a chair over to the side for when the questions started, was our host for the evening, Boggy.

What were the stakes of this event? I could repair my relationship with the fans, or ruin it. Build or break. Grow or go. Marry, fuck, kill. There was no immediate danger of being sacked. Unless I fell all the way off my trolley, MD would give me the rest of the season. Strangely, the highest stakes were with Emma—if I behaved myself I could spend three days a week with her. That thought was almost enough for me to behave myself. Almost.

Seeing the fans there, judging me, resenting me, was getting on my tits.

Unedited transcript of the Chester Fans Trust Mid-Season Forum dated Friday, February 2.

On the panel: Mike Dean (MD); Joe X (club secretary); Max Best (DoF, men's first team manager); Jackie Reaper (women's first team manager); Ryan Jack (player); Boggy (host).

Boggy: Ready to begin? [cough] Good evening, ladies and gentlemen. I'd like to offer you a warm welcome to this Fans Forum. My name is Boggy and I'm the host of *Seals Live,* the official Chester podcast. I don't think anyone on the stage needs an introduction except for one. This is Emma, Max's lawyer. She'll be making sure he doesn't say anything interesting.

[laughs from the stage; dead silence from the audience]

Max: Can I say something real quick? That woman who just came in isn't a Chester fan. She's a journalist. Let's boot her out like she wants to boot out my mum's care workers. Out of the country, that is. Then we can get going.

Secretary Joe: Oh, sorry, Max. She's a member.

Max: Holy Christ. You let anyone in if they give you twelve quid? That's crazy. Second point. It's very dangly up here. We have a women's team, you know.

Jackie: Bonnie was booked to be the player rep but she swapped with Ryan so he'd get a bit of attention.

Ryan: Get bent.

Max: Class, Bonnie mate. You can do one of my post-match interviews instead if you want.

[inaudible retort]

[laughter]

Boggy: I think we can all agree it's going to be a busy night, so we'll skip most of the pleasantries. Perhaps a quick recap of the season so far is in order. The men are top of the league and into the Cheshire Cup semifinal. They had a memorable FA Cup run, which included an astonishing win over Salford City and our very own Benny scored in the second round.

[applause]

Boggy: The women's team, led by Jackie Reaper, are keeping track with league leaders Altrincham and only a last-minute Altrincham equaliser stopped us from beating them and topping the table. There has been some rare silverware in the youth system with the under-twelves winning in Liverpool.

[applause]

Boggy: All in all, the club is in fine fettle and robust health.

[a pin drops]

Boggy: Right. To the questions! We thought we'd start with an easy one.

Max: Hold up. Easy one? How do you know what the question will be?

MD: The questions have been vetted.

Max: MD, what are you doing? They'll think I've insisted on that! Like I'm fucking Stalin. Let them ask what they want.

MD: We thought tempers might run high and we want to make sure there's a civil, productive discussion. I'm sure that everyone will behave themselves and when they've heard what you have to say everyone will leave here happy and optimistic. This is merely precautionary. We have microphones for the audience so if you want to have more of a discussion with an individual fan, we can do that.

Boggy: It's also a time issue, Max. Normally at these things, fans preface their questions with lengthy descriptions of their history as a supporter. It can get quite repetitive and doesn't add much to the discussion. So, first question is for MD. The bathrooms in the Harry McNally Terrace aren't cleaned enough. What do you plan to do about it?

MD: That's something that's a top priority—

Max: Scuse me. Is that seriously the first question?

Boggy: Yes.

Max: [laughter] If you've organised the questions in terms of increasing unhappiness so that I have to end with a rousing speech to win the fans back, then mwah. Chef's kiss.

MD: So, the bathrooms. The current issue is—

I tuned out. Delaying the inevitable might have seemed like a good idea to MD and Boggy, but for once I wanted to rip the plaster off. Get the unpleasantness over with!

I contemplated the worst-case scenario. If I got sacked that evening, I'd lose the £500 a week income I had from the club. Ruth wouldn't kick me out right away, but I'd find myself homeless soon enough. The Brig would get his money and I'd be left with a few thousand to tide me over. I'd played for two teams this season, so unless I got special dispensation, I wouldn't be able to sign for a third one.

What could I do? Be the assistant manager at Tranmere—except Facegate had caused a huge stir and Mateo might want that to die down before inviting me back to his gaff. So that left taking over as manager at some other club. I wasn't stressed about getting an offer. The curse said my reputation was "very poor," but the teams we'd been thrashing 4– and 5–0 didn't see it that way. If they could get me, they would. My talent was undeniable.

And my skills had increased even further in recent weeks.

In January, I'd powered through to get the 10,000 XP I'd dangled in front of Old Nick. There was only one match where it felt like work—that was a long

Monday night drive to watch Brighton on the south coast. It was good I did that, though, because far from getting to 10K on the twentieth or twenty-first like I'd blithely expected, I had to scramble for last-minute five-a-sides to grab the final few hundred XP I needed. Wondering if I'd find those last matches felt very much like the old days when I was scrambling to get the XP needed for Super Scout.

With my wallet bulging, I'd made two purchases.

For the discount price of 1,000 XP, I bought Masterpiece Theatre, which would allow me to more precisely position players at set pieces. I hadn't used it yet.

Then I'd used a five percent voucher and bought Contracts 2. That was hilariously overpowered. I had it in time for Liverpool Women versus Arsenal Women and the results were shocking.

One Liverpool player was earning £350 a week, the same that I was paying Charlotte to be part-time. Liverpool's foreign stars were better paid, including one on £1,000 a week. Arsenal were paying a lot more. Their star striker was earning £6,000 a week. Way, way below her male equivalent, but pretty decent.

The contract screen had some other tasty morsels.

Squad Status told me how important each player was with phrases such as *invaluable to the club, important first-team player, used in a squad rotation system, backup for the first team, hot prospect for the future,* or *decent youth player.*

Bonuses was a space for things like goal, assist, or clean-sheet bonuses. They were less common than I expected.

Clauses showed scenarios that would change the contract. A few older players had a manager release clause: A club could sign that player as their manager and not have to pay compensation. Many had a release clause like Raffi Brown's. The ones I saw were too high to be interesting but if Christian Fierce was worth £100,000 and he had a release clause for £70,000, that was an obvious source of arbitrage. Many players had relegation clauses. If their club went down it would trigger a release clause (so the players could escape). But the clubs had their own protections, too. Most players would get an immediate twenty-five percent pay cut if Scenario B happened.

Most useful to me, maybe, was the contract expiry date. If Christian Fierce had a contract until 2027, it was going to be hard to get him out of his club. But any players whose contracts ended this summer could be signed for free! With young players I'd have to pay compensation—set by a tribunal if I couldn't agree to terms with the club—but for guys over twenty-four there was no cost.

In theory, I could sign eleven out-of-contract players and have a whole new team ready for the first match in August. There was even an expiring contracts filter in the player search screen. All I needed to do was re-scout everyone I'd ever scouted and hey! Dozens of players who I could negotiate with.

Just top, top stuff. I was going to be one of the football world's biggest nuisances!

Unlocking Contracts 2 led to two new perks becoming available in the shop.

The Future perk was 900 XP and promised to tell me how players felt about their future at a club. It made sense that I needed to unlock Contracts

2 and Morale to get to that one. That perk felt like a medium-priority buy. It would be amazing to grab it and scout Mo Salah. The Saudi Pro League had tried to buy him again, and again Liverpool had rejected an enormous bid. He'd probably have doubled or tripled his salary if he'd been allowed to leave, same as the many stars who had moved from the top European leagues in January. What would Salah's Future say? *Would quite like to go somewhere warm, actually?*

Contracts 3 was 1,300 XP. Bit of an odd one. It would simply tell me who a player's agent was. I would discover that pretty soon after I started the process of trying to sign someone, but maybe it would be worth the cost to know in advance. If a player had Bradley Rymarquis as an agent I probably wouldn't bother, right? And who knew, maybe there would be some other advantages to knowing.

I nodded to myself. It was intriguing and I wanted it, but it'd have to wait. Next stop was Wibwob, which would cost 9,000 XP after I used my ten percent voucher.

XP balance: 5,024

There wouldn't be any more 10,000-XP months for a while, but it very much looked like I'd get Wibwob by the end of the season. I thought back to the imps chattering "get Wibwob, get Wibwob." Soon I would, unless the February perk was so enticing it blew a hole in my wallet. Angel shook her hair just then and I felt sure the perk would land on Valentine's Day.

Hadn't it been like that last year? Or was February the month the Fantasy Football perk got upgraded? Another upgrade to *that* would be irresistible.

"Max?"

"Mmm?" I said, reluctantly taking my eyes off Angel. Emma was just as easy on the eye, thankfully. "Bebs?"

"They asked a question."

"Who?" I blinked as I realised 350 Chester fans were staring at me, arms still folded. "I was miles away. What was the question?"

Boggy: The question's on the very topic of you being miles away. From Ollie. Why did you leave us in the middle of the season?

Max: Oh! It's happening. It's happening, Jackie, are you ready?

Jackie: I was told there'd be popcorn.

[laughter]

Max: Can we get Ollie a microphone, please? No, I'm serious. Ollie, good? All right. I went because it was the solution to lots of problems and for personal reasons. You might remember that I was murdered and while I was on my deathbed, I was told I was the new Chester manager.

Ollie: That was terrible, shocking, course it was. Course it was. But you can't use that as an excuse forever.

Max: Excuse? That's a loaded word. That's for when you're saying sorry. I'm not saying sorry. This isn't an apology. I haven't done anything wrong. So I wake up, learn to walk, and then it's full on, twenty-four-seven Chester Chester Chester Chester for months and months and months. I'm managing the men's team, the women's, going to schools to scout kids, looking for coaches, watching video of our opponents, writing the match programmes. Think about it. It's bonkers. Did I complain? What, about doing everyone in this room's dream job? No. But it's tiring, isn't it? It's a punishing pace I was doing. So Tranmere was a break. A change is as good as a rest.

Ollie: But—

Max: Ollie, be honest, now. Are you actually listening to me?

Ollie: I am.

Max: What did I do? I played one game a week, trained in the morning like a normal player without having to wonder why D-Day is dogging his sprints or having to take a break from a drill to sign some document. I used their coaches and facilities in the afternoons. Got myself sharp. Cleared my head. It was great. I needed it.

Ollie: But why Tranmere, though?

Max: Why not?

Ollie: They're rivals.

Max: Ah. So here's one thing we're going to learn tonight. You and I are very different. We think differently about everything. I don't hate Tranmere, and I never will. Ditto Wrexham. When you sing your anti-Wrexham songs, I get demotivated. I don't want anything to do with that. After my murder the football clubs that helped me most were, number one, Chester. Thanks! Two, Tranmere Rovers. Three, Wrexham. Four, Manchester City. I mean, what a list, but that's the truth of it. No one told me hating Tranmere was a prerequisite for this job, by the way. That didn't come up in the job interview, do you know what I mean? So you can bin that whole thing. Tranmere were unbelievable to me. Unbelievable. And I've gone there and repaid them. I'm very, very pleased with myself.

Ryan Jack: Tranmere's a top club. Great people.

Jackie: I like Tranmere. I'm made up they're safe. There's football rivalries and there's real life. Max chose real life, for once. I'm proud of him.

Max: Thanks, mate. Listen. I spent a lot of time walking around Merseyside in the past month and there's a bit of nice stuff and there's a lot of poverty. A lot of deprived areas. Places and people abandoned by this government, left to rot. It's like where I grew up but where I grew up there's a posh bit next door. There's no posh bit there. There's destitution. It's proper shocking. What they've got that keeps them going is their football teams and if I brought a few smiles to a few faces then yeah, pleased with that. Pleased with that. The far-right journalist at the back is writing this down under examples of me promoting Marxism or some tripe, but I don't think working class people should turn on each other. Complain about my friends all you want. They're my friends and when they're in trouble I want to think I'll be there for them.

Ollie: Are you telling us to stop singing about other teams?

Max: It's your club. Do what you want.

Ollie: What we want is for our manager to be with us for the whole season.

[applause]

Max: Why?

Ollie: What?

Max: Why?

Ollie: Because.

Max: Because why?

Ollie: For a start, it's the transfer window.

Max: We'd done our business. Got ahead of it, sorted it all. The rest of the month's just noise. You think loads is happening because there's rumours and fake Twitter accounts and all that shit, but there's not. We said we were done, and we were done.

Ollie: You didn't replace Ryan when he got injured.

Max: Ryan is irreplaceable. If we had infinite cash like the Premier League or the Saudis, we would have done it. The cupboard's bare but that's fine. Sandra and I will find creative solutions. You're talking like the entire club fell off a cliff because I popped out to Asda to buy some Hobnobs. We're top of the league, mate. We're smashing everything. We've scored the most goals of any team in the top six divisions. I didn't wake up one morning and leave a note on MD's desk, did I? I planned it. Got replacements, got everything sorted. It was smooth as silk.

Ollie: It's embarrassing, though, isn't it? We're a laughingstock. Our manager's scuttling around the pitch at Tranmere like an obedient dog.

Max: Do you reckon they're laughing at Bradford Park Avenue?

Ollie: Yeah.

Max: Four–nil home, four–nil away. Are they laughing in Farsley? Five–nil. Boston? Six–nil. We did this last year, Ollie. You were worried about fans laughing at us. We're never going to agree on it. We've got our foot on the accelerator and we're leaving this league far behind. Soon you won't be able to hear them, mate.

Ollie: What about York? Four–nil. If you'd been playing, we'd have won that, and we'd be six points clear.

Max: What's it like being a multimillionaire?

Ollie: You what?

Max: You've made tens of millions of pounds betting on sports. What's it like?

Ollie: I haven't. What?

Max: But you're a hundred percent sure we'd have beaten York. I just think you're missing a trick if you haven't monetised that skill yet. And you could come help us pick the teams. If we're going to win five–nil with this lineup, what happens if we rest Glenn Ryder? Does it go to two–nil? We could really optimise the season if we could harness your powers.

Ollie: You know what I mean. We wouldn't have lost four–nil and been embarrassed.

Max: There's that embarrassment thing again. Teams lose matches. I seem to remember us losing a few matches last season. Did I . . . ? [Quietly] Stop poking me, bebs. I'm being nice! [Normal volume] Here's my promise to you: As long as I'm manager we'll continue to lose matches heavily. Four–nil's nothing. Because here's another difference between you and me. I was proud of that match.

Ollie: Proud?

Max: Yes, mate. One–nil down, it's tight, York are playing great, what do we do? We try to smash them. We try to win. They hit us on the counter. What do we do? The same. Nothing's changed. We can get three quick goals, easy. Let's slap! York get a third. Nothing's changed. We can get four quick goals, easy! We want to win every game. We play to win every game. We'll lose some. So what? It's three points for a win. Mathematically, it's better to play to win than to try to scrape some draws. And that's why I know we're going to win the league. Because we played against one of the best teams the way we play against the worst. Because we know we can win every single game. And I'm proud that it happened when I wasn't there. It shows that Sandra and the players believe in me and trust what I'm doing.

Ollie: At least someone does.

Max: What?

Ollie: Look at your questions, there. You'll find a lot about trust. About honesty. And loyalty.

[applause]

Max: Boggy, give me that list.

Ollie: There's a lot of hurt, Max. You've hurt people by leaving. You've hurt people by diving into Tranmere's fans to celebrate like you've never done here. You've hurt us by turning our club into a circus. We can't trust you, but you seem to have free rein to run the club as you want. You've turned it into your own little playground, and you don't talk to the new board. You were a little prick last year, too, but at least you talked to us. You had a plan for the worst-case scenario, and it was reassuring. You don't talk to the current lot. You keep saying it's our club, but you act like it's yours. In every respect, whether it's chucking money around like there's no tomorrow and breaking your promise not to do another Boost the Budget this year, you're unreliable. You won't sign a contract, you've run off for a cushty little jolly at our rival, and you've bought a small team and sent our players there to line your own pockets. And you've turned down huge bids for Raffi Brown that would make a huge difference to a club like ours. I mean—[laughs]—I could go on.

[standing ovation]

Boggy: Perhaps we could—

Max: Ollie. What do you want? Do you want me to quit right now?

[murmur of discontent]

Ollie: Er . . . No, Max. I think you're a prick, personally, but I like watching the team. And when you're smashing Darlington, you're our prick. Every football fan wants a prick like you on their team. But you're not our prick. You're your prick.

Max: What do you want?

Ollie: I want you to commit to the club.

[applause]

Max: Boggy, give me one of those mics so I can walk around like Gordon Gekko. Thanks. All right. I get the picture. Ollie's spoken for you all, sounds like, and there's these questions. Where's the money going? How can we trust someone who leaves on a whim? Why can't you ever be honest with us? Fine. Let's get into it all. You ready? This is going to be fucking epic. Got a spare pen, Beth?

MD: Max, maybe we should—

Max: Let me tell you about money first. My weekly wage is five hundred pounds a week right now. I get a little bit from my clients from when I was an agent, which I remind you you all knew about when you offered me this job. The Tranmere gig was pretty substantial, financially. I got the money today and I've never seen those sorts of numbers. It'll keep me going for a while. It'll let me stay at a low-paid job for longer. It'll let me stay here for longer.

Secretary Joe: You got paid already?

Max: Yes. Why?

Secretary Joe: But . . . nothing. Sorry.

Max: I know I'm not going to get rich managing Chester. I know that. And it's fine. I'll make enough from side hustles, I think. If the Saudi Pro League asks me to go and manage one of their teams next January and the money's right, I'll go! Why wouldn't I? One month there could keep me fed for a year.

Jackie: What about your morals, Max?

Max: My morals are why they have to pay double. Right, what else? How about . . . loyalty. Lots of complaints about my loyalty in these questions. What happens when I lose five matches in a row? I get sacked. Okay. Please explain to me what loyalty means. Five defeats equals the sack. We could go down the ninety-two teams in the football league and ask how many would survive losing five in a row. Pep would. Klopp would—and did, I think. Man United's guy would, but that's only because the owners wouldn't even know it had happened. Most of the ninety-two are getting sacked. We're going to win our league this year. Next season it's the National League. Bigger teams, harder opponents. We'll struggle at the start of the season and you lot will be out for blood. So I'm always two weeks away from being unemployed and I get punished for bringing you to a higher level. Loyalty? You have got to be joking.

Ryan Jack: That deserves applause, if you ask me. You're bang on, Max. Bang on the money.

Max: Communication. You want me to talk to the board and talk to fans more, not just on podcasts. Right. Okay. Why? There's three hundred and fifty people in this room who think they can do this job better than me. I can tell you two who might have doubts: Jackie and Sandra. Because they know how fucking hard it is. Everyone else knows better than me. The board, incredibly, comprise seven floating megabrains who have very strong opinions on the rotating of goalkeepers, of formations, and which players should be bought and sold. It's astonishing! You'd think I'd be delighted to have such a resource, but no, because I'm being sarcastic.

[inaudible]

Max: Yeah, I know, babes. [sigh] Okay. Deep breath. I don't want to have football conversations with you. Because they aren't conversations, they are diatribes where you tell me what I'm doing wrong. You don't listen when I explain that the thing you think is true is false. You hear things on talkSPORT and podcasts and you believe the last thing anyone told you. You go to matches and scream at the players to do the exact opposite of what I've told them. A midfielder gets close to the box? Shoooooot! After I've screamed in his face and risked my relationship with him because that's the last thing we need. What do you cheer? Tackles. So players want to do tackles. After I've been paying elite coaches to train them not to tackle. What do you hate? Passing backwards to draw teams out. Which is a great way to win football matches. What do you do when a player makes a mistake? Bury him. It's savage. And me and a team of specialists have to spend three days building his confidence back up.

Boggy: It's ingrained, Max. I've learned a lot in the last year, but I still love a good, old-fashioned crunching tackle.

Max: Sure, who doesn't? But it's my job to know what helps us to win and what makes us lose. I know that down to the Nth degree. The balance of risk and reward is insanely complicated and constantly changing, even within micro passages of play. I think about it nonstop and I'm amazing at it. You can have your opinions and shout them all over the pub, but don't waste my time with them. That's got to be fair enough, right? The board's job is to make sure I've not got my hand in the till. It's to make sure the club's stable and the fans' needs are being met. They simply don't have the expertise to question me on footballing matters. It's not a very nice thing to say, but there we have it. If you want someone on the board to represent you on football matters like signings and formations, then you need to elect a former player or someone with a coaching badge.

Boggy: Would you want to meet such a candidate and give him the okay, so to speak?

Max: That's absurd. I can't tell you who to elect. Just don't send racists. You don't need a former player on the board to check my work—you can ask Jackie or Ryan or another player. Does this guy know what he's talking about? How's training? Are you fit? Are you being treated fairly? And so on. The board could do it like that. Or they could look at the league table and say oh that's weird we were nearly relegated ten minutes ago how's he done that?

Jackie: They want you to talk to them, Max. That's all.

Max: That's not all. They're football fans. They always want more than they've got. They always want more than I can give. So how about I give them nothing? They're equally unhappy but at least I've saved some energy to do the job.

Jackie: You're exaggerating a little bit. You could talk more than you do.

Max: Like what? December twentieth. Tweet from Max Best. Hey guys, deep in negotiations with Banbury trying to sign one of their players. You'll never guess who! Lol! Oops their fans are outside the stadium trying to block the deal. Oops another team is bidding. Might be better to do deals in private, don't you think?

Jackie: Not every signing is that controversial. Chris Beaumont was a lot of money. You could explain why you value him so much and you could explain what you're thinking about upcoming games. Let fans know what tactical problems you face.

Max: Or I could just call the other manager and tell him my lineup and what we're going to try to do.

Jackie: Come on, lad. If this lot knew how much effort you put into what looks effortless, they'd have a different opinion of you. They don't see the graft and the hours. Give them a hint about how hard it is and how good you are.

Max: But why? Just cheer the team, enjoy the goals, enjoy the wins.

Jackie: They want to be involved.

Max: Yeah? I want to involve them. But Ollie wants the moon on a stick, and I don't have a moon and I don't have a stick. Right. Last big topic. Trust. Loads of questions on this list about trust. How can we trust you? I want to think you turned the Raffi bids down for a good reason, but I can't because I don't trust you. And so on. Trust. Mmm.

Secretary Joe: What? Sorry, I just got a . . . I have to go check something. I'll be back.

Max: Got to do it in an Arnie accent, mate. Trust is hard, isn't it? Because I don't trust you lot to take my work and continue it. When I lose five matches in a row, and I will, you'll sack me and then you'll dismantle everything I've done. You'll sell Raffi for peanuts, you'll sell Youngster for buttons, and Pascal will be put on a shelf somewhere. The youth teams will be neglected and the next time there's a bit of a cash shortage someone will break my promise to the women and use their budget to prop up the men. I want to build something at this club but sometimes I wonder what the point is. You're all mad at me for something absolutely trivial that didn't hurt the club in the slightest. Where was that anger when the youth system was a smouldering wreck? Where was that anger when the football was reactionary dogshit? When injured players were forced to play? You're mad at trivial shit and you don't value things that are actually important.

Jackie: Fucking hell, Max. [sigh] But when you're right, you're right.

Max: You don't trust me? It's hilarious. Before me, decisions at this club were mostly terrible. Now, they're mostly perfect. I started out fighting for the youth team, fought for the injured players, fought to improve the culture, fought to improve standards in training. I've been fighting and fighting and when I got to my limit I went for a break and that's when you found your voice. That's when you had an opinion. What's funny is that I have extra motivation to get you onside because if I stay in Chester, Emma will come and stay with me half the week and that's something I need to happen. I need it. But even with that carrot, I can't stand here and hear all this crap about loyalty and trust. You came to ask me questions. Let me ask you one.

MD: Go on.

Max: Where is everybody?

MD: What do you mean?

Max: I mean last season we were getting two thousand a match. This season it's up a bit. What's the average home attendance? Twenty-one hundred? More against Warrington, obviously—local rivals, and they brought a fair few. Most of the bigger crowds have been because teams like York brought a lot of away fans. We're top of the league, we play incredible football, we use kids, it's exciting, we do loads of community stuff, yeah we've had some media attention—that other clubs would kill for, by the way—and there's no one here. Ollie asked why I went into the crowd at Tranmere. Because there's seven thousand people going crazy! Even I couldn't resist. I want that here. The fans we get are noisy. It's a noisy stadium when you get going and I love it. But I want more. I want it full. I want to be so sucked into the moment that I don't even know what's happening. I want to be bombarded with questions about expanding the ground. But there's two thousand people who come, watch the match, have a great time, and go home and tell absolutely no one about it. We're on track to score a hundred and twelve goals this season. Why aren't we getting three thousand? Four thousand?

Jackie: Only Max would turn a Fans Forum into a Manc Inquisition.

[nervous laughter]

Max: Hey, I get that my tone might be belligerent or fractious or whatever but I'm genuinely asking. I know the ticket prices went up but it's still top value for money. Why aren't attendances going up?

Boggy: I think it's very fair to ask.

MD: I don't know.

Max: Ollie?

Boggy: He doesn't have the mic.

Max: I want to play football in front of seven thousand people. Seventeen thousand people. Seventy thousand people. I'm not like most players, but even I had my mind blown by the sheer fucking euphoria of scoring that equaliser in front of seven thousand crazy fans. Players want to play for big clubs in front of big crowds. It'll be easier to sign players when the stadium's full and rocking. Can I get that in Chester or not?

MD: Can I ask a question?

Max: Yes.

MD: What did you mean about building something? You mean getting into the EFL? Expanding the stadium? I'm not sure you've ever spoken this ambitiously.

Max: Okay, interesting. Crunch time. I was thinking this was like a relationship. I'm the gorgeous blonde lawyer with the EQ and the barely legal smile. You're the needy Manc twat who can't keep his mouth shut but is somehow still in with a chance.

Ryan Jack: If this kicks off can you all remember that I can't run? Thanks.

Jackie: If this is a relationship then you cheated on us with the club who bullied us in school.

Max: That wasn't cheating. We just danced a little and there was one kiss that got out of control.

Ryan: And she paid you.

Max: And she paid me. Wait.

Jackie: For those at the back, Emma's got questions about Max's definition of cheating.

Max: What I'm saying is that, failed similes aside, I am willing to work on our relationship. For the babies.

Jackie: Is that the youth team now or what?

Max: I don't know. I just said it because it felt good. One sign of a healthy relationship is honesty, isn't it? So I'm going to try being honest and we'll see where that gets us.

Jackie: We just got a double blast of honesty. Not sure we can take much more.

[laughter]

Max: The truth is, I haven't been completely open. Is everyone excited? Here's the deal. I've been looking at the history of Chester City. Before and after World War II, you were always a solid third-tier side. The sixties were a big dip into tier four, roaring back to three, crash, recovery, and then it gets terminal about where you got that shitty owner. Overall, a third-tier team which gets sucked into trouble every now and then. That's Chester. Am I right, MD?

MD: Yes, I'd say so. Historically.

Max: As far as I can tell, the average attendance in the third tier last year was around seven thousand. So to sustain itself in League One, a club should be looking to have seven thousand fans going to every home game. MD?

MD: Logical.

Max: I personally have very little interest in staying in non-league football for very long. If you guys want to stick around tiers five and six then I'll stay to the end of this season, grab my trophies, my medals, and my Manager of the Year award, and then I'll fuck off somewhere else, no big deal.

Secretary Joe: Sorry. I'm back. Max, can we talk? It's urgent.

Max: In a second. I'm on one. We're going to win the league this year. If I'm still in charge, we're going to struggle at the start of next season but sort it out in time for a late charge into the playoffs. Hate the playoffs, but we should be pretty good by then. Let's say it's three tight matches and your boy Max Best steps up with last-minute winners in every one and celebrates or doesn't as he wants because he's a free man. Boom, we're in League Two. Mate, League Two is a joke. Three teams promoted automatically and one playoff spot? Are you fucking joking? After the National League, that's a piece of piss.

MD: Hold on. Are you saying you want to take us to League One? In how many years?

Max: In three years. Weren't you listening?

MD: One promotion per year?

Max: The only hard one is next season. If there's a team like Wrexham or Notts County who are going to get a hundred and ten points, then we'd need a fast start and we won't get that. Bromley got into the playoffs on seventy-one points. I don't see how we play forty-six games and fail to get seventy-one points. Come on.

MD: But how would we do it? Wrexham and Notts County had massive investment. If we get promoted, our budget will be mid-table.

Max: We do it by using our resources well. Using our brains. Buy low, sell high. We do it by having a full stadium of nutjobs scaring opponents, intimidating referees, and urging our players to grab a last-minute winner. We do it with those goosebump moments where a young player makes a mistake and after a disappointed moment, the crowd fucking roars support and encouragement. That's how. And I reckon my haircut's worth about seventy points a season.

MD: You lifted us in the National League North, that's obvious, and we've even got a good shot at winning it. But the National League has some big hitters. There's whoever drops from League Two. Not Tranmere anymore. Grimsby are in danger. They're big! Forest Green Rovers have money. Look who's already in there. Oldham, Chesterfield, Rochdale, Southend. The competition is fierce. It's cut-throat.

Max: Cut-throat? I'll eat their babies. The only question is: Can we do it fast enough? Because I'm not interested in sticking around for consolidation seasons. It's up or out for me.

MD: Max, it needs money.

Max: We've got assets. We'll sell Raffi in the summer. There's other players making a name for themselves. And there's ways to improve the squad on the cheap. There's the exit trials. There's young players. I'm coming at it from all angles. The details don't matter right now. You guys, you've got a choice. You let me take you to the third tier or you start looking for a new manager to take over next season.

Boggy: League One seems ambitious, to say the least.

Max: I've already started. There were questions about why we let certain players go and haven't renewed contracts. It's because I'm building a League One team. I reckon we've got seven players who can play in League One.

MD: Seven?

Max: Well, one of them is Ryan. He'll have to turn the clock back a little bit, but I reckon he can do a job for us. Stanley Matthews was the best player in Europe in his forties.

Jackie: What about the women?

Max: The women's ceiling is way higher than the men's. If we don't go up this year, it'll happen next, and it should be a pretty straight line.

MD: We're not set up to be a League One team. I'm in a panic just thinking about it.

Max: We do it step by step. This summer, we don't need much. We add a reserve team and more youth teams. Every age group for the boys, half for the girls. We need a kitchen and staff. We need some new toys for the training ground. Cameras and stuff.

Jackie: We bought some.

Max: What?

Jackie: Pitch one has cameras all round, now. Sandra films training and cuts bits up for the lads to look at. And we got some ball machines and some bits and pieces.

Max: Okay. Sounds good. Where's Joe gone? He looked worried.

MD: Er . . . popped out again.

Max: I want to hear from Ollie. Get him the mic.

Boggy: There's other voices.

Max: Ollie speaks for the masses. Everything he says gets applause.

Ollie: If you want to be here for three years, sign a three-year contract.

[applause]

Max: There we go. You're not listening. You want loyalty that you won't give me. I'll sign a three-year contract if everyone in this room puts five thousand pounds, each, into escrow so that if I'm fired after losing five in a row, I'll get that money. It's a marriage you want? Sack me and I get half the club. You wouldn't ever do it. You can't have more from me than you're willing to give, Ollie. I'm the Emma of this relationship and that means that if I get the chance to go off and play in Japan for a month for big money, I'm going to go. If they ask me to manage Ghana at the next African Cup of Nations, that sounds fun. I'll prepare Chester some packed lunches and oven meals and leave notes about which bills need to be paid, go and do my side hustle, come right back, blast you into orbit. That's what I'm offering.

Ollie: Jackie. Help me out. Tell me you're on our side.

Jackie: Max is on your side if you'd only listen to him.

[smattering of applause]

Jackie: It's almost funny watching this. It's like the village has come together to talk about cooking the golden goose.

Max: What?

Jackie: It's an old saying. You don't know that one? But what I think is really funny is that Max is trying to take this relationship to the next level and watching him flirt is incredible. He's always passing himself off as a sort of Mister Lover Lover, but turns out he's read that pick-up artist book and all he knows is negging.

Ryan: He could learn a thing or two from you, Jack?

Jackie: Reckon so.

[they laugh in Scouse]

Max: I'm not trying to flirt with or seduce Ollie. I'm not in love with Chester Football Club. I want a trophy wife. That's a wife who picks up my trophies.

Ollie: Ah, here we go. This is good. There's a lot of people who can't get past the question, why us? What happens if Man United come calling? If you're as good as you think, that could happen. Will you be off? What about if Tranmere offer you the job? You'll be off then, and we'll be stuck with loads of players you rate that no one else does. Or loads of tiny midfielders on eight-year contracts and we play nice football and ship two goals a game from corners.

Max: You went off track a bit there. Why Chester, right? Emma, is this one where I'm honest? She's not sure. Me neither. Let's try honesty. There's no special reason why it's Chester. You're fan-owned, which is very important to me. You say Tranmere and I think the owner there is fantastic and a great guy but he's a guy and if I make the club successful he'll bag his profit and I'll be stuck with some arsehole. Amazingly, Ollie, I prefer you.

[some laughter]

Max: As for other teams . . . In April 2021, six English football teams conspired to annihilate English football. They took sledgehammers to the ankles of the sport, tried to nuke the pyramid, tried to end the very concept of competition. Those six clubs got a tiny slap on the wrist from the other fourteen Premier League teams who were too cowardly to kick them out of the league like they deserved. I will never, ever manage Arsenal, Chelsea, Liverpool, Manchester City, United, or Tottenham and while I watch United and hope they do well in a general, vague sense, it doesn't move me if they win or lose. Whatever passion I had, they snuffed out that day. If they get new owners and beg and beg, they'll have to do something immense to show their contrition, like give every EFL team a million pounds. So that's them. Newcastle United? Emma knows how I feel about climate criminals and despots. The rest of the Premier League and the Championship is owned by ghouls, hedge funds, billionaires whose faces make my skin crawl. Is it possible one of them makes me an offer I can't refuse? Maybe. But it's a long way down the pyramid till you start finding clean clubs. My standards are so high I've been brought this low. So of all the fan-owned teams it's Chester because Jackie brought me here, and while I've been pissing you off since day one, you've let me get on with the football stuff. Oh, another relationship thing. You were a mess when I came and, like all incurable romantics, I thought I could fix you. If things were more solid, were working better, it might have been hard to switch things round to my way. I can achieve my goals here in a way that might be much harder at some other clubs.

Ollie: Okay, I respect the honesty about us not being your dream club.

Max: I've never said otherwise.

Ollie: I know, but . . . But what about Raffi? You need money to get players. Why would you turn down bids that we haven't seen here since Ian Rush?

Max: When I scouted Raffi the first time, I knew he was a great prospect. He's got the steel that Ian Evans liked and the silk that I like. Almost a perfect central midfielder. But what even I didn't realise was how great he is at getting goals from midfield. We've always had a problem here that teams can shut Aff down and we look uninspired. What I've worked on is Aff left, one of three different guys right, Henri and now Chris up front. Right? So you've got menace from all angles. It's very dangerous. But good defences will cope, even with that. So you add Ryan Jack to get more craft. Amazing, but they might pull a midfielder or striker deeper to try to close up some space. Then! Raffi Brown makes a late run into the box. How do you defend that? You can't stop us if we're coming from all angles. We'll get you one way or another.

Ryan: And if you try a low block, Chris makes mincemeat out of you. [laughs] He's trying to build the perfect football team and you're trying to bin him off!

Max: When I came to Chester as Raffi's agent, I said I wanted an eight-hundred-thousand-pound release clause. MD and Ian didn't think twice because it would never get triggered. I knew better, and I think it will get triggered this summer, or someone will get close enough, maybe with some add-ons. But again, that was the Raffi I thought I saw. How much is goalscoring Raffi worth? Goals from midfield have a cash value. It's my job to make hard decisions and there's always an element of risk if you hold out for more money and it never comes. If Raffi leaves this club for free, you'll call me incompetent or corrupt or whatever but that's a risk I'll take because I know his value. And by the way, we need him for the rest of the season. I think it's obvious we're relying on him, big time. And if there are no bids in the summer, ouch. But we've got him for next year and wow, wait till you see him then. He'd wreck the National League. Is him shooting us up to the EFL worth four hundred thousand? I've no idea. I'd prefer the money, I reckon, but it's not clear cut. I'm his agent and he trusts me, and there are win-win solutions all round. But don't ask me to accept lowball offers because I won't.

MD: I find it stressful to turn down such offers but it's also exciting that we have players like that at the club and that's because of Max.

[applause]

MD: Max, you know I understand your point of view and totally accept that you went to Tranmere for good reasons and left us in good shape, and I know you're going to do more controversial things in the future. So it might just be nice for everyone and for me to hear that although we're maybe not your dream woman, you're happy to be here.

Max: I love managing Chester. I'm a builder and I want to build something awesome, and that's happening. It'd be a gut punch to leave now, but if you don't like what I'm doing, that's fine. It's your club. I keep saying it because it's true. Here's . . . Here's what I've been thinking today, because of my girlfriend, mostly. I realised that I can build a team that takes this club to League One. I know it sounds loopy to some of you, but I'm really fucking good at it. Can I get eleven players on the pitch who will win most games they play? Yes. Can I organise them so they'll actually win? Yes. Can I find five subs and backup players and young guys to come in like a production line? Yes. All that is various shades of easy.

[inaudible]

Max: Cocky? What's cocky about that?

[laughter]

Max: But what I can't do is sustain that after I've gone. To get to the third tier we're going to need to expand the stadium and buy our own training facilities and equip it and hire chefs and nutritionists and data nerds and media ghouls. I'll make us a profit in the transfer market and leave you with some assets, but what then? We need to work together to fill the stadium. To turn my, let's say unconventional ability to generate media attention into cash. To make sure the culture I've created lives on. Some of you might not like it but the players do and that's why it needs to stay. The board needs to support MD in driving revenue and working out stadium expansion plans and finding land for a training complex and hundreds of things like that—and leave me to manage the football side.

MD: And you won't pop along to tell us how to do our jobs?

Max: Of course not, mate.

[laughter]

Max: That's all future stuff. This season . . . it's like we've just moved in together. You're staring at my toothbrush on your bathroom sink and you're thinking . . . not sure about this.

[laughter]

Max: And I'm thinking, you know what . . . I could do better.

[laughter]

Max: But I'm here. I'm young but I'm old enough to know the grass isn't always greener on the other side. This relationship could work. It really could. [pause] I'm a human being and I need things. I need breaks from work, I need money, and I need new experiences. I'm open to mad offers, but this is my job. This is my home. I'll be here on the final day of the season. We're going to parade around with our league trophy, our Cheshire Cup, our women's league, our youth trophies. [laughs] I'll bring you my League Two Player of the Month for January, too, if you want to see that. I assume I'll get it. I was fucking amazing.

Jackie: Read the room, Max, Jesus Christ.

Max: Fine, I'll just stick it on my fridge. Hang on.

MD: What? What?

Max: Why do you have tartlets in your fridge if you don't like them?

MD: Who are you talking to?

Secretary Joe: Oh my God! MD! Max! It's really happened.

MD: What has?

Secretary Joe: Just before, I got a big deposit in the club's account. A big one. Eight hundred thousand pounds!

Jackie: The fuck?

Ryan: Eight— Has anyone seen Raffi today?

[inaudible]

MD: Sandra's shouting that he was at training.

Max: Why are you talking about Raffi?

Jackie: Max!

Max: I'm his agent. He can't . . .

Secretary Joe: You got some money today. Does the amount . . . ? I mean . . . it's too soon to be from Tranmere.

Max: The fucking transfer window is closed. Everybody calm the fuck down!

Secretary Joe: It's the Saudi Pro League. Their windows are longer. They can still buy players. Max, he's gone. They paid the release money and the paperwork's done. He's gone. Here we go! I mean . . . sorry.

Max: Saudi? Why would they want a non-league player?

Jackie: Because he's a goalscoring midfielder with a high ceiling, like you said.

Max: But he's not famous. This is all a big misunderstanding, right? Can everyone stop shouting for two seconds? [pause] The buyout fee to change agents is exactly the same as what I was expecting from Tranmere. What the hell . . .

Secretary Joe: Exactly the same? Did you include taxes?

Max: No. Taxes, right. I won't get full whack from Tranmere. And that explains why the money came from the Cayman Islands. [pause] He's binned me off without a word. He wouldn't, though. Joe, has he really gone? [pause] Oh, shit. Oh, fuck. Oh, fucking shit.

MD: Let's take a short break.

Ollie: Is it a break or the end?

MD: It's a break.

Ollie: It's just that Max has run off.

MD: It's just a break. We'll be back in ten minutes. Okay? It's not the end.

THE END

15

EPILOGUE

Saturday, February 3. Match 28 of 46: Chester versus Banbury United.
The ball came to me on our right. My first touch killed the ball, but it felt
wrong. The ball was heavy and sullen. Beside me, the community stand was
quiet, like a heavy blanket had been draped over it. The little away section
on this quarter of the ground was deserted; the few dozen Banbury fans were
behind the goal I was attacking.

Attacking? Hardly.

I rolled the ball under my foot, away from the defender, evaded the onrush-
ing midfielder, and clipped a pass back to Carl. He waited to see if I would
surge down the line. I didn't. He passed square to Steve Alton; the move would
happen down the left or not at all.

A moment later I realised my hands were on my head, and not from any
particular physical exertion. I had been doing my defensive duties, but with our
highest-CA defender behind me—Carl was fast becoming one of the best in the
league—there wasn't much need for my services. I pulled my hands down and
resolved to look like a professional footballer.

Not long after, I had forgotten my resolution and was on my haunches,
scanning the pitch and the stadium, looking everywhere except for the centre
of midfield where a giant blood-soaked sinkhole was gently throbbing.

"Max!" called Sam Topps, with some urgency.

His need bypassed my mood; I sprinted away, past the startled left back, to
give him an option. Sam leaned back and did his best Ryan Jack impression,
trying to roll the ball into my path like a snooker player—Ronnie O'Sullivan
coaxing the white behind the blue, sweet as a tartlet. His attempt lacked a bit of
pace, so suddenly the left back was favourite to get there first. I competed but
the defender was strong enough to hold me off and he played the ball back to
his goalie. Henri jogged towards it to stop them wasting time, and then the ball
was launched long.

Banbury's average CA had actually improved without Chris Beaumont in
their lineup, but they were much, much less dangerous. They'd found a big,
strong boy to replace him so they could keep playing the same way. The new lad
had good heading and was more mobile, but he didn't have the X-factor. Glenn
and Steve took it in turns to carry him around in their pockets.

MD, Sec Joe, Boggy. Even Ollie. "Look on the bright side," they'd said.
Trying to cheer me up. Cheer? Up? In *Indiana Jones and the Temple of Doom,*

when the evil priest tears out a victim's heart and shows it to him, still beating, at least no one says, "Cheer up, mate. Could be worse."

Raffi Brown, who I'd plucked from obscurity—no, fuck him. He was dead to me. Find *Raffi* replace *traitor*.

My hands were on my head again. I'd been trying to use the screens less when I was playing. Playing *au naturel* helped with fatigue and I had Sandra to help me with in-match decisions. I opened them now, though, to glance at the match ratings. Nothing stood out; it was a pretty drab game that we were dominating, but there had barely been any shots.

William B. Roberts was a new name on the Banbury bench. Sometimes the curse added initials to player names, especially if they were pretty common—it avoided confusion. Had it added the B. because we had Robbo Robson on the bench?

One reason we weren't creating much was that Aff was struggling. Banbury weren't playing a low block but were strung out in a defensive 4-5-1. They'd tasked their right mid to drop back and help the right back deal with Aff, and it was working. Of course, if they were doing double coverage against Aff on their right and were doing the same against me on their left, then the middle should have been badly exposed.

The middle. Where Ryan would have picked their lock with angled, well-weighted passes. Where Raffi—

"FUCK!" I screamed.

I looked on the bright side.

The bright side of losing the £150,000 a year I would have got when he made it to the Championship. The bright side of having no midfield threat. The bright side of being dumped, not even by text, but by bank transfer. The bright side of having my heart ripped out in public. Worst of all, I had to go through the motions of playing a football match before I was allowed to die.

Nothing had been resolved at the Fans Forum. Both sides had said their piece, but nothing had been accomplished. Perhaps my relationship with the Chester fans was slightly worse. I'd told them off for not turning up and now the stands looked even sparser than usual; I'd know the definitive attendance when the second half started. Not only did I never get a honeymoon period, but also the wedding was off. One of us was doing it wrong!

The bright side? We'd nearly tripled Chester's record sale for a player. Back in the olden days, Chester City had sold a young hotshot called Ian Rush to Liverpool for £300,000; £800,000 was insane money for a small club. In most scenarios, it would have felt like a miraculous injection of cash but today the mood was sombre. This wasn't a football match. This wasn't a wedding. This was a funeral.

It was all Old Nick's doing, that was clear. My human enemies were low-rent: Bradley Rymarquis and Richard Carling. Folke Wester and the media twat I'd kicked in the face. There was no connection between them and the Saudi Pro League. No chance. Unless . . . unless Rymarquis had developed a relationship with a scout for the SPL over the last four weeks. Perhaps they had been coming to every match to check on Raffi and if I'd been around, I'd have seen it and would have been able to swerve out of danger. But I'd been in Tranmere.

My own fault?

What could I have done differently? The transfer window was closed. Like, proper closed. Who could have imagined in a million years the SPL would be interested in Raffi? He'd been called up for England C, yes, and his numbers were good. Serious English clubs had been bidding on him. So the Saudis had overpaid by thirty or forty percent—so what? That's what they did. But who could have predicted it?

The ball came to me again. I shaped to pass inside to Magnus, dipped my shoulder, went around the defender and was immediately tackled by the covering midfielder. The ball went out of play, and I threw it back to Carl with an urgency that didn't fit the rest of the match or my own personal performance.

We were miles better than Banbury. We should have been able to grind out a result. I'd sat with Sandra to go through our options, but we didn't have many. Ryan was done for the season. Joe Anka was a couple of weeks away from training. Chris Beaumont couldn't play against the team that owned him.

In addition, our morale had been squashed like an organically grown orange. We normally had much higher morale than every team we ever played. Today was the first time we'd been lower, the first time we were collectively below the midpoint, and the first time I'd had to leave someone out of the lineup because of morale.

That person was Pascal, and Pascal was a wreck. If anyone was taking Raffi's betrayal worse than me, it was him. Raffi had been like an older brother to the German, who was an only child. The only child had spent the whole morning one stray thought from blubbering, but kept it together enough to ask, "Has anyone heard from him? I've tried to call. He doesn't pick up. Has he texted anyone?" His morale was on abysmal, the lowest.

Hence why I was playing right midfield.

We were doing 4-1-4-1 with Ben in goal, a defence of Eddie Moore, Glenn Ryder, Steve Alton, and Carl Carlile. Three silvers and two golds in that group.

Youngster was the holding midfielder. Under the tutelage of a coaching megabrain (Sandra) and with his number of minutes being carefully managed by another megabrain (me) he had eased to CA 49. Silver, but in touching distance of gold.

Sam and Magnus patrolled the middle. Sam was so, so close to platinum, which was great. But it was also his limit. And he couldn't pass like Ryan or score like . . . like . . . the traitor. Sam was a very good, very solid destroyer of enemy attacks. And so was Magnus. His CA had crept up to 48 and I could play him anywhere in defence or midfield. But that central axis of Youngster, Sam, and Magnus was sorely lacking in creativity.

Fortunately, we had Aff on CA 58. If we could get him into the final third with a bit of space, he'd mess teams up and fire crosses and low passes to Henri, CA 63. Henri was stuck again, but we just had to live with it. Our schedule was Tuesday/Saturday almost nonstop until the end of the season. Managing availability was my new challenge, not squeezing every drop of talent out of my star players.

While the team lacked a bit of magic, it had an average CA of 52.4. And there was one flair player in the blue and white stripes . . .

Unfortunately, that was me. I reckoned I was around CA 90, physically. Mentally I was CA 1, morale 1, traitors unmasked 1, number of hearts left in body 0. And that was the problem with me having influence 20. If I was in a black mood, it spread to the rest of the team.

We ran and competed and did our jobs. We were professional. But with low morale, there was no spark; we didn't do the extras. We didn't make the selfless runs that cost us energy but opened just a fraction of a yard of space so someone could get a better angle on a pass or someone could get a second to put some quality on a shot. We didn't do the extra covering, didn't call out danger, didn't suffer or sacrifice in any way. We were so much better than the oppo that it didn't much matter, but one day it would.

The bright side? We were top of the league with a game in hand. We had £800,000 in the bank. Money that would be bugger all help in the rest of the season. We couldn't sign players apart from free agents and none of the ones in my database were over CA 32. Even if I did pick up a decent out-of-contract dude, he would need weeks to get up to match fitness. Vivek and Michael were doing well at West, impressing the manager and other players, but were far from ready for meaningful National League North action.

No, the squad was the squad. And that's why I had Bark on the bench instead of D-Day. Our loan deal for Chris Beaumont was set in stone, but if we didn't give Bark minutes or weren't seen to be developing him, Tranmere could recall him, and we'd be struggling even more. Mateo and James wouldn't do it, probably, but why take the risk? D-Day had taken my decision well. He knew he'd get minutes, he knew he'd be involved, he knew I was under the cosh. He was a dick but when it came to the crunch, he was a team player.

Youngster and Glenn combined to deal with a long ball to the Banbury big boy. Youngster scampered away with the ball and fizzed it to Magnus. It was the sort of pass he had been playing to the traitor, but Magnus had a totally different style. He lost the ball and Sam Topps stretched and threw himself into a sliding tackle to recover it. A Banbury guy did the same and the two players clattered into each other.

Both guys' pace went red and both injury screens said *potential foot injury.*

Well, wasn't that peachy?

I made the sub signal to the dugout while I waited for Dean to come and check out the sitch. Sam, naturally, said he wanted to stay on. I bent and loomed over him. "Mate. We've got twenty more games this season. Shut the fuck up and start getting ready for next Saturday."

"What about Tuesday night?"

"Are you fucking stupid?"

He slumped back to the turf. "No, Max."

"Dean, give me a minute."

"Yes, boss."

I meant that he should keep Sam there so I could talk to Sandra about the subs. She wanted Tony on to support Henri, maybe moving to 4-3-3. I wanted to get our loanee on to show his club that I would use him. "Let's stick with this. Bark right mid. I'll go in the centre."

So the team became much more youthful, much less experienced, and much less dense in CA. We fell to under 49. Still well ahead of Banbury's 40, but now within the range where losing wouldn't be such an upset.

From the centre of midfield I kept things tidy, moved the ball around, and made interceptions. But my heart wasn't in it. My heart, you'll remember, had been ripped out and tossed aside and unless the cleaners had been, it was still on the stage in a drab conference room.

The ref blew for halftime and I trudged, slow as a toddler who doesn't want to leave a puddle, towards the tunnel. Two of the imps were there in their favoured spots. Tactics Imp was wearing smart trousers with a fancy belt, a plain white shirt rolled up at the sleeves with two buttons undone at the neck, and he had a black jumper wrapped around his neck like a scarf. Around one wrist sat a very chunky, very expensive-looking watch. The effect was ruined or enhanced, depending on your point of view, by one of those plain plastic bracelet things that support some good cause or other.

Snake Imp had gone for a different vibe. He was in a baggy black T-shirt with words in a chunky yellow font: *JUST A MAX THANG*. He had at least thirty gold chains around his neck, a gold watch on one wrist, gold bracelets on the other. The inevitable snapback was far too big for him, but perhaps that was to get the embroidered letters as big as possible: *MBFTW*.

Old Nick had leveraged my January XP well, then, and there were plenty of Hell Points to go round. At least someone in the stadium was happy. When they saw me looking, both formed their fingers into W signs. W for Wibwob. It looked more congruent coming from Snake Imp.

In the dressing room, I checked on Sam—he would be fine by next Saturday—and sat on the cramped bench—cramped apart from one unoccupied section with an empty hook—and wallowed in misery. Glenn barely spoke. Aff didn't call anything deadly. Henri was in a distant world of his own. Sandra gave us a few minutes to collect our thoughts; we would need a lot more than that.

The door opened and Jackie stepped in. He asked for Youngster. Behind Jackie, Kisi poked her head in and waved at Sandra. She was pulled back by Meghan, the Butcher of Burnage. I knew she had a crush on Youngster. Whatever this was, it was kid's stuff; I ignored it.

So I was pretty surprised when Youngster went to the tactics board and coughed to get our attention.

"I would like to give the halftime team talk," he said. The level of astonishment was on par with the events of the night before.

Sandra looked over; I shrugged. Why not? Life couldn't get any worse.

Youngster looked over at the doorway. Jackie was nodding, while Kisi and Meghan were holding each other's hands, unable to believe their luck. "When I first came to this country," said James Yalley, a player who now represented almost the entirety of my financial hopes and dreams, "I knew there would be things I would not understand. Tea with milk. Cricket. *Doctor Who*. Ben's inability to park within the lines."

"Oi!"

"But I never expected the taps. One is hot. One is cold. The system is quite stupid. What if you would like some warm water?"

His goofy smile made everyone turn to me. They saw some tiny tears and one big smile. "James, you weren't there. How do you know the words?"

"Kisi repeats it often. But, Mr. Best . . . I have something I would like to say and I would like to use my own words, not my father's. I am not sure I have the courage. I do not think everyone will like it."

"If everyone likes what you're doing, you're doing it wrong."

"Do you believe that?"

I scoffed. "I'm Max Best. I have to."

"Very well." He took a deep breath. "What has happened is unfathomable. It is beyond belief. But we know Raffi Brown to be a good man. If he left us without a word of explanation, there must be a reason."

"Yeah," spat Sam. "For five grand a week on a four-year contract." The numbers slapped me in the face. They sounded *right*. The only way to be sure would be to go to Saudi Arabia and watch a match featuring the traitor. Yeah, veto.

"Oh," said Youngster. "Perhaps. But regardless, I believe that if Jesus were here, he would want us to forgive Raffi Brown."

I shook my head. "No one has ever said this before or even *thought* this before, but I think Jesus was a better person than me." Kisi thought I was being hilarious, but Jackie made the girls leave and followed suit, giving me a little nod before departing. "But thanks, James, bro. Someone needed to say something and God knows it wasn't going to be me." I smiled. "And I needed the laugh."

The squad did, too, even if most didn't know about the taps. They'd reacted to my reaction, and they somehow knew Youngster had played one of his aces. The average morale had gone up. A little bit more might be the kick we needed to get a goal in the second half and keep our lead at the top of the table. Something told me we couldn't afford any slip-ups.

"Max," said Sandra, gently pushing Youngster away from the tactics board. Sam gave him a fist bump as he went past. My assistant manager had her little book out. "Would you like me to give the lads some notes?"

"Yes please, mum," I said.

The noise was deafening. Shouts, calls, whoops. Morale went green all across the board. Angles hugged Sandra then Goliath gave her a high five. Sam, Tony, and Henri were in fits, side by side on the bench. Gerald, Magnus, and Glenn stood so they could fall into each other. Pascal was laughing so hard Livia was worried about him.

When the mayhem subsided just enough, the Brig stepped in front of D-Day. "Pay up, lad."

D-Day looked panicked. "What?"

"I wagered on Max."

D-Day started to reach into his kit bag. From what I had heard, this bet was big news; was he carrying around over a thousand in cash? But he stopped and pointed from the Brig to me. "Fix! It's a fix!"

"Pardon me, sir?" The Brig fixed him with a steely gaze that Donny would normally have withered under.

Not this time. "You told him! He did it on purpose! What a swizz!"

There's a song for Portsmouth Football Club, nickname "Pompey," that sounds like a church bell and goes "Play up, Pompey, Pompey play up!" Someone—I think it was Glenn—started singing:

"Pay up, D-Day! D-Day pay up!"

We all joined in, even Sandra, Dean, Livia, and Vimsy.

Morale went up up up.

D-Day, the only one with red morale, snatched his bag, snatched the money, and tried to snatch it *into* the Brig's hand, which is linguistically impossible.

The Brig held it up and we fell silent. After a beat—incredible timing—he yelled, "Big night out if we beat Banbury!"

Green green green! Sam and Tony pushed and pulled Donny, uttering nonsense at him until he broke into a reluctant grin. He had lost, but in a good way. The story would be the stuff of legend. Well worth whatever his cut of the takings was going to be.

I slapped my hands together and went to the tactics board.

"Lads? New plan. You ready?" They were. I slapped the magnets showing our 4-1-4-1. "We do the same, but this time, we do it right. That's it. Get the fuck back out there."

"Come on, Chester!" yelled Glenn, and with a final roar, the lads charged out of the dressing room.

When it was mostly just the senior staff left, I looked at Sandra. "See that? You know who can't do that? Your boy Pep. You're in the big leagues now."

She shook her head, mock exasperated. "Thanks, Max. Very educational. I'm learning a *lot*. Now do you think we might push Youngster up to CM and get you into more advanced areas? And tell Carl to stay back to cover Bark? And get Eddie farther forward like you did with the guy at Tranmere? Without breaking him?"

I cricked my neck left and right. "No. We had it right first time. We just needed a thumping motivational speech."

"What was all that about taps?"

"That?" I said, laughing, putting an arm around her shoulder. "Didn't I ever tell you? That was how the Beth Heads beat you."

As the second half kicked off, I saw the attendance: 1,812. Meagre. Demotivational. But I'd used my morale amplifier and couldn't let it go to waste. We had to win today and then we'd have a few days to work on our, like, feelings or whatever. Then on Tuesday night we'd hit crosses to Goliath and win at a canter, rotating the squad, conserving energy. Simples.

The match restarted with us attacking the Harry McNally stand where our noisiest fans were. Banbury kicked off and I sprinted at the ball carrier, slid in front of him, collected the ball, and danced away from a couple of challenges. I waited for movement—Bark was sprinting down the right but was blocked off the ball by the much more experienced fullback. Henri was scampering ahead. I knew he'd drift left so that my pass could curve between the centre backs.

The goalie knew it as well, and he took a few steps forward, ready to sprint out and be a sweeper keeper. So I cocked my leg and struck the ball miles to the side of the goal. It took the keeper a second to understand the danger, but that was nearly enough. He scrambled back across his six-yard box, and at full stretch flung his arms out. He got fingertips to the ball just as it finished its final spinning bounce. It would have crept in at the near post, but he pushed it onto the upright. It bounced back onto the back of his head and dribbled towards goal. He twisted and flung himself on it, breathing heavily.

A lucky escape, but he'd think twice about coming off his line again.

The incident spooked the away team and they dropped a little deeper. A point against us would be a fantastic result for them, so I expected them to go low block as soon as we got our gander up.

But for now they were still in the match on their own terms. They won a couple of headers, put a few passes together, forced us back. Youngster cleaned up a bit of a Steve Alton mess, Magnus slid the ball out to Bark, and he did a cute trick to get past the left back. Bark sprinted ahead and had Henri up in support. Bark wanted to hit a low pass or get into slapping position at the side of the box, but he lacked conviction. He slowed, hesitated, and when the defender got back, he turned and passed to Magnus. Chance gone.

"Come on, man," I said, in a rare moment of on-pitch annoyance. Generally, I was very good at being a positive presence and not slating players for minor mistakes or missteps. The moment clarified that I had a decision to make about which CM to be. By default, I'd taken Sam's place near Aff, and he and I combining could cause havoc. Or, I thought, it could allow Banbury to flood that side of the pitch and shut us down, making us reliant on the right. Bark was talented but he looked like a boy playing against a man, to the point where it was hard to imagine him impacting the game. Subbing him off, being a sub himself, would make his confidence even worse. Me going over there would be frustrating if Bark kept making shit decisions.

A few more minutes passed and our match ratings had increased all round. Lots of sevens, now. We were getting a grip. Banbury sensed that, and one of their players took it upon himself to take decisive action.

Henri jogged over to force a Banbury centre back into clearing the ball. He aimed it high to the left, towards his number 3 and Bark. Bark had poor heading and jumping but he wasn't short by any means. The elbow he took was aimed up, *into* the face.

I lost my mind, had the 3 in my grip, was snarling at him. The Brig was there to separate us, and I cooled enough to check on the kid. He was lucky— no broken nose, eye socket, or jaw.

And no red card for the assault. The ref bottled it completely, giving a throw-in.

I bent to ask Bark if he was all right. He said yes. Dean said it might be best to take him off. "No," I growled. "We need him. Get up, mate. We're gonna fuck these cowards up."

Did my voice get louder as I spoke? Was I right in front of the Banbury bench? I couldn't say. But by the time Bark got to his feet, my blood was pumping and I'd reorganised the whole team.

Aff was now playing at left back. Eddie Moore was left centre back, partnering Glenn, and Steve at right back. Carl was the DM. I'd basically rotated everyone one space. That left Magnus and Youngster as the CMs and Bark at right mid. On the tactics screen I started as the left mid, but I had no intention of playing there, which was the whole point.

"Max!" called Sandra. "What are you doing?"

What I was doing was playing as a *second* right winger. I'd probably only get a minute or two of freedom until Banbury realised, but for now every attack would be an overload.

We competed for the throw-in and there was an untidy phase of play. Typical non-league fare until Carl, enjoying his unexpected day out in midfield, literally put his foot on the ball like he was, I don't know, *me*. He touched it to Youngster, who skipped past one tackle—he was getting really good at that line-breaking move—and played a short pass to me.

That was decision-making 20 because I was absolutely white-hot with rage and ready to slap. I sprinted and passed the ball down the line for Bark to run onto. Then I cut in front of the defender and made him barge into me. Don't run into a fucking brick wall, mate! The prick was lucky I didn't elbow him in the grille but I couldn't afford a suspension while the squad was so thin, and I was already in hot water with the Football Association for Facegate.

Bark realised he was free and accelerated. I untangled myself from 3 and pumped my legs as hard as I could trying to give Bark an option. Henri darted to the near post. Bark shaped to pass. Henri turned and zipped to the back post. Bark didn't panic—he swept the ball diagonally back, into my path, and his eyes widened as I clipped it first time, full of side spin, through the defenders, where Henri was dynamically lurking and—GOAL!

I raced to Bark and bearhugged him, lifted and tried to spin him around. He was a lot heavier than Emma and I wasn't as strong as I once was, so I only succeeded in moving him a few feet, but his ecstatic laughter was worth it. Henri arrived, we screamed at each other, we screamed at Youngster and Magnus and the others as they came flooding in. A river of us.

Once the huddle broke, I walked towards the left midfield slot, doing my patented position disguise, but on the way a lot of emotions hit me at the same time. Anger, betrayal, frustration, relief, and what's this? *Even more* anger. Fists clenched, I almost doubled up as I roared defiance.

Smash my boys I'll smash you.

Wreck my plans I'll improvise.

Block my path I'll overcome.

Fuck. You.

The ref whistled to get the game back underway, and I walked right. The match went on around me like I'd been inserted into a cool movie sequence where one guy—Paul Blart: Mall Cop, for example—is on an escalator while the world around him zips past. But then the ball broke and the world flipped: I was the speed, I was the energy, and everyone else was in slow motion.

I passed to Bark. He touched it back. A tackle came in. I booped the ball over the outstretched leg and moved forward five yards. I passed to Bark again. He touched it back, fell into a sprinter's start, retreated, and we repeated. More tackles came in. I dodged and weaved and when it was time to nutmeg the fullback, I pointed, feinted to touch the ball, laughed as he closed his legs, and twisted my body to thrash the ball on a slight diag into Aff's path. With me attracting all the aggro, he was one-on-one for the first time in the match.

Aff surges forward with the ball on his favoured left foot.

He drops a shoulder and moves past the defender with ease.

He keeps going. Now he needs support.

Lyons comes square. They exchange passes.

Aff seems to miskick a pass with his right foot.

No! It has gone straight into the path of Youngster.

He's clean through! He dabs the ball to the right of goal . . .

Hits the post! The rebound is loose . . .

Saved! A defender clears.

But only as far as Barkley. He sends it back in . . .

Lyons is beaten in the air.

It falls to Aff on the volley . . .

Blocked!

Chester can't believe they haven't scored.

I abandoned all pretence, then, and lined up right next to Bark. If Banbury tried to overload the other side, I'd cover. No problem.

The goalie played it short to the right back Aff had just skinned, and he smashed long. It was too easy for Ryder to head away, and the ball was cycled to me. The lads knew now. They knew I was the pass.

Magnus looked up and played it to me. I shifted my body weight left, then right, then let the ball go through my legs, leaving 3 bamboozled, but Bark had read my intentions. He was callow, but he was smart. He was in place for my dummy, dribbled forward, used me as a decoy to get some space, and chopped left, Ronaldo-style, as he moved from the edge of the box to the D. A retreating midfielder took him out.

The ref gave a free kick in what future historians will call "Max Best Territory."

Two perks kicked in. First, the offer of a Free Hit. Yes, please. Smash that.

Second, Masterpiece Theatre. It was pretty cool—it was basically a mini-map with eleven circles that I could move around to some extent. I used it now to leave three players back and everyone else to the left of goal. Banbury erected a two-man wall, which I found quite insulting. Two? Try ten, you pricks.

When was the last time someone had underestimated me from a free kick? Had it been my trial at Chester, when I'd used Raffi to turn an indirect free kick into a direct one?

Raffi. Raffi, mate, what have you done?

The ref blew his whistle; I got the impression he'd been doing so for a while. I gave him a little thumbs-up and settled into my stance. Beckham or cannonball?

I pumped my legs like I was running on the spot, released the brake, and slapped that ball as hard as I could. It flew to my right, the goalie's left—he would save it comfortably—but then physics kicked in and it veered away, away, away . . .

The Harry McNally stand leapt, jumped, and hugged. Limbs everywhere. I didn't hear it, didn't feel it. It was just a goal. There was no emotion for me. I noted with vague interest that the player who'd been involved in the tackle with Sam, who had stayed on the pitch despite being equally injured, was being helped off. His injury was worse than Sam's now. He'd miss more games, come back less fit with more risk of being reinjured.

I was on the right track. I was doing the right things. But as I'd learned at the start of my adventure, no good deed goes unpunished.

My players enveloped me, surrounded me, and took care of the celebrations. I let them; it was my job to suffer.

At 2–0 down and with me targeting his left back, Banbury's manager decided to shut up shop. He went low block, tried to keep the score down, and subbed off his 3.

I raced across and told them what I thought of that. "Hey! Hey! I'm not finished with you. Get back here! What the fuck! Get fucking back here, you prick!"

Bark and Magnus combined to pull me away and the last I saw of 3 was him heading down the tunnel behind some high-number rando on the touchline waiting to come on instead.

It didn't matter who the rando was. Banbury were shit and now they were pulling their necks in like scared little turtles. They could fuck off home. Two hours and thirty minutes of guys asking 3 why he had wound me up. Why he had decided to crash his elbow into a young man's face.

Banbury kicked off, played a half-hearted long ball to their big boy, and when he was outmuscled by Carl, fell into the low block. I swapped things back to the default formation for the day, pretending to call out to people so Sandra wouldn't get suspicious.

Then I went to CM to take the piss without attracting the ire of the Sentinel.

Starting with . . . a long-shot bombardment. I took the ball forty yards from goal, shaped to pass to Bark, and instead launched an absolute fucking howitzer that the goalie batted away before shaking his head like a boxer who'd just been punched.

I was snarling again, I realised, and while the thought did occur to me that I should maybe relax, I was also enjoying it. Let the anger make you strong!

Next time I got the ball, I burst past one tackle and had Bark to the right, Henri moving smartly across goal, and—this confused me—Eddie Moore and Aff racing each other down the left. I decided to do a cheeky little chip to the left to see . . .

Two sets of pain hit, one after the other. The first, on the back of my calf from where he kicked me. The second as I crashed into the turf, totally unprepared, totally off balance.

I stayed down to let Dean come and check me out before I tried to move. If I *was* injured, now would be a pretty good time to go off. Who could come on? Andrew Harrison, probably. He needed minutes.

That could wait, though. Dean said everything looked fine and helped me to my feet. I stayed bent for a second while I checked I could wiggle my right toes. When I looked up to see the prick who had fouled me, I fell right back down again.

The ref came over. "Are you timewasting or not, Best? I can't tell."

"Got a bit light-headed. I need ten seconds."

My assailant was right there, and based on the fact I'd never heard of him, he was making his Banbury debut. Fifteen years old with a B in his name. B for booking. The fine for the yellow card would be thirty pounds. Did he have it? He was registered with Banbury but he didn't have a full-time contract.

What he did have was the fucking nerve to foul me on my own patch. He had an almost palpable will to win; steam was coming out of his ears, so frustrated was he at the dire performance of his team and his own inability to catch me up. Looking at his attributes, it might have been the first time he'd ever played against someone faster than him.

WILLIAM B. ROBERTS		
Born 10.03.2008	(Age 15)	English
Acceleration 16		
	Handling 1	Stamina 12
	Heading 11	Strength 12
		Tackling 6
	Jumping 9	Teamwork 14
Bravery 16		Technique 10
Creativity 14		
	Pace 16	preferred foot B
	Passing 9	
Dribbling 8	Positioning 6	
Finishing 14		
CA 4	PA 185	
Forward (RLC)		

The PA made me dizzy again. He was better than Dani. Better even than Youngster. And he was a forward. That meant goals. Marketing. Money. Glory!

The ref wanted me to take the free kick. Who gave a fucking shit about one measly free kick? This match was as good as over.

And I'd just had an absolutely absurd thought. I hadn't quite been able to work out why Old Nick had engineered a move for Raffi. A move I couldn't block or talk him out of. With Raffi gone, I'd have to play more matches. I'd have to play every match, and that's the last thing Nick wanted.

Unless, though . . . Unless the absolute most important thing this month was that I was here. On this pitch, against Banbury. If Raffi had been available today there was a risk—a low risk, but still—that I'd have left Sandra in charge and gone, I don't know, tobogganing with Emma. (Euphemism accidental.)

But Raffi was gone and I had to stay at Chester to clean up the mess. And more importantly, to play. And to meet William B. fucking Roberts, one of the hottest prospects in the country, on his debut, before anyone else in the world of football even knew about him! It was the chance of a lifetime.

The smile came of its own accord and I changed from a cannonball to a Beckham. I stepped, struck, and this little Roberts yob turned to watch as it flew into the top left corner. I strode toward him and gave him some friendly advice. "You've just cost your team a goal because you're a selfish prick. You wanted everyone to notice you? Great. Everyone knows you're a fucking undisciplined little shit who puts himself above his team. Foul me again, I'll score again. Get bent!"

"Fuck off!" he yelled. "Fuck you!"

My players got between me and the furious Banbury guys, tried to pull me away so we could celebrate, but I just wanted the game to restart so I shrugged them away. Banbury kicked off and I positioned myself ten yards in front of Roberts. When he got on the ball, I pounced, surging towards him. He played a simple pass away and I backed off. That move broke down and the ball was sent to my feet. I put my knee on the ball and got up, all my body weight left. I'm going left! I'm going left! Roberts came at me, expecting the trick. At the last second he stuck his leg right.

So I nutmegged him.

I ran around him and he grabbed me. It was like being hugged by a wheelie bin full of bricks, but he let go because of his yellow card. He'd done enough to slow me down without risking the referee's wrath. Self-regulation! Maybe he wasn't aggression 20 as I'd initially thought. There was a good way to check—I dribbled over to the left with him tracking me, snapping at my heels.

"Henri!" I called, and my mate came short.

Roberts, the dick, reacted by getting too tight to me. I backheel nutmegged him and ran off, cackling. Still the kid kept tracking, kept in my wake, kept at me like a greyhound chasing a rabbit. He wasn't a greyhound, though. He was a human being with, theoretically, a brain.

"Give up!" I yelled as I exchanged passes with a bemused Carl Carlile.

"Fuck you!" came the reply.

I opened my body to spread a pass out wide to Aff and Roberts slid in to block it. I popped the ball up and rested it on my shoelaces, two feet above the grass. I bent down. "Give up," I said, and as I moved away, he slapped the pitch in frustration.

We used our last two subs to give minutes to Andrew and Tony, and I played the rest of the match pretty straight. No dribbles, no taunts. Truth be told, I spent most of the match staring at Roberts's player profile. Not just because it was pure sex, but because one of the attributes had turned green. After I'd given him a piece of my mind, his teamwork had popped to 15 and his CA had risen. He was a complete sponge. Whatever I poured into him, he'd absorb.

Holy fucking shit.

Three–nil, three points, and three stud marks on the back of my calf.

I ignored the fans, my mates, my opponents. I had Sandra to do my diplomatic work. I went straight for Roberts.

He was stocky with a face that couldn't decide if it wanted to be round or rectangular and ears that couldn't decide if they were in or out. He had broad shoulders and big powerful thighs that with his low centre of gravity gave him a vaguely Maradona-esque vibe. The comparison was absurd, of course. But then again, PA 185 and two-footed. It was close enough!

"Did you enjoy that?" I said.

"No," he said. His voice had broken and he was gruff. He was a little ogre, this guy!

"Come on. You did a bit."

He glared at me in a show of bravado, but while he almost had the body of a man, he *was* just a kid. He smiled cheekily. "Yeah." The scowl was back. "Don't like losing."

"Is that right?" I mused. His Contract screen had some interesting words. *Currently considering a contract offer from Banbury United*. I could get in trouble for what I was about to do, but so the fuck what? Some risks were worth taking. "Don't sign that contract, then."

"What? How did you know about that? You been scouting me?"

I looked around, then realised that was making me look suspicious. "Just don't sign it yet, all right? I want a friendly chat. That's all right, isn't it?"

He considered me. Gave me a very mature look, very thoughtful. "Friendly chat? If I want a friend, I'll get a puppy."

I smiled. "All right, then. Nice knowing you." I walked away, heart thudding alarmingly hard in my chest. Relationship anxiety. Welcome back, old friend!

After a few yards, I was stopped by a cry. "Max!"

But it wasn't the kid. Chris Beaumont had been down the away end, posing for selfies with and chatting to the few Banbury fans that had come. He was very much their star player and the club's talisman. The money I'd paid to have him on loan for a few months would pay their entire tax bill. "Chris, mate. What did you think? Enjoy that? Must have been weird. Who did you even want to win?"

"Fuck all that. I can't wait to get on the same side as you. You're something else. What were you doing when the kid came on?"

"Who? Roberts?"

"It was like one-on-one in the back garden for a minute, there. Hilarious. Never seen owt like it."

"Just seeing if he's got what it takes."

"And? Does he?"

"I've seen worse," I said truthfully.

Chris smiled at Roberts as he went past us on his way to the dressing room. "Made your debut. How's it feel?"

It was clear Roberts admired Goliath. "Good, Chris, thanks."

"And you got to meet your idol. He megged you a couple of times, I thought."

Roberts turned red and mumbled something, then kept going.

I couldn't believe it. "Idol?" The kid had fouled me and run around like a whirling dervish trying to compete with me. He didn't *like* me, did he?

Chris laughed. "Max. Come on. You know how you play."

"Is he a good kid?"

"Yeah. He was at grassroots scoring a few, had a growth spurt and he hasn't been right for a while but looks like he's sorted himself out since I've been gone. He's absolutely football mad. It's all he does. Extra practice, extra coaching, ball boy, clearing snow off the pitch. Anything to be around footy. He's got it bad. And he plays *Soccer Supremo* nonstop, too. He's always tweaking his formations and asking the coaches what they think. Drives them mad because they don't understand what he's on about. That's why he's got that nickname."

"What nickname?"

Chris Beaumont had one of the best nicknames going. Goliath. But William B. Roberts had a nickname that nearly blasted me off my feet. "You don't play *Soccer Supremo*, do you? It's an acronym thingy. You tell your players what to do *with* the ball, and what to do *without* the ball. And his name sounds just like it."

I felt like if he didn't say the fucking nickname already I would fall flat on my face and simply give up the ghost. The tension was killing me. Literally. But I already knew what this nickname was going to be. It had all clicked. It explained why the imps were there. All this time, they hadn't been encouraging me to get a perk, they'd been steering me towards getting something *completely* different.

"We all call him Wibwob."

APPENDIX

February 3 League Table

	TEAM	P	W	D	L	F	A	GD	PTS
1	Chester	28	21	2	5	75	27	48	65
2	Kidderminster	29	18	8	3	51	20	31	62
3	York	30	16	11	3	49	30	19	59
4	Darlington	29	16	10	3	45	28	17	58

Chester Men's First Team

			AGE	WAGE	CA	PA
1	Robbie "Robbo" Robson	GK	34	500	44	45
13	Ben Cavanagh	GK	26	425	48	67
25	Steve "Angles" English	GK	36	500	19	80
4	Glenn Ryder	DC	30	750	54	54
2	Carl Carlile	DCR	25	400	57	77
12	Magnus Evergreen	D, DM, M	26	500	48	−2
5	Gerald May	DC	29	700	38	38
	Vivek [LOAN]	DC	17	0		66
16	Steve Alton	D CR	25	500	46	53
20	Eddie Moore	DL	22	900	42	75
	Lucas Friend	DL	16	0	7	62
6	Sam Topps	MC	28	750	59	60
17	Andrew Harrison	MC R	22	500	24	?
18	Michael Harrison [LOAN]	MC R	18	350	12	?
19	Ryan Jack	MC	35	750	INJ JAN 2025	151
11	Diarmuid "Aff" Dubhlainn	ML	27	525	58	70

14	James "Youngster" Yalley	DM, MC	18	500	49	181
	Dan Badford	CM	15	0	5	−1
77	Max Best	Omni	23	500		
15	Joe Anka	MR	28	600	INJ 2 WKS	40
22	Calabash "Bark" Barkley	AMRC	17	0	23	130
	Tyson	AMRC	15	0	13	58
7	Donny "D-Day" Dorigo	AMLR	33	500	39	55
18	Pascal Bochum	F (RLC)	18	500	43	133
21	Chris Beaumont	S	36	1000	29	33
9	Henri Lyons	S	28	800	63	90
10	Tony Hetherington	S	26	600	44	44
26	Benny		15	0	14	40

Transfer Value of Men's Squad
(Estimated by Max): £170,000 (+£105,000 year on year)

Chester Women's First Team

1	Robyn Wright	GK	19		14	14
13	Queenie	GK	16		4	94
16	Erin Barnes	CB	19		12	12
22	Mel Robinson	RB	18		15	15
15	Mo Walsh	CB	18		21	21
23	Lucy	LB	42		21	90
4	Bonnie	CB	25	350	26	41
18	Diane	DM	22		3	60
14	Gracie Davies	LM	20		17	17
6	Pippa Hoole	CM	32	200	28	111
7	Dani Smith–Smithe	M, AM LRC	16	350	33	177
12	Susan Butler	MC	18		21	21
11	Maddy Hines	MRC	17	200	25	80
8	Charlotte	MC	21	350	40	101
17	Kisi Yalley	AM RLC	15		24	143
9	Beatrice Pearce	S	18		27	36
19	Julie McKay	S	17	150	17	53
10	Angel	S	16	350	9	155

Notable Youth Prospects:

		Age	PA
Chas Fungrieve	S	14	83
Future	CB DM	12	99
Stephen Watson	DM	10	146
Mark Nelson	D RLC	10	70
Tadpole	GK	10	130
Big Sam	GK	12	61
Simon Black	S	10	77

Max's Private Clients:
Ziggy – £45/week
Youngster – £50/week

R.E.M. Clients/Agency Cut:
Bark – £50/week
Dani – £35/week
Angel – £35/week

Max's Assets and Liabilities
£20,000 from traitor
£20,000 (minus taxes) from Tranmere
The Duchess (a brown Subaru)
West Didsbury and Chorlton AFC
One superfast laptop
–?,000 to the Brig for services rendered

Estimated % of Merch Sold in Chester with Chester FC Branding: 4

ABOUT THE AUTHOR

Ted Steel is the author of the Player Manager series, which features a charming but secretive main character. He also wrote *Nerves of Steel*, a LitRPG featuring a charming but secretive main character. When asked to provide a bit of color for his biography, Steel was charming but . . . secretive. Learn more at www.ted-steel.com.

RESPAWN YOUR CURIOSITY

follow us on our socials

podiumentertainment.com

@podiumentertainment

/podiumentertainment

@podium_ent

@podiumentertainment